SHADE ME

JENNIFER BROWN

SHADE ME

KATHERINE TEGEN BOOKS
An Imprint of HarperCollins Publishers

Katherine Tegen Books is an imprint of HarperCollins Publishers.

Shade Me

Library of Congress Cataloging-in-Publication Data
Brown, Jennifer, date.
  Shade me / Jennifer Brown. — First edition.
    pages cm
  Summary: "A teenage girl with special cognitive abilities becomes embroiled in
a mystery surrounding the brutal attack of a high-profile classmate and a sexy yet
dangerous relationship with a stranger"— Provided by publisher.
  ISBN 978-0-06-232443-6 (hardback)
  [1. Mystery and detective stories. 2. Synesthesia—Fiction.] I. Title.
PZ7.B814224Sh 2016   2015010020
[Fic]—dc23   CIP
                                                                                  AC

Typography by Carla Weiss
15 16 17 18 19   PC/RRDH   10 9 8 7 6 5 4 3 2 1
❖
First Edition

FOR SCOTT

PROLOGUE

W HEN SHE WAS being honest with herself, she
knew she had chosen the drop site based mainly on
how she'd seen it done in movies. Laughably typical, she
thought—every part of her life had always been so very
Hollywood. Dazzle and dysfunction, spritzed with expensive
perfume. Every secret, every scandal, every stitch of clothing
and fancy car had a glam front to it. Emphasis on *front*. Her
life was nothing if not faked. That was, after all, the main
problem.

Of course, needing a drop site in the first place was
almost as millionaire's-daughter cliché as choosing the loading dock of an abandoned Italian grocery in the middle of
the night. Lord knew she'd spent enough of her life in the

tabloids—*Daughter of the Acclaimed Producer*—but if she kept playing into the moneygrubbing rich-girl stereotype like this, she could end up being paparazzi fodder for the rest of her life. God, for the tiniest moment, she wished to be one of those boring girls in small towns where nobody even knew a film director or makeup artist to the stars.

She'd asked for five million. She could have asked for more. Maybe she *should* have asked for more. Maybe five million would be gone before her twenty-first birthday, and she would wish she'd asked for ten. Or twenty. God knew, twenty was doable.

She hadn't heard the purr of a car engine since she shut hers off. The loading dock wasn't just isolated—it was completely abandoned. Flattened cans and discarded fast-food bags drifted in the corners of the dock, rocking and shivering in the breeze. It was a clear night, but it felt foggy somehow, as if danger were physically pressing down on her.

Paranoid. She was being paranoid. She had chosen carefully who would make the exchange. He wouldn't let her down. He was the only one she could somewhat trust.

But it was the *somewhat* that had her worried, wasn't it? He was good for booze and bitch sessions and the occasional cover-up, but he was hardly an upstanding citizen. She knew enough of his dirt to know she couldn't *totally* trust him.

Maybe she should leave.

Definitely she should leave.

But just as she started to step out of the shadows, she heard the familiar crunch of tires on gravel. It was his car. Her heart sped up as the car slowed to a stop, the headlights dying before the engine. In their absence, her eyes seemed filled with black ink; she rubbed them with the heels of her palms, fighting panic.

Why had she trusted him? She knew how he could get. *You trusted him because this affects him, too,* she reminded herself. *Even if he won't accept it yet.* But still, out here where nobody would hear her scream, his not accepting the truth seemed to make all the difference in the world.

Mistake. This was a huge, huge mistake.

She would call. She had to call. It was too soon, but she'd told herself she would, if she started to think things might go south. If she didn't call now, she might never get the chance.

She fumbled her phone out of her pocket and hesitated.

He got out of his car and began walking toward the dock, but stopped as another pair of headlights clawed open the darkness. She got a momentary glimpse of him—cocky, expensive, athletic. A briefcase swung casually from one hand—way too casually, she thought, given what she knew was in it—the Figaro bracelet she'd given him for Christmas two years ago glinting in the headlights.

He'd promised not to bring anyone else with him. He'd betrayed her.

"Where is she?" a voice said from the direction of the new car. She heard a door softly shut.

"I just got here," he answered. "She's here, though. Her car's here."

"We'll find her," the other voice answered. Now two sets of feet were scuffing through the gravel toward her.

She pushed herself deeper into the corner, no longer caring if there were rats or used condoms or dirty hypodermics underneath the trash and leaves. She woke the phone, slid to the only number in her contacts list, and hit call. It rang what seemed like an impossible number of times, during which she clearly heard the words "Right there" come from the direction of the cars, though from which one of the men, she couldn't be sure.

"Hello?" a voice said on the other end.

Suddenly, she didn't know what to say. The men were moving quicker now, the one who'd just arrived walking with a cane. She thought she recognized his silhouette, and that was bad news. Her mouth went dry and her mind went blank as she tried to figure out where—how—to start.

"Hello?" the voice repeated.

"Hey," she said, panicked. "Listen, I . . ."

"Put the phone down," the man with the cane said. He didn't bother to yell it, which scared her even more.

"What?" the voice on the other end of the phone said. "Hello?"

Her throat seemed swollen shut. She could have sworn her every breath whistled as it tried to force its way into her lungs. All the things she needed to say—the instructions she needed to give—swirled nonsensically in her mind. "Nikki," she said, but the men were climbing up the dock steps now, so close she could make them out clearly.

"Put the phone down," the man with the cane repeated.

She hung up and stuffed the phone back into her pocket, tried to look tough, even though she was trembling and pouring sweat. "You're late," she said. "I was about to leave."

The man with the cane grinned. One of his side teeth wore a silver cap, which matched the silver ball cane handle he was gripping.

"We show up when we want to show up," the boy said. But there was something funny about his voice. She thought maybe the briefcase trembled.

She crossed her arms over her chest so the two wouldn't see her hands shake. "You seem to have forgotten that I'm the one who can destroy your life," she said to the boy.

Worry flickered in his eyes. "Who did you just call?" he asked.

She tossed her hair back. "Don't worry, golden boy, I didn't out you yet. You play nice, and I'll play nice. That's how it works. Just give me the money and I'll be out of your life forever." *Or at least until I need more money,* she finished in her head.

The boy swallowed; then the man elbowed him. "Go ahead," he said. "Who cares who she called? Do it."

The boy held the briefcase toward her. She made no move to take it.

"It's all here? Five million?" she asked, staring into his eyes, refusing to look away.

"You don't trust us?" the boy said.

She laughed out loud. "Not for a second."

"It's all there," he said.

"I want to see it."

After a brief hesitation, he turned the briefcase so it was flat against his forearm. With his free hand, he popped open the clasps, and then slowly eased it open. The man with the cane let out a low whistle. Finally, she tore her eyes away from the boy's and gazed at the neat stacks of new bills within. Tears pricked the corners of her eyes. Her ticket out of Brentwood. Her freedom to finally live a real life. Maybe she would go to the Midwest. Get as far away from this life as humanly possible.

She nodded, and he reclosed the case, the snap of the clasps especially loud in the abandoned lot. Wordlessly, he extended the case toward her and she took it, her hand brushing up against his.

"Pleasure doing business with you," she said, though it

had been anything but. The only pleasure now would be getting the hell out of there.

Somehow she found the strength to move her shaky legs. She could feel more sweat roll down between her shoulder blades. She felt almost weak with relief. She'd done it. She'd gotten the money and gotten away. Away from them all. Forever.

She stopped just before passing her so-called protector. She was shorter than he by at least six inches, but she knew that for him, it was all about attitude. She gazed at him through the darkness, his dark-brown eyes nearly black. His betrayal hurt. So very disappointing.

"You can pass on this message. Do not. Fuck. With me," she said through gritted teeth. Satisfied, she sauntered slowly toward the stairs, her heart thrumming as if she'd been sprinting for miles.

Just as she reached the top step, she heard the rustle of swift movement, followed by a sharp cry of "Wait!" She turned at the top of the stairs, just in time to see the cane singing through the air toward her.

Her eyes shut involuntarily, and she brought her hand up to shield her face. There was time only to suck in a great gust of air, but never to let out the scream.

1

IF I WERE a conscientious student, I would be studying for my chem quiz instead of sitting on a window ledge, chain-smoking. But it was beautiful outside—clear, starry, kind of chilly. I loved the way the air in Brentwood smelled on nights like this. It was crisp and still and promising, and if you closed your eyes and inhaled deeply enough, you could even fool yourself into thinking you were catching a little whiff of the beach five miles away. So much better than the aroma of the high school, which smelled like old food, new money, and competition. And phoniness. So many fake people. Sometimes I wondered if a real feeling actually existed in this city, if you could trust the words of anyone here. I sure as hell didn't. When you lived in a town where it seemed like everyone claimed to have a sister in a music video or an uncle who was so-and-so's agent, it was hard to know who was real and who was a wannabe.

But I didn't give a crap about being a conscientious student, so instead of studying, I was sitting and smoking, my legs hung over the ledge, the backs of my shoes thunking, soft and rubbery, against the side of the house in time to the music pulsing through my computer speakers. I'd already dropped three butts to the rock landscaping below. Dad would have a shit fit later; would blame the gardener. But at the moment I didn't care. I was enjoying myself. I would finish my smoke, and then, I promised myself, I would go back inside and cram. Enjoyment over.

Who was I kidding—the air could have been choked with pollution, unbreathable, and I still would've rather been sitting on the ledge than hunched over a textbook, scratching notes onto index cards and memorizing formulas. I only had a semester and a half left until graduation, thank God, but that also meant I only had a semester and a half left to try to salvage my pathetic GPA. At the moment, my graduation status was iffy. The school called it *academic probation*. I called it hopeless.

Not that *academic probation* was a surprising new development for me. School had never exactly been my forte. I pretty much avoided being there every moment I could. Hence, the grade issues.

When I was a kid, I always wondered why nobody else talked about words and numbers looking magenta or brown or blue or yellow or silver. I never understood why emotions didn't have colors to other people, or how someone could be depressed without seeing a field of sickly greenish yellow everywhere, or why nobody else seemed to understand that happiness was pink.

Turned out I was the weird one. When I got to kindergarten, I couldn't concentrate on the alphabet, because I was too dazzled by all the colors. Math was torture, because threes were purple, but so was the letter *E*, and I was always getting them confused. And I hated it when teachers would say things like, "Roses are red," because while the right color for the word *red* was definitely red, the color for *roses* was more orangey pink.

And then there were the colors of feelings. My mom always called me "sensitive," but I learned later that she really meant "intuitive." Most people missed the little hints that we all give off when we're feeling sad or angry or happy or uncertain. But those feelings also had colors for me, so I couldn't miss them, even when I desperately wanted to. Where other people knew a room felt awkward, I knew the same room was blushing dusty pink.

But as a kid, I didn't know all this yet. Like all my friends, I didn't consciously realize that my second-grade teacher had red-rimmed, puffy eyes and a voice that turned down at the edges and hands that shook. I only knew that the putrid brown that her white chalk left behind made me cry. I didn't necessarily notice that the PE teacher's fists were balled up and his face tense with anger when he yelled at us, only that the numbers on his jerseys were always electric pulsing rage-monster red and they scared me.

And the worst, Mrs. Hinton, the art teacher who wrote her name so neatly in cursive. Later I would piece it together that, of course, there had been hints that she was sick. But at the time all I knew was that her room felt dull olive to me, and that halfway through the year, she was absent for a few days and never came back. I asked and asked if any of my friends had seen the ugly color in her room, but they hadn't. Only me. I felt responsible, like I had *made* her sick. She was probably dead, and I might have made her that way, too. Because of my colors.

After Mom died, and I became too afraid of letters and numbers to go to school, Dad bounced me around from doctor to doctor, trying to figure out what was wrong with me. I was only eight, and I was nervous and upset, so I couldn't describe what was going on any better than that the room felt brown or green or that the word *color* was like a flashing dance of primary hues. Most of the docs seemed to think it was an eye problem. One sent me off for brain scans. Two suggested therapy. And another insisted I was making it up; that I was trying to get attention. I learned quickly to put doctors on my People Not to Be Trusted list. When people in charge couldn't seem to figure out what was wrong with someone, they assumed that person was messed up in the head. God forbid we didn't have all the answers.

Dad was about to give up when we finally found a doctor who'd seen cases like mine before. He told us that some people's senses combine. They might hear a scent or see a feeling or smell a shape. Or, like me, see a color in a number or letter or emotion, or all of the above. It was rare, and pretty much impossible to treat, but at least we had a name for what was going on with me: synesthesia. He said it wasn't uncommon for someone to have more than one kind, like I did. He also said synesthetes could be highly intuitive, which explained why I could "see" Mrs. Hinton's sickness and the PE teacher's rage in my colors, even though nobody had ever exactly told me that Mrs. Hinton had hepatitis or the PE teacher had a short fuse. According to the doctor, this was like a gift. According to him, I was special. And in case I didn't like feeling special, I would eventually just get used to it. I would get to a point where I barely even noticed it.

That was third grade. A grade I got to be in twice, thanks to my special little gift. I was now just months from graduation and still avoiding my homework, so I guess that doctor was wrong. Instead of getting used to it, I learned to hide it well. The only person besides me and Dad who knew about it was the high school counselor, who Dad forced me to "open up to" after I started failing enough to make gradu-ation look iffy.

"You never know, Nikki," Dad had said. "He might be able to help you through a lot of old emotions, and then maybe this will go away." Because sometimes even Dad didn't get that my synesthesia wasn't just an emotional prob-lem to be solved.

But ten seconds in the same room with Mr. Ear Dan-druff or whoever the counselor was, I was wishing that he would just go away. It was clear that (a) he didn't believe a word I was saying, and (b) even if he did, he didn't exactly care.

"So you're saying you're too distracted thinking about colors to concentrate on your work," he'd said.

"Not really," I said, hating that I was having to talk about this once again, and that I hadn't gotten any better at explaining it at eighteen than I had been at eight.

"Not really," he repeated, his voice vaguely sarcastic. He wrote something on a piece of paper. I glared at him.

"It's not that I'm too busy thinking about colors to think about what we're doing in class," I said. "I'm trying to con-centrate, but the colors just . . . push in."

He nodded as if he'd just cracked the code to the uni-verse or something. "Push in." He was great at repeating stuff.

"Yeah, so I'll have to think, 'Is this a three or an *e*,' and by the time I've figured it out, I've completely lost my train of thought."

He wrote something else down, nodding. I shifted, starting to get irritated. "So you're working, and then you start thinking about what colors things should be, and you get distracted," he said.

"Yeah. Well, no. Not like you're saying."

He arched an eyebrow at me, pooching his lips together in thought. "Have you ever been tested for ADHD, Nikki?" he asked.

I sighed. "Yes. And I don't have ADHD. It's synesthesia."

He nodded, flipping back a few pages in my file. "Yes, yes, I see that." He glanced up at me and pasted on a patronizing smile. "I think we would be wise to look at ADHD again, since it's affecting your schoolwork. Testing has come a long way in the past ten years. They could have missed something when you were tested before. You might find a new, treatable diagnosis to be more satisfying to your grade card."

I stared at him, stunned. A *new, treatable diagnosis more satisfying*? Did he really think my dad and I were that dumb? That we just went with synesthesia because ADHD seemed too hard to deal with? Rusty starbursts began to glow in my vision. I imagined my eyes—dark, deep-set, intense—filling with those starbursts. I imagined my untidy straight brown hair floating on them, my angular features sharpening to rusty points as I became a starburst myself—my anger as visible to the counselor as it was to me. "You know," I said, gathering my things, "you can shove your ADHD test up your ass. Flunk me if you have to. Won't be the first time. I'll live." And I stormed out.

I half expected him to call Dad, and for Dad to read me the riot act for throwing away a chance to get help so that I could graduate. But he must not have. He must not have told anyone.

And I sure as hell wasn't telling anyone. I was an excellent secret keeper. They should hire me for the goddamned CIA. The colors were still there. Just nobody but me knew it.

When does anyone use chemistry in real life, anyway? Or math? Or Western Civ? You know what they should teach in school? How not to become a bitter, mistrustful ball of numb when life shits all over you. How to survive your mother's murder and never get any answers and still somehow come out the other end a useful human being. How to keep people at arm's distance so you don't lose your mind when they leave you, because no matter what they say, they always, always, always will, no matter what. That would be a useful class.

I dragged on my cigarette, pulling hard down to the filter, and used my thumb to flick it onto the rocks below with the others. It landed with a little fireworks show of sparks. Like a celebration. *Congratulations, Nikki, you are officially a chain-smoking, nonstudying, academic-probation, failing freak show. Let's throw a party for your bad self! Pow!*

I turned my face upward and slowly and ceremoniously exhaled, making my lips into a tight O to send a funnel of smoke into the sky, then reached into my pocket to pull out a new cigarette. Screw my promises to go in and cram. I wasn't going to get any chem done anyway.

But just as I reached into my pocket, I felt the familiar buzz of my phone against the side of my hand. I groaned. It was probably Jones again.

Jones was my ex. Newly ex, actually, and I didn't have the energy to talk to him. I'd been avoiding him at school ever since we broke up. Or rather, since I broke up with him. I could see rotting brown pulsing onto the cinder-barf school walls before he even rounded the corner to my locker or the lunchroom or the gym. The same decaying brown that made me cry when I was in kindergarten just made me hide now. Every time I saw Jones coming I doubled back, ducked into a restroom, rushed away. School was bad enough without enduring some schmaltzy romance novel scene in the hallway, starring heartbroken Jones and the cold bitch who broke his heart.

We'd been dating for months, and I was into him, I really was. He thought I was beautiful, even though I thought I was too skinny and plain. Overlookable. He had an excellent body, a killer smile, and an eager attitude that made him super easy to manipulate. Violet was the color I associated with lust, and I felt like a lit-up violet Christmas tree every time I came near him. Like a neon bar sign: *Nikki Kill on Tap Here!* Jones and I had so much passion I sometimes felt my very skin would light up when he touched me. And that passion didn't go away after I broke it off with him. I still wanted Jones. I just didn't want the same thing he wanted.

He ruined it all by falling in love, an adorable puppy trailing after his master. I knew it was getting bad when I started seeing color change around him—violet to pink to magenta. His heart practically beat out of his chest every time we were together. Fantastic.

I liked Jones. But I didn't love him. After seeing what happened to my parents, I didn't believe in it. Love, too young, spelled disaster, and I didn't want any part of it.

Jones had taken to calling me three or four times a day, begging for another chance, telling me how devoted he was, pleading to make things right between us. He had no idea that professing his love was exactly the wrong way to make things right. I'd taken to silencing his calls.

But I was four cigarettes in and feeling generous, so I pulled out my phone without even bothering to look who it was.

"Hello?"

There was nothing. Scratch that, there was something that sounded like rough footsteps in the distance, and some tight breathing.

"Hello?" I asked again. Irritated. If this was Jones's new method of trying to get me back, it was lame as hell. The heavy-breathing stalker method, Jones? Really?

"Hey," a voice said. It was quiet, the pitch high, like a girl's voice, or maybe a child's. "Listen, I . . ."

I heard something else, then. A man's voice in the distance, saying something that I couldn't quite make out.

"What? Hello?" I asked again.

The breathing got faster, more urgent.

"Nikki," the voice said, and while it was still unclear if it was a girl or a child, something about it itched with familiarity in the back of my mind.

The man in the background spoke again, and this time it was clear. "Put the phone down." And then the connection cut off.

I looked at the screen. The numbers were all their standard "correct" colors—two was green, nine was yellow, three was purple—but it wasn't a color order I recognized, and I was really good at recognizing and remembering color patterns. It wasn't Jones's number. I had no idea whose it was.

I held the phone in my free hand, waiting for it to ring again, but it never did. I lit a cigarette, the weirdness of the phone call dulling any real enjoyment I would have gotten out of it. I eventually flung it to the ground with the other butts, the night air now feeling cold and as if I didn't belong in it.

"Weird new tactic, Jones," I said softly. Even I didn't believe myself, though. He had a younger sister, one who might have been talked into giving the old ex a call, but subtlety wasn't exactly Jones's strength. He would've called back. He would have capitalized on such a chilling mystery by offering to come over and hold me until I calmed down or some other soppy bullshit like that. Jones was pathetic, but he wasn't this pathetic.

Who had it been, then? She'd said my name. It was hard to pretend it had just been a wrong number when the person said your name.

I pulled myself back into my room and tried to concentrate on chem, ignoring the rainbow of letters and numbers as they swirled around the page, wishing for a memory miracle. The doctor once told me he read about a patient who could remember every meal he'd eaten for the past nine years. I could totally believe it. I remembered strange, random things that normal people wouldn't, the colors associated with a date or an address or God-knew-what sticking tight to my brain, and I was great at memorizing things like phone numbers. Yet I couldn't seem to remember the other name for *antimony* to save my life, or whether magnesium or gallium was liquid at room temperature. Synesthesia was funny that way—always either a distraction or a tool, and only it could decide which it wanted to be at any given time, it seemed.

I accidentally pushed too hard with my pencil and broke the lead. Growling, I tossed it onto the desk. God, I hated homework.

I went downstairs and found Dad in the living room, cleaning out his camera bag. He glanced up.

"Done with homework already?"

I flopped onto the couch and propped my feet on the coffee table. "Sure, why not?" I said. "Pointless anyway."

"Ah, must be working on chem," he said, vigorously wiping off a lens with a cloth.

"What else?" I said. "Just distracted, I guess." I sat up. "Hey, the house phone hasn't rung or anything, has it?"

His brow furrowed. "No. Why?"

"No reason," I said. "I thought I heard it is all." I definitely hadn't heard it, but figured it was worth a shot. "I got a weird call on my cell."

He put down the lens and picked up another. "Weird? How so?"

"Someone said my name. I'm sure it was just a prank," I said.

"They still make prank calls these days?"

Come to think of it, not really. In fact, I had never gotten one before in my life. Caller ID made prank calling too difficult. Or maybe people just didn't get that bored anymore. But that only served to make the phone call even weirder. "I guess so," I said.

"Well, no wonder you're distracted," Dad said. "Want to help?"

"Sure." I scooted down onto the floor next to him and began pulling camera supplies out of his bag, sorting and cleaning them, the whole time Dad grilling me about my grades and how I was going to make sure I would graduate. A topic that he never stopped talking about, and one that always wore me out.

When we finished, I checked the clock. It had been an hour. If ever there was a time for a smoke break, it was now. I headed back upstairs, shut my computer, and started for my cigarettes, but was interrupted by the buzz of my phone again.

I grabbed the phone and fumbled it, catching it at the last minute between my arm and stomach. It was the same number as before—I still didn't recognize it, but whoever it was, they were way desperate, a realization that made orange start creeping over the numbers, blotting out their correct colors. I recovered the phone, gripped it tightly, and hit the answer button, half expecting to feel the heat of that orange against my cheek.

"Hello?"

"Uh, yes, is this Nikki?" a woman's voice on the other

end said, and then went on before I could even answer. "I'm trying to reach Nikki. It's an emergency." Definitely not the same childlike voice that had called earlier.

"This is Nikki," I said. "Can I help y—"

"You must come quickly," the voice said. "She's in terrible shape, barely hanging on."

"What? Come where? Who is this?"

The woman on the other end took a frustrated breath. "This is Ronald Reagan UCLA Medical Center calling," she said. "You need to come right away. She might not make it through the night."

"Who?" I asked. There was no "she" in my life. The only real "she" who had ever been in my life was my mother, and she had died long ago. "She who?"

"We were hoping you could tell us," the voice said. "We've brought a girl in. An anonymous caller found her, but he was gone before the ambulance got there. You're the only contact number in her phone. She has no ID, no nothing."

I paused, pulled the phone away from my ear, and studied the numbers again. "I don't . . ." *I don't have any friends,* I wanted to finish, but that sounded too pathetic to divulge, even to a stranger. I didn't have any. Not real friends. Not in this fucked-up town full of plastic dolls and expensive wannabe whores. I had my stock of social media "friends," and my sparring "friends" at the *dojang,* and maybe even some of

Jones's idiot bro-gang "friends," but anyone I'd actually hang out with? Anyone who would have me, and only me, in their phone contacts list? Never. "I think this is a mistake."

"Would you be willing to at least come and see if you can identify the girl? We really need to get ahold of the family."

"It's that bad? She's, like, not conscious?"

"Yes," the nurse answered. "And I can't stress enough that you need to hurry. Please, Miss . . ."

"Kill," I supplied for her. "I'm Nikki Kill."

She cleared her throat, the way so many people do when they hear my last name. "Please, Miss Kill. She may not have much time."

"And this isn't a prank."

"Absolutely not. This is the hospital calling. I've—"

"Because if it is, and you're just messing with me, you are some kind of sick jerk," I interrupted.

There was a pause, and then the nurse's voice came back, sounding very serious. "I can assure you, what has happened to this young lady is no joking matter. You'll see when you get here. If you're going to come, you should do so soon."

I stared out the window, considering my options. "Okay, I'll be there," I said reluctantly.

This was too weird. It couldn't be a mistake—the nurse knew my name—but it sure as shit could be a joke. I mostly flew under the radar at school, but maybe Jones had finally gotten angry about the breakup and had turned some of his bro-gang and bro-gang sympathizers against me. Was Jones capable of that? I didn't think so. Jones was much more the follow-you-around-begging type.

Out of habit, I pulled out another cigarette, but just as I held the lighter up to it, I froze. I couldn't ignore what I knew. The orange. Something in the caller's voice had made me feel orange. My cynical side told me this was a setup. But the orange in my head told me this was a true emergency.

And I was just curious enough to find out what kind of emergency we were talking about.

I T WAS AFTER midnight, but the TV was still droning downstairs, so I knew Dad hadn't gone to bed yet. I would have to sneak out. Not that I was too worried about it. I'd been an expert at sneaking out of my house since middle school. It wasn't too hard to sneak out on a guy who pretty much didn't notice what I did on a daily basis anyway.

I crept down the stairs as softly as I could, prepared to make up something if he should catch me and grill me about where I was going on a school night.

I have to borrow chem notes from a friend, I practiced in my head. *I left something in my car. No big deal. I'll be right back.* Or how about this one: *Dude, I'm eighteen, I can leave whenever I want.*

No, that would probably just open up some sort of "conversation" that I definitely didn't want to get dragged into. When Dad wanted to "have a one-on-one conversation," things got pretty agonizing pretty fast. Also, I didn't like to hide things from him. Dad was mostly a cool guy who'd been dealt a really raw deal in this life. And we had a pretty easy system going. He didn't mess around in my business, and I didn't give him reason to want to.

I reached the bottom of the stairs and peered around the corner into the living room. Dad's leather recliner was empty. I could see light spilling from his study onto the wood hallway floor, could hear his fingers tapping on the computer inside the study. I grabbed my jacket and slipped through the front door, turning the doorknob so it wouldn't click behind me. He'd have no idea I'd ever left.

I got into my car, put it in neutral, and coasted down the hill before starting it, then took off toward the hospital.

Driving had always been a challenge for me. If there was ever a time I was surrounded by letters and numbers, it was while driving. I'd learned to ignore most of it but still got distracted by the occasional house number or name on a mailbox. But tonight I had no time for distraction. And even if I did, I was already preoccupied enough by thoughts of what I would find at the hospital. Would the mystery girl already be dead?

I sped through the night, talking to myself. "Okay, Nikki,

this is weird. But you've done weird before, right? Your life's default setting is weird, so you've got this." What was I talking about—this was weirder than weird. The woman on the phone hadn't even told me what had happened to this so-called dying patient. Was it a car crash? An accident at home? Was she mangled, missing body parts, burned, bloody? *She might not live through the night*—that definitely sounded bloody. Dear God, could I even do bloody? I remembered bloody. Bloody was terrifying. Bloody was life-altering.

My phone buzzed, and thinking it might be the hospital again, I quickly hit the Bluetooth button on my steering wheel.

"Yeah?"

"Hey, Nik." Jones. Cripes.

"Listen, Jones, now's not a great time."

"I just want to talk," he said.

I let out a deep, calming breath. It didn't work. I was still irritated. "We've talked. And talked and talked. There really isn't anything else to say."

"You in the car?" He sounded like he'd been drinking. A little aggressive, a little slurred. "Shit, Nikki, are you on a date? The body's not even cold yet and you're already with somebody else? What the fuck?"

A shiver went down my spine. *The body's not even cold yet.* I hoped that wasn't a harbinger of what I would find at the hospital.

I bit down on my annoyance. Part of me wanted to tell him, *Yes, we're on a date. We plan to park in your driveway and screw our brains out to that stupid* Say Anything *song you were always making me listen to, and then we're going to fall in love and get married and have tons of babies and maybe we'll name one Jones just so you can be even more pathetic than you already are. Will that make you stop calling me?*

"Relax, I'm not on a date," I said instead.

"You're in the car. I can hear it."

I sighed, flipped on my turn signal. I could see the hospital in the distance. "Yes, I'm in the car, but I'm alone. Can't we do this later? At school tomorrow?" *When I can see you coming and run away from you?*

There was a noise, almost like choking, which turned into a drunken sob, and I nearly groaned out loud. "I thought you loved me, Nik. What happened?"

"I don't have time to talk about this right now, Jones. Go home and sober up. And I never told you I loved you."

"But I love you."

"I know. You've told me. And I've got to go."

Before he could respond, I hit the end call button on my steering wheel. If the phone rang again—and it probably would, if Jones was being true to form—I would just ignore it, no matter who might be on the other end.

Soon I was turning into UCLA Medical, scanning for a parking space in front of the emergency room.

The lobby was mostly empty, except for a couple sitting in a corner, the woman holding her head in her hands, the man rubbing a wet washcloth on the back of her neck. ERs always made me think of neon green—pain. I held my breath while I walked by just in case it was contagious pain.

"May I help you?" a nurse at the front desk asked.

I let out the breath I'd been holding. "I'm looking for someone," I said. "I'm not sure who. They called me. I'm Nikki Kill."

"Nikki Kill," the nurse repeated, typing into her computer. Her eyes went wide. "Oh, yes. You're here for the one who came in on the ambulance. She's in Bay Nineteen. Go through those doors and take a left."

Suddenly nervous, I wiped my palms on my jeans and followed where she was pointing to a set of double doors. I pushed a button on the wall, and they swung open slowly. I went through and turned left and walked past bays filled with moaning patients and beeping equipment until I found Bay 19. The curtain was pulled closed around the bed, and I could hear the hum and tweet of machines, but no voices within.

I quickly scanned the area for a nurse or doctor who could maybe give me some answers, but none were around. I turned back to the curtain.

"Hello?" I called out softly. "Is anyone in there?"

There was no response. I pulled back the curtain and stepped into the bay.

Immediately, my breathing went ragged, and the room began to swoop and swim.

The girl's face was swollen, puffy, distorted, nearly unrecognizable. Her hair was caked with blood and lying stiffly across the pillow underneath her. Bandages, soaked through, were wrapped around her head, her neck, her upper arm. And the machines. There were so many machines—wires and tubes snaking out of her, the color of the numbers on their readouts so strong it was practically blinding me. The blood pressure monitor, the oxygen reader, the pulse monitor. Forget their correct colors—all of them were shaded a deep crimson. I felt surrounded by it. I checked my own shaking hands and saw that they, too, were crimson, reflecting the lighted numbers from the machines. I knew this color.

Instantly, I was eight. I was coming home from my friend Wendy's house. I'd had dinner with her family, and it was late evening when her dad dropped me off in my driveway. I was carrying a sack filled with Tootsie Rolls and singing the song that had just been on the car radio, totally relaxed, totally happy.

So relaxed and happy, in fact, I didn't even notice that the front door was wide-open, the house completely dark and silent. Didn't notice, until I felt my shoe slide on the tile and looked down to see my mother's outstretched arm, lying in the same pool of blood I was standing in. The numbers on her watch were covered, too, making them deep crimson.

Mom's hand twitched, the crimson pulsing at me. My hands relaxed, the Tootsie Rolls splashing in the blood. I looked at her face. Her eyes rolled to meet mine.

"Nikki . . . go . . . ," she wheezed.

But I couldn't go. I could only stand there, feet frozen in her blood, and stare at her watch as its pulsing crimson numbers followed my mom's heartbeat. They skipped fast while she turned her head to look directly at the ceiling, then slowed as her eyes closed. I watched in horror as time stretched between the beating of the numbers. The pulses got more uneven, and then shone a steady, thick crimson. I knew then that she was going to die.

Crimson meant death.

If the color in my head was right, if my intuition was spot-on, the girl in Bay 19 was going to die. And seeing her there like that—seeing all that crimson—practically knocked me down. Her face bent and swirled into my mother's face, her blood my mom's blood, the lifeless hand lying across her stomach my mom's hand reaching for help on the tile floor. I blinked, trying to steady myself, trying to clear my mom out of my eyes. I wanted to vomit, to pass out, to run—all the things I didn't, and couldn't, do when I found my mother.

"Oh, God," I rasped, as my breathing got faster. It felt like my heart was going to squeeze my chest dry. I pressed my fingers against my eyes and tried to push away the woozy feeling. But it wasn't working, so I backed out of the bay, accidentally knocking into the wall that separated Bay 19 from Bay 20. My cell phone fell out of my jacket pocket and slid across the tile floor, coming to a stop under her bed. I didn't go after it. I just needed to get out of all that crimson for a minute.

I took two steps back, three, four, half doubled over. I felt myself bump into something from behind again. Scattered, I whirled to find myself face-to-face with a cop.

"Jesus!" I breathed.

"Whoa," he said, holding his hands out toward me. "Got to watch where you're walking in here." His forehead creased into concern. "You okay?" He took my elbow and led me toward a wheeled office chair at a computer station. "Here, sit down. You look faint."

I followed his guiding hand and eased into the chair. I took three deep breaths and willed my heart to slow, willed the images of my mother's lifeless body out of my mind.

"Stay here, I'll be right back." The cop stepped away, during which time I closed my eyes and focused my breathing, trying to get back in command of the situation. I hated being out of control. I hated going back to that place with my mother. Back to the worst day of my life.

Why was I even here? I wasn't meant to be here. Not for *this* girl. Despite her bloodied and puffy face, and despite the little side trip down memory lane, I'd still recognized the girl in the bed, and it only deepened the mystery of why in the hell they'd summoned me.

She was Peyton Hollis, lovely, doe-eyed daughter of noted film producer Bill Hollis. As if his power and money didn't make him sexy enough, Bill Hollis was known for having trotted out Peyton and her brother for the tabloids and entertainment shows, holding their tiny hands in his big, important ones, dolloping ketchup on their fries at the Malibu Country Mart, petting bunnies with them at Studio City Farmers Market. Most people, including me, couldn't pick Peyton's mom out of a crowd of two, but anyone who'd ever read a magazine in a dentist's office would recognize the salt-and-pepper-haired movie executive and the beautiful children he doted on.

Admittedly, I hadn't seen Peyton in the press for a long time. And she definitely wasn't a child anymore. In recent months, she'd gone from sweet little rich girl to punk rocker with a trust fund. She wasn't Hallmark-card cute anymore, but she also wasn't rehab-scandalous. Translation: too boring for the gossip pages. She was still queen of our high school, though—popular, head of Drama Club and Choral Group, but she was also popular for other things now, too, like hosting epic parties at her house—a place all of us knew as Hollis Mansion. Most notably, she was lead singer for Viral Fanfare, an underground garage band that played at pretty much every A-list party in Brentwood. Not that I was an A-list partier by any stretch. But when Peyton Hollis was involved, everyone in the free world had to know all about it. Including no-listers like me.

I knew who she was, but I didn't *know* Peyton. We weren't friends. We weren't even in the same stratosphere—the weirdo flunk-out and the ruler of all that is high school. Yet my number was the only number in her cell phone? It didn't make sense.

I didn't need this shit. Not right now. Not with Jones hassling me and with trying not to fail my senior year. Not when I'd finally gotten to a place where I didn't think about my mother's murder every day.

I should've told the nurse who called me that this wasn't my problem, that my phone number being in that phone was a mistake. I should have stayed on my window ledge, where I was happy with my crisp air and cigarettes. Peyton Hollis had so many friends. So many other people to be there for her. People who would fall all over themselves to keep vigil in that pulsing crimson room. What was I supposed to do here, anyway? I couldn't stop someone from dying. It's not like Peyton would help me if I were dying. She was royalty and I was no one.

I opened my eyes and started to get up. *Fuck it, I'm out,* I said to myself. *Let the Hollis family deal with their own problems.*

But before I could make a move, the cop reappeared,

holding a Styrofoam cup in my face. "Here," he said. "I brought you some water."

"I'm fine. Just leaving, actually. I'm not the one who should be here." But he didn't budge, and I couldn't get up with him blocking me. "Excuse me?" I said pointedly.

"Just have a drink first," he coaxed. "You looked like you were about to pass out over there. I don't feel good about you getting behind the wheel of a car just yet."

Impatiently, I grabbed the cup and sipped from it as I studied his police badge. Detective Chris Martinez. Kind of cute. Definitely young, maybe early twenties. Close-cropped black hair, muscles, stubble. Something behind his eyes looked wounded, or maybe just jaded, not that I could fault him for it. I was the most wounded and jaded person I knew. Hell, I was so wounded and jaded I was about to bail on a battered girl. But there was something about the erect way he stood—important and eager—that made me think of sparkling gold. His badge numbers came across as bright yellow. If my instincts were right, he believed in the whole serve-and-protect thing, heavy on the *protect*. Too bad I didn't need his help, because this was not my problem. Peyton needed his help. I needed a cigarette and some distance. Let Detective Martinez handle the Peyton situation.

"Your color is looking better," he said, and at first I was confused, thinking maybe he had synesthesia, too, and what were the odds. But then I realized he was talking about the color of my face. My hairline was ringed with cold sweat, but the burning in my cheeks had stopped.

"Great," I said. "So I'll be going now." I started to get up again, but he still didn't move.

"Just curious, what had you so rattled in the first place? You looked like you'd seen a ghost."

I squared my shoulders and tried to look confident, unfazed by how close his assessment was. "I just didn't expect to see her looking like that, I guess. I didn't know how bad she was."

His eyebrows went up. "Her?" He motioned toward Bay 19. "You know her?"

I nodded. "It's Peyton Hollis. Everyone knows her."

"Hollis?" he repeated. He seemed to be searching for the name. "As in Bill Hollis?"

I nodded. "The producer. That's her dad. Like I said, everyone knows her. I have no idea why I'm here."

He arched one eyebrow. "You're part of everyone, aren't you?"

I cocked my head to the side. "Not to Peyton Hollis. I'm no one."

He gave me a long look, then flagged down a nurse and whispered to her. The nurse nodded, pulled a piece of paper out of her pocket, jotted Peyton's name on it, and hurried away.

I set the cup on the counter behind me and finally stood, forcing him to shuffle back a step. "What happened to her?" I asked.

"I was hoping you could tell me that," he said.

I glanced at the curtain again. I had left it open a crack when I'd backed out of it, and I could see crimson glowing out, could see one of Peyton's closed, swollen eyes. I swallowed. *Confidence, Nik. Cold confidence. That's not your mother in there. It's not.* "I have no idea."

"You're not friends at school?"

"No. Not at all. I mean, I knew her. *Know* her," I corrected, realizing I had just spoken about her in the past tense. "I actually haven't seen her at school in a couple of weeks."

Now that I thought about it, the last time I saw her at school was the day she showed up with her perfect, shiny blond hair chopped into uneven, dry-looking hunks and dyed mousy brown. Everyone was talking about it, and saying she'd also gotten a tattoo on the side of her neck. On someone like me these changes would have looked "gross" and "skanky" and everyone would have assumed I was suddenly on drugs or had joined a gang or something. But on Peyton Hollis they were cool rebellion, and soon everyone would be cutting their hair that way and begging their parents for neck tattoos.

The next day, she was nowhere to be found. Some

people said she quit school, but nobody really believed it. Royalty like Peyton Hollis didn't quit school. Crowds were their lifeblood.

"You never hung out?" Detective Martinez asked.

I shook my head.

"Ever meet her family?"

I shook again.

"Know of any enemies Peyton might have had? Anyone who might want to hurt her?"

I thought it over. Did Peyton Hollis have enemies? Yes, and no. Everyone envied Peyton. She was so popular, everyone wanted to be her friend. Hell, everyone wanted to *be her*. But her popularity also made everyone hate her in their own way. Wasn't that how it always worked? People killed themselves to put you up on a pedestal, just so they could watch you lose your balance and fall, and even pull you down when you weren't falling fast enough. When the whole world idolized you, did that mean the whole world was your enemy, too?

But the phone call I'd gotten before the hospital had called. The one that had said my name and hung up. I didn't have the first clue why, but I was now sure that call was Peyton. And, if it was, there had been a male voice in the background. Was that person an enemy?

How on earth would I know? And why would I want to? Why help this cop, when cops had never done anything to help me? Hadn't I asked as many questions about my mom's death ten years before? Hadn't I gotten big old shoulder shrugs from everyone? Whoever was in the background of that phone call was presumably still out there. It seemed safer to just stay out of it.

I shrugged. "Not that I know of. Like I said, I wasn't . . . *am not* . . . part of her group or anything. Um, shouldn't someone contact her family?"

"We're working on that. Having someone identify her definitely helps."

Detective Martinez stared off toward the curtain, chewing one side of his lip. I wondered if he knew something he wasn't telling.

"Any idea why you're the only number in her phone?" he finally asked.

"No," I answered. "No idea at all."

"Mind if I leave you my card? In case you come up with information we should know about."

Yes, in fact, I did mind. I didn't want to be part of this at all. But I would be lying if I said I wasn't a little curious about what had happened to her, too. "I doubt I will. Like I said, I don't know anything about Peyton Hollis's private life at all."

"Can't hurt to think on it some, though, right?" he said. He fished around in his pocket and pulled out a business card, then fished again and cursed. "Forever losing my pen.

Here, you mind?" He gestured toward the double doors and I followed him to the front desk, where he borrowed a pen from the nurse he'd spoken to earlier, who was just hanging up the phone when we got there.

"I've contacted the family," she said, and the detective nodded. "Someone's on the way now."

He wrote something on the back of his business card, and handed it to me. I turned it over. His cell phone number had been written there, the digits every bit as yellow as the ones on his badge. "You have a number where I can reach you? In case I need to ask some questions?"

I gave him my information, and he wrote it on the back of a different business card, which he tucked into his shirt pocket.

"Thanks for your help, Miss Kill," he said. He gestured to the card still in my hand. "You think of anything, just give me a call. You never know which details are important details."

I nodded and watched him stride through the automatic double doors and get into his police car, which was parked in the tow-away zone at the curb.

I stood there for a long while after he left, listening to the cars pull in and out of the parking lot, letting the night air calm me down and clear my mind. Being outside the hospital, away from the crimson, was far less frightening than being by Peyton's bedside, but something was keeping me from just walking to my car and leaving. There was something so curious about the whole situation, and somehow I felt obligated to stay, even though I knew this was so not my problem and that Peyton wouldn't stay there for me, and even though I'd heard the nurse say the Hollises were coming to be with her, so I knew she wouldn't be alone.

An ambulance pulled up to the curb, lights flashing, and I took a few steps back, my mind trying to eel its way back to all that crimson, back to my mom. I was in the way here. I wasn't needed. More importantly, it wasn't good for me to dredge up all those horrible memories.

I stuck Detective Martinez's card, which I hadn't realized I was still holding, into my jacket pocket, then had a panic moment. My phone was missing. Frantically, I patted all my pockets until I remembered it rattling on the floor and skidding under Peyton's bed.

Damn it. I was going to have to go back and get it. I wasn't sure if I could make myself do it. I didn't want another scene like before. But I needed my phone. Even if I spent most of the time dodging Jones on it.

Slowly, my stomach clenching with the very thought of it, I turned and went back to Bay 19.

3

A NURSE PLOWED through the curtain and nearly bowled me over as I approached Peyton's bay.

"Sorry," she said. "We're getting ready to move her upstairs. You want to see her real quick before we go?"

Not really. But I nodded and pushed through the curtain, steeling myself for what I would find on the other side. *The worst color. There will be the worst color, Nik, a whole lot of it. But you can handle it. You handled it before. You can get a grip and deal with whatever it is you see. It's not your mother in there. It's Peyton Hollis. You know this. You are prepared this time.*

But I was wrong. I wasn't prepared at all for what I found on the other side of the curtain.

Peyton was no longer alone. A boy was sitting next to her bed, clutching her hand. He turned to look at me when I stepped through the curtain, and I felt my face flush.

Dru Hollis. Peyton's brother. He was a year older than me—had graduated last year—and was something of a legend at our school, mostly for his aloof and mysterious, live-on-the-edge lifestyle. While Peyton disappeared from the tabloids, they seemed to eat him up, always catching him on a volcano scuba trip, or in a Vegas hotel gripping the hands of barely dressed, beautiful women twice his age, or zipping along the Marrakech loop on a motorcycle. With his looks and connections, a lot of people had him pegged to be the next big star of one of his father's movies. But he didn't seem to have the temperament for it. Where Bill Hollis was the sexy, powerful, charming face of Hollywood, his son, Dru, had a reputation for being ruthless, not as likely to smile for the camera so much as break it, and your nose with it. Instead of going away to college, Dru just went away, moving into his own apartment, constantly traveling, picking up a half-dozen bit parts in movies, where he looked bored and slightly bitter to be there, everything else he did with his time the subject of a great many awe-filled rumors. But mostly Dru Hollis was known for being unknowable. He kept his public life and his private life very separate.

And I could see why girls would line up to be with him. His expensive sport coat and khakis were so perfectly fitted, they wrapped around his tan skin like butter. Styled to look careless, he practically reeked of influence and adventure, as if he was ready to climb a mountain or negotiate a business deal or lay down a royal flush any second of the day. I had noticed him at school—everyone noticed him at school—but had never been this close to him before. He was flawless, perfection. I had to remind myself to breathe and do my best to ignore the violet thoughts that wanted to push into my brain. I liked to think of myself as immune to obvious guys like Dru Hollis, but nobody could truly ignore who he was.

After a beat of surprise, he let go of Peyton's hand and stood, the khakis sliding along the lines of his muscles.

"Sorry," he said, wiping tears from beneath his eyes with his fingers. He gazed at Peyton. "It's just . . . she looks so bad."

I didn't say anything. I was too struck by him to open my mouth. I'd never been alone in the same room with Dru Hollis before, and I was suddenly thirteen again. It was seriously starting to piss me off.

He held his hand out. "Dru," he said. "I'm Peyton's brother. They just called me. Thank God I was close by."

I took his hand, feeling a jolt run through me as I met his eyes. Despite looking tired and red-rimmed, they were searching, as if he was accustomed to always being allowed entrance into souls, just because of who he was. Something about the way he gazed into me made me feel naked. The violet I was ignoring pulsed brighter. I let go of his grip, tried to compose myself by staring at his hand. His knuckles looked red and swollen around the tan line of a ring, a scuff of raw skin skidding across the back of his hand. That was probably what most girls loved about Dru Hollis—he was rich but rugged. Privileged without being pampered.

"I'm Nikki," I said. "They called me here, too."

I saw a flicker of something strange pass over Dru's face. Confusion, maybe? Irritation? He went back to her bedside and sat, grabbed the same hand he'd been holding before, and pressed it to his cheek. "Who would've done something like this?" he asked. "Why? Why would someone hurt Peyton? If she dies . . ."

He trailed off, but I could have just about finished the sentence for him. I knew what he was thinking. *If she dies, I'll die, too. If she dies, someone will pay. If she dies, will I ever be fixable?* There were a boatload of ways to finish *If she dies,* and I knew every last one of them, because my mom did die, and I lived through that same loop of horrible thoughts. I spent more sleepless nights with *why* than I could count. I felt another squeeze in my chest, but this one was different from the one before. It was pity for Dru. I knew how his heart was breaking, because mine had broken just like it ten years ago. And as far as I could tell, I was anything but fixable.

"She won't," I said, moving a step toward him. "She's strong." I said this like I knew her, and then I realized that, in a way, I did know at least that much about her. I'd seen how she'd worked the school, students and teachers alike. I'd seen the way she'd organized everything from parties to protests. Let nobody get in her way. Peyton Hollis was strong as hell. A force to be reckoned with. "She's a fighter. She'll fight."

But somebody out there was stronger, a bigger force. Somebody out there had beaten the fight right out of her. She didn't look like a fighter right now. Pale and lifeless, with all those tubes and wires wrapping her up, she reminded me more of a fly in a spider's web.

Who was your spider, Peyton?

"Yeah," Dru said. "She definitely knows how to survive. She's a Hollis, after all." He was quiet for a moment, and then seemed to shake off a thought. "I haven't ever seen you around. You two hang out much?"

I shook my head. "No. You?"

He gave a breathy chuckle. "She's my sister."

"Oh, right," I said. "I wasn't thinking. Sorry."

The curtain rustled open again, and the nurse who'd nearly knocked me down before came in. Dru backed up to make room for her. "Okay, guys, we're going to move her upstairs," the nurse said. "I can get some blankets and pillows for you."

"No," I said. The thought of spending a whole night bathed in Peyton's crimson lights and Dru's dark, electric stare terrified and nauseated me. I needed air. I needed space. I needed time to think, to process. "I'll just grab my phone and go."

I bent to retrieve my phone, and that was when I saw the rumors were true—Peyton actually had gotten a neck tattoo. It was small and had the sharp lines of new ink, all in black and gray, which seemed an odd choice for what it was—a rainbow, surrounded by clouds. The words *Live in Color* were scripted beneath the curve of the bottom stripe. To me, it was beautiful, the words jumping out in vibrant gem tones, especially against the gray of the rainbow. I wanted to reach out and touch it, as I so often did when words took on a particularly stunning hue. But Dru stepped toward me, and I resisted.

I tore my eyes away from the tattoo and bent all the way down to the floor, lowering myself to my hands and knees so I could find my phone.

When I stood up again, Dru had gone back to Peyton's bedside. It seemed like the perfect time to leave. "I'm really sorry about your sister."

I didn't wait for him to respond but ducked back through the curtain and practically raced out of the emergency ward and through the double doors into the waiting room. Only then did I slow down a little to collect myself.

But just as the sliding doors swished open in front of me, I heard a voice calling from behind.

"Nikki!" I turned. Dru was rushing through the doors

after me. I waited. "Hey," he said when he reached me. "Did you drive here?"

"Yeah, why?"

"Let me walk you to your car." He gestured toward where we'd just come from. "This has got me a little on guard, you know?"

He wasn't the only one. In general, I wasn't easily shaken, but I would admit that seeing Peyton's injuries had me eyeing the parking lot a little closer than I normally would. I felt like eight-year-old Nikki again—afraid that the bad guys who'd killed my mom might jump out at me and take me out, too. Not that I had any reason to trust Dru Hollis, but another warm body was better than nothing.

"Consider it a thank-you," he said. "For coming."

"Sure," I said. "Of course."

We walked to my car, awkward silence stretching between us. Away from the heavy hospital smell, I was able to catch his scent. The night air commingled with his cologne and drifted through me, practically carried me. He smelled rich, rugged, sexy, and like he didn't know it, which only made him even sexier. I was conscious of everything—the way I walked, the wrinkles in my shirt, the catches in my hair from being windblown on the window ledge earlier. I wondered if I smelled like smoke.

Once we got to my car, I finally spoke. "This . . . didn't happen at your house, did it?"

Hollis Mansion was huge, and the setting of a museum of epic parties. If someone came to school laughing about having lost anything from shoes to car keys to their virginity, chances were high that it happened during a party at Peyton's. The mansion was like Pleasure Island—the place where fun happens and nobody has to answer to anything. It was weird to think of the boy standing beside me being part of that scene. Even despite the rumors about him. It was even weirder to think an intruder might have gotten in there and tried to kill one of them.

"No," he said. "The nurse told me someone found her in a parking lot, called it in, and split." He wrung his hands together. "I don't know who it was. I'm just glad she got some help."

We fell into silence again, and I wasn't sure if I was supposed to get into my car now, or if he had more to say.

"What happened?" I asked, to break the tension. I pointed at his hand.

He glanced at it, splaying his fingers out, and then covered it with his other hand and let them both drop in front of him. "Basketball game," he said. "Got a little rough. Also took an elbow." He rubbed his cheek, right below his eye, and I noticed for the first time that it was bruised and swollen as well.

"Damn, tough game."

He stared back toward the hospital. "Better than being

on one of my father's job interviews, which was where I was supposed to be," he said.

"Job interview?"

"Nothing," he said. "My parents think I need some *direction*." He said the last with a heavy tinge of sarcasm.

"So you burn off energy by beating up basketballs?"

He turned to me, and I got the patented Dru Hollis guarded stare full-on for the first time.

My cheeks burned. "Sorry. It's been a weird night."

"Yeah," he said. "It has. I don't understand it. Why would someone want to hurt Peyton?"

"I have no idea," I said. "And they said I was the only contact in her phone. Why? Why not you? Or your parents?"

"I don't know," he said, looking surprised. "My dad's going to be shattered. They're really close. I couldn't get ahold of him. He has no clue. None of this makes any sense."

"Maybe it was an accident?" I said hopefully.

"Maybe," he echoed, but he sounded doubtful. "Listen, I really appreciate you coming." He reached around me for the door handle. Instinctively, I tensed, fixing my eyes on the point on his throat that I would punch if he did something fishy. But then he smiled at me and I relaxed a little. That smile. It was so disarming. Alarmingly disarming.

"No problem."

He pulled open my door and stepped back so I could get in. He licked his lips—*God, they looked so soft!*—and we locked eyes again, a gaze that swept through me, made me breathless.

"No, I mean thank you for everything. For being there with Peyton. For reminding me what she's made of. You made me feel a lot better. I can maybe have a little hope."

"I've sort of been there," I said. "I get it."

His eyes narrowed, as if he were studying me. "You really do, don't you?"

I couldn't answer. I could see the letters on his key fob, a leather souvenir from the Dominican Republic, which hung out of his front pocket, begin to glow lavender, then purple, and then violet so bright I could feel it in my throat.

I wasn't the only one feeling that current between us.

Or was I? That violet could have been all me.

I swallowed again, tearing my eyes away from the fob, trying to put Cool and Controlled Nikki back in place. "I should go. My dad doesn't know I'm gone."

"It is pretty late," he said.

I squeezed past him and got into my car. "See you."

"Yeah. It was nice meeting you, Nikki," he said. "And thanks for"—he shot me a look that was part grateful, part wary—"everything." He pushed my door shut with a thud.

I started the car, put it into gear, and took off, glad to be free of the unnerving Hollis pull.

I TOSSED AND turned all night, seeing Peyton's face morph into my mom's, and when I woke up all I could think about was what I'd seen in Dru's key chain, which I'd regretted about ten seconds after I pulled away from the parking garage. Everything felt wrong, like I was being played. Like I was involved in something I shouldn't have been. Like I had let myself be sucked in by his charm like some swoony, desperate girl. And I was generally not big on being "involved" in things to begin with.

I had no idea what I was doing on my chem quiz, but I didn't have time to care about that. I still had a D in the class, and if I didn't screw up my finals, I just might pull out enough of a grade to graduate. I had time.

Not that it was possible to concentrate on schoolwork anyway. Word had already gotten out about what had happened to Peyton, and everyone was talking about it.

"I heard she rolled her car, like, ten times," a girl said in first period. "They say she was running from drug dealers when she did it. You saw that tattoo on her neck, didn't you? Who does that?"

"Nuh-uh, it was cops she was running from. And I heard she got run over by a truck," someone else said.

"I thought it was that she was dating some college guy and he beat her up because he caught her cheating. With a girl," yet another person chimed in.

Killed themselves to put you up on a pedestal, just so they could watch you lose your balance and fall, and even pull you down when you weren't falling fast enough.

I wanted to turn on them, tell them all to shut up because they had no idea what they were talking about, and just yesterday they were all wanting to be her and talking about the neck tattoos they were going to get. But then I remembered I actually had no idea what had happened to Peyton, either, and they could have been right for all I knew, not to mention why on earth would I be sticking up for Peyton Hollis anyway? *Stay out of it, Nikki,* I told myself about a thousand times. *It's not your business.*

Still, I wondered how her night had gone—if she was still comatose, or if she'd stirred and asked for me, or if she hadn't made it after all. Would anyone have found a way to tell me if she'd died? And should I even care? Before last night, would I have cared? I thought probably not.

By the end of the day, people were talking about going to visit her after school. Some of her friends had collected money during lunch shift for flowers. There was going to be a carpool. A caravan of carpools. So predictable. They'd probably show up with entire greenhouses full of flowers, with cashmere teddy bears, these people who'd spent the day relentlessly passing around rumors about her. Brentwood was dangerously close to Hollywood in so many ways.

The last thing I wanted to do was be in the middle of that bullshit. Especially if Dru was there. Awkward City.

So instead of going to the hospital with everyone else, I went to open gym at LightningKick, the tae kwon do academy where I'd been training since I was twelve. I liked LightningKick. It centered me, made me feel strong and powerful, capable. I couldn't score an A on anything at school to save my life, but I could kick the ass of a grown man without breaking much of a sweat. Knowing I could do that didn't make the bad guys who'd killed my mom go away, but it made me less scared of them. Plus, when I was perfecting an eagle strike or memorizing my patterns, the synesthesia didn't matter, because I wasn't even seeing letters or numbers. I wasn't feeling emotions. I was focused inside my head, inside myself. Maybe the vacation from a color-coded world was why I was so good at tae kwon do. I didn't do it to be good, though; I did it to be myself. And myself liked to beat the snot out of unwitting sparring partners on a Tuesday afternoon at the *dojang*.

I pulled open the glass doors and inhaled the familiar smell of LightningKick—a mixture of sweat, muscle ointment, and bare feet. A gross combination, but one that I associated with taking control, with self-preservation; so immediately, I felt better. I couldn't pinpoint it, but something about the events of the night before made me feel like I needed to brush up on my self-protection skills. I headed for the changing room, where I unloaded my backpack and cell phone, took off my shoes, and changed into my *dobok*. My muscles twitched with anticipation.

"Everything okay, Nik?" Gunner, my *kyo sah nim*, asked as I walked across the padded floor toward the heavy bag.

"Yes, sir, fine," I said. I squared myself up next to the bag and roundhoused it so hard it swung back and forth on its hook. The connection rattled my whole body. It felt good, so I did it again. And again. And another dozen times, before switching to my left foot and starting over. Peyton's face flashed in my mind, the crusted blood around her nostrils and crimson monitors trying to edge in on me, shake me up. The memory of how Peyton blurred into my mother stirred into focus. I blitzed the bag with everything I had— royal-blue strength bubbles popping around me—gritting my teeth to keep them from clacking together with the impact, and the image shattered to pieces and floated away. I tried, instead, to imagine her perpetrator, who had somehow, in my mind, morphed into my mom's nameless, faceless culprit, fantasize about finding him in Bay 19 and kicking him over and over until he coughed blood and teeth. But it was impossible to conjure an image of someone you had no clue about. I'd been trying to take down an anonymous bad guy since the day I slid in my mom's blood on the tile entryway floor. The frustration ramped me up and I kicked harder and harder—blue, blue, blue—my foot stinging and then going numb.

Kyo Sah Nim Gunner appeared on the other side of the bag and held on to it to stop its swing. I paused, bouncing on my toes, breathing hard. "You sure you're all right?" he asked. "This bag is crying uncle."

"Sorry," I said. I felt sweat trickle down my back and disappear under my belt. I didn't want to lose my momentum, so I moved to the sparring dummy and practiced a few elbow strikes. "It's been a long day. Late night last night. Was at the ER with a fr—with someone I know."

"Ouch. Your friend come out okay?"

She's not my friend, I wanted to say, but instead I just nodded. "She'll be fine."

"You want to spar?" he asked. "I can find Justin if you think you're up to it."

I reared back and hit the dummy with a palm heel, and followed it up with a tornado kick. The dummy tipped so far the weighted base couldn't counterbalance, and it fell. Justin was a skinny kid, not much of a challenge, but he was a live body. One I could pummel guilt free. "Yes, sir," I said. "I'm up for it."

For the next hour I punched and kicked until my legs were wobbly and my arms felt like they'd been filled with sand and even the blue faded. I was drenched with sweat, my hair lying in a limp ponytail down my back, my *dobok* wet through at the shoulder blades. I felt good. Like I could take on anyone, even anonymous bad guys. I felt like me again.

After, I went back to the changing room and peeled off my *dobok*. I used a towel to wipe myself off, then sat on the bench, trying to cool down and catch my breath.

I couldn't get Peyton out of my mind. I felt guilty for not going back to the hospital. I didn't know why she'd asked for me, but she had, and it was shitty of me to just leave her lying there in a hospital bed because I was too afraid of running into her friends or her brother or whatever other dumb excuse I'd been giving myself for staying away. I still didn't want to, but I had to go see her. Just suck it up and go.

PEYTON'S ROOM WAS just as I had expected it to be. There were flowers on every flat surface, as if a celebrity had died. There were stuffed toys and so many balloons they were like cloud cover along the ceiling. In the middle of the jungle of get-well wishes, looking sallow and broken in a nest of crisp white blankets, lay Peyton. Sitting next to her, just as he had been the night before, was Dru.

He had been leaning his forehead against the mattress but looked up when I walked in. I suddenly felt smelly and gross and wished I had showered after my workout. And then I was pissed for being worried about something as stupid as Dru Hollis thinking I smelled bad. I could wrap him up and take him down before his muscles could twitch a response. Why would I worry about what he thought?

Because he makes you see violet, Nikki. Even more than Jones, my brain tried to answer, but I shoved the thought away. That was last night. That was me in a weak moment.

"Where is everyone?" I asked.

"Who?"

I gestured at the plants all around. "For starters, these people. And, I don't know, your family. Don't you have another sister?" I knew he did. She was younger than me. A sophomore. She was fragile and wispy, with creamy actress skin and perfect everything. She was Peyton: The Starlet Version, waiting to happen in full force the minute we crossed the graduation stage. I'd seen her a few times, in the halls. She was always giving this sweet little smile and giggling like a tween, but there was something calculated about her. I couldn't stand her.

"Half sister," he said. "Luna. She came earlier." His mouth turned down when he said this, and I wondered if maybe she'd been a big, dramatic mess, and he wasn't very good at crying scenes or something. I could definitely see a Hollis being unable to handle emotion. Emotion and the press didn't always go together.

"What about your parents?"

"Out of town," he said. "In Monaco. They're trying to get back right now."

I tried to imagine what it must be like to have something like this happen while you're on vacation. I couldn't do it. When Mom died, our lives stopped. Dad shut down, seeming to wrestle with so many regrets and memories they practically bowled him over.

Ever since, he'd been an emotional desert. He never talked about Mom. A freelance photographer, he wandered through life clutching his camera like a safety blanket, without even seeming to notice when a model hit on him or an actress threw herself at him. He was just a void. Half the time, he ignored me. The other half, he tried to be my friend. But I knew he would come to my side if something happened to me. Instantly.

Wouldn't he?

He never solved Mom's murder, I thought, for the thousandth time. *He tried,* I reminded myself. *But every lead was dead.*

"Anyway," Dru said, "a few friends have been in and out. But that cop has been hanging around and making everyone feel uncomfortable, so they haven't been staying."

"The same one from last night?"

His jaw tightened. "I guess. Crew cut, stubble, major superiority complex." Again, there was something in his voice I couldn't quite place. Something severe, off-putting.

"Detective Chris Martinez," I supplied. "Seems pretty harmless. Has he found any suspects yet?"

"Not that I know of. He's all about chasing his own tail. I told him he should be out there, asking around, interviewing people, following leads, or whatever it is cops do. Not in here, watching her . . . die. It's not like Peyton's attacker is going to be hanging out at the hospital."

I stepped closer to the bed. At the moment, the monitors were all shrouded from my line of sight by balloons and plants. I was trying to keep the colors at bay. But I could feel the crimson edging in on me. My palms started to sweat.

"That would be pretty stupid with you sitting right here. I'm guessing you wouldn't mind it, though, getting a chance for a one-on-one with the person who did this."

He raised his eyebrows. "Yeah."

I took another step. The crimson was flooding my peripheral vision, but I ignored it. My mouth was dry as I went all the way to Peyton's bedside and eased into the chair across from Dru. I focused on her tattoo, letting those colors dazzle the crimson away. *Red is an apple. Blue is the sky. Yellow is the sun. Orange is a tabby cat. Green is the grass. . . .* "Have there been any changes?"

He shook his head, still not looking at me. "Looks like it was a blunt weapon. A board or a baseball bat or something. Messed up her brain pretty bad. I wish I could have stopped it. In some ways she's the centerpiece of our family. When she moved out, it upset everyone."

"She's the centerpiece of a lot of things," I said, thinking about the conversations at school, my voice coming out more bitterly than I'd intended it to. Then it sank in what he'd said after that. "Wait a minute. She moved out? Where?"

Dru paused and squinted at me. "Why are you here, Nikki?"

I ignored his question, my mouth moving faster than my brain. If people knew she'd moved out, they weren't talking about it. Which was odd. "When did she move? Where is she living?"

He shrugged. "A couple of weeks ago. I don't know where. Nobody told me."

A couple of weeks. Right around the same time she got her hair cut and stopped coming to school. This seemed like more than a coincidence. Something had clearly been going on with Peyton Hollis before this happened. "Can't you ask your parents where?"

"I told you, they're in Monaco. I don't know what was going on. Why are you here, Nikki?" he repeated a little more forcefully.

"They called me," I said.

"Yeah, last night they did. But why are you here today?"

That, really, was the question of the hour. Why was I there? Why, after the sucker punch of reliving my mom's murder in that bay last night, had I come back?

A distant part of me realized that maybe that sucker punch *was* why. Maybe because I had to prove to myself that it wasn't my mom lying there. Maybe to keep the nightmares from coming back, or even just to assure myself that, even though my mom's killer had never been found, Peyton's attacker would be. Maybe, somehow that I couldn't explain, coming back today made me feel safer.

But how could I explain all that to Dru? There would be no explaining it in a way that would make sense to him. And I wasn't big on sharing life experiences with others. Of course he would be curious about me. Suspicious, even. Dad had treated everyone like a suspect for years after Mom's death. Because anyone could have been.

"I wanted to see if she was okay," I said.

"I get that." He stood and placed his hands on his hips. "But you said that you two weren't close. I've never seen you hanging around our house or with my sister at all. Is there more to it that I'm not seeing?"

Yes. There was more to it. More, even, than just the memory of my mom. More than being shaken by seeing a classmate snaked up in all those wires. More than any sort of morbid curiosity or even the fact that part of me wanted to see him again.

It was more than Peyton calling me.

It was that she had called *only* me. She had called me when she had scores of friends, admirers, bandmates, and her own family right here in Brentwood. And that wasn't even accounting for the army of official legal help I was guessing the Hollis family had on call.

She had called me.

Me.

Someone she had no ties with.

"It's just . . ." I scratched the back of my neck, trying to decide how much to let him in on what I was thinking. "I know that Peyton tried to call me last night. I don't know why, and I don't even know for sure it was her. But I know that somehow I became involved in something that it makes no sense for me to be involved in. I know that Peyton—or someone using Peyton's phone, but my gut tells me it was her—called me about an hour before she was brought here. She didn't try to call you or your parents or your half sister. She called me. Why, Dru? How am I involved in this?"

He didn't respond, just shook his head helplessly.

"I don't know either," I said. "And maybe a lot of people

could walk away from that, but apparently I can't. So that's why I'm here. So I can get answers when she wakes up."

"And if she doesn't make it?" he asked, his voice rough and unsteady.

I swallowed, considered Peyton's form. She was so bruised and battered, it would be difficult to believe that she could possibly survive, even if I hadn't seen the crimson pulsing through Bay 19 last night. "Then I really can't walk away," I said.

He sank back into his chair, but instead of picking up Peyton's hand, he leaned his elbows on the mattress and rested his forehead in his hands. He rubbed his eyes with his palms and slowly looked up at me. "You're going to find her attacker," he said. Not a question. Not a suggestion. A fact.

Live in Color. Live in Color. Live in Color.

Red. Blue. Yellow. Orange. Green.

Peyton's tattoo pulsed at me, so beautiful, so brilliant. The black-and-gray rainbow surrounded by undulating letters. Lying in that bed, her chopped brown hair greasy-looking against the softness of the pillow, rings of dried blood around her nostrils, her face misshapen and discolored, Peyton didn't look like the edgy girl-in-charge who I'd always known her to be. I could still hear that frightened voice—the one I'd mistaken for a child—coming through my phone the night before. Peyton was in trouble, and for some reason she'd thought I could help her. She wasn't frightening or frustrating or annoying here—she was dying.

I couldn't walk away. Not this time. Not like we'd all eventually walked away from my mother.

I supposed this was the conclusion I had been arriving at ever since I'd gotten the mystery phone call the night before. Dru hadn't been the only reason I'd wanted to show up at the hospital today. I'd wanted to show up because I couldn't just let it go.

"Yes," I said. "I'm going to find out who did this to Peyton. And why."

5

DRU DIDN'T HAVE much to say after I told him I was going to find Peyton's attacker. He seemed so tired. And maybe a little afraid.

"I'll talk to my dad," he said. "See about offering a reward." But the words were monotone, emotionless, and I actually felt kind of sorry for him. What must it be like to be the only one in the family who was there to stay by Peyton's bedside? And why was it I would never have thought Dru Hollis to be the sitting-by-someone's-bedside type?

So I sat opposite him, cataloguing the visible wounds on Peyton. There were two obvious blows to her head. One had split the skin under her eye and blackened the entire side of her face. There was bandaging around her head that suggested trauma to the back of it as well. One arm was now casted. The hand on my side of the bed was swollen, the palm a fist of purple and green. Clearly she'd tried to defend herself with it.

A few stragglers came in here and there. They hung their heads with appropriate sadness—some of the more artistic girls actually wiped the corners of their leaking eyes—and left behind cards and more balloons and flowers. Some of the girls had obvious histories with Dru; others were obvious about their desire to create histories with him. But, without exception, we could hear them giggling or gossiping in the hallway before they'd even left the unit. *How hot is Dru Hollis, you guys? Think we could get into Exchange tonight? God, her hair was the grossest.*

Fake.

Fake. Fake. Fake.

I wondered who among them could have been her attacker. Who had Peyton pissed off? Maybe someone who'd gotten trampled at one of her concerts or wasted at one of her parties. Someone she'd insulted or left out or turned down. Or a boyfriend she'd dumped. Maybe it wasn't about her at all—maybe someone had auditioned for something and blamed her dad for not getting the part. Maybe Dru had loved and left the wrong girl . . . or the wrong girl's mom. God, the possibilities were endless.

Dru had just gotten up and announced that he was

going down to the lobby to find a soda when Bill Hollis burst through the door, crisp tan slacks and navy Club Med polo looking far too fresh to have been on an airplane for fifteen hours. Behind him came a bored-looking blonde, petite and tan, pressed into a skintight wrap skirt and sandals. I'd never seen her before, but I assumed she was the elusive matriarch of the Hollis family: Vanessa.

"So what's the situation?" Bill Hollis barked before Dru or I could even speak, striding to Peyton's bedside. He looked down at her, his hands on his hips, the way he might regard a film location or a testy set. "Christ," he mumbled.

"Oh," the woman breathed, scurrying to the other side of the bed, where she bent over Peyton, brushing stray clumps of hair off her forehead. "My God. Look at her." She turned to Dru, reached up to cup his head in her hands. "Oh, Dru." He ducked away from her touch.

"The situation?" Bill repeated, clearly annoyed at having been interrupted. He finally saw me in the room and gave a curt nod—what I guessed was his version of hello. I stood up, feeling awkward, and maybe even a little starstruck—Bill Hollis was standing two feet away from me. I opened my mouth to excuse myself from the room.

Dru's eyes flicked to me, uncomfortable, but he didn't give me time to speak. He gestured toward Peyton. "This is the situation. She's been like this since they brought her in."

"And what are they saying about her prognosis?" Bill

Hollis asked, checking his watch, still all business, as the blonde settled into the chair Dru had vacated and began tapping on her cell phone.

"They're not," Dru said. "Not to me, anyway. Still too early to tell, I guess. But it doesn't look good."

"No, it doesn't." Bill Hollis turned to me, his icy blue eyes turning my insides cold. "And you are?"

But before I could open my mouth, Dru answered for me. "A friend of Peyton's." I gave him a curious look. Why the lie? But I guessed maybe I knew why. Bill Hollis was not in a mood for games—and who could blame him?—and he might consider it a game for someone who wasn't exactly a friend to be there. Fern green feathered around us, giving me an itchy feeling I always got in awkward situations.

"Were you the one who found her? Do you know who did this?" Bill Hollis asked, his gaze penetrating me. And then, as if flipping a switch, his eyes softened and his mouth curved into a pleasant tilt—the man from the magazines. "Should we be thanking you?" He held out his hand. "There will be a reward, of course."

I stared at it, unsure what to do, my head shaking of its own accord. Bill Hollis was probably not the kind of guy whose handshakes went unreciprocated, but something about him oozed minty distrust that made my heart pound, even more so than with Dru. I was too scared of him to touch him.

"No," I said, meaning no, to all of the above.

The blonde suddenly sprang from her chair. "Dru. Baby," she said, her voice a purr. "Have you eaten? Have you slept?" She ran her hand over his head, down his cheek, resting it on his shoulder.

Dru rubbed his palms over his face, sidestepping away from her. "No, not much," he said. "I've been waiting for you." This he said mostly to his dad.

"Well, you should get something," she said. "I'll drive you. We don't need two of you in hospital beds." She stood, bent over the bed, and ran a knuckle down the side of Peyton's face. "The poor dear," she said, and then she was gone.

"You should go with her," Bill Hollis said. "I'm going to find a doctor. Get some information." He glanced around the hospital room. "We need to get her moved. I'll call Cedars-Sinai. Someplace a little more private. This is no place for one of ours. The press."

"Dru," the woman called from the hallway.

Dru nodded, and then, with a glance at me that was both wary and warning, followed the woman out of the room.

"I should go, too," I mumbled, and hurried out, wondering what I had just witnessed.

DAD WAS GONE when I got home. He'd left a note on the kitchen counter that he was on a shoot in Santa Monica and not to expect him home until the following night. With some single dads, "being on a shoot in Santa Monica" could be code for just about anything, but with my dad, it meant he was actually taking photographs in Santa Monica and would be coming straight home after. Ten years was a long time to get over losing your wife, but Dad was still married. Married to his camera. Married to a ghost.

Some people would probably really hate it if their dad was sleeping around, finding someone new, but I actually wanted my dad to move on. I worried about what might happen to him after I moved out. In some ways, I thought Dad's inability to move on was part of why I was chronically failing. If I didn't graduate, I wouldn't have to leave him. If I didn't leave, I wouldn't have to worry about him being alone. It was a fucked-up system, but the Kill family was nothing if not fucked-up.

I went straight to my bedroom and dropped my things on my bed, then shucked off my clothes and headed for the shower.

I leaned forward against the tile shower wall and let the water massage my screaming back muscles.

"Who could it be?" I muttered to myself, my words echoing off the walls. "Who hurt you, Peyton? Was it one of your friends?" My head jerked up. I brushed the water off my chin. Her friends. Of course. Peyton Hollis had about a billion Facebook friends. I knew this because pretty much every single person on my paltry friend list was also connected to her, even though not a single one was actually connected to her in real life. I didn't get on Facebook very often—social media was a little too social for my taste—but it seemed like every time I was on there, one of Peyton's posts was staring me in the face. Most of the time it felt like I was the only person I knew who wasn't friended to Peyton, but it didn't matter because I saw all her stuff anyway, through her adoring fans.

I rinsed the conditioner out of my hair and soaped myself up quickly, then got out and dried in record time. I slipped into a pair of sweats and a T-shirt and plopped into my desk chair, opening up my laptop at the same time.

"All right, Peyton," I said, logging onto Facebook. "Let's see what you've been up to lately."

I had zero messages and zero notifications. Typical. The top post in my feed was by Jones, a link to some video of an "epic prank." Assholes being assholes. Typical. Not surprised at all that Jones liked it. Wouldn't be surprised if one of Jones's bro-gang perpetrated said epic prank.

But Jones was a good enough starting point. I knew for a fact that he was friended to Peyton, so I followed his post to his page, scanned his friends list, and clicked through to her page. Easy.

Her last post had been on October 7, which, now that I thought about it, had to be right around the time she disappeared from school.

Must get to the bottom of things.

The post was, of course, filled with worried questions from 240 of Peyton's closest friends. The only hint that Peyton would give, though, was in a comment halfway down the thread that provided a single word:

Family

So Peyton had been frustrated with her family just before chopping off her hair and disappearing from school. But so what? We all had family drama, right? In some ways it was the most normal post Peyton had ever put on her page.

I scrolled down. There were links to songs and a shitload of memes about being wasted. There were tongue-out, Solo-cup-wielding party selfies and a photo of her last pedicure. Everything she posted—everything!—was treated like it was the most profound thought all of Brentwood had ever heard.

And then there was this:

u will not win dis.

The post was written by Gibson Tally. I didn't know him, but I knew of him. He was older, a notorious drug-head dropout, who'd gone out epically, smashing lockers and kicking dents into the sides of Assistant Principal Elliot's Mercedes on the way. He was everyone's hookup for weed and once got arrested for supposedly calling in a bomb threat during an antidrug assembly. He was constantly in fights and in jail and reportedly carried a gun with him everywhere he went.

He was also the lead guitarist of Viral Fanfare.

Was he more than that to Peyton?

I clicked on his name and it took me to his profile, but it was too private for me to see anything other than photos of him playing his guitar. He'd acquired a few tattoos and facial piercings since I'd last seen him. He'd also acquired a hard look in his eyes that sent a chill through me. *u will not win dis.*

I went back to Peyton's page and read the comments under his post. Most of them were asking what was going on; a few were making typical Facebook jackass jokes. Only one stood out, from a girl named Liz who I'd seen clinging to Peyton's orbit.

I heard about you and the band. Is it true?

But Peyton hadn't responded to her, and nobody else seemed interested. I scrolled through the comments again, looking for anything I might have missed, wondering what it was that Liz had heard about Peyton and the band. What Peyton was trying to "win" against Gibson Talley. Was he joking or threatening? I'd assumed he was threatening, because of his bad-news reputation, but with Facebook, you never could really tell who meant what they were saying. Facebook made my head hurt. It was like a jumpy mishmash of colors. This was why I didn't hang out on it much. It was impossible to follow anyone's true thoughts there. It was impossible to block out the rainbow.

I wondered if Detective Martinez had been through Peyton's Facebook yet, and, if so, what he made of Gibson Talley's remark. Or did the police only do things like that if someone died?

I scrolled down farther, past a few more parties and one throwback picture of Peyton in a black leather fringed bikini.

Wait a minute. I went back to the bikini. It might or might not have been black—it was the photo itself that was black-and-white. Peyton was standing shin-deep in a spar-kling swimming pool, her hip cocked out to one side, the rope of a life preserver draped over her shoulders and snaking down her hip. Her hands were on her hips, the life preserver ring draped casually around one wrist, the letters SO a soft glow across the top of the ring—SO, *yellow, pink*. Peyton's face was dwarfed by sunglasses, her lips painted a deep color that came across as slick black in the photo.

She looked amazing.

As usual.

I clicked on the picture, and it took me to a photo- and art-sharing website. Aesthetishare.com. Peyton had been posting for three months. I scrolled down to her earliest posts. One of a moppy little dog. A nearly nude bathroom mirror selfie. One of a pair of shoes—a scuffed and worn pair of cherry-red Chucks—with kneesocked legs still in them. The toe of one of the shoes was lifted by a sizable rock. Pretty standard. I'd seen a zillion photos like these on Instagram.

I scrolled up to the next one. Peyton, with Viral Fanfare. She was grasping a microphone, her mouth wide open in one of her high notes. Her eyes were scrunched shut, her hip jutted out. I scrutinized the other band members, but they all looked totally in their own zones. All except Gibson Talley, whose eyes were on Peyton as he played his guitar. I stared into the photo, trying to glean anything I could from it—love, anger, scorn—but got nothing. If Gibson Talley was battling Peyton over something, which his post suggested, it could have been any number of things. I continued to scroll. The three photos above that one were similar—more Viral Fanfare performances—and in none of them did anything look abnormal.

But the one above those was different. They weren't performing. Instead, they were standing inside a recording studio, in a line, their arms wrapped around one another like a bunch of kids at camp. The bassist and the drummer were smiling like it was their birthday. But it was Gibson I couldn't quit looking at. His face was set in a smug look of victory, his eyes looking away from the camera. His guitar was draped across his body—the word *Hendrix*, printed on the strap, jumped out at me in tie-dye letters. His left arm was casually resting on the drummer's shoulder, but his right arm . . . his right arm was crooked around Peyton's neck, his fist practically under her chin. A pose of conquest.

Peyton was the only one in the photo not smiling. Her eyes were pointed toward the floor. I could practically feel the tension coming off her. Whatever had been eating Peyton had already been going on when this photo was taken.

There was a date printed on the bottom of the photo. October 15. There were only five photos after that, all taken in black and white. A new artistic phase, I guessed.

In the first, Peyton stood in the pool with her life preserver.

The next showcased Peyton and her sister (*half* sister, my mind corrected, in Dru's voice), Luna, standing in front of a plate-glass window. Definitely not in Brentwood—maybe New York? A neon sign in the window promised violet SEXSEXSEXSEXSEX. Luna's head was tilted back, mugging, her hand buried in her hair, while Peyton jutted her chest out toward the camera seductively, a giant gold-glittering dollar sign on the front of her T-shirt. She had titled the photo *Double Rainbow*. For some reason the words immediately brought to mind the tattoo on her neck. Only the word *rainbow* didn't come out at me in its usual colors. I had a hard time describing the color it made me think of in this photo. Glitzy cherrybomb, maybe? I sighed, rubbed my eyes. I hated when I got so tired even my synesthesia got confused.

Regardless, I pressed on. The next was a family photo, standing on a pier, the ocean rolling behind them. I zeroed in on Dru, who looked at home in the sun, his shirt unbuttoned and revealing a chiseled chest and a dark shadow of hair under his belly button. I blushed, cursed at myself, and quickly flipped to the next photo.

In this one, Peyton sat at a bus stop, her face turned away from the camera, her free hand caressing the back of her new haircut. She stared pensively at a cigarette butt on the sidewalk, her profile blocking out most of an apartment rental ad and some graffiti behind her head. A square of gauze covered her new tattoo. The overexposed black-and-white pixelation made her skin look grainy and pocked. She might have been mistaken for someone homeless in this photo, an effect I found to be brilliant and shocking. One of the richest girls in the city, mistaken for a homeless girl? Would she have died to know that was what someone would see in this photo, or was it what she'd been going for?

She'd given the photo a title: *Fear Is Golden.* Which made me chuckle, because the first thought in my mind was, No, *it's not. Fear is bumpy gray and black, like asphalt.*

But then I remembered I was the only person who knew that.

The final photo looked like a mistake. This was the only one in color, but it might as well have been black and white. It was a close-up of a stucco wall, the bottom of which was gobbled up by foliage. At the very top left-hand corner was a pinprick dot of reddish orange—a tiny light of some kind. I squinted at it, tried to zoom in, but nothing would work. It was as if she'd accidentally snapped a photo while she was walking by a building. But she'd given this one a title, too.

What Lies Beneath

I felt a familiar tickle, a sneeze coming on. The word *beneath*, the color of dust, always did that to me. But the tickle was soon forgotten as I saw the rest of the title.

It was a date.

October 20.

The date of her attack.

I WAS JARRED awake by the buzz of my cell phone against my cheek. I jerked upright, confused, blinking. I was still sitting at my desk, Peyton's YouTube channel pulled up. After a few seconds, I remembered. I'd fallen asleep poring over Viral Fanfare videos, watching every move Peyton made. Every time I saw even the tiniest flicker of something stand out, I backed up the video and watched it again, never sure if I was just imagining things.

I looked at my phone. It was 6:03 a.m. It was also the familiar color sequence of Jones's number on the ID. I sighed. Might as well get it over with.

"Hi, Jones."

"Hey, beautiful." He sounded sleepy, and I took a

moment to remember what Sleepy Jones's skin felt like—warm, smooth, muscles somehow rock hard without him even flexing, as if they were ready to spring into action at any moment. I loved waking up in Jones's arms. For those first few moments after blinking into consciousness, I could even pretend that maybe I wasn't in hate with love, and that our bodies fit together perfectly for a reason. That feeling only lasted a few seconds.

"What do you want?" I asked, cutting him off before he launched into kissy noises or some other sappy bullshit.

"Did I wake you up?"

"It's six o'clock in the morning, Jones, what do you think? I wasn't out running a marathon."

"Wow, someone woke up on the wrong side of the bed this morning," he said. "I'm just checking in. Just because we broke up doesn't mean I stopped caring about you."

I wish you would, I thought. "If only I'd woken up on a bed," I mumbled instead. I rubbed my cheek. I could feel creases in my skin where the phone had been pressed into it for God-knew-how long. I yawned. "I fell asleep at my desk."

"Chem? You need help?"

"No. I mean, sure, I always need help with chem. But no, I wasn't doing schoolwork." *You probably should,* the voice in my head reminded me. *Academic probation, remember?* But I ignored that voice. It had been a long time since I could be guilted over not doing schoolwork. "I was watching videos."

"Oh," Jones said, his voice going up into that obnoxious falsetto he got when he was trying to be flirtatious.

"Not those kind of videos, you freak," I snapped.

"Kidding, kidding," he said. "You gonna be like this all day? Just asking so I can avoid you at school."

"Yes," I said, relieved. At least I could cross dodging Jones off my to-do list for the day. "I'm planning to be a huge bitch all day. Avoidance is a good idea."

"You could never be a bitch," he said. "That's why I love you."

"Try me."

He yawned, and again I could imagine him, his bare chest tan and warm, his amazing abs descending to a V right where the sheets pooled deep around his hips. I needed to stop thinking about it. "I'm not too worried. I know you better than you do, sometimes," he said. He groaned as if he were stretching. "I probably should get ready. I just wanted to say good morning. I'll see you at school."

"Okay, whatever," I said. Gibson Talley's paused face stared at me, his hand in a downstroke on the rhythm of "Your Mother Loves It." I started to hang up, but stopped myself. "Hey, Jones?"

"Yeah?" Hopeful. Eager. I rolled my eyes, hating that do-anything sound in his voice, and hating even more that I was about to take advantage of it.

"You know Peyton Hollis, right?"

"Of course."

"Do you know the guy from her band? Gibson Talley?"

He made a humming sound. "I think I might know who you're talking about. Dropout, right? With the green Mohawk?"

"Yeah, that's the one. What do you know about him?"

"Not much," he said. "Only that he lives in those apartments by the storage place. What's it called? Fountain something. Come to think of it, I saw Peyton Hollis walking over there not that long ago."

I sat up straighter, the cobwebs suddenly blasted out of the sleepy corners of my mind. "When?" I asked.

"I don't know. It was probably a week or so ago. I only remember it because everybody was talking about how she freaked out. Had some sort of mental breakdown or something. You saw her hair, right?"

"Yeah, I saw it," I said. "And you're positive that it was her you saw walking there?"

"Totally positive."

"You're not messing with me just to get me back, are you?"

"Nikki, I can't believe you think I would do that."

"Are you?" I repeated.

"No."

"Because we're not getting back together, Jones. Not ever."

He sighed. "So you've told me. Time and time again. Why are you so interested in Peyton Hollis all of a sudden, anyway?"

Instantly, the image of Peyton lying in her hospital bed flooded my mind. Dru, sitting there next to her, looking at me with a mixture of gratitude and suspicion. "Never mind," I said. "But thanks for the information."

I hung up and headed for a shower, my back stiff and aching from sleeping bent over my desk. I pushed my hands into the small of my back and stretched, mulling over what Jones had told me. It felt like important information, but I couldn't quite figure out why.

Halfway through my shower, it hit me.

When she moved out, it upset everyone, Dru had said.

When she moved out . . .

I shut off the shower, dried myself, and slicked my sopping hair into a ponytail. It was now 6:42. School started in an hour, and I still had yet to get dressed and get my shit together. But how was I supposed to think about world history or English literature, or—the worst—chem, when I had just been handed a clue that might lead me to what happened to Peyton Hollis?

I wrapped myself in a heavy robe that Dad scored for me at Four Seasons Chicago last year and hurried back to my desk.

Just as I sat down, the doorbell rang. Glancing down

at myself in my robe, I decided to let it go. Probably just a delivery. But a few seconds later, it rang again, followed by insistent knocking.

"Fine, fine," I muttered as I hurried down the steps, pulling the robe tight around me as I went. "You can just leave it on the porch, you know," I called.

There was a pause, and then, "Miss Kill? It's Detective Martinez. From the hospital. Mind if I talk to you for a moment?"

Alarmed, again I glanced down at myself, my hands instantly flying up to my dripping hair. I wasn't one of those perfect-princess types of girls who always had to look like she just stepped off a runway when she left the house, but a robe with nothing underneath was maybe just the tiniest bit too casual for conversation with strangers.

"Miss Kill?" he called again. "Nikki?"

Groaning, I accepted the inevitable and opened the door a crack, awkward fern turning into all-out-embarrassed pine in my vision. There was Chris Martinez, smiling and holding up a steaming cup of coffee.

"Mind if I come in?"

Now, standing next to him in his pressed khakis and button-down shirt, I felt really naked. "I'm kind of busy," I said.

But he was unflappable. "It'll only take a minute. You like French vanilla?"

Eyeing the coffee, I sighed and backed up, opening the door wider for him to come in. He stepped through the threshold without a word and pressed the coffee into my hand.

"Sorry to bother you so early. I thought I might try to catch you before school." He paused and looked me up and down. "I apologize if I've caught you at an inappropriate moment."

My face burned—I might as well have been standing in the middle of a pine forest at that point, I was so mortified—and I crossed my arms over my chest, just in case my robe might get any ideas. I sipped the coffee, which was—frustratingly—really good.

"Is there a place we can sit?" he asked.

"Not really," I said. I didn't love cops to begin with. And Dad absolutely hated them after they botched Mom's case so badly. If he found out I'd let a cop into our house for a cup of coffee, much less let one sit down, he would probably flip. "Can we make this quick?" I gestured at my hair like I needed to do something with it. As if I ever did anything with my hair.

He shuffled his feet, shifting his gaze down to them momentarily, and then nodded. "Okay. I just wanted to ask you some questions about Dru Hollis."

"What about him?"

"Well, for starters, what was his relationship with Peyton like?"

I rolled my eyes. "Detective, I already told you. I'm not friends with the Hollises. I don't know anything about Dru Hollis."

"But you've spent some time with him since the incident," he said.

The smell of the coffee wafted up, intoxicating. "Well, yeah, but it's not like I'm sitting there asking for details of his childhood."

The detective nodded and licked his lips. I ran my fingers along my robe belt, just to make sure it was still intact. "Fair enough," he said. "Do you know anything about whether or not he's been traveling lately? Maybe to Vegas? Or anyplace else, recently, where he might have caught up with some old friends? Or has he been pretty much staying around Brentwood? What has he been up to these days?"

I shrugged. "We haven't talked about that, either," I said. "We're not spending our time sharing our secrets like besties. His sister is lying in a hospital bed."

He raised his eyebrows. "Does he have secrets to share?"

"No, I didn't mean . . . How would I know?" I squinted. "What are you getting at, exactly? Do you think Dru had something to do with Peyton's attack?" He remained maddeningly straight-faced, and instantly I was taken back to those early days after Mom's death. All questions, no answers, and a ton of jumping to conclusions that never got any of us anywhere. Dad was right—cops were all alike, no matter how much yellow I saw when I was around one. I cocked my head to one side. "He's been by his sister's bedside since she was brought in. He has been worried sick. He's cried. I've seen it myself. That's what I know about Dru Hollis."

"Yes, he's been very interested in Peyton's care," Detective Martinez said. But his face was grim as he brought his coffee to his lips.

"You know, I really need to get ready for school," I said. I opened the front door, holding the knob in my hand, hoping that my robe wasn't gaping open, but too irritated to really worry about it too much if it was.

He hesitated, then gave a single nod and headed toward the door.

"Oh, and here. You can have this back," I said, holding the coffee out toward him. "I don't like French vanilla."

He took the coffee and stepped out. I slammed the door after him, then watched through the window as he pulled the lid off my drink and dumped it out in the grass. And kept watching until he got into his car and left.

I leaned against the front door for a moment. Clearly he was suspicious of Dru. But was it normal check-out-the-family suspicious, or was there something more to it? Or was he, like the cops on my mom's case, just completely clueless and reaching for anything he could get his hands on?

After I stopped shaking, I took a deep breath and decided on the latter, and then went back upstairs. Something I'd seen in Peyton's pictures was gnawing at the recesses of my brain, and had been since my conversation with Jones. Something blue.

BACK AT MY desk, I pulled up Peyton's Aesthetishare account and scrolled through the pictures once again. There it was, the one at the bus stop. Peyton was turned away, her free hand touching her hair. She was pensively staring at something on the ground. All stark black and white. Except behind her, the partially obscured apartment rental ad. Fountain View Apartments, which shone out to me in what I liked to think of as dolphin blue—the color I always associated with water words. Jones had seen Peyton walking near Gibson's apartment complex. He'd thought they'd been called Fountain something. But just above the ad, scrawled on top of the word *apartment*, someone had written something. I'd thought of it as graffiti last night when I'd first seen it, but my brain had catalogued something else about it. The silver.

Three numbers—412. *Silver, brown, pink.*

My fingers felt cold against the keys of my laptop. Were the numbers a clue?

It seemed so unlikely, so impossible. But it made sense in a way I couldn't explain—just like I was eight years old again and trying to tell a doctor about my colors. I couldn't ignore it.

Dru and I had exchanged numbers the last time we were at the hospital together, just in case. I picked up my phone and dialed.

"Hello?" The voice sounded gravelly with sleep. I had forgotten how early it still was.

"Dru?"

"Who is this?"

"It's Nikki Kill."

"Oh." There was rustling, followed by beeping that I knew all too well. "Hey," he said after a pause. "Sorry, I'm at the hospital."

"Any changes?"

"No. She's still unresponsive. My dad wants to have her moved. Wants some specialist he knows to look at her, but it's too risky. The doctor said the brain swelling is not going down, either. It's bad, Nikki."

Words stuck in my throat. I remembered my dad, pulling me into his lap in a special room at the hospital ten years ago, saying the same words. *It's bad, Nikki.* But he hadn't had to tell me for me to know. I'd slipped in the blood. I'd seen the crimson all over the room. I'd already known she was going to die.

"Hello?" Dru asked. "You still there?"

I cleared my throat. "I'm here."

"Are you coming by today?"

"I have school," I said. "But, um, that's actually why I was calling you."

His voice went grim. "I graduated a year ago, remember? You couldn't pay me enough to go back into that place. I'd take one of my dad's stupid acting jobs if I had to."

"No, not that. You said Peyton moved out of the mansion, right?"

He paused. "The mansion? What, are we royalty?"

Just about, but I let it slide. "Sorry. But you said she moved out, right?"

"Yeah, why?"

"And you don't know where she went?" I felt a trickle of sweat run down the side of my face into the raised collar of my robe. I realized I'd been clutching the phone so tightly my fingers ached. I took a breath and eased up.

"No." His voice took on that wary tone again. "What are you getting at, Nikki?"

"I think I might know where she went."

There was another pause. "Where?" he asked.

"I don't know if I'm right," I said. "Do you have her keys?"

"I think so," he said. "The hospital gave them to me that night. They were the only thing she had on her, besides that phone. So I have them, I just don't know what they unlock."

I stood, shook off my robe, and let it drop to the floor. I raced across my room and grabbed clothes out of the closet without even paying attention to what I was grabbing. Not that my closet offered a lot of variety—worn jeans, concert T-shirts, a couple of Jones's button-downs. "Meet me at Fountain View Apartments in twenty minutes."

"What about school?"

"I just decided I'm skipping."

"How do you know it's the right place?"

I hopped on one foot, trying to get a sock on the other, almost dropping the phone in the process. *I'll explain later,* I opened my mouth to say, but I knew that wasn't true. I wasn't in the habit of telling anyone about my dolphin blue, or any other color, and I wasn't going to start today. "I just know," I said, which turned out to be as close of an explanation to my synesthesia as there was anyway.

I heard the murmur of voices. Maybe nurses. And more beeping, getting closer, as if he were walking toward Peyton again. I closed my eyes and practically saw it on the insides of my eyelids—*crimson, crimson, crimson,* pounding with my pulse. *It's in your head, Nik. It's all in your head.*

"So are you going to meet me?" I asked, realizing how husky and desperate my voice sounded.

"Okay. I'll be there in twenty."

T HE FOUNTAIN VIEW Apartments were a squat cluster
of straight lines and brown stucco with cream-colored
balconies tacked on like teeth. Sandwiched between bone-
rattling railroad tracks and a drugstore, and surrounded
by what seemed like miles of storage sheds and a grocery,
they felt worlds away from Hollis Mansion. Hell, they felt
worlds away from where I lived, too. Dad and I weren't rich,
by any means, but we had enough. My neighborhood was a
place where families settled down—new carpet in the living
room, a wet bar in an alcove off the kitchen, a flat-screen
wall-mounted in the den. Fountain View Apartments was a
place where people lived by necessity rather than by luxury.
The type of place a Hollis wouldn't even know existed.

Yet Peyton did. I was sure of it. I couldn't explain how exactly—and I wasn't even sure I was right—but the photo had told me that this was where I'd find clues to Peyton's attack.

I waited for Dru in the parking lot, fiddling with the radio dial until I finally became frustrated and antsy and turned it off. I watched as a man came out of an apartment, carrying a hard-shell lunch cooler in one hand, and got into his truck and rumbled away, leaving a polluting cloud of old country tunes in his wake. A few minutes later, a woman in a pair of shorts and a T-shirt with a ratty knee-length robe tossed over it came outside and loosed a tiny dog onto the ground. I thought about Chris Martinez barging in on me in my robe and felt a pang of embarrassment again. The little dog scampered, picked a spot, and squatted. The woman watched on as she smoked. My fingers itched to hold a cigarette.

Just when I'd almost convinced myself to get out and bum a smoke from the lady in the robe, a silver Spyder crept into the parking lot—all chrome and shiny paint and wheel-waxed tires, dubstep thumping angrily through its speakers—and pulled up next to my car.

I sucked in my breath. My God, you could smell the posh. Dru must have really felt like he was slumming it here.

Not that I was caught up in money, but there was something seriously sexy about seeing him behind the wheel, his hair ruffled from the top being down, his sunglasses hiding identity and emotion, the glint of midmorning sun reflecting on his watch. He stepped out and headed toward me, his button-down tucked loosely into his jeans. I felt myself flush but rolled down my window with shaky fingers.

"Nice car."

"Birthday present," he said, glancing at the Spyder.

"Wow, happy birthday, huh? I got a laptop."

He shrugged. "I guess. If you're into that sort of thing." Again, he glanced at the car, and I could have sworn the look on his face said that he kind of wasn't into that sort of thing, which went against every rumor that ever floated about every Hollis. He reached into his pocket and pulled out a set of keys. He held them up, jangled them. "You ready?"

I nodded, rolled up my window, and got out, walking toward the buildings, trying to ignore the violet feeling of being pulled toward Dru. I was almost tempted to trade exploring Peyton's apartment for exploring each other instead.

"You want to explain how you know this is where Peyton lived?" Dru called after me.

I scanned the numbers on the doors, kept moving. "Nope."

"Don't you think it might be important information for her family to know?" Emphasis on the word *family*.

I stopped, and he nearly walked into me. "Not really," I

said. "I found it—isn't that the important part? Besides, it's just a hunch."

"You brought me out here on a hunch?"

I rolled my eyes. "It's an apartment complex, not Siberia, for God's sake. And it's . . . well, it's more than a hunch, but I can't explain it. Or more like I won't. And this is the one," I said, pointing to the door we stood in front of, stickers misaligned so that the 412 looked like it was riding a wave. *Silver, brown, pink*—just as it had been in the photo, of course. But seeing them here gave me confidence that maybe I was right.

He looked at the door, then at me, skeptically. "This is where Peyton moved to? My spoiled sister? You're sure?"

"Well, I won't know for sure until we open it. But that's your job. Unless you want me to kick it in?" Doubt settled into the pit of my stomach. All my life, I'd been intuitive. I never lost things. I had a pretty good memory. And I could get a feel for a room or a person or a mood pretty much the moment I was near. I'd never tried it with a photo before, but why couldn't it work?

His mouth dropped open, and he slid his sunglasses down the bridge of his nose to look over them at me. "You mean we could open this and someone else could be in there?"

Yes. It was possible—if Jones was right—that Gibson Talley could be in there. And I hadn't really thought through that part until just now. He seemed like just the kind of guy who waited around for opportunities to shoot people who came trespassing into his space. But Peyton's family had every right to go into her apartment, no matter who she shared it with. Especially if she were to die, they would need to pack up her . . . I shook my head, remembering the cleaning ladies Dad had hired to box up Mom's things, how vulture-like they'd seemed to me. I didn't want to go there. "If it's not hers, the key won't work," I said, evading the subject.

A grin pushed up one corner of Dru's mouth. "You are a little mystery, aren't you, Nikki Kill?"

I felt myself blush down what felt like the entire length of my body, which pissed me off. I hated when I blushed. Made me feel like a little kid. I pressed my chin down toward my chest to hide my face. "Just open the door before I grow old and die waiting," I said.

Dru stepped around me and stuck a key in the door. Nothing.

"Try another one," I said. He did. Still nothing.

My heart pounded, waiting for angry footsteps on the other side of the door, waiting for Gibson Talley to whip it open and rearrange Dru's half grin permanently. "Try another one," I said again.

"This one's a car key," he said. "There's only one more."

He stuck the last key into the lock. At first it stuck, and

I felt my shoulders sag with disappointment. I'd been so sure. Well, not *sure* sure. But it would have been cool for me to have figured out where Peyton lived based on that photo alone. *Serves me right,* I thought. *I stop fighting my synesthesia for the first time ever and it lets me dow—*

But Dru jiggled the key a little and it sank all the way in, giving a crunching sound that the others hadn't. It was the sound of key teeth meeting home. We glanced at each other, and then he turned the key and grasped the doorknob.

It turned.

We were in.

"Holy shit," I said, pushing past Dru and stepping through the doorway. "I was right. Hello?" I called out tentatively.

"Who's going to answer you? Peyton's in the hospital, remember?"

Dru had followed me in and shut the door behind us. I found myself fumbling for a light switch. "Just a precaution," I muttered, though inside I was thanking God that nobody had answered. There was a difference between being able to defend yourself if you had to, and wanting to actually have to. "Find a light, would you?"

Instead, Dru whipped back the curtains that had been pulled tight across the front window, letting in a flood of morning sun. I held my breath. Then looked around and let it out.

Other than the heavy gray linen curtains, the apartment was stark. A plain beige sofa sat across from a small television, which was perched atop a nondescript side table. There were no decorations on the walls, no photos on the mantel, and, most importantly, nothing that looked like a heavy-duty rocker slash hard-core drug dealer lived there.

I walked down the hall toward the one bedroom in the back, half bracing myself to find a passed-out Gibson Talley sprawled across the bed, or waiting for me behind a door with a baseball bat decorated with Peyton's dried blood.

But the bedroom was as bare as the living room. The bed was unmade, a white sheet set and plain gray blanket tousled across the mattress. The closet door stood open, showing off an impressive array of designer jeans, silk shirts, purses—the only nod to Peyton's former lifestyle. I pawed through the clothes, recognizing a few pieces. The white J. Mendel sleeveless V-neck dress she wore on the first day of school, everyone losing their freaking minds over how tan her legs looked against the fabric (A *month in the Dominican*, I'd overheard her purr countless times that day). The Isabel Marant leather top with the lace-up sleeves that she told everyone she got at Barney's during spring break. The rows and rows of Blahniks on the floor—what Jones, with not a little bit of disgusting awe, used to call her screw-me heels.

But not one stitch of men's clothes.

Not one hint of Gibson Talley at all.

Peyton had moved out, but she clearly lived alone. Why? And, more importantly, this was obviously a temporary place for her. She planned to set up house—real house—somewhere else.

Dru had joined me in the bedroom and was leaning against the door watching me. "You planning on raiding my sister's closet?"

I let out a derisive snort. "Please," I said. I held up a lace baby-doll top—pink, of course. "Like I would be caught dead in this." I twirled my finger through my hair. "Have the maid bring me up a cosmo, Dru. With the imported vodka, of course."

His face darkened. "That's not what it's like, you know."

I hung the shirt back on the rack and knelt in front of a suitcase on the floor. "What?" I unzipped the front pocket of the suitcase. There was a small stash of photos inside. Peyton clearly liked her photography. Underneath them was a pocket-sized notebook filled with what looked like poetry. At the bottom of some of the poems, she'd written ©Hollis/Talley. Song lyrics. I dropped the notebook back into the suitcase.

"We're not all ordering our maids around and living lives of luxury all the time," Dru said. "Rich people have problems, too."

"I'm not exactly poor," I snapped. "There's a long distance

between rich and Hollis-rich. What problems could the Hollises possibly have?"

But as I stood and turned, looked at him, it hit me how insensitive I'd just sounded. Peyton lay in a bath of crimson monitor readouts a couple of miles away right at that moment. The biggest problem I'd ever had—seeing someone I loved die from random, avoidable violence—was exactly what Dru was going through right at that moment.

"I'm sorry," I said. "Of course you have problems. I didn't mean that."

He ducked his head, crossed one foot over the other. "It's okay. Most people think we have the perfect family. People don't understand the pressure of being lorded over by someone as powerful as my dad. Someone as rich. In a way, I don't blame Peyton for wanting out." Again, I heard that same derision in his voice that I'd heard earlier when he'd told me that Luna was his *half* sister. The words felt a confusing mix of putrid brown and rust. "This place is so empty," he said, pushing away from the door frame and walking over to the squat dresser that sat near the window. He ran his fingers over its sleek surface. Nothing on it but a small jewelry box and a single bottle of perfume. "I know she's only been here a couple of weeks, but it's like she didn't really move in. You should have seen her bedroom at the house. She had so much shit in it, you could barely walk through it, you know? She left most of it there. It was like she left, but only part of her left." He raised his head but seemed to be looking at something beyond me. A memory, maybe, or a thought. "Seeing this place, I can see how unhappy she was. Seems so desperate here. I don't know." He pushed a thumb against each eye. His jaw had a bitter set to it, one I recognized in my own face sometimes. "I'm probably overthinking it."

I went to him, put my hand on his arm. His skin felt clammy, his muscles tight under my fingers. I thought I could almost detect a tremor running through them. Fear, or grief, or both. Maybe it had been a mistake to bring him here. Maybe I should have just called Detective Martinez and told him my suspicions that Gibson was somehow involved in what happened to Peyton, no matter how unbelievable he might have thought them. Maybe it was colossally shitty of me to put Dru through this, just because of my own distrust of the police.

"Hey," I said. "We'll figure out who did this to her." *And hopefully we will figure out why I'm involved,* I added internally, even if I recognized that my need to know made me selfish.

His eyes met mine, bright with wetness and deep with gratitude, and in that instant, every defense I'd placed around myself regarding Dru Hollis dropped, whether I wanted it to or not. Even sitting next to Peyton's bedside, he'd been so guarded, so distant. Still, the only things I knew about Dru Hollis really revolved around his reputation. But now I could see something else in him. Tenderness, maybe. Perhaps even a little bit of awe.

As soon as his hand settled over mine, I was overcome by the connection I'd been trying so hard to deny. I could smell him—not the cheap aftershave that Jones used to slap on, but something luxurious and exotic. Something probably brought back from one of his family vacations in Saint-Tropez or Hvar or wherever the hell the Hollis family jetted off to when they wanted a break. Every time I inhaled, the purple in my mind glowed brighter and brighter, blocking out the mystifying brown he'd filled the room with and curling into a violet I knew well.

I started to pull my hand away, sensing what might happen next if I didn't get a handle on the charge between us. But the moment I lifted it off his arm, he grabbed it and pulled me in.

I didn't fight. It was so wrong to be doing this in Peyton's apartment. So wrong to be doing it at all, but I didn't fight. I didn't have any fight in me. The pull was too powerful. I wanted him too much.

His lips were soft and warm up against mine, and moved more in strokes than in the full-on attacks that I was used to with Jones. They were feathery light—the kind of kisses that pull sighs out of parted lips—and insistent. His breath tasted sweet, and there was an underlying strength in his grasp that should have been frightening, but when he wrapped his

arms around my waist, I was the calmest I'd felt since getting that first phone call two nights before.

Maybe it wasn't wrong. Maybe it was exactly what
needed to happen.

"We don't . . . ," I said, but trailed off as his lips moved
down the side of my neck.

"It's okay," he whispered into my hair. He pulled back
and brushed a finger down my cheek, staring deep into my
eyes. "You amaze me a little, you know that?"

I shook my head. "I'm not amazing."

He rested his thumb on my chin, tilting my face up with
his forefinger so he could look into it. I could still feel the
ghost of his lips against mine. I bit my lower lip to keep it
steady. "Look what you're willing to do for someone you don't
even really know," he whispered. "It's amazing. It's brave. I've
never known anyone as brave as you, Nikki Kill." He bent so
that his lips were right up against mine. "It's so sexy."

I closed my eyes and fell into him, pulling at the buttons
on his shirt. We paused only long enough for me to unzip
my boots. When he pushed me back onto the bed, I barely
even registered that we were lying across Peyton's mattress. I
was only aware of my desire.

He paused, held himself above me. "Do you want this?"
he asked, the kind of question I would never have guessed
Dru Hollis would ask. I wondered if it was earnest; if he'd

ever had a woman tell him no. I wondered, if I were to shake my head, would he have handed me my shirt and gone on with searching Peyton's apartment? Maybe. Dru Hollis seemed full of surprises. Full of colors I couldn't quite read. Colors that confounded and frightened and exhilarated me.

But I wouldn't test the theory that he would stop if I asked him to.

Because I did want him. Despite my mind nagging at me with doubts brought on by my conversation with Chris Martinez just that morning, I wanted him.

I reached up and curled my arm around his neck, pulling him down toward me.

ONLY AFTERWARD DID it start to feel a little strange. The violet had blinked out, all at once, just as it always did, and then we were left in Peyton's stark room, the door to her closet yawning open a mouthful of colorful textiles. I lay next to Dru, trying to read him, but it was impossible.

I traced some yellowing bruises on his ribs. "What happened here?"

He flinched, touched them with his own fingertips, without looking. "Same basketball game," he said.

"You sure it wasn't football?" I asked, noting a scrape across his elbow, thick with a crusted scab. Once again, Chris Martinez pushed into my mind. Would he have thought these bruises somehow proved that Dru had something to do with Peyton's attack? I could feel the awkwardness in my own voice.

He studied me, his eyes almost black in this light. "You're not thinking . . ."

I shrugged. "The timing is pretty weird, wouldn't you say?"

"Ah, I see," he said, leaning his head against the wall. "Well, I can assure you it's not at all unusual for me to have bruises. I'm not as pampered as they make me out to be. I play hard. And these are no big deal, even by my standards. Nothing like the bruises my sister has right now. Not even close."

I supposed he was right. I'd seen plenty of photos. Dru was always doing something rugged, something dangerous. He was physical. And besides, if someone started combing my body for bruises after a long sparring session at the *dojang*, I'd shudder to think what they'd find.

He let out a dark chuckle. "One thing you should know, Nikki. Hollises leave it all on the court." He shifted so that he was lying on the bruises, facing me, and kissed my forehead. "You strike me as the kind of girl who knows what it means to play all out."

"Every day," I said, thinking about the way I'd pummeled the heavy bag just yesterday. "But remind me never to play basketball with you."

Dru gazed at me for a long while. So long, I started to get uncomfortable. I fumbled for the sheet, which had been kicked to the far side of the bed, and pulled it over my chest, surly. "What?"

"I'm just wondering who you really are."

"What do you mean? This is who I am. No mystery here."

He arched an eyebrow. "Oh, I disagree. You're a hell of a mystery. You're a girl who shows up at a hospital for someone you don't really know, and then goes on a hunt to solve a crime that has nothing to do with you. And"—he pulled himself to sitting, his back propped against the wall—"on your first attempt to follow a clue, you're remarkably good at it, with no explanation of how."

I gathered myself up, keeping the sheet pulled around me as I turned so I was facing him. The green was back, only this time it had morphed into wisps of mint green. Dru was suspicious of me. I had seen it before—when I was talking to Detective Martinez that night at the hospital, it had tried to edge in around us, but I'd been so shaken by the crimson bleeding out of Peyton's bay to pay attention to it.

"What are you getting at?" I asked.

He shrugged, the protective wall he liked to hide behind coming up again. "Nothing. I'm just saying it's a little crazy how you figured out so fast where Peyton lived."

"So?"

"So . . ." He looked away, his hands twisting against each other. "So I think there's more to your story than you're telling me." He grinned and leaned in toward me. "I'm not saying a little mystery isn't sexy."

My mouth dropped open and I edged away from him. "You think I had something to do with Peyton's attack?"

His jaw tightened. "I'm not saying that," he said in a low voice.

I slid out of bed and pulled my jeans on. He wasn't saying that outright, but it was clear that was what he'd meant. He thought it was possible that I was somehow responsible for Peyton being in that hospital bed.

Of course, it wasn't lost on me that there actually *was* more to my story than he knew. Especially when it came to figuring out where Peyton lived. But he didn't need to know that.

And that was exactly why it was such a bad idea for the two of us to have hooked up in the first place. Neither of us would ever be able to trust the other. Not truly.

I slipped into my bra and tugged my shirt over my head, swatting at my flyaway hair. "I should have known better than to do this," I said.

"Nikki, come on, that's not what I meant," he said.

"I know exactly what you meant. And getting me naked is not going to get me to let my guard down, you know. I'm not going to curl up in your arms and baby-talk you all my dirty little secrets."

He grinned. "You have dirty little secrets?"

"This is a game to you?" I was shouting now. "You're cracking jokes while your sister is dying? What the hell is wrong with you?"

He winced, putting his hand over his bare chest. I could hear myself breathing in the silence.

"Of course it's not a game," he said. "Nothing about this is funny."

"No shit," I said, but the fire had gone out of my words. A part of me felt bad for hurting him, even though I was stung by him.

Just as he reached for his shirt, there was a pounding on the door. My heart jostled. We'd gotten so caught up in our own personal stuff, we'd completely forgotten that we were in Peyton's apartment. That we were trying to find an attempted killer. This was no game.

Of course, my mind immediately returned to Gibson Talley. Jones thought that Gib lived in this complex. I had definitely not searched the whole place—maybe we missed the part where all his stuff was.

Dru and I looked at each other, wide-eyed. He was as surprised by our visitor as I was.

The pounding continued. I put my finger over my lips

to shush Dru and crept, still barefoot, into the hallway. I could see nothing through the front window, so I kept going, thinking maybe I would stop in the kitchen and find a knife on the way.

I had reached the door and placed my ear against it, Dru right at my heels, when we finally heard a voice.

"Open up! Police!" We exchanged confused glances. Why were the police looking for Peyton? And then the voice came again, this time all too familiar. "Come on, Miss Kill, I know you and Hollis are in there. Open the door."

8

I STOOD RAMROD straight, my mind searching for a plan. Dru had gone white, the swagger zapped from him. He shook his head at me, a slight movement that might have actually been my imagination.

The police were looking for us? But why? We didn't break in. We had a key. Dru was family. This was no crime.

"What the hell?" I whispered. Dru shrugged, at a loss, but the pale edges around his lips told me otherwise.

Maybe the police were only looking for clues here, just like we were. But they knew I was inside. Which could only mean . . .

I whipped open the door. "Oh my God, are you following me?"

Detective Martinez stood on the other side of the door, one hand pushed into his pants pocket, the other still raised to knock again. He edged past me into Peyton's apartment, a uniformed officer trailing behind him. "Excuse me, Miss Kill," he muttered.

I shut the door and whirled on him. "I mean it. Are you following me? You obviously knew I was here. How?"

He bowed his head and rubbed his top lip contemplatively. "No," he said. "I'm not following you. Though I do find it pretty curious that you're here. With the person I *am* following. Funny that you didn't mention you were meeting up with him when I was just talking to you this morning."

"It wasn't planned yet," I said. "What business is it of yours who I meet up with, anyway?"

"It's my business when you're meeting up with a suspect in an assault and battery case."

It took me a minute to process what he was saying. I glanced up at Dru, who looked as surprised as I felt. "Dru's officially a suspect now? Why?"

Detective Martinez turned toward Dru, pulling something out of his waistband. I caught a glimpse of shiny metal, and recognized the rattling sound of handcuffs. The silver rippled with bumpy gray and black. "Dru Hollis, you're under arrest for the attack on Peyton Hollis." The other officer took two steps toward us.

I gasped as the rest of the color left Dru's face. "I didn't hurt her," he said. "I didn't touch her."

"What's going on?" I asked. When nobody responded, I shoved between Detective Martinez and Dru. Detective Martinez might have thought he was Scary Hero Officer, but I wasn't frightened of him. I'd dealt with plenty of cops over the years, and I wanted answers. "Hello? Tell me what's going on."

The other officer made a beeline toward me, but Detective Martinez held out a hand to stop him. "Get out of the way, Miss Kill. You don't want to get involved in this."

I threw my hands up in the air. "In case you couldn't tell, I'm already involved in this." I flashed on my fingers trailing the bruises on Dru's naked side and realized I was involved even deeper now than before. I'd managed to complicate things for everyone, especially me.

"I didn't hurt her," Dru repeated. "And I want my lawyer."

Detective Martinez stepped toward me. "I don't want to have to arrest you too, Miss Kill," he said. "But if you don't get out of the way, I will do it." As if on cue, the other officer produced a pair of handcuffs as well.

"What do you have on him?" I asked, knowing I was pushing my luck. How brave was I, exactly? How far did I think I could push Detective Martinez? Was I willing to spend the night in jail? Was I willing to have to explain things to Dad?

"You have ten seconds to get out of the way," he responded.

"They have nothing," Dru said. "It's not possible for them to have anything on me."

"Eight . . . ," Detective Martinez intoned.

"This is crazy," I said, though I didn't just mean Dru's arrest. I meant all of it, from the phone call to the *silver, brown, pink* numbers leading me here to the violet and mint green of lust and suspicion to watching Dru get arrested just minutes after being in bed with him.

"Six . . ."

My mind swirled with color. Sunshine yellow, bumpy gray and black, the orangish-pink innocence I often saw when I was in the same room with a baby. It was too much. I didn't know which colors to trust, and which were just my own wrong interpretation. I took a deep breath. "Fine," I said, and stepped aside.

"Mr. Hollis, you have the right to remain silent," Detective Martinez said, squeezing the handcuffs over his wrists. They made the clicking sound I'd heard a million times on TV and in movies, but never had it sounded so loud, so real, so final as it did in that moment. I didn't hear anything else the detective said. My ears were ringing from the noise of the handcuffs. My mind was blinded by the rainbow.

None of this made sense, and for the first time since getting that phone call that night, I had a feeling of being in over my head. Who could I believe? Dru Hollis? Detective Martinez? Neither one? My own gut instinct that there was more to this than any of us knew?

Dru's guard had dropped when we were in bed. I'd felt it. Yet he still had those bruises.

Detective Martinez seemed so up-and-up. But for ten years I'd been waiting for the cops to find my mom's killer. And for ten years there had been nothing. *No concrete evidence* were words I practically lived my life by. I'd heard that phrase more times than I could count. Did that mean he had concrete evidence against Dru?

And what if there was concrete evidence against Gibson Talley instead? Would he even bother to look for it if he was so sure it was Dru?

I still didn't know who was behind Peyton's attack. But I knew that my intuition was telling me there was more to this case, and I was going to have to have more than a few vague Facebook threats to go off of.

Otherwise, I would never know the truth. Not so Detective Martinez could get his concrete evidence. I wanted to know the truth for myself.

"Nikki," Dru said. I looked at him. Detective Martinez had opened up the door, but had paused. "What happened today . . . I wanted it to happen. I know you had nothing to do with this."

I nodded, mute, while Detective Martinez walked Dru

through the front door. I raced to the window and watched as they walked through the complex toward the parking lot. A few of Peyton's neighbors had gathered on their balconies to watch. "Drama whores!" I shouted at the window, but none of them heard me.

The apartment seemed even emptier now that Dru was no longer in it. And since I had seen that Gibson Talley definitely didn't live here, I didn't really have any reason to keep searching. Going through Peyton's designer clothes only made me feel like a creepy snoop. Not to mention it reminded me of all the reasons why someone could hate Peyton Hollis, including me.

I walked back to the bedroom to retrieve my boots, which lay unzipped and collapsed like a monster with its belly flayed, next to the bed. I could still smell Dru in here. I wondered if I would be another number on his list of conquests. I wondered if I'd see him again, and, if I did, what would happen. Most of all, I wondered if he was guilty.

I sat on the edge of the bed and stuffed my feet into my boots, then bent to zip them. My eye caught a flyer lying halfway under the bed. I pulled it out.

Junk. The kind of crap somebody handed you as you walked by a strip club. It was advertising someplace called Hollywood Dreams Ranch, an instant scandalous *glittery, shimmery lilac* connection. There was an expensive-looking, leggy blonde in a plunging neckline promising an evening

with an escort to "rival even the most luxurious of dreams."
Gag.

I dropped it back on the floor and went back to zipping, but the flyer turned over as it fluttered to the carpet. I stopped, mid-zip. Peyton had written something on the other side.

I picked it up and studied her handwriting, trying to concentrate on just the words and numbers.

There was an address that I didn't recognize, followed by a time—11:00.

And then, in the lower left-hand corner, a doodle. A simple drawing of a sun, just a circle with lines coming off it, sunglasses and a big smile plastered across it—the kind of picture a kid might draw. Or someone who was doodling while on the phone. Above the sun, she had written, in whimsical letters, *Mr. Golden Sun. Golden* was underlined three times.

I squinted at the word. I especially hated reading color words, because the color never matched the word, and it was confusing. *Golden* wasn't golden to me. It was—

I sat up straight. I had had this thought before, not that long ago.

I racked my brain, trying to remember when. So much had happened recently, everything was starting to meld together.

Maybe it was something on Peyton's Facebook page. Or

something Martinez had said. Or maybe . . .

The photo. Yes, I had thought it while looking at Peyton's photos on Aesthetishare. The ominous one, the one with her address graffitied above an ad for these apartments. She'd titled it.

Fear Is Golden.

And I'd had the thought that it wasn't. Fear was bumpy gray and black, like asphalt, but the only person who would know that was me.

Forgetting my partially unzipped boot, I stood up, like someone had zapped me with electricity.

I avoided color words. I despised them. They were confusing and distracting, and I would never say something like "the sky is blue" because *sky* was definitely white, or "grass is green," because green didn't really describe the word *grass* specifically. No synesthete would ever utter a sentence like "Fear is golden," because that lie would be so frustrating.

Unless, of course, to them, fear really was golden.

I stopped in my tracks and stared down at the flyer.

Mr. Golden Sun.

It was a message. *Fear Is Golden; Mr. Golden Sun.* Two sentences, using that same color word. My heart pounded in my chest like I was running a marathon. If I was reading this correctly, then whatever was going down at that address at eleven o'clock had Peyton afraid. But was I reading it correctly, or was I reading into it as a synesthete?

A synesthete would use a sentence like that if they were actually describing the color of a word. *Sadness* is brown. *Cheating* is turquoise. *Fear is golden.*

Live in Color. A neck tattoo, with a black-and-gray rainbow, and words, also inked in black and gray.

But they were beautiful, colorful words to someone like me.

Jesus.

Was Peyton Hollis a synesthete?

I paced through the apartment, looking for more clues. More words that might stand out. I found none. In fact, I found almost no words, no letters or numbers at all. Which was as much of a sign as anything.

If Peyton was a synesthete . . . was that why she had my number in her phone? Was she reaching out to me because she knew I suffered the same color issues she did? But how? Nobody knew about my synesthesia. Nobody.

Yet it made so much sense. And I couldn't explain it any more than I could explain how I knew that the 412 graffiti meant Peyton lived in this apartment.

Peyton Hollis had synesthesia. Somehow she'd found out that I did, too. She must have known someone was trying to hurt her.

And she left me clues.

Peyton Hollis wanted me to find her attacker.

I RACED BACK to Peyton's bedroom and quickly rifled through her dresser drawers. Nothing. I checked under the bed again. Nothing. I went back to the closet, felt along the top shelf, pawed through each and every shirt and dress and pair of pants. Nothing. It was as if she'd left her apartment purposely bare. Or as if she didn't expect to be here long.

After a quick check through the bathroom and kitchen, I went back to the bedroom closet and opened the front pocket of the suitcase. I pulled out the photos I'd found there before and shoved them in my back pocket. I didn't know if they would offer any clues, but they were all I had to go on.

Dru had left Peyton's keys on the kitchen counter, and I grabbed those, too, on my way out. I needed to go back to the hospital. I needed to find out if she had more tattoos, or something in her clothes, or . . . or just something. And I definitely needed to get out of there before the police came to search her apartment, now that they knew where it was.

I stopped to zip my boot the rest of the way, then hurried outside, locked Peyton's apartment, and walked down the sidewalk. I tried not to notice Dru's Spyder still sitting next to my car as I headed toward the lot. Just looking at his car now gave me a queasy, unsure feeling.

Instead, I concentrated on shoving Peyton's keys and the flyer into my jacket pocket, barely paying attention to where I was going until I almost tripped over the woman with the dog.

"Excuse me," I mumbled, stumbling to keep from plowing into her. I veered off the sidewalk to edge around her as she pulled letters out of a mailbox.

"No problem," she said. "Not like I'm dying to get to these bills anyway." She chuckled, a rattling smoker's laugh, and I smiled and made agreeing noises as I kept walking.

And then, ten steps away, it dawned on me.

Mailboxes.

I hurried around a corner, hoping it wasn't the direction she was going to be headed, and pressed my back against the wall between the corner and a window. I leaned forward and peered toward where I'd just been. She was still standing there, pulling out letters with one hand while juggling the dog with the other.

Of course. Mailboxes. How easy.

I waited there, flattening myself as she came back toward the buildings, prepared to bolt if she came my way, but fortunately she turned and disappeared inside an apartment in another building, talking to her dog all the while.

I waited a while longer, listening for every rogue sound I could pick up, my muscles twitching, my breath sounding exceedingly loud, firecracker gold—the color of adrenaline—popping in my peripheral vision. Twice I thought I heard someone coming up from behind, and I instantly tensed, but twice there was nothing there. Once, police sirens had me sure that they were racing to Peyton's apartment to search and arrest me for taking things, but of course, that was my own paranoia getting to me. The sirens passed on by, hurrying to someone else's emergency. The Fountain View courtyard was as still as a cemetery.

Finally, I figured it was as clear as it was ever going to be, and I slipped out from behind the building, hurrying toward the mailboxes, walking as lightly on my feet as I could. *Be cool, Nikki. For all anyone knows, you're a new girl here checking out your own mail.* I took a deep breath, relaxed, and slowed my walk to something more nonchalant.

Not all the mailboxes were labeled. Peyton's box—412—was

only marked in *silver, brown, pink* numbers, which, of course, I expected. The ones that were tagged were a mix of terrible handwriting, their letters jumping out at me in confusing hits and misses as I tried to figure out what they were.

P. Simms

Hanson

K Abendroth

Daniel Cattaneo

I ran my fingers along the names to steady the colors, a trick I had learned sometimes worked in English class. I blew a puff of air out, about to give up, when I finally saw it.

VF c/o Talley

Gibson's apartment.

Underneath the name were three numbers, 503. *White, black, purple.* Easy to remember.

I was so pumped about finding his place—and knowing that I was right . . . well, technically, Jones was right, but I'd been right to go with my gut—it was hard to look casual as I hurried back down the sidewalk. I would feel much more at ease once I got close to the shadows of the buildings.

I stopped when I neared Peyton's apartment and diverted to the left. Peyton's number was 412, so I guessed the 500s building to be next door. It took me only a moment of searching to realize that Gibson's apartment was on the second floor. I hiked up the outside steps, found the door, and before I could even think about what I was doing, swallowed the lump in my throat and knocked softly. *White, black, purple* blinked at me amid the scratches and dents and the one Viral Fanfare poster that clung to the outside of the door.

I waited. Nothing. I knocked again, harder this time. Still nothing. I tried the handle. Locked.

Shit.

I knew a lot of things. I knew how to find pressure points that would take an attacker to his knees. I knew how to get out of a wrist grab. I knew that the word *danger* was, oddly, kind of sparkly and white when you would totally think it would be flashing red or something. I knew how to break a knee with just one kick.

But I definitely didn't know how to pick locks.

I stood and gazed at Gibson's door for what seemed like forever, as if staring at it would suddenly make it open. In the meantime, I heard someone either coming out of or going into an apartment downstairs. I had to do something. I couldn't just hang around here all day.

"It can't be that hard, can it?" I whispered to myself.

I had a penknife in my car—a gift from Jones when I'd passed my black belt test. I'd kept it in the glove box, thinking I would never use it, but I hurried out, grabbed it, then came back and knelt in front of Gibson Talley's door. Now I looked really suspicious, so I knew I had to hurry, which made my hands shaky and clumsy.

"Come on," I whispered to myself as I jiggled and straightened the knife around in the keyhole. "Come on."

But nothing.

After ten minutes of trying, I capped the knife with exasperation and crammed it into my pocket, hating that I would have to just go home.

I stared at the door, hoping for one last-ditch bit of inspiration.

It came to me.

Earlier, I'd joked with Dru that I could just kick down Peyton's door. I didn't know if I could actually do such a thing, but at the moment it seemed like the only option I had left. I lifted my knee, turned my body, and side-kicked the door, hoping it would pop open without much racket. It shuddered, and I thought maybe I'd heard some wood splinter in the door frame, but it stayed intact, and the noise was definitely of the variety that would tempt nosy neighbors to poke their heads out.

I could have sworn the squeak of a door opening downstairs sounded again. Time to get out of there.

I was three steps away from Gibson's door when I realized I had Peyton's keys in my pocket. Dru had tried several before one worked in her door.

It was an outside chance, but . . .

The first one worked. When I heard it hit home, I stopped and stared in disbelief. Who would have guessed? Peyton had a key to Gibson Talley's apartment. Of course it made sense. But it also meant that I was right—they were close. Very close.

I held my breath while I turned the key and then the doorknob.

Just like Peyton's had been, Gibson's apartment was dark and shadowy, with thick curtains drawn across the window. But unlike Peyton's, Gibson's apartment was filled with crap. Papers and magazines and mail and clothes and tons of used Solo cups. Filled ashtrays and piles of trash and dirty dishes and musical instruments. A scraggly cat came out of nowhere and mewed at me, causing me to jump half out of my skin. In the quiet apartment, his meow sounded like a roar.

"Hey, kitty," I said, squatting and holding out my hand, but the cat hissed and ran away, ducking behind a half-broken table in the kitchen area. I stood, closed the door behind me, and tried to figure out where I would look first.

What was I even looking for? I had no idea.

I started by listlessly pawing through some of his mail, but found nothing but junk and letters from what looked like bill collectors. I drifted through the kitchen, looking for a cell phone or a whiteboard or . . . anything. But there was nothing. The cat came out again, this time close enough to rub across my leg one time before scurrying away.

I went back into the living room and sat on the very edge of the futon that served as half couch, half garbage can. I tried to imagine Peyton feeling at home here and couldn't do it. This was so far and away different from Hollis Mansion it had to feel like a whole other life to her.

Or maybe that was what made her comfortable here.

Must get to the bottom of things. Family.

On the floor, tucked most of the way under the coffee table, was an ashtray, filled with cigarette butts and blunts. I scooted it with my foot and saw a notebook underneath it. Curious, I picked up the notebook, holding it close to my face to read it in the dim light.

The first page was filled with what looked like more song lyrics, similar to the ones in the notebook I'd found in Peyton's apartment. I wished I had taken hers with me, for comparison. But in this book, most of the words were scribbled over and rewritten. I tried to make them out, but the handwriting was so bad, and the light so dim, I could only decipher the occasional word. *Trees. Cocaine. Steps. Love. Laying there.* Half the words misspelled. From the looks of things, whoever had written this was not comfortable doing so.

I flipped back several pages—more and more lyrics, more and more scratch-outs. Nothing useful. Nothing to do with Peyton. I started to put the notebook back where I'd found it and a business card fell out, landing in the ashtray. I picked it up.

Leo Powers
Producer
(323) 555-0140

I turned the card over, but there was nothing written on the back side. I turned it over again and studied it. One corner had an outline of a pair of headphones. Could this possibly have something to do with Peyton? Probably not. Probably Gibson had picked up a card from someone and stuck it in the notebook, forgetting about it, and it had nothing at all to do with her. But then again, Bill Hollis was a producer. Could that be a connection?

I was still deep in thought when I heard thumping. It took me a minute to place what the sound was. It was almost to the front door before I realized it was the sound of footsteps coming up the stairs outside, voices trailing the steps.

My eyes darted around the room, looking for an escape route. There was no way out but the front door, which was now rattling with someone turning the doorknob.

Shit.

I jumped up, accidentally upending the ashtray with my foot. The notebook fell to the floor on top of the spilled ashes, and I shoved the business card that I'd found into my back pocket. I raced toward the darkened hallway, nearly tripping over the cat, toward what I assumed was the bedroom. I was barely out of sight before the door opened and the voices were in the apartment.

". . . all those songs will go with her," one voice said. "Some of them are half mine, but she's the one listed as the writer. Her fucking dad insisted."

"Can you sue for them?" the other said. "You were there. You cowrote them. You'd think you'd have some rights, you know?"

"Hell if I know. I'd have to get a lawyer, and I ain't got money for that shit. Guess we'll find out, though, won't we? We are hosed without that music. I can't write without her. And you and Vee suck at writing. Might as well give up. Fucking Peyton. If she hadn't just been such a bitch about everything . . ."

My ears perked at the mention of her name, as I slipped through the first doorway on my right. It was a bedroom, as filthy and cluttered as the living room, but with an underlying smell of body odor and pot. I wrinkled my nose, my heart pounding in my chest.

"So what about the meeting?"

"We go. We don't need her. Or her dad."

There was the noise of someone dropping keys on a table. Someone—I was guessing Gibson—asked the other if he wanted a beer, and then there was the sound of cans popping. I crept across the room, fumbling for an idea. I couldn't stay here forever, but it was sounding like these two were settling in.

There was what looked like a door or window on the other side of the room, the light blocked out by a comforter pinned across the top of it. I remembered the balconies I'd seen from the outside—the ones I'd thought looked like teeth—and headed for it, praying I'd find a balcony on the other side of the blanket.

"Dude, are these your lyrics?" one of the voices asked, giving me pause.

"What are those doing there? And what the hell happened with this? Fucking cat," the other voice answered.

I gulped, imagining them bent over the spilled ashtray, hoping I hadn't left anything else. I patted my pockets. Shit, shit, shit. The penknife.

"Where did this come from?" I heard.

I sprang into action, racing across the room in the dark. My feet got tangled in a heap of dirty clothes and I tumbled, hands splayed out in front of me, right into a dresser. Something leaning against the dresser scraped slowly along the wall and then landed with the soft clang of guitar strings being jarred.

"Dude, did you hear that?" one of the voices said, and then there were footsteps coming down the hall, the hallway light blinking on and nearly blinding me.

A voice, loud, commanding. "Whoever the fuck you are, if I find you, I'll kill you."

I didn't have time to think. I got to my feet and lunged for the comforter. I tore it away, revealing a door. Blindly, panicked, I clawed at the lock. I flipped it up, flung open the door, slammed it closed behind me, and climbed the balcony fence.

No time to think. No time to plan. Just act.

The balcony seemed a lot higher from up here than it did from the ground. But as I heard the door yank open behind me, I dropped to the other side of the fence, dangling by my hands for only a few seconds before closing my eyes and letting go.

I hit the ground with a jarring thud, my teeth clacking together, my ankles creaking with a distant pain. The momentum rolled me backward over my shoulder, and I found my feet again.

"Hey! Who the hell?" I heard, but I didn't dare look up. I just ran so hard for the parking lot my chest felt like it was going to burst.

I threw myself into my car and jammed it into gear, seeing Gibson Talley and another guy running down the sidewalk toward me, their angry, shouting faces growing smaller in my rearview mirror as I roared away.

PEYTON LOOKED MUCH smaller and frailer without Dru sitting next to her. Her face was so pale, so swollen. She looked like a dying person.

The flowers and balloons had grown overnight as well. Now they were the first thing you noticed when you came into the room. I caught an orderly leaving with a cartful of greenery as I was coming in, my ankle nagging me with every step.

He grinned, shrugged one shoulder. "Doctor's orders," he said. "Too many."

I remembered my mom's funeral. There'd been flowers. What had seemed like so, so many of them. Enough that my dad had to enlist the gardener to pawn some off on friends and family. *I don't want them here*, I remembered him saying, his voice ragged, a sweating glass of whiskey in his hand. *That smell is depressing as hell.*

But even though there'd been a ton of flowers at Mom's funeral, there hadn't been as many as were in Peyton's room right now. How many would there be when Peyton died? *If, Nikki, if!* I tried to correct myself. I squeezed my eyes shut to block out the crimson to make it easier to believe.

I walked around the room, idly checking the cards poking out of the flowers. Where were these people? Where were Abby and Sutton and the Drama Club? Where was Mr. Benecio, the Choral Group instructor? Where were her grandparents? Luna? The hordes of gorgeous guys always falling over themselves to be with her?

I pulled a card out of a vase filled with black daisies. Where in the hell did someone find black daisies?

The card read, *Vee.*

Vee. The singularly named bass guitarist for Viral Fanfare.

I turned it over, looking for more. A kind note. A get-well wish. Something. Anything. But that was it. *Vee.*

Where were you, Vee? Where was the rest of the band?

Black daisies. A hell of a strange choice.

I put the card back into the flowers and continued

looking through the rest of them. None of them meant any-thing to me. My mind kept going back to Vee. Mint green. Sharp edges. Vee.

Finally, I went over to Peyton and stared down at her for a moment. Somehow she'd figured out that we shared this very important thing. Somehow she'd gotten my number. She'd tried to call it. She'd left me clues. I knew this with everything I had. But I still felt like I was invading her per-sonal space by being in here.

"Hey," I said softly. I moved her hair off her tattoo. "I live in color, too. How did you know?"

I sat down next to her, where Dru had been sitting the day before, and picked up her hand. I turned over her arm, searching for more tattoos. Nothing. Just the scratches and bruises from being beaten. I looked at her other arm. Noth-ing.

"So what am I supposed to do next?" I asked. "I think I'm onto something, but I'm not sure how to get proof. I don't suppose you have any other clues to give me."

I stared at her face for so long, I almost could have talked myself into believing that I saw it move. But of course it didn't. The steady drip of the IV into her lifeless arm told me that much.

A nurse bustled into the room. She jumped, surprised.

"Oh! I wasn't expecting to find anyone here," she said, placing her hand over her heart. "Other than Peyton, I mean."

"Just me," I said.

"Well, that's okay. I'm sure any company is appreciated. I'll be right out of your way." She checked the IV bag.

"Do you still have the clothes she was wearing when they brought her in?" I asked. "I can take them home for her," I added sheepishly, to keep from sounding as creepy as I was afraid I did.

The nurse hesitated, seemed to think about it, and then shook her head. "They gave everything to the police. But honestly, all she had on her were her keys and a phone, and they gave those to her family. Who would have ever thought our Jane Doe would turn out to be Bill Hollis's daughter? Crazy, huh?"

She moved to Peyton, picked up her wrist, and counted her pulse. "Just goes to show your mama was right."

I blinked. "I'm sorry?"

She smiled warmly, checking various tubes and machines swiftly and expertly, as if she could do it in her sleep. "You know how your mom always said to wear clean underwear because you never knew if you were going to get into an accident?"

I shook my head sourly. "My mom died when I was a little kid."

"Oh. I'm sorry. That's terrible." She wrote something on a pad she kept in the front pocket of her scrubs. "Well, my mama always said it, and she was right. You never know what's going to happen to you when you wake up in the morning."

Not true. Peyton knew what was going to happen to her. *Fear Is Golden.*

"Has she had any other visitors? I mean, besides her family?"

"Well, I only work the day shift, so I don't know what happens when I'm gone at night. She has a lot of kids come in after school, but they usually only stay for a few minutes."

"You see anyone with spikes running through her ears? Lip piercing? Dreads?"

The nurse thought about it, and then brightened. "I think I know who you're talking about. The girl who brought the black flowers. She wasn't here very long, either." She took a couple of steps toward me and leaned in. "Between you and me, she was a strange one, that girl. She asked if I knew whether Peyton had a will for her intellectual property. Isn't that a weird thing for a young person to ask?"

Not if that young person is trying to kill Peyton, I thought, remembering the conversation I'd heard in Gibson's apartment. *All those songs will go with her.* Was that what this whole thing was about? Was this a fight over song lyrics?

The nurse checked some other monitors and then straightened the blankets, tucking them under Peyton's ankles. She stopped, patted Peyton's foot through the blanket.

"Poor thing. So young and pretty. You related? You look a little like her." She swirled her fingers in front of her face. "It's the nose."

"No. I'm just a friend," I said, and then, realizing that the only Hollis I'd ever really spoken to was Dru, and that we'd so much more than spoken, added, "Of the family." I felt myself blush and wanted to pluck my own tongue out and burn it.

"Well, you must be a good friend."

"Have the police been around much?"

"Just the one. The one with the brown hair. Was just here this morning, in fact. This girl sure is surrounded with lookers, isn't she?" She squeezed Peyton's toe, patted her foot again, and then turned to leave. "Should be motivation for her to come back to us, huh?"

So Martinez had come here first, ready to arrest a man at his sister's deathbed. Nice. What kind of asshole did that? I didn't care what he looked like—he was clearly a heartless honor-and-glory type who didn't care about tact and feelings one bit.

I sat by myself for a while after the nurse left but then decided that I wasn't going to solve anything by sitting here. I checked the clock on my phone. There were still two hours of school left.

And I needed to see someone there.

"I'll be back," I said to Peyton. "Don't worry. I'll figure

this out." I stared at her a moment longer, willing her to open her eyes. Wishing that she would answer me. Just tell me . . . why me?

I left, thinking it was weird how I felt closer to her somehow. Nothing had changed. Not really. I wasn't the close relationship type, at all. Plus, we were still in totally separate worlds. We had nothing in common. And we'd never spoken. Not directly.

But she'd spoken to me through that photo, hadn't she? She'd talked to me through her tattoo.

We'd communicated in color—the most intimate way I knew how.

I got into my car and headed out of the parking lot, concentrating on what would be the quickest route that would get me to school. I was so focused, I almost didn't see the beat-up car parked two slots down from mine.

Or the man standing next to it, smoking a cigarette, the smoke wafting up in curlicues around the tattoo on his jaw. Curlicues that popped into rusty starbursts.

But he noticed me. He peered at me as I crept by, never losing eye contact, never looking away. He had an angry crease in the center of his forehead. His lips were set in a tight line. We locked eyes, and my skin crawled with goose bumps.

It was Gibson Talley.

I dropped my gaze and punched the gas pedal, watching

in the rearview mirror to see if he would follow me. He didn't, but the uneasy feeling that had washed over me wouldn't let go. *Bumpy gray and black, bumpy gray and black.* Was he there for Peyton, or had he followed me from his apartment?

Either answer wasn't a good one.

I KNEW RIGHT where Vee's locker was. Everyone knew where Vee's locker was. It was the battle site of a long-time war between Vee and the custodian, the door scrubbed to bare metal where it had been tagged with Vee's Sharpie about a thousand times over. Angry bumper stickers had been half scraped off, flyers for grunge bands pasted on and ripped down. It was a disaster area, which was just the way Vee liked it.

I sort of knew Vee a little bit. She'd been in my family and consumer sciences class in junior high. It was one of the few classes that I did okay in, because I didn't have to read to sew a pair of mittens (a stupid-ass project for a bunch of California kids, by the way) or to open a can of biscuits or diaper a fake baby. I could zone out in there. One of the few places.

Vee was who Peyton would be without her rich Hollywood parents and their celebrity-studded parties. Punk, without the posh. Even back then, Vee had a troublemaker side to her. She was forever sabotaging her own cookies just to watch the teacher's lips pucker in disgust during the taste test. Her mitten boasted an obscene middle finger. Occasionally, she would catch my eye while she was doing something she wasn't supposed to be doing, and we would laugh together. Which didn't exactly make us friends, but it was probably as close to friends as Vee or I ever get.

Vee played bass guitar. She had biceps to beat most of the boys in our school. And she had the rattiest, nastiest-looking dreadlocks I'd ever seen, with feathers and shit hanging out of them. She was so crazy she was cool. And when she hooked up with Viral Fanfare, she got even cooler. But untouchable cool, like Peyton. Only Vee was about a million times more unlikable than Peyton. Nobody envied Vee; they feared her.

She loped to her locker about ten seconds before the tardy bell rang, clearly in no hurry to get to the next period, which I knew was PE because I normally had health at the same time.

"Hey," she said, flicking her eyes to me. I was leaning against the locker next to hers—the only two people left in the hallway.

"Hey," I answered.

She opened the door—22, 3, 19, *black-and-white checkered, purple, mauve*—and a bunch of papers fell out. She bent to retrieve them, wadded them up, and crammed them back on the shelf. The inside of her locker smelled like smoke and pork chops. She shoved a book on top of the papers, crammed her messenger bag into the bottom of the locker, then slammed the door shut and crossed her arms, leveling me with her stare. "What? You lost?"

Probably half the kids at our school would have pissed themselves if Vee were standing in front of them looking the way she was looking at me, but I wasn't half the kids at our school. She didn't scare me. I could identify girls like her a mile away. She was all talk and no action. One chokehold and I would have her pounding the floor for mercy.

And her attitude irritated me. It had been a long enough day without dealing with her crap.

"Peyton Hollis, that's what," I said.

She blinked, recovered quickly. "What about her?"

I narrowed my eyes. "You know exactly what about her. Someone beat the shit out of her, and I think you might know who."

"I might know who?" She snickered derisively. "Someone's been watching too many cop shows. Why would I know who'd want to turn Peyton into a high-dollar smear on parking lot pavement?" She started to walk down the hall, but I followed her. "I've been done with that bitch for a while now."

"Not true. I saw the black daisies," I said. "I know they came from you. What's going on? Did she do something to Viral Fanfare?"

She whirled around on me, the sleeves of the flannel shirt she had tied around her waist smacking me in the knees. "And this is your business, why?"

I ignored her question and fired back one of my own. "Gibson Talley?"

She threw her hands in the air. "What about him?"

"'You won't win this,'" I recited. "Sound familiar? He said that on her Facebook page. What wasn't she going to win? What did she do to him? Was it about the songs? Or were they something more than bandmates?"

She smirked and shook her head as it dawned on her what I was saying. "You don't have a clue," she said, and started walking again. "But you would be wise to stay out of it. Gibson Talley is not somebody you want to piss off."

"Answer my questions. I saw him at the hospital. Why is he after her?" I touched the back of her arm and she wheeled on me, smacking my hand away angrily. Instinctively, I curled it into a fist, shifting my weight back onto my right leg, fight-ready.

"He is not 'after her,' and if that's what she's telling people, she's lying. You need to leave this alone. It has nothing to do with you. And nothing to do with Peyton's current problem."

"Problem? It's not a broken fingernail. She's not telling anyone anything, because she's barely hanging on. But I guess you knew that, since you sent black flowers. Classy, by the way."

She grinned, her entire body tensed. "Why are you bothering me about this, anyway? Haven't they already arrested someone? I heard it on the radio on my way here. Oh yeah, it's Dru. I also heard you been hanging around the hospital a lot, so you probably already know all about Dru Hollis's legal problems. He letting you pretend you're screwing for love?" When I didn't answer, her grin widened. "Aw, a happy romantic couple. How cute." She poked a finger in my face, all of a sudden serious. "You need to find a new hobby. And leave me and Gibson Talley alone."

This time when she walked away, I simply watched her go, my fists clenched at my sides, my shoulders tensed. Her vile words washed over me. I wanted to chase her down, rip her backward by her hair, and side-kick her to the face. I wanted to show her how wrong she was about me, about Dru, about all of it. But the worst part was I wasn't sure how much she was actually right about. I knew she was right about one thing, though—Dru was in jail. And I wasn't sure yet what exactly that meant.

"I don't screw for love," I yelled.

She turned. She was still smiling. "Just so you know, Nancy Drew, we have a song called 'Black Daisy.' Peyton wrote it two years ago. It was my favorite. I special ordered the flowers. I thought it would be a nice touch. Would make her smile when she wakes up. Mystery solved. Seriously, you should stay in the clubhouse with all the other little kiddies playing Clue." She walked backward a few more steps, wiggling her fingers at me in a good-bye gesture. "Tell Dru I said hi."

She turned and was gone. I paced back toward her locker, then screamed and punched it, leaving a dent right in the middle of a piece of a bumper sticker, the only letters still visible—*ass*. A teacher poked her head out of her classroom.

"What's going on here?"

"Nothing," I said.

"You should get to class, then. The bell has rung," the teacher said.

I turned toward Vee's locker and started spinning the dial. "I know. I've just got to get my book," I said.

The teacher gave me a disapproving look, and then, after a pause, said, "Do it quickly," and went back into her room.

I rolled my eyes at the space where she'd just been and started to walk away. But *black-and-white checkered, purple, mauve* flashed in the back of my head. *Checkered, purple, mauve.*

I turned back to Vee's locker. She would absolutely kill

me if she knew I was even thinking what I was thinking.

But somebody was hiding something. Maybe it was Dru, maybe it was Gibson, maybe it was Vee. Maybe it was Peyton herself. All I knew was I was too far into it to just give up now.

I turned the dial a few times, and then went to *checkered, purple, mauve*—22, 3, 19—and pulled open Vee's locker. Those same few papers dropped to the floor, but I didn't bother to pick them up. Looking over my shoulder, I quickly opened Vee's messenger bag. Hesitating for only a second, I lifted her laptop out of her bag, tucked it under my arm, shut her locker door, and walked out of the school.

THE NEXT DAY, I made it a point to go to school, mostly because when you're on academic probation and you start skipping class, the school calls your house before your first-period chair is even cool.

I knew they had called my dad because when I woke up he had left a note on the bathroom counter for me in his uneven, all-capital-letters script: *WE NEED TO TALK.*

I rolled my eyes and wadded up the note, tossed it into the trash can. The last thing I had time for was to make my father feel like a legitimate dad with some schmucky talk about staying in school and trying my hardest and *blah, blah, blah.* He would lecture me for a few minutes, feel guilty about it, try to make up by being my friend, and then disappear on another shoot.

Sometimes I wished my mom was around to yell at me about stuff. I would've taken the yelling over not having her at all.

I couldn't remember a lot about my mom. She had long, dark hair and prominent cheekbones, just like mine, and she was really pretty. She had a job, but if I ever went there with her, I couldn't remember it. Most of my memories of her were of warm days sitting outside, sipping sodas together while I showed off cartwheels or how high I could swing or whatever dopey little-kid thing I wanted to show off. She always laughed. Always indulged me. I literally could not remember a single time of ever being in trouble with my mom. But probably that was just because my brain chose to wipe out those memories after she died. Was murdered.

My mom never went to college—I knew that much for sure—but I was pretty sure she graduated high school, which would make her one up on me if I didn't get my act together. Sometimes I liked to pretend that she had synesthesia, too, and that was why she didn't go to college. Sometimes I liked to pretend that the colors I saw when emotions hit me out of nowhere were sent by her to help me make sense of them—an astral gift. But on some level I supposed I knew that wasn't true, because I'd always seen those colors, even before she was gone.

Had I ever told her about my colors? I couldn't remember. But I didn't think so.

I showered and dressed, trying not to think about what would happen if my path crossed Vee's today at school. Would she suspect I had stolen her laptop, or would she just assume she'd lost it? Part of me would have almost welcomed her questioning me, though. *He letting you pretend you're screwing for love?*

I'd spent most of the night before combing Vee's Facebook page for information. Anything I could sink my teeth into. Anything that would make sense out of what had happened with Peyton. But all her page turned up were a lot of links to indie punk bands and some snarky articles that were supposed to be funny. Her private messages were pretty much wiped clean, and her friends only talked about getting wasted and missing Viral Fanfare. *When are you going to play again?* seemed to be the question everyone was asking. Vee's answer, across the board, was simply *idk . . . idk . . . idk.* Vee didn't have nearly as many friends as Peyton, and from what I could tell, hadn't really had any interaction with Peyton in weeks.

I'd gone to bed exhausted and confused, giving up.

But by morning I was refreshed, ready to try again. So Vee didn't like Facebook. Fine. I tried all the others—Twitter, Instagram, even the photo-sharing site Peyton had been using—but nothing. Finally, desperate, I pulled up her email account. I needed a password. Great.

I sat back in my desk chair, trying to channel Vee's mind. I didn't know enough about her to know what she would choose as a password.

I tried "ViralFanfare" and got nothing.

I tried just "Viral" and just "Fanfare." Nope, and nope.

Tapping my fingernails on my desk, I thought some more. I tried "punk," "punkrocker," and "punkgirl," and was still locked out.

I was just about to give up, when out of desperation I typed in "BlackDaisy."

To my surprise, the account opened.

It was full of junk. Spam. Notices from bands. Invitations to connect on various social media. Newsletters. The occasional assignment email from a teacher or another student. Nothing worth seeing.

I was just about to log out and give up completely when an email from Peyton caught my eye. The subject was "Big Break!!!!!" and it had been sent two months ago. I opened it, noting that the email had gone to Vee, Gibson, and someone else named SethMonster123.

> You guys,
>
> I did it. I got my shithead father to finally agree to call in some favors and get us in front of that guy I told you about. Guess maybe there's hope for the daddy from hell

after all. Don't tell him or he'll just go off on another one of his power trips and probably try to make us all wear matching uniforms or something. I'm still working on him about the lyrics, tho, I promise. He's so greedy—even the lyrics we wrote together have to have the Bill Hollis stamp of approval. He's gotten some lawyer on it, but I promise, Gib, I will make sure the guy adds your name to them. Even if I have to pay him myself.

So here's the deal. Leo is on a project until October, and then he can meet with us. Right now we're saying Clear Lake on the 23rd at two p.m. Work for you? It better, because this is our only shot. I would not expect the great and powerful Bill to do us any more favors. It's sort of a miracle he did this much for us. I mean, without the press watching, at least.

You guys, can you believe it? Getting in front of Leo is, like, impossible. It's your ticket out of Brentwood, Gib! And maybe I can finally tell Vanessa I don't need her. I can get my own acting job.

Oh, and btw, I have some new songs for us. I've run them by my father and he said they're right up Leo's alley. I'll bring them tomorrow.

    P

I reread the email. The name Leo kept sticking out at me. After a minute of trying to place it, I went to the hamper and pulled out the jeans I'd worn the day before, then rummaged through the back pocket for the business card I'd taken from Gibson's apartment.

"'Leo Powers,'" I read aloud. "That's where I've heard of you before."

I Googled Leo Powers, the search turning up what I'd already guessed. Leo Powers was a record producer, known for signing huge punk bands like Salt and Vinegar, Dead Man Bitches, and Ello. Leo Powers took grungy kids and turned them into stars.

I checked Vee's search history and found a website for Clear Lake, a recording studio on Burbank Boulevard.

What about the meeting? one of the guys had asked at Gibson's apartment. *We go. We don't need her,* the other one had answered.

I reread the email for a third time. October 23. Today. If that was the meeting they were talking about, I wondered who would be there. All of Viral Fanfare except Peyton?

I had time, so I grabbed a cigarette, opened my window, and sat on the ledge. The morning air was never as satisfying as night air, even if it was as crisp and cool. But still, the cigarette helped calm my nerves and sharpen my focus.

I tried to imagine what Dru was doing at that moment. Was he awake, staring at a jail wall, or was he home, sleeping it off in his big mansion? Once again I found myself wondering what the hell I was doing. He was a Hollis—so many miles out of my league I couldn't even see the dugout—and he'd just been arrested for attacking his own sister. Not to mention he put out a serious sketchy vibe half the time. But there was something between us that I couldn't ignore. A pull. I couldn't stay away.

Too soon, I was down to the filter, so I flicked my butt into the rocks and bushes below (those damned gardeners!) and lit a second one, checking the time. I would have to smoke fast if I was going to make it to first-period economics class. God, more numbers. Just what I fucking needed.

JONES WAS WAITING for me. Only this time he was smart—waiting for me right outside my classroom door rather than by my locker. He'd apparently figured out that the locker was a high-visibility area and I could see him before he could see me. But the classroom was at the very end of a basement hallway, tucked into a little alcove. I couldn't see him until I was right on top of him. No chance of running away.

I groaned. His shoulders were hunched practically to his ears. I knew Jones well enough to know that he was pissed. My mind lit up with blinding red. What the hell was going on?

He pushed off from the wall as soon as he saw me and shifted so he was in my way.

"Not now, Jones, I'm going to be late." I tried to edge

around him, but he moved with me. He smelled delicious, like sweat and soap and cloves. But even smelling delicious wasn't enough to make me want to talk to him.

"Dru Hollis?" he said, ducking to speak conspiratorially.

I bumped my shoulder into his and stepped back, irritated. "What about him?"

"You hooked up with him," he said. Not a question; a statement.

My mouth dropped open of its own will. I was so shocked to hear him say it out loud, I didn't have time or the presence of mind to cover it. Still, I tried. "Who told you that?"

He gestured around the hallway. "Everyone is talking about the two of you. You've been hanging out with him. You dumped me for Hollis? He's so . . . skeevy," he said, a look of disgust pinching his face. "I never would have taken you for someone to get all caught up in that kind of thing."

"First, I didn't dump you for him," I said. "His sister is in the hospital, and I'm helping him find out who did it. We didn't . . . hook up. You'll have to get your rocks off on some other little fantasy." I bumped him harder and actually made it past him. "Second, not that it's any of your business at all even if we did."

"That's the thing," he said, talking at my back, but in a desperate catching-up way. "Some people are saying he's the one who did it. Somebody said he's already in jail for it. It's on the news."

My gut twisted at those words. On some level, I knew Jones had a point, and I hated him for it. "Whatever. Since when do you sit around gossiping so much, Jones? It's a bad look for you." I turned, looked him up and down with a sneer. "Very unmanly."

He grabbed my arm to stop me. I shot his hand an impatient look. Two girls pushed past us into the classroom, their eyes big, their heads together as they whispered. Were they whispering about Jones holding on to my arm, or was the gossip all about Dru and Nikki hooking up over Peyton's hospital bed? I thought I could probably guess which it was.

"What do you want, Jones? Yes, we hooked up, okay? Will that finally make you get the hint?"

"Listen," he said. "This may make me stupid, but I care about you, Nikki. I don't want you getting into something you can't handle. Dru Hollis is not good for you. He will hurt you."

I twisted my fist upward against his thumb and wrenched my arm out of his hand. "And you're here to save me, is that it? News flash, Jones. I don't get hurt and I don't need saving," I said through clenched teeth. "I can handle Dru Hollis and anyone else who comes my way. Including you. But thanks for the concern."

Jones seemed to take in what I said slowly, almost as if he were only now fully digesting what I'd been telling him for weeks. It was over. Finished. Forever. I almost felt bad for him as I saw his heart slowly break in front of me, almost as if it were shutting down piece by piece. He straightened, let his hands drop at his sides, and nodded.

"I hope you know what you're doing," he said.

"I always know what I'm doing," I answered, though an annoying lump had formed in the back of my throat, the slate of nerves—nagging that maybe, just maybe, I didn't know this time. I was stealing laptops and dangling from balconies, and living with all this bumpy black and gray all the time, and worst of all, sleeping with a guy I knew absolutely nothing about. Except the one thing I did know for sure about him—he was a suspect in the attempted murder of his own sister.

"A few weeks ago, I was at the Hollises'," Jones said, as I tried to make my way into the classroom. I stopped, curious. He looked eager, excited to have a reason to keep talking to me. Did Jones really care about Dru hurting me, or was this just more of the same—Jones trying to get me back? I guessed it was the latter, but if he had information, I was willing to play along to get it out of him, whatever his motives.

"You were at the mansion?"

He nodded. "Huge party. Dru bought the alcohol. Maybe the drugs, too, I don't know. There was plenty of Molly there. Some blond chick was selling it. Peyton was there, and she passed out pretty quickly, but first she kept saying all this weird shit."

My ears perked up. "What kind of weird shit?"

He shook his head. "I don't remember exactly. I was pretty messed up. It was right after you and I . . ." He hung his head, took a breath, and started over. "Some shit about not being able to trust anyone."

I took a step toward him, forgetting about class, ignoring that the bell had just rung and that Mr. Torres had closed the classroom door, which meant I was going to have to go back to the office and get a tardy slip if I wanted to be let in. "Did she mention names?"

"I don't think so. Before she could say too much, the blond chick with all the Molly was all over her, putting her arm around her, talking some shit about them both being groomed to be actresses and Peyton totally owning the part of an alcoholic soap opera diva. I laughed, but she didn't even smile. She looked completely serious."

"Was it Luna?"

"Sophomore? Blonde? Eyes dead like a crocodile. Does that make sense?"

I thought of Luna (*half* sister), and while I'd never thought about it before, yes, his description fit. I nodded.

"Anyway, she passed out, and the girl and Dru hauled her off to some other part of the house, and then later I saw them arguing in the kitchen when they thought they were alone."

"Who's 'they'?"

"Dru. And the crocodile girl. And another blond woman, who I never saw before or after that. They didn't see me, so I left." Immediately, I thought of the bored-looking blonde who'd shown up at the hospital. *Dru. Baby. Have you eaten?* Vanessa Hollis.

"*Left* left?"

He nodded. "The whole party felt weird. Like, dangerous or something. Shit you see on TV. I don't know. I had a lot to drink that night. I may not be remembering things right. But I remember how I felt, Nikki, and I'm just . . . I'm telling you. It was weird. He was weird. Stay away from Dru Hollis."

I laughed. "Because he bought alcohol for his sister? Or because he protected her after she passed out? Do you realize how ridiculous you sound right now, Jones?" Although the truth was I really didn't know Dru, and in the back of my mind wondered if maybe I sounded like the ridiculous one. Especially since this whole conversation was making me think of ice cream and toothpaste and other things mint green. *Suspicious much, Nikki?*

"Whatever. Do what you want." He waved me off and started down the hall.

"Jealous much?" I said to his back, but unlike Vee, Jones didn't bother to acknowledge that I'd said anything at all.

I supposed that meant I had finally succeeded. It was officially over between Jones and me. A relief.

After he'd turned the corner, I headed after him, walking slowly toward the office. This was such bullshit, and if Jones, or Vee, or anyone else in this school thought they were going to scare me away from hanging out with whoever the hell I felt like hanging out with, they were all sorely mistaken. I thought about the two girls who'd whispered as they'd passed us in the doorway. Fuck them and their whispers. I practically vibrated with eagerness to walk down the classroom aisle in front of them. I couldn't wait to hold their stares, to dare them to talk in front of my face.

I heard Jones's footsteps fade and picked up my pace, fuming, muttering under my breath.

I was so busy being furious, I walked head-on into someone rounding the corner. I jumped back, letting out a surprised noise as he held out his hands to keep me from falling over.

"Watch out," I snapped, but then my eyes landed on who'd nearly bowled me over.

"Miss Kill, I was just thinking about you."

Damn it. Chris Martinez. I would have rather kept talking to Jones.

"Well, what a coincidence, then, that you should just happen to show up at my school," I said.

"I was actually here to look through Peyton Hollis's locker, but yes, it is fortunate that I ran into you while I was here."

I crossed my arms over my chest and cocked my head to one side. "Literally."

He smiled, reminding me of holding that steaming coffee while talking to him in my entryway at home. Something about that smile made my teeth grind together. "Well, I hadn't intended to actually run into you, no."

"Detective, I don't know what you want from me, but—"

"Answers," he said simply, cutting me off. I didn't respond. "I need you to come down to the station. Is now a good time?"

I glanced at the lockers, the fluorescent light that was flickering above my head, shadows deepening on the ceiling around it.

"Actually, I have to get to class," I said. "I'm already late. Sorry." I offered him a sarcastic smile and maneuvered around him.

He sighed. "Sure, I understand. When do you think you can come? I just need to ask you some questions."

I turned back. "I don't know what you think I might be able to help you with. I've told you a thousand times I don't know anything."

"But you seem to still be very involved," he said. "I'm asking right now, but at some point it may no longer be a question."

"What does that mean? That you'll arrest me?"

He stepped close to me, so close I could smell his

cologne, and leaned toward my ear. "If you keep showing up in apartments you don't belong in, I may have to. Trespassing is a crime," he whispered. My face burned, but I tried not to let it show. Was he talking about finding me in Peyton's apartment, or did he somehow know about Gibson's?

I swallowed and took a couple of steps back, tossing my hair over my shoulder as if I hadn't a care in the world. "I have a lot of homework to catch up on, Detective," I said. "I really doubt I'll be able to come down this week. But thanks for the invitation."

I walked away, turning the corner quickly and getting out of sight before I let out the breath I'd been holding. For a few moments, I stood in the middle of the hallway, shaking my head in disbelief. As if I would waltz into the police station and spill my guts on everything I knew about Dru Hollis just because some die-hard detective wanted me to.

As if I knew anything about Dru Hollis anyway.

The thought made my palms grow cold and clammy. Made the mint green crawl up my skin.

I tried to shake it off, continuing toward the office. Class would be half over before I got in there, and my rage at those girls had worn off a little. How tough would I look, how sure of myself, if the door burst open halfway through class and I was escorted out in handcuffs? Walking through the aisles would feel much more exposed than I'd originally thought. Much more like maybe they could be right.

But of course they weren't right. I knew this because I knew about Gibson Talley. I knew about the threats and about the way Vee reacted when I confronted her and about the black daisies and seeing Gibson in the hospital parking lot.

Instead of turning into the office to get my tardy slip, I blew right past it and through the front doors of the school.

If Detective Martinez wanted to talk, we would talk.

DETECTIVE MARTINEZ'S TOTALLY obvious "unmarked car" was still sitting in front of the school when I left, so I knew I had some time to kill. I decided to drive slowly and take a little detour.

Hollis Mansion was on a street that featured sprawling houses guarded by a sea of undulating hedges and decades-old trees. Everything sculpted, everything pristine, expensive. Dad had a guy we called a gardener, but he was really a guy who mowed the lawn once a week and weeded our flower beds three or four times a year. People on the Hollises' street probably had fleets of actual gardeners, the type who were as much artist as landscaper.

I'd never been inside the Hollis house, although, truth be told, I probably could have shown up to any number of parties and nobody would have even noticed I was there. I wasn't comfortable around all this opulence. I didn't like show.

I pulled up in front of the house and parked. A gleaming white monolith that seemed to laugh at me with its enormous arched windows, Hollis Mansion was impressive, even to someone who'd grown up driving past million-dollar houses. Balconies and porches jutted out from every room, wrought iron and white picket and stately navy-and-yellow-striped awnings. Palm trees swaying gently against the chimneys. Concrete benches and statuaries and fountains. I could only imagine what it looked like inside.

I didn't know what I expected to do here, what I expected to learn. Maybe I was hoping that Peyton would have left a clue in a window or I would learn something more about Dru by studying the front of his house. But all I really saw was a shiny estate that looked like the perfect place to grow up.

I was just about to leave when the garage door began to rumble open, an SUV pulling into the driveway. But before the SUV could make it all the way to the garage, Bill Hollis stormed out of the house, stepping into the driveway so that the driver had to slam on the brakes. The door popped open and Vanessa Hollis stepped out, stilettos first, followed by long legs that seemed to end in a postage stamp of a skirt. Tucked into her skirt was a deep-V shirt, which showed most of a hot-pink lacy bra underneath. Make no mistake—Vanessa Hollis had some crazy curves, and she was proud of them.

I slid down into my seat and opened the window.

"Fine, you can park it," Vanessa yelled, throwing up her hands and stomping up the driveway past Bill, her purse dangling from her arm.

"Did you even go to the hospital today at all?" Bill demanded.

She stopped. "I have to work. As you already know. My clients' needs don't stop just because someone's laid up. You've been there. Dru's been there. I've actually been there, if you'll recall."

"Once. You've been there once."

She shrugged, her purse bumping against her thigh. "I thought you were having her moved to someplace closer to home. More comfortable for us."

"I'm working on that. In the meantime, it would be nice if you would make the occasional appearance."

Vanessa slid her sunglasses down her nose, peering up at Bill, pouty. "She's not my biggest fan. I'm sure she doesn't mind my not being there."

"Do you know how it makes us look?" he boomed. "Do you know how important it is for all of us to be there? The media has gotten ahold of the story. By tomorrow, this place will be crawling with cameras. I can only deflect so much. Show up."

She turned, walked back to him, and ran her finger down his chest while slowly moving her knee up his inner thigh. I had to lean closer to the window to make out what she was saying. It sounded like, "Don't you fret about a thing. It's all fine." She leaned in, nuzzled his neck, and then abruptly turned and waltzed back through the front door. "Seriously, you worry too much," she tossed over her shoulder before going inside.

After a few minutes of standing in the driveway, Bill Hollis climbed into the still-running SUV and pulled it into the garage. The door swung down, leaving the house looking as perfect as ever.

I watched a while longer, turning over their conversation in my head. Peyton had called him the daddy from hell in that email, had said he liked power trips. Vanessa seemed to be more concerned with herself than with Peyton. Dru was sitting in jail. Peyton was clinging to life.

All I could think about while pulling away was that this was one strange family, and I might be Peyton's only hope.

THE POLICE STATION was crazy busy, even for a weekday midmorning, and at first I had the inclination to just turn around and walk right back outside. I was never in the mood for fighting crowds—too many things to try to shut out of my mind if I wanted to concentrate on anything, and in a police station crowd, the color of the room was so ugly it was almost unbearable.

Dread. Grief. Bitterness, confusion, rage. *Brown mist,*

bruise-violet swirls, sickly green waves, rays of black and gray and pulsing reds. I clutched my stomach, nauseated.

"Can I help you?" asked an officer at the front desk.

It took me a minute to realize she was talking to me. I swallowed against the bile that was trying to rise up in my throat and stepped closer.

"I'm looking for Detective Martinez," I said. "I'm Nikki Kill. He's expecting me." Not technically true—I had pretty much told him expressly not to expect me—but she didn't need to know that.

She gave me a long look, like maybe she wasn't sure if she was supposed to believe me or not. I wondered if she gave everyone that look—if that's what being a police officer in a busy city did to everyone—but started to feel myself glower the longer she stared at me. For all she knew, I was here to report a crime.

I opened my mouth to say something, but she picked up the phone and punched in a couple of numbers before I could. Probably a good thing. The last thing I needed was to be in a cell adjoining Dru's. Dad would really think we needed to talk if I got myself arrested. The "discussion" would be interminable.

The officer mumbled something into the phone and then hung up, moving on to the person behind me without so much as telling me to move over, hold on, or piss off. I scooted to the side and kept myself busy by staring at a single white tile on the floor. If Martinez didn't come out soon, I was going to bolt.

And do what? I asked myself. Go back to school? No big, I just missed first period to hang out down at the police station. Go home and talk to Dad? No thanks. Go to the hospital and wait for Peyton to wake up, trying to block out all that crimson around me? The thought made my throat feel dry.

"Miss Kill," I heard. I looked up. Detective Martinez was coming toward me, his shirtsleeves rolled up, a gun clinging to his waistband. I hadn't noticed it at school, but he'd gotten a haircut—the buzz a little closer to his head. How weird it was to think of him having a regular life that involved normal stuff like haircuts. I tried to imagine him doing ordinary things like mowing the lawn or folding a T-shirt. Impossible. "I thought you weren't coming."

"Surprise," I said, pasting on my shittiest smile. I gestured toward the door. "But I can leave."

"No, no, I'm glad you came. Follow me."

Every fiber in my body told me not to follow him. Cops had failed me before. Cops had failed my mother. Yet there was something about this one. Something about the way he held himself, the way he followed me around, almost as if he was pursuing this case as hard as I was, the way he made me think of baby-chick yellow and sunshine yellow and the yellow of trustworthiness.

We went into what looked like a small conference room, a square table in the center, with three chairs surrounding it. I wondered how many criminals had been questioned in here. How many had broken under the accusations. My eyes flicked up toward the ceiling, looking for the video camera that was almost certainly pointing at me.

"Nobody's listening in," he said, as if he could read my mind. He pulled out a chair. I stared at it, obstinate, and after a few seconds he went over to the other side of the table and sat in his own chair. He leaned back and crossed his leg so casually over the other one, I began to feel uncomfortable standing there. He gestured toward the chair. "Please, have a seat. There's no need for you to feel worried. Are you worried, Miss Kill?"

I cocked my head to one side. "Why would I be worried?"

He shrugged, turned his mouth down in a thinking frown. "Most people get pretty nervous in here," he said. "Nobody likes to be in this room. Not even me."

"Well, I'm not exactly jumping for joy, either," I said. "But I have nothing to be worried about."

"All right, well, let's just get down to it, then. What do you know about Dru Hollis, Nikki? Okay if I call you Nikki?"

I glared. "No. And I know enough. What do you know?"

He ignored my question and fired another at me.

"So you know about his involvement with Arrigo Basile, then, I assume?"

"Who?"

He grinned, a spider-to-the-fly kind of grin, and slid an open file toward me. Inside was a photo—a mug shot—of a bulky middle-aged man with a bad comb-over. He didn't look like the kind of guy anyone would be afraid of if they walked past him on the street, but there was something in the way he peered up at the camera from beneath his bushy eyebrows that was chilling. "Maybe you don't know him as well as you thought," he said. He uncrossed his legs, leaned forward, gestured to the empty chair again. "Please, have a seat, and I'll fill you in."

I didn't want to. I didn't want to let the good detective, Chris Martinez, tell me what to do, ever. But I was curious. I sat on the very edge of the chair, keeping my arms crossed over my chest.

He reclined against the seat back and folded his arms to match mine. "Arrigo Basile is a prominent member of the Basile family. They're a pretty dangerous family with lots of connections."

"Mafia," I said.

He nodded. "They've been on our radar for years—we think they have some ties to drugs and prostitution, but we can't pinpoint what or where. We're also not sure what

Arrigo's role is in the family, but we know that he likes to hang around women and drugs. And he likes to hang around Dru Hollis."

"So Dru has a friend that you don't like, but you don't really know why you don't like him, so you arrest Dru? What kind of sense does that make?" This actually sounded like the police work I'd grown to know and hate.

"It's more complicated than that."

"Sounds to me like the most complicated part about it is you trying to figure out how to pin something on Dru. Who cares about this Arrigo Basile anyway? Just because he likes to sleep with hookers doesn't mean he beat up Peyton. Don't you see what a huge leap this is? Why?"

Chris Martinez leaned forward over the table again, concern creasing his forehead. I scooted backward in my chair, not wanting to be any closer to him than I absolutely had to be. "Arrigo Basile is no stranger to assault and battery."

"Neither are a thousand other guys in this city," I said. "What does it prove?"

"Listen, Nikki—"

"Miss Kill," I corrected, narrowing my eyes into steely slits.

He took a breath. "Miss Kill. Peyton Hollis's wounds are consistent with blunt force trauma. To be more specific, they look like they were inflicted by a smooth, rounded object, like a baseball bat or possibly a cane."

"So?"

"So, Arrigo Basile's signature is a cane."

My stomach dropped. As much as I wanted to deny all this, as much as I wanted to believe in Dru, it was becoming more and more difficult.

"I take it Dru mentioned none of this to you."

"It didn't come up," I said through numb lips. "It's not like we're dating."

"Were you with him the night of Peyton's attack?" Martinez's voice had taken on a sudden professional tone.

"No. We hadn't met yet."

"Were you with anyone that night?"

I flashed onto the memory of sitting in the window, chain-smoking. "I was studying for a chem test."

"So your parents can confirm that?"

I shot him my iciest look. "My father can. My mother is dead," I said.

He looked down. "I'm sorry to hear that."

"Are you suggesting I might have had something to do with this? I didn't have anything to do with Peyton Hollis before that night," I said.

"You seem pretty immersed in her business now, though." His voice was flat, impersonal.

I threw up my hands. "I don't know why, though! I have no idea why she had my phone number, or how she even got it. We weren't friends."

"But you're pretty friendly with her brother now."

I blushed. I could feel it. My ears got hot and my eyes burned with it and the familiar prickly pine hue swept in on me. I silently cursed myself and willed the feeling to go away. But when I sneaked a look at Martinez, I could have almost sworn I saw a blush high in his cheeks as well. "That was an accident," I said, wondering how much Martinez really knew about my life. It seemed like he knew an awful lot. I tried changing the subject. "A one-time thing. Are you sure he's the one? What evidence other than Arrigo what's-his-name's signature weapon do you have?"

He leafed through some papers. "That's why you're here, Nikki. Help me out. I know you've been following leads of your own. Why? And who are they? What have you found out?"

I didn't correct him on using my first name that time. My mind was spinning. Should I tell him what I knew about Gibson Talley? Would I ever find out the truth if I let the police get involved? Would I end up in trouble if I kept looking for answers? But I had a feeling he already knew more than I wanted him to, anyway. After all, I still had that unnerving feeling he knew I'd been at Gibson's.

"Have you ever heard of Viral Fanfare?" I asked.

"I hadn't until I started investigating Peyton's attack. It's her band, correct?"

I nodded. "She is . . . or was, I'm not sure . . . the lead

singer. Something happened a few weeks before the attack. I haven't been able to figure out what yet, but I'm working on it. Gibson Talley is involved."

At the mention of Gibson's name, Martinez's eyes perked up.

"I take it you have heard of him," I said.

He nodded. "Of course I have. Drugs, assault, breaking and entering, petty theft. You name it, he's probably been in here for it. We consider him one of our regulars."

"So that's basically it. You now know everything I do. Peyton moved out of her house and into that apartment where you arrested Dru, and I thought maybe she'd moved in with Gibson, but I was wrong."

"But how do you know he's involved?" Detective Martinez asked, his face a tight and intense question mark of scrutiny. "What makes you so sure? There's something more, Nikki. Something you don't want to tell me."

There was plenty I didn't want to tell him. It was one thing to tell him about Gibson, but there was no way in hell that I was going to tell him about my synesthesia. About the apartment number left behind in that photo of Peyton. About the tattoo on her neck and what it meant to people like us. Those were things the police didn't need to know—especially Detective Chris Martinez.

"Are we done?" I asked, but my voice was weak. I hated the sound of it.

He licked his lips, thought about it, and then finally nodded. "You're not in any sort of trouble, if that's what you're asking. So, yes, you're free to go. But I might have more questions for you later. You know, we could solve this faster if we had all the information."

"I've told you everything I know."

I could see in his eyes that he didn't believe me, a look of suspicion that reminded me of cold wintergreen. I shivered.

I pushed away from the table, my chair making a great scraping noise along the floor. But before I could stand, Detective Martinez reached across and put his hand on top of mine. I started to pull away, but his hand wasn't there menacingly. It was gentle, warm.

"I can see that you're not going to let this go," he said. "Although I would highly advise that you do. You're in over your head. So I will just say this. If you find yourself face-to-face with Arrigo Basile, get away from him and call me. He is not someone you want to mess with alone."

I pulled my hand free. "I'll be fine. I always am."

He left his hand where it was before, now empty of my own. "I don't want to see you get hurt. You don't know what it's like to be in real trouble." We locked eyes, and I could see it deep down—a woolly, brown-tinged white that told me there was more to Chris Martinez than he wanted people to know. He was asking me to trust him. But how could I when

I knew for certain I wasn't the only one hiding something?

"I can take care of myself," I mumbled.

"You don't know Arrigo Basile," he said. I stood and made my way to the door. "And, Nikki?" I turned. "You don't know Dru Hollis, either."

I didn't respond. Why did everyone keep reminding me of that?

He was trying to scare me. He wanted to trick me into telling him something to incriminate Dru. He must have thought he was some baller detective, manipulating Dru's tough little wrong-side-of-the-tracks slut into handing him over. He was wrong. I wasn't going to give him anything. I didn't have anything to give.

I walked briskly back the way I had come, but then stopped short once I reached the lobby.

Dru was leaving the station, Bill Hollis, wearing a shiny silver suit, leading him out with a hand on his arm.

Once again, the Bill Hollis of the entertainment pages was gone; this was the Bill Hollis I'd seen in the hospital room and in the driveway of Hollis Mansion. He reeked of money and importance and, at the moment, rage. Dru's head was ducked down, all the confidence I'd seen in him drained away. I waited for them to push through the doors and then crept out after them, staying in the shadow of the doorway as I watched the older Hollis lead his son away.

"Your mother is fit to be tied over it," Bill Hollis was fuming as they walked across the parking lot, his fingers digging into Dru's arm now.

"Sorry, I wasn't getting arrested for the fun of it," Dru answered. He shied away from his father's grip but didn't try to pull free of it. "Besides, they have nothing on me. That's why they had to let me go."

Bill Hollis stopped, yanking Dru to a stop as well. "You're going to try to be cavalier about it, too, you little shithead? Do you know what this can do to us? To your future? To my future? What am I supposed to say to the press?" He shook Dru, clamping down on his arm harder.

Dru winced. His eyes flashed with anger, his jaw straining. "I said I'm sorry."

"Well, what if 'sorry' won't do it, huh? You ever think about that? Think about your mother? About me?"

Dru gave a sardonic chuckle. "There it is. It's all about you. Always."

"It's about you, too. How are you supposed to get anywhere in this business if you're getting arrested for bullshit like this?"

"I don't want to get anywhere in this business. I've been telling you that for years, Dad," Dru said. "I want to live my own life. Why is it so hard for you to just respect that?"

Bill Hollis's jaw pulsed. "You have to earn respect in this life. So far you're not doing a great job of that."

"Trust me, this is all—"

"Why on earth would I trust you?" Bill Hollis said.

"Peyton trusted me," Dru said, his voice pure ice.

"Yes, and look what happened. Get in the car."

Bill Hollis shoved Dru's arm then. Dru didn't budge. Didn't stumble or even back up a step or two. He remained in place, digging into Bill Hollis with hatred-filled eyes, his fists clenched at his sides. Bill stepped off the curb and walked around to the driver's side of a white Cadillac, so expensive-looking it practically hurt my eyes. Dru stayed in place. I sank back into the shadows of the doorway, hoping he wouldn't see me spying on . . . whatever that was I'd just witnessed.

Nobody would expect Bill Hollis to be thrilled about having to fetch his son from jail, but there was something about the way he had gripped Dru's arm, something about the language he'd used, the way he'd torn into his son, that made his anger seem a little over the edge. This, combined with the weird scene with the SUV that I saw in front of their house, hardly seemed like the happy family unit I had once believed the perfect Hollises to be.

My dad is going to be shattered, Dru had told me that first night. Yet Hollis didn't seem so much shattered as inconvenienced. And worried about how his daughter's attack would affect his reputation.

"Get in!" I heard. I peeked around the corner again to see

that Bill Hollis had backed out of the parking space, pulled up to the curb, and rolled down the window. "It's bad enough that we've lost your sister's car. Let's go get yours before that apartment complex has the son of a bitch impounded."

Dru turned in slow motion, as if fighting against a tide, his shoulders tensed as he made his way to the other side of the car. Slowly, he got in and slammed the door shut.

Hollis's window rolled up, the tint making it impossible to see more than a couple of shadow heads within. He pulled away from the curb, and I pushed off the wall to watch him go. Two women breezed through the glass doors and right past me. Just as I stepped out of the shadow, glittery, shimmery lilac caught my eye.

I did a double take, peering at the Cadillac as it pulled out onto the street.

The vanity plate read DREAMS.

13

'D SPENT SO much time at the police station, I'd missed
lunch, and I figured since that meant most of the school
day was gone and it would be pointless to show up now, I
might as well go and get myself some proper food. I hit the
highway and headed up toward the city, rolling down the
windows to let the fresh air in.

I knew exactly what I wanted, and cruised right toward
MacArthur Park.

The line at Langer's was so long it snaked out onto the
sidewalk, so I took my time browsing Alvarado Street, with
its open-air shops and the Westlake Mall, while I waited. I'd
been expecting the line. Langer's had been one of my mom's
favorite delis, and she always said a hot pastrami as good as

theirs was worth waiting for. Langer's hot pastrami with cole-slaw was an institution, and it was my comfort food. The sun felt good on my head. And, like Mom, I didn't mind waiting.

Just when I neared the counter, my phone buzzed. Dad's face popped up on my screen.

"So you're not at school," he said when I answered.

"Sorry," I said. "I started out there, but things happened."

"Do I want to know what kind of things happened?"

"Not really."

"And where are you if you're not at school?"

I hesitated. He would not be thrilled to hear that I'd gone all the way to L.A. instead of just going to class like I was supposed to. "At Langer's," I said.

I heard him sigh on the other end. "I'm not far," he said. "Get a booth."

I got pastrami with tomato and a soda for each of us, and waited for one of the brown vinyl booths to open. By the time I was sitting down, he was coming through the front door, pulling off his sunglasses and tucking them into the V-neck collar of his shirt. He searched, found me, and headed in my direction.

"Well, at least I'm starving," he said, scooting up to the table. "So there's that."

Suddenly I felt too ashamed to eat. I stared at my sandwich guiltily as he bit into his, my plate growing brick-colored with my shame.

"What?" he said, looking at my plate. "Go ahead. You might as well."

"I'm sorry," I said again. "I really intended to go today."

He chewed, swallowed, and nodded, looking over my shoulder at the bustling crowd inside Langer's. "So is that what I'm supposed to tell them when they withhold your diploma? She intended to go, but it just didn't work out? Things happened?"

I stared at my sandwich sullenly. "Tell them whatever you want."

"Dare I ask what's so important that you just couldn't go to school today?"

I shook my head, mulling over what I could tell him. I couldn't tell him everything. I couldn't tell him that a stolen laptop was in my bedroom at that very moment, or that I'd slept with the suspect of a pretty high-profile crime, or that I'd just left the police station. Dad was patient, and lenient, but even he had his limits.

"There's this girl who goes to my school. She's been in a pretty bad accident. I've been visiting her at the hospital."

Dad stopped chewing. "So this is a friend of yours? Have I met her?"

"We're not exactly friends. I just . . . know her," I said. "And being there has brought up a lot of bad memories."

Dad looked up at the ceiling, sucking food out of his teeth. "Ah," he said. "So that's why the pastrami, huh?"

I nodded. "Sometimes it seems like Mom's been gone forever. And then other times it seems like it was just yesterday. It gets confusing. I guess I just needed to be close to her in some way." I knew this was only partially true—that everything I was telling him was only partial truth—and the brick-colored guilt was seeping up behind my eyelids, but it was the best I could do at the moment. I knew that bringing up Mom would shut him down.

"Well," he said. "I get that. Maybe more than you'll ever know. You know, I used to love the way her hair shone in the sun when we came here to eat. She was the most beautiful woman I'd ever met, and the fact that she could wolf down a pastrami with tomato faster than I could only made her more beautiful." He paused, dabbing at his mouth with a napkin. "But here's the thing. I still need you to go to school. Mom is gone, no matter how much it can sometimes feel like she's still here. And you have a future to think of. Promise me that tomorrow you'll do more than try."

I nodded.

"Okay. Now eat your sandwich. You can't wait in line for a Langer's pastrami and let it go to waste. That would for sure disappoint your mother."

We spent the rest of the meal eating in mostly silence, Dad thinking about whatever, and me contemplating Bill Hollis's vanity plate. I'd seen the glittery lilac before. Peyton had written an address and a time on the back of a

Hollywood Dreams Ranch flyer. I hadn't realized it at the time, but the words on the front were glittery lilac, the color of eye shadow. Was the message she'd written only part of the clue? Was the flyer itself a clue?

Did Bill Hollis have something to do with Hollywood Dreams? It seemed unlikely. Why would someone like him need to go to an escort service? He probably could have had any number of women in Brentwood, not to mention he was married to bombshell Vanessa. It was probably all a huge coincidence, and my synesthesia was tricking me. It had happened before. Especially when it came to the colors I associated with emotions. I wasn't perfect, and neither were the colors.

But there was no mistaking the grip that Bill Hollis had on Dru's arm. There was no misreading his words. He was blaming Dru for everything that had happened, and what was worse, he was pissed about how this was making him look. And what nagged at me the most was that Dru had claimed that his dad would be shattered to find out about Peyton. Yet clearly he wasn't. Why had Dru lied to me? Because Chris Martinez was right and he was guilty?

Finally, Dad wiped his mouth, checked his watch, and threw his napkin on the table. "Jesus, it's going on two o'clock." He pushed his chair away from the table. "Listen, I have one more quick shoot today, and then I'm headed home. How about I'll make dinner?"

I nodded. "Sure."

"You'll be there? Even if things happen?"

I rolled my eyes. "Yes, of course."

"What do you plan to do with the rest of your day?"

It was almost two o'clock and I was already in L.A. I remembered Peyton's email about the meeting with Leo. *We go. We don't need her.* I didn't have anything close to a plan, but something told me I needed to be there. "I'm going to stay in the city for a little bit," I said. "But I'll be home for dinner."

Dad raised his eyebrows. "And homework?"

"Yeah, sure," I said, though I honestly had no clue what homework I even had anymore, I was so behind.

He regarded me for a long moment, trying to talk himself into being satisfied, I supposed, and then stood. "Okay, I'll see you at home."

I waited until he pulled out of the parking lot before I went into planning mode.

FROM THE OUTSIDE, Clear Lake was an unassuming building—white brick, old-fashioned, tucked in alongside auto and hardware shops on busy Burbank Boulevard. I parked across the street and waited before getting out, watching the cars to see Gibson Talley pull up. It was just after two o'clock, and nobody seemed to be coming or going at Clear Lake. Maybe Gib had changed his mind about coming to the meeting without Peyton.

I'd stopped at a pharmacy on my way there, picking up a baseball cap, some huge touristy sunglasses, two bottled coffees, and a tube of bright-red lipstick. I realized it was about the dumbest "disguise" anyone could put together, but I was in a pinch, and it was the only idea I had.

I let my hair out of its elastic and vigorously scrubbed my hands through it, trying to give it messy volume. Satisfied, I plunked the Angels cap down over it, making sure to let some of my hair crowd the sides of my face. Pulling down the car visor so I could look in the mirror, I painted my lips with the bright-red—*ragemonster*, I thought distantly—lipstick, and then tore the tag off the sunglasses and put those on as well.

I still looked like me. But what could I do?

I got out of the car, shucked off my jacket, tugged my shirt up so that my belly button showed, and rolled up the cuffs of my jeans. I studied my murky reflection in the car door, then picked up the coffees and headed toward the front door, walking as if I belonged in the place.

My mouth was dry and my hands shaking with nerves. I wished I'd stayed in the car for a smoke real quick before going in, but there was no time now. The guy at the front desk had already spotted me.

"Hey," I said, trying to sound perky, and like someone other than Nikki Kill, even though this guy wouldn't know the difference anyway. I stuck out my hand. "I'm Angie. Leo Powers's assistant?"

The guy's eyebrows shot up. "Oh, okay," he said. "You here with the band, then?"

I nodded. "Viral Fanfare. Going to be huge, Leo says. Huge. They here yet? I'm so excited to hear them." I hoped that wasn't a completely stupid thing for a record producer's assistant to say. I held up the coffees apologetically. "Had to stop for Leo. He's so addicted."

He jumped up. "The band's here, but Leo's not yet. We, uh, actually don't have him on the schedule. Someone must have forgotten to write it down. But fortunately we didn't have anything else scheduled, so we could still get the band in. They're setting up in studio A while we try to sort this out. I'm glad you're here. Follow me."

I followed him down a short hallway into a huge studio. My feet got cold when I saw Gibson Talley, who was busy plugging his guitar into an amp. He only briefly glanced up when we came into the room. I ducked my head, hoping the visor of my cap hid my face, and scurried after the guy into the sound booth.

"You can wait here for Leo," he said. "Unless you want to talk to the band. There's only the two of them here so far. I think they said the bass player is on the way from Brentwood right now. I'll be doing your engineering, by the way. I'm

Zach." He held out his hand, but I was holding the coffees and we both chuckled and shrugged. He turned awkwardly, scratching one arm, and then said, "So just make yourself comfortable, I guess. You can hang on that couch over there. And I'll go back out front and wait for Leo to get here. Unless you want to . . . ?"

"No, that's okay. Couch sounds good."

I watched Zach leave the room. He stopped and talked to Gibson and another guy, who I recognized from the photos and videos as Viral Fanfare's drummer. They both glanced toward the booth, and I blazed with nerves. I looked away, as if I were busy studying something important in the booth, but I could still feel Gibson's eyes on me. After a beat, they went back to work and I was able to relax a little. I set the coffees on a small table and went over to the engineering table, looking for any sort of switch that looked like it might be an intercom. I flipped a few; nothing happened. But then the third button—a mic button—worked.

". . . dude doesn't show up?" the drummer asked.

"He will, man. No way would she have been stupid enough to cancel on me," Gibson answered. He picked up his guitar and tested it.

"I don't know if *stupid* is the word I'd use to describe Peyton," the other guy said. "Maybe she canceled on you just to be a bitch."

"She didn't."

"Why isn't he here yet, then? I'm telling you, something is up with that."

"Relax, man, producers are late all the time. Just get your set out and don't worry about it."

The drummer went back to unpacking his drums, but I wasn't relaxing. I still hadn't figured out how I was going to cover my story when Leo Powers got here and his "assistant" was already in the booth, waiting with his coffees.

Just then the studio door burst open and a flurry of dreads and flannel burst in. I slouched down in my seat. My lame disguise might fool Gibson and the drummer—two people who didn't know me—but no way would it fool Vee, even for a second. "Sorry I'm late, guys. Got here as fast as I could. Did I miss him?" Vee asked breathlessly, her bass case thumping against her leg. "What did he say? Are we in?"

"Not here," the drummer said without looking at her.

"What?" She glanced at the sound booth. I ducked even lower. "Why?"

"He's not here yet," Gibson said. "He's late. Just get your shit out and let's stop freaking out about it like a bunch of fucking preteens, okay? His assistant's here, so he's coming."

Vee glanced at the booth again, only this time her gaze stuck a little longer, her eyes narrowing curiously. I tensed, ready to run, but eventually she looked away. She set her case down and bent to unlatch it.

"Any update on Peyton?" she asked.

"I ain't talking about her here," the drummer said. "Not right now anyways."

"The songs?" Vee pressed.

"What more do you want me to do about her?" Gibson snarled. "We're gonna stick to the plan. Technically, they're my songs, too, no matter how much she's tried to screw me over. So we play them today and worry about the legal stuff later. Things will come out fine."

I froze. *What more do you want me to do about her?* What did that even mean? What had Gibson already done?

They all stood around staring at one another, and then Gibson sighed. "Would you two stop acting like such babies? This is our big break. Don't even think about Peyton. She's nothing." I thought about the photos I'd seen—the ones where Gibson was watching Peyton, where his arm was crooked around her neck. She hadn't been nothing to him then.

"Gib," Vee said. "She's in the hospital."

"Don't you think I know that?" he snapped. "Of all people, don't you think I'm very well aware that Peyton is at death's door right now? But I can't let it tank my one shot. I can't let her do that to me. Do you want this or don't you?"

"Of course I—" Vee started, but the door opened again, and Zach came back into the studio.

"So I called Leo Powers," he started, and I didn't wait to

hear the rest before I was moving, gold adrenaline flashes bursting in my brain. I scanned the room for a place to hide, afraid that I was stuck and would have to fight my way out of Clear Lake. I grabbed a bottle of coffee just in case I should need to improvise a weapon.

Fortunately, there was a door on the back wall. I raced to it and ducked through, just as I heard the drummer say, "What do you mean, canceled? His assistant's in the booth."

The door opened into a different hallway than I'd originally come down. I wasn't sure where to go, but I didn't have time to waffle about it. I speed-walked, hoping I had chosen the right direction.

I could hear voices coming from the other side of the sound booth door. "Hey, Angie?" I heard Zach call to me. I dipped my chin into my chest and walked even faster.

I was just turning the corner to the original hallway Zach had taken me down earlier when they came through the sound booth door I'd just come out of.

"Dude, is that the chick from your apartment?" I heard the drummer say.

"I know who that is," Vee piped up, before Gibson could respond. "That's not Leo Powers's assistant. That's Nikki K—" I didn't wait for her to finish. I sprinted, my car keys already in hand, the bottle of coffee falling to a broken mess in the Clear Lake lobby.

■ ■ ■

I WAS SO glad to get home, I skipped steps up to my room. I dropped my backpack, grabbed my cigarettes, and threw open my window in one clean motion. I smoked three in quick succession before I felt satisfied enough to climb back into my room, the outside air still clinging to my skin.

The conversation among the bandmates raced through my mind on a loop. Something had happened with the song lyrics, and Gibson was definitely pissed about it. So pissed he'd had a plan. So pissed he thought Peyton was nothing.

So pissed he wanted her to die? It seemed possible.

Yet I could find nothing in the clues Peyton had left that answered my questions. Was Gib more to her than a band-mate? Was it about more than the lyrics?

I had so many things to do, I didn't know where to begin. I started by going through the photos I'd stolen from Peyton's suitcase. There were three of them, all snapshots that looked to be taken without the knowledge of the people in the photo. The first was of a couple, hidden deep in the shadows of what looked like a home office, a door partially obscuring the camera lens. They were leaning against a glass-topped desk, kissing. Only they were *kissing* kissing, the woman's hand fisted around a tangle of the man's hair, which went nearly to his shoulders, her leg curled around his hips. His face was completely shadowed, as well as the top half of his body. Really, the only thing visible about him was one arm, curved around her backside, a bracelet glinting under the soft light of the lamp behind them. Whoever they were, they looked well past the point of no return. And why Peyton had a photo of them was beyond me.

Another photo showed the torso only of a young woman, her hand extended toward a hairy man's hand, her fingertips splayed with a delicate charm dangling from the tip of one. In the girl's outstretched palm was a rainbow of pills, each stamped with a different image—a Buddha, a crown, a Pac-Man, a ghost.

A drug deal? It didn't make sense. Why would Peyton be taking a photo of a drug deal? And where?

The third photo was a blur, a partially rolled-down car window in the foreground, as if it had been taken from a moving vehicle. It was mostly lights—the lights of a building front and what looked like a front door, the back half of a well-dressed man disappearing inside. I squinted, searching for clues, but there was nothing. This, like the others, looked more like a mistake than an actual photo. Maybe they weren't so much hidden in the suitcase as forgotten there. Maybe these were simply the errors of a budding photographer.

I tossed the photos onto my bed. None of this made sense, and I was beginning to think that maybe I had been "finding clues" where there had been none. I'd gotten lucky with the apartment, but to be fair, Jones had helped me out with that. I still knew nothing more than I'd known before.

I rubbed my eyes. There had to be something more. Something I was missing.

I wondered if Dru was at the hospital tonight, keeping vigil by Peyton just as he had been before, or if his arrest, and his parents' return from Monaco, had changed things. Was Peyton alone in there now, surrounded by the sea of gifts and a marching squadron of efficient nurses?

. . . all she had on her were her keys . . .

I remembered the nurse saying that as she checked Peyton's wires and tubes, squishing the IV bag between her stout fingers, her voice morphing into Bill Hollis's voice, as he pulled away in a glittering lilac cloud: *It's bad enough that we've lost your sister's car.*

Of course. Even if the photos made no sense, I still had keys to solving Peyton's attack. Literally.

I raced downstairs to find my jacket, which I'd left on the hook by the front door. I hadn't realized how late it had gotten until I reached the bottom of the stairs and smelled the tomatillos.

Shit. Dad's promise of dinner.

I stood at the bottom of the stairs for a few moments, then, with a sigh, decided to get this over with.

"*Chilaquiles?*" I asked, coming into the bright kitchen. Dad was standing at the black granite countertop, so polished it reflected the kitchen spotlights onto his glasses so that I couldn't see his eyes from some angles. His fingers expertly pulled cooked chicken into shreds.

"Which came first?" he asked, just as he always did when he made my favorite dish of quartered tortillas, green salsa, shredded chicken, and fried eggs.

"The chicken, of course," I answered, the way I always did. In Dad's *chilaquiles*, the eggs always came last, sitting on top, lovely and jiggling, the last thing placed before serving.

Dad grinned. "Age-old mystery solved." I could have recited that line with him. If Mom were alive, she'd have been able to recite it, too. "Are the *totopos* soft?"

I poked at one of the tortilla triangles. It broke apart. I nodded. He reached across me and let loose a handful of cheese, then broke two eggs into a separate pan.

"Sunny-side up?"

"Yep."

Our shoulders bumped, and the proximity combined with the rusty peach banners of nostalgia waving in my mind started to make me feel queasy, so I crossed the kitchen to get two plates out of the cabinet, turning my back to him so I could breathe.

I scooped half of the *chilaquiles* onto each plate. Dad slid an egg on top of each one. I took mine and headed for the table, fumbling for the remote that we kept in a basket in the middle of the table.

For years, this was how Dad and I had eaten dinner

together—to the drone of early evening newscasts, to make us feel less alone.

A car commercial was just ending as the TV flicked on, some idiot prancing around a dealership lot in a suit and a pair of those giant plastic sunglasses. I concentrated on eating my food and was so into it I didn't even notice that the news had come back on until Dad spoke.

"That family," he mumbled. The steam from his plate had clouded his glasses.

I glanced up at the screen, and there was a video of Dru Hollis being escorted into the police station by Detective Martinez. Obviously from yesterday, when he'd been arrested.

". . . say that the film producer's son was arrested in connection with his sister's brutal attack, which took place late Monday night. Sources say police were alerted by an anonymous caller, who reported finding a woman severely beaten in an elementary school parking lot. . . ."

"What did you say?" I asked.

Dad looked startled, almost as if he'd forgotten I was in the room with him. "Oh." He tried to wave it off. "I said that family thinks they're untouchable. It was just a matter of time before one of them ended up in trouble."

I pressed the mute button on the remote as the news switched to another story, about an apartment fire in a nearby town. "You know the Hollises?"

He stuffed another bite into his mouth, keeping his eyes rooted to his plate. "Not really. I did a shoot with Bill Hollis once. He was an arrogant asshole. Thinks if he throws around a few dollars, he can own the whole world. And his wife is a real piece of work."

While that assessment of Hollis certainly fit with what I'd witnessed that morning at the police station, there was something about Dad's reaction that seemed . . . off. "That's it?"

He finally looked up. The steam cloud had cleared from his glasses. "Yeah. That's it. Why? Do you know something about that?" He gestured toward the TV, and his face blanched. "Is that the friend you've been visiting in the hospital? What's her name? Peyton? The daughter?"

I didn't answer. I could tell he wasn't going to be happy with the truth.

He pointed his fork at me. "Nikki, you stay away from that family. Okay? No more visiting the hospital. You want nothing to do with that mess. You hear me?"

"How do you know it's a mess?" I asked.

He moved his fork so it was pointing at the TV now. "That's how I know. And, like I said, I worked with those people. I don't want you putting yourself in some kind of danger. Not for that family."

"I'm not in danger," I said, but he cut me off.

"Stay out of it, Nikki."

"Okay, sure, whatever," I mumbled, even though I knew it would be impossible for me to stay away at that point. I was already too far in. Plus, the truth was, if I wanted to keep going to the hospital, there wasn't anything he could do about it, and we both knew it. We finished our meal in silence—the news rolling along on mute—and then I took my plate to the sink.

"I have to run out real quick," I said. "Is that okay?"

"Is your homework done?" he asked, which was cute, but totally not believable from a dad standpoint. He sounded like he was reading from a cue card. A tired, over-read one.

"I'll get it done."

"You're not going to that hospital," he said.

"No," I answered honestly. "Nowhere near it."

He seemed to think this over, his lips pursing in displeasure. "Just be home at a decent hour."

"Sure thing," I said.

"And Nik?" he asked. I turned. "You sure there isn't anything you need help with? Homework? Or any other problems? I know you'd rather have Mom help you, but I'm a good stand-in. You seem to be . . . struggling with something."

I went over and kissed him on top of the head. "Everything's fine, Dad," I said. "Promise." I felt a little bad for him. He had to know I was lying.

■ ■ ■

I GRABBED MY jacket from the hook by the door and headed out to my car, digging out Peyton's keys as I walked. Where was her car? Was it truly lost, as Bill Hollis had said it was, or was it simply left?

The news had said the anonymous caller had found Peyton in an elementary school parking lot. There were probably a dozen elementary school parking lots in Brentwood. Maybe more, who knew? And I had no clue in which parking lot Peyton's body had been found.

But I had an address on the back of a Hollywood Dreams flyer.

And it seemed like a good start.

I T WAS ALREADY dark outside by the time I reached the address. It was no elementary school. I pulled into a severely neglected parking lot, my headlights sweeping over what looked like an abandoned supermarket. Damn it, I had gotten the address wrong.

I turned on the dome light and inspected what Peyton had written again, which was difficult with the bumpy gray and black undulating under my fingers. *Golden. Golden. Golden.* My heart beat in time with the word, getting stronger and faster with every propulsion of blood through my veins. *Golden. Golden. Fear. Fear.*

I looked at the building again, and the screen on my GPS, which showed that I was at the end point. This was definitely the address she had written down.

Peyton had met someone here? At eleven o'clock? Morning or night, that was the question. In the morning, it would be sketchy enough, but at night, it would have been downright terrifying. I had assumed I was coming to the place where she'd met her attacker, but if she'd been attacked at an elementary school, then this wasn't it. She'd had an appointment here for something else.

Golden. Golden. Golden.

Slowly, I pulled around to the back of the building. My headlights revealed drifts of detritus shifting around an old loading dock—trash and old clothing, broken bottles, the kind of stuff the derelicts sometimes dropped behind the *dojang* on summer nights. I pulled up to the dock and let the lights shine on it, trying to take in every detail, trying to imagine Peyton Hollis standing ankle-deep in the muck in the middle of a fall night, frantically pushing buttons to call me.

I couldn't get there in my head.

I turned off the car and got out.

It was impossibly dark behind the building now, adding to the ominousness, and immediately goose bumps popped up on my arms. I was in full alert mode. I heard fast-food wrappers rustle in the wind, or possibly shifted by a rat, I smelled the exhaust from my own car, I saw the letters on a Dumpster pulsate with a dull glow. Slowly, as I settled down, my eyes adjusted and I was able to make out the parking lot better. A cloud drifted away from the moon, and I could see individual pebbles on the ground.

And, at the foot of the steps leading up to the loading dock, a pool of dark pebbles. I switched my phone to flashlight mode and shone it down onto them.

Blood. A lot of it.

I shone the light in a circle around them.

The darkened stones trailed off toward the middle of the lot, and I followed them until they abruptly ended near a set of tire tracks.

My hand shook.

Jesus. She had been here. This was where it had gone down, whatever "it" was. Peyton hadn't been attacked in an elementary school parking lot. She'd been attacked here and moved to an elementary school parking lot. But why? And by whom? Did the police not know this? Or had they been withholding it, hoping someone would slip? Either way, it was probably something they should know. Something I should call Detective Martinez about as soon as I got back to my car.

Shaken, I held up the light and stood up straight, trying to take in everything I could see, wishing the light would penetrate farther across the parking lot so I could stay near the safety of my car. But my phone could only light up so far, and I found myself crunching through the gravel toward the

Dumpsters and the tree line behind them. I felt a familiar lump try to edge its way into my throat. A panicky constriction settled in there. My eyes kept trying to pull back to that pool of blood. Kept trying to see it, to feel it under my shoes, slipping, slipping, Tootsie Rolls soaking up the red, the numbers of a watch pulsing slower, slower, slower. *Cool it, Nikki,* I told myself. *It's not your mother's blood.*

I caught a flicker of something through the leaves, far back in the trees. I swept the light back and forth a few times, trying to catch it again. Nothing but foliage, rustling in the night breeze. I had almost convinced myself that it had just been my imagination, when suddenly the light caught it again. A flash. Or more like . . . a reflection?

I walked all the way across the lot, until I'd finally hit grass. Holding the phone out in front of me, my entire body on high alert, I slowly arced the light across the woods.

There it was. Again.

Red. It was definitely a red reflection.

"A taillight," I whispered to myself. "There's a car in there."

For a moment, my body was seized with fear. Was there someone back there, watching me? Maybe the same person who had attacked Peyton, just waiting for me to get close enough? I took a deep breath. Clenched and unclenched my fists. Closed my eyes and tried to imagine *Kyo Sah Nim*

Gunner standing by my side. He would be calm, ready to defend.

I wanted to run. To turn around, get into my car, and drive straight to the police station, find Detective Martinez, and tell him what I'd found. Admit to myself that I was in over my head and this was best handled by the police now. But I couldn't not go into those trees. Bill Hollis had been yelling about having lost Peyton's car. The reflected taillight was hers. I just knew it down deep in my bones. I had to go in. I could find the answers I was searching for. The answers I would probably never get if I turned this over to the police.

Deciding that I might need my hands, just in case my theory about the car being Peyton's was wrong and someone was waiting for me inside, I pocketed my phone and plunged into the tree line, feeling somewhat protected by the same dark that had frightened me. The brambles wrapped around the toes of my shoes and tried to keep me back, but I kept to the flattened and broken areas where the car tires had gone through.

Although it seemed like I was completely cut off from the rest of the world back here in the woods, it was no time before I was on top of a cherry-red Mustang convertible with vanity plates reading *FNFAIR*—the car that everyone who was anyone knew was Peyton Hollis's car.

"Shit," I whispered as I stared at it. Clearly, whoever had

attacked Peyton knew what they were doing when it came to covering tracks. By moving Peyton's body and hiding her car in the woods behind an abandoned supermarket, they'd just about guaranteed it would never be found. Except . . . why not hide her body in the car? She probably would have died.

The only reason I could think of was that whoever had moved Peyton's body did not want her to die. But why? Was this a warning to someone? Was Peyton an example? Was Detective Martinez right? Was Arrigo Basile behind this? And if so, did that mean Dru was, too?

I reached into my jacket pocket and pulled out Peyton's keys. The car key was easy to find—it was the only one attached to a fob with buttons. I pressed the unlock button and the car sprang to life, the interior light blinking on.

I gulped, peering through the driver's-side window. I couldn't see anything out of the ordinary. Definitely no bad guys crouching on the floorboard. Maybe there was nothing in there at all, but I wouldn't know unless I opened the door and got in. But if I opened the door and got in, I was reaching the point of no return. My prints would be all over the inside of this car, and if the cops found it, Detective Martinez would really have some questions for me.

I could still turn back. Give up. Get out of this. Let Peyton's problem be the Hollises' to solve. They were back in the country now anyway, and they had some deep, deep problems. That much was clear. My dad was right—there was something particularly repulsive about someone with major issues and an untouchable superiority complex.

But then something caught my eye on the floorboard of the passenger side. A snippet of a word, swirling with tie-dye. I'd seen it before. *Hendrix.*

"Christ. Gibson," I breathed, making my way to the other side of the car, where I could see more clearly the guitar strap that Gibson Talley had been wearing in one of the Viral Fanfare photos. I recalled the date on the photo. October 15. It had stood out to me, the way all dates did. It wasn't that long ago. He had been in this car. And recently. "I knew it," I said. "I fucking knew it."

I opened the passenger door and picked up the guitar strap, turned it over. Sure enough, there was blood along the edge. God, was that Peyton's blood? Had Gibson picked it up after he attacked her? Had he ditched it in her car to hide evidence? I felt sick, like I shouldn't be touching it. I rolled the strap into a loose wad and stuffed it deep into my pocket. I wasn't sure what I would do with it, only that it seemed like an important thing to have. I had now removed evidence from the victim's car. Any chance that I might be able to ask Chris Martinez for help was gone.

Otherwise, the car seemed exceptionally clean. I slid inside and shut the door. An iPod was plugged in. A few Starbucks Splash Sticks and a tube of lipstick littered the center console. I opened the glove box. Nothing. Car manual and two service receipts.

The dome light blinked out, and I was once again bathed in eerie darkness. I could see if anyone pulled into the parking lot behind me. I pressed the door lock button, feeling safer after hearing the reassuring click of all the locks finding home.

I turned onto my knees and peered into the backseat, blinking a few times to help my eyes adjust.

There was something on the floor.

I bent to pick it up. It was a point-and-shoot camera. Was this the camera that had taken all the strange photos? Hopefully there were more on it. If the photos were the clues Peyton wanted me to find, the camera was a gold mine.

I fiddled around with it until I located the memory card slot. I pushed my finger against it. Nothing happened. I pulled out my phone and shone a light on it. There was an empty slot where the memory card should have been.

Strange. I continued to examine the camera with my flashlight but found nothing on it. The battery was dead, so I couldn't turn it on, but even if I could, with no memory card in it, there would be nothing to view.

The light from my phone bounced off something else on the same floorboard. I bent over the seat and grabbed it, held it up.

A bracelet dangled between my thumb and forefinger. It was gold, Figaro link, the clasp smashed and broken. I dropped the bracelet into my palm and shone the light on it full force. A brown crust looked brushed over it. Blood.

I dropped the bracelet into my jacket pocket with the guitar strap, my heart beating fast. I needed to go back through Peyton's photos. If only I could find one of Gib wearing this bracelet, I would have enough to go to the cops with. In the back of my mind, I remembered seeing it in one of the pictures. I just had to find which one.

I started to get out of the car and then had a thought. I reached over the driver's seat and found the button for the trunk. My heart sped up as I pressed the button. God knew what I would discover in there, but I had to know.

I stepped out of the car and shut the door softly, pausing to listen to the night air. I almost thought I could hear a car coming down the road. I squinted, peering through the woods back the way I'd come, but saw no headlights. My mind was playing tricks on me.

I stood there long enough for the dome light to go out again. Something moved in the weeds to my left, causing me to tense, bend my knees, and get ready to bolt. I stood that way for a long time, just listening. I felt watched.

But after hearing nothing else, I went around to the open trunk and looked inside. A quilt, soiled with grass stains and some leaves, was wadded up in one corner. A set of jumper cables was coiled neatly on top of it. A flashlight. A bicycle tire pump. A spare tire. Standard trunk stuff.

In frustration, I picked up the corner of the quilt and let it drop again. I didn't know what I'd been hoping to find, but it wasn't in here.

And then I saw it.

A manila folder, peeking out from under the corner of the quilt I'd just messed with. A file, filled with papers.

I slid it out and opened it, holding it low under the trunk light.

Kill, Nikki A.

What the hell?

I scanned down the first page inside the folder, unsure what I was looking at. My name, address, date of birth. My dad's name, cell phone number. I turned the page—my vaccination records, going all the way back to kindergarten. After that, my last report card.

It was my school record. The original, typed on official letterhead. Somehow Peyton had gotten hold of it.

I flipped through everything, my gut dropping as I read about myself, and then I got to the last page. It was the school counselor's report, from the one time I'd talked to him, earlier this year.

I scanned his stupid report:

Student reports seeing colors associated with letters and numbers. Each letter and number has what she considers a "correct" color, and certain words have specific colors as well, which may or may not be related to the colors of the letters contained in the words. She reports being unable to control this phenomenon. Student excels at memory tasks and is ambidextrous, but has a hard time concentrating on math and reading. I recommend a full eval to treat possible ADHD and also suggest therapy for attention-seeking behaviors. Student used foul language during our session and ended it abruptly. I recommend continuing with academic probation, possibly offering help from the tutoring lab or behavioral education services.

"Asshole," I muttered, ragemonster red and black swirling a little dance across the page, but as I started to flip the file closed, I realized for the first time that several words of the report had been highlighted. In the margin, in very curvy script, someone had written the word *synesthesia*.

I stared at the writing, everything becoming completely clear.

Peyton had somehow gotten her hands on my school file and had read the report. I was right—she knew I had synesthesia.

She knew because she had it, too.

The clues I'd found were clues she'd been deliberately leaving.

How had I even ended up on her radar in the first place?

Just as I flipped back through the pages, I heard a noise.

This time it was no small animal in the woods beside me. This time it was the distinctive crunch of car tires on gravel. The telltale hum of an engine. I gazed through the trees. There were no headlights. Quickly, I dropped the file back into the trunk and softly shut it.

I heard the sound of a car door shutting, followed by the scuff of footsteps on gravel.

I had a bad feeling, the paint of Peyton's car turning bumpy gray and black under my hand.

I needed to get out of there.

SILENTLY, QUICK AND fluid, I swept through the woods toward the parking lot, trying to formulate a plan, but none would come when I didn't know what the threat was, or even if there was one at all. When I'd almost reached the gravel, I veered off toward the Dumpsters. I found them and crouched behind, ignoring the stench of who-knew-how-old garbage that lined their insides.

Squinting through the crack between the two Dumpsters, and past the gold sparkles that were now blooming in the air like fireflies, I was able to see my car. It wasn't that far away. I could close the gap in just a few long strides. I moved to the far end of the Dumpsters and poked my head around the corner. I didn't see another car anywhere.

I no longer heard footsteps, either.

I let out a breath and eased out from behind the Dumpster.

Two steps away from it, someone slammed into me from behind. A hand closed over my mouth, an arm snaking around my throat, forcing out a muffled grunt. I was instantly paralyzed with surprise and fear.

"Don't fight me," a man's voice said right behind my ear.

There was something about the word *fight* that must have kicked my subconscious into motion. The part of me that had been kicking the shit out of sparring dummies for five years took over.

I stomped the arch of his right foot with everything I had, then immediately followed it with a mule kick to the groin. A burst of air flew past my ear as his grip loosened around my mouth. I could just about hear Gunner in my head, shouting, *Move, move! You have the momentum now, don't give it up!* Without giving the man even a second to recover, I jammed my elbow into his ribs, hard, then peeled his hand off my mouth.

"Fuck!" he wheezed.

But he was saying this on the way down. I twisted his hand into a wrist lock, popped his jaw with my elbow, and dropped him to the ground.

That was when I saw who I was dealing with.

Gibson Talley.

My insides turned to jelly, but I didn't stop. Instead, dread gave my muscles an extra burst of energy. Growling, I forced his arm into an arm lock and flipped him over to his stomach, leaning into him with every ounce of body weight I had.

He yelled again, struggling against me. I jammed the arm up higher, using pain to equalize our size difference.

I was out of breath but felt strangely invigorated. "What do you want?" I panted. My eyes darted toward my car. The scuffle had taken me several feet away from it, and what was worse, my keys were still in my pocket. I didn't know if I could outrun him. I would have to fight him if I let him go.

He turned his face to the side, his eyes squeezed shut in a wince, blood wetting his lips where I'd elbowed him.

"Answer me," I said, giving his arm an extra shove. I thought I might have felt a pop in his shoulder. "Why are you here?"

"I was going to ask you the same thing," he said. "And why were you at the studio? And my apartment? Stop! Stop!"

I laughed in his face. "You attack me from behind, and now you want me to stop? I don't think so, dude. You're lucky I left you conscious." I thought I could probably knock someone unconscious, but I'd never done it before, which made my threat mostly bravado, but he had stopped squirming, so it must have been believable. I supposed any threat was believable when someone had your shoulder half out of its socket. "Now answer my question. Why did you come here? Did you follow me?"

"Okay, okay," he said, going completely limp. "Yes. I followed you."

"Were you going to beat me up like you did Peyton?" I shifted my weight so that my knee was on top of his twisted wrist.

"No." He stopped, swallowed, squeezed his eyes shut with pain, opened them again. "I was going to threaten you. I didn't touch Peyton. I had nothing to do with what happened to her."

I laughed again. "You expect me to believe that? I saw what you said on Facebook. I saw Peyton's email. I heard what you said about her. 'She's nothing'? 'What more do you want me to do about her?' Sound familiar?"

"I know," he said. "You sicced the fucking cops on me, too. Vee told me all about it after that detective showed up at my apartment. Storming in all questions and bullshit."

"Martinez arrested you?"

"No, man, he didn't have anything on me. I didn't do it. I have an alibi. Two of them, actually. I was at band practice that night."

I considered this. "Vee would give you a false alibi. She's in on the threats, too. Besides, I saw you at the hospital. I heard the conversation at the studio. I know you want Peyton out of the picture for some reason. And I have the guitar strap with the blood on it. How did that get in her car?" His arm had begun slipping down again, so I renewed the grip, shoving it up farther and eliciting a new roar of pain from him.

"What the fuck are you talking about? Yeah, I showed up at the hospital. So did all her other friends. And I gave Peyton the guitar strap to celebrate her first tattoo. It's got blood on it because the tat was fresh when she first tried it on. I'm telling you, why would I want to hurt Peyton?"

"She did something to you," I said. My breath was coming slower now, and the gold fireworks had begun to subside, but the gray and black were still there, still undulating in the gravel. I still didn't feel like I had the upper hand. As much as I hated to think it, even to myself, his story made sense.

"Yeah." He spit a wad of blood onto the gravel next to his face. I leaned in on him harder. "God! Bitch! Yeah, she walked out on us, okay? She was our songwriter. And when she left the band, she took the songs with her. Even the ones I cowrote. Those are half mine—she had no right to take them. And I haven't been able to write since. We have no singer, no songs. We had a meeting with a producer, and she fucked us. The guy worked for her dad. Big money. Huge. She said she didn't want anything to do with blood money, and she walked away. We were going to make it to the big time, and she left us hanging. And now I'm stuck being a nothing in a shit apartment, and it's all Peyton's fault. So, yeah, I've been pissed. But not pissed enough to want her dead, man."

"When?" I asked. "When did this happen? When did she take everything and screw you over?"

"I don't know, about two weeks ago. Right around the same time she cut her hair and got the tattoo. She moved into my apartment complex, too, but she wouldn't even fucking answer her door when I tried to talk to her. It was like she had this enormous freak-out all of a sudden. A nervous breakdown or something. I knew she was nuts. Should've never let her into the band. I have video of our band practice the night she got attacked. Time-stamped video. I was at practice. And now we don't know what happens to those songs if she dies. Maybe it seems selfish or some shit, but I don't want to be where I am right now forever. Dude, I was pissed, but I didn't want her dead."

It didn't make sense. None of this made sense. But then again, it made total sense. Everything he said added up. Added up into blazing orangish-pink innocence.

"Jesus," I whispered.

"Let me up," he said. "My arm!"

"But what about the bracelet?" I asked, more to myself than to him at that point.

"What bracelet? What are you talking about?" he said, his voice laced with equal parts agony and anger.

"I found your bracelet in Peyton's car. It's got blood on

it, and the clasp is smashed. You moved her car, didn't you?"

"I've never owned any fucking bracelet!" he roared.

"Don't lie to me," I said. "I've seen it in the photo. . . ."

But as I said the words aloud, I flashed onto the photo that I'd seen the bracelet in. It wasn't one of the band photos after all. It was one of the photos from Peyton's suitcase. The man and woman embraced in a deep kiss, the man's hand cupping low on the woman's waist, his bracelet the only thing about him visible.

He might have been only a silhouette in the photo, but there was one thing about the man that was clear. He didn't have a Mohawk. Gibson Talley's signature look.

"Shit," I said.

"Yeah, shit," Gibson cried with another agonized grunt. He wriggled again, almost getting out of my grasp. "Now let me go."

Someone else had been in Peyton's car the night of her attack. Someone else had hidden it, had lost his broken bracelet in the backseat while removing the memory card from her camera. Someone else had moved her.

That someone else was the man in the photo.

But how on earth would I ever figure out who he was?

"I said let me up, goddamn it!" Gibson shouted, wriggling with such force now I could barely hang on. If I didn't make a move soon, he would be out of my grip. And pissed. And gunning for me.

I resituated myself and put all my weight on my knee, which pinned his wrist in the high middle of his back. With my free hand, I reached over until I found a good-sized chunk of concrete that had been chewed up at the edge of the parking lot.

"Sorry," I said. I swung the rock down on the side of Gibson's head, making him go limp.

WAS STILL sore a couple of days later, but I was guessing I was nowhere near as sore as Gibson Talley, who'd most likely come to with a monster headache and a jaw full of loose teeth. Not to mention super pissed off at me. Even more so than before.

In a way, I was surprised that I was sore. I'd sparred against more competitors than I could count, and I felt like I never held back. But on the other hand, this was my first actual fight-or-flight encounter, and there must be a difference between not holding back in the *dojang*, and actually not holding back.

Either way, it was Saturday morning, the *dojang* would

be open until noon, and I felt a need to work out some of the kinks.

Gunner took one look at me hitting the heavy bag and excused himself from a new kid he had been showing some basic blocks. He came around to the other side of the bag and held it, peeking around at me.

"Come on, Nikki, you gonna hit it or you gonna play tiddlywinks with it?"

I clenched my teeth and hit the bag harder, wincing as my sore pecs twinged.

"That's not a hit. I've seen six-year-olds work harder," he taunted. "Come on."

I whaled on the bag again, letting out pained grunts as my punches landed. The bag barely moved. I just didn't have the muscle behind it today. But all I could see on the face of that heavy bag was Gibson Talley's face. All I could hear was his voice behind my ear as he pressed his hand over my mouth. If he were to decide to surprise me again, I would be ready.

"What is this? You're hitting like a girl," Gunner said, shoving the bag toward me. "You here to play around or be serious?"

I was used to Gunner's taunts. Telling me I couldn't do something was the best way to ensure that I absolutely would do it. I was just built that way. *Oppositional*, my dad used to call me. *Determined*, my mom used to correct him.

Maybe she was oppositional, too.

I'll show you how a girl hits, I thought.

I hopped back a step, my whole body readying itself into a parallel stance. Light on my toes, muscles flexed, lips pulled taut. With a growl, I went at the bag, hitting it fast with both fists, with elbows, and then lunging in for a kick that went wild and knocked me off my feet. I hit the mat with an *oomph.*

"Whoa," Gunner said, coming around the bag and reaching out a hand. "Never seen that happen before. Not with you, anyway."

I started to lift my head, then flopped back onto the mat to catch my breath. After a moment, I took his hand and let him pull me up. I felt nauseated, my shoulders aching.

"Seriously, Nik, everything okay? What's going on?" Gunner asked. He placed his hand on the small of my back and led me to a spectator's chair off the mat. "You are definitely not yourself today."

I collapsed into the chair. "Got in a fight last night," I said.

Gunner raised his eyebrows at me. "I assume you came out on top?"

I nodded. "But it was a guy. Bigger than me. My muscles are shredded."

Gunner rubbed his index finger down one side of his goatee, and then the other. "Sure, sure," he said. "A guy, you said? You okay?" He leaned over, grabbed a water out of the mini fridge next to the front desk, and handed it to me.

I took the water and gulped it. "Yeah. Just sore. And sc . . ." I trailed off. *Scared.* I was scared. Scared of Gibson Talley, sure, but more than that. Scared of whoever had hurt Peyton. Scared because I was now pretty sure Gibson Talley hadn't been the one who did it, and scared because that meant that maybe Chris Martinez was right and Dru had been the one. And scared because, no matter who it was, I was definitely caught up in it now. Admitting fear was not one of my strengths. I hated feeling weak. Weak girls stood in their mother's blood and trembled and sobbed and pounded at the crimson in their eyes. Weak girls didn't get out of bed for weeks. Weak girls were afraid to be home alone, afraid to go to bed at night. Afraid of the murderer who had never been caught. "Scraped up a little," I finished instead.

I lifted the leg of my *dobok* and showed him the scabbed knee, where I'd knelt against gravel while subduing Gibson. There was a bit of bruising around the scrape, but it was the part of me that hurt the least.

Gunner inspected my knee, and then sat next to me, stroking his goatee and nodding, as if he were contemplating what all this meant.

"You were attacked," he said, matter-of-factly.

I nodded.

"Did you contact the police?"

I took another drink and shook my head, ignoring the guilty feeling that wanted to press in on me. "I left him unconscious in a parking lot." In truth, I'd also dropped his guitar strap on top of his back. A message that if he was guilty, I could prove it.

"Do you know this guy?" I could sense irritation in Gunner's voice. We'd known each other for a lot of years. We'd trained together. We'd sweated together. We'd bled together. He was protective of me. Of all his students, actually. Gunner was single and in his early thirties. Tae kwon do was his life.

"Yeah, I know him," I said. "But it's taken care of now." *I hope*, I added internally.

"I can give him a visit, send a message."

"No," I said. "Leave it alone."

"He'll never know."

"Of course he will."

Gunner leaned forward in his chair, resting his elbows on his knees, his fingers tenting together. He turned his head toward me. "What are you in the middle of, Nikki?"

I pressed my lips together. Squeezed the water bottle so the plastic crackled under my fingers. "I'm not sure," I said honestly. "But I'll be okay."

"Can you guarantee me that?"

I felt a familiar wave of steel wash over me, driving out

the fear that had tried to set up shop. Gibson Talley had come after me in the worst possible way—by surprise, from behind, in an abandoned parking lot. And I'd taken care of it. I'd been fine. Nobody could defeat me. Not Gib, not Vee, not the shadowy man in the kissing photo. I believed that. I had to. I was too far in to ask for help now. "Yes, I can," I said.

To prove that I knew what I was talking about, and to shut Gunner up, I went back out onto the mat and spent the next hour pummeling the sparring dummy with everything I had. Elbow strike. Mule kick. Elbow strike. Mule kick. Mule kick, mule kick, mule kick—the moves from the night before rolling off me over and over again until I could feel the crunch of Gibson Talley's ribs, hear the wheeze of him taking my foot to his groin. My arms and legs groaned from all the work, and I was covered with so much sweat it dripped down into my eyes and off the end of my nose. But the soreness was gone. The fear was pushed away.

Gunner put his hand on my shoulder just as I geared up for another elbow strike. I whirled on him, grabbing his hand and turning, angling my body so that his arm was stretched, palm up, his elbow resting on my shoulder. One sharp tug downward and I could have put some serious hurt on him.

"Whoa, I tap, I tap!" he said, patting my back with his other hand. "*Dojang's* closing for the day. Time to call it done."

I let up. "Next move, broken elbow," I said, bowing.

He bowed in response, then cocked his head at me. "You sure you're okay?"

"Yes, sir," I said. "Better than ever."

He looked unconvinced. "Go on in and get changed. I'll see you next week."

"Yes, sir." I bowed again on my way out, feeling much better.

I made my way to the changing room and grabbed my things out of my cubby, sliding my taxed limbs into my clothes.

Gunner was waiting for me by the front door, ready to lock up, when I was finished.

"Have a good afternoon, Nik," he said as I slipped through the door past him. "And be careful, okay?"

I turned and gave him a devious grin from the sidewalk. "I don't need to be careful. I just need to be deadly."

He chuckled. "Be a little of both, you hear?"

"Of course," I said, and headed for my car.

I stopped in my tracks when I saw who was leaning against it. I rolled my shoulders back and kept walking reluctantly. Chris Martinez was apparently not on duty. He was wearing a Stussy baseball tee—white with blue sleeves that made his skin glow. A pair of mirrored aviators kept me from seeing his eyes. I couldn't see one, but I imagined a gun was tucked into the waistband of the relaxed jeans he was wearing. Two violet wisps danced across the yellow I'd come to associate with him. I blinked, hard. That violet was not okay. I was clearly going crazy.

"Detective," I said. "I wish I could say I was surprised to see you here, but you seem to be showing up everywhere."

He pushed away from the car and slid his hands into his pockets. "Miss Kill. Have a good workout?"

"I did okay in there," I said, stopping a few feet away from him and crossing my arms. "But something tells me you didn't come all the way over here to ask me about my fitness."

He smirked, and I wished I could see his eyes so I could know what he was thinking. "Nope, you're right, I didn't. I just wanted to talk to you."

Of course he did. He was always *just wanting to talk* to me. I held up my car keys. "I would love to, Detective, but I really have to go."

He took a side step away from my door, and I moved around him.

"Really interesting coincidence happened the other night," he said to my back. I stopped. "That guy you were telling me about? Gibson Talley? Showed up in the emergency room with a laceration to his head." He paused to assess my reaction, so I was careful to keep my face guarded. "Twenty-six stitches on his scalp."

"Wow," I said. I swallowed, sure he was going to reach

around and pull out a pair of handcuffs. "That's too bad."

"Yeah, said he got drunk and fell, hit his head on an amp."

I let out a breath, white specks floating in front of my eyes. "Really?"

Martinez snapped his fingers and pointed one at me, shaking it up and down. "That was exactly what I said. I mean, this guy's had a hell of a week, you know? His bandmate gets beat up, he's questioned about that by me, someone breaks into his apartment, and then he has this . . . freak accident."

"That's a crappy week," I agreed. "But why are you telling me about it?"

He rubbed his chin with his palm, his other hand on his hip. "I don't suppose you were anywhere near the amp he fell on, were you, Miss Kill?"

"Why would I have any reason to be near him?"

"You don't appear to need a reason these days, it would seem. Did you know that he gave a description of the person who broke into his apartment?" I didn't answer. "Tall, thin girl. Long, dark hair. Dark jeans, black jacket, black boots. Very familiar style, wouldn't you say?"

"Sounds pretty generic," I said. "But I'll keep a lookout. If I hear anything, I'll let you know."

He nodded, then leaned against my car again, crossing one leg over the other. "I'm warning you again, Miss Kill. You need to back out of this. Let me do my job. If I keep having to watch after you, I can't watch for Peyton's attacker."

"Then stop watching after me," I said. "I don't need your protection." My mind briefly flashed to Gibson coming at me from behind, and how, for a moment, I was sure I was in real trouble. How I'd kept thinking maybe I needed to let Chris Martinez know what I'd found, until things got so complicated.

"That's not going to happen. What you're playing with here, it's not a game. Whoever attacked Peyton meant business."

"I thought it was Dru who attacked her. Isn't that why you arrested him? You should probably make up your mind, Detective. Either Peyton's attacker has been arrested, or I'm in danger."

"Or both," he said, his voice taking an annoyed edge. "Just because we didn't have enough evidence to hold him doesn't mean he's innocent." He bit his bottom lip. "Listen, I can't sit by and watch you get hurt. I can't go through that aga—" He broke off.

It was the first time I'd seen his cool crack, even a little bit. I'd suspected before that there was more to the detective's past than he wanted me to know. Now I wondered if maybe my guess was right.

He pulled out a pen and placed it in my palm. My heart skipped a beat. I recognized it—shiny black with silver trim.

The penknife I'd left in Gibson's apartment. He pulled his sunglasses down so that our eyes locked. "I'm doing you all kinds of favors right now and you know it," he continued. "But I will take you in if I have to do it to keep you safe."

I rolled my eyes, as though his threat didn't worry me in the least. "Thanks for the warning," I said, curling my fist around the pen. He was doing more than favors; what he was doing could get him in trouble. But why? "Now if you don't mind . . ." I motioned for him to get off my car.

Reluctantly, he did, stepping up onto the walk as I got in.

"Be careful, Nikki," he called just before I shut the door.

I gave him a wave, tossed the penknife back in my glove box, and turned the key in the ignition.

I backed out of my parking space and threw my car into drive. Just before I started moving, my phone buzzed with a text. It was from Dru.

I'm out. Want to get together tonite?

I chewed my thumbnail, Detective Martinez's warning still fresh in my mind. Maybe he was right and I'd be wise to just ignore that I'd ever gotten Dru's text. Stay away from Gibson, stay away from Dru, stay away from this whole thing.

But that would mean staying away from Peyton. And if I did that, I might never know what she had wanted from me.

Sure. Where and when?

There was a pause while I waited for him to respond—long enough for Gunner to come out of the *dojang* and give me a long, questioning look as he locked the doors and went around the building, where his bike was parked. He had his phone tucked between his shoulder and his ear, so thankfully he couldn't give me the third degree about why I hadn't left yet. Gunner was a good friend, a big brother, almost, but he could be a little overprotective sometimes. And I wasn't the biggest fan of overprotective.

Finally, my phone vibrated in my hand.

7? Lujo on 18th

I had heard of Lujo. Overheard, really, was more accurate. Most of the spoiled girls with their fancy manicures and their sports cars spent their Monday mornings in the school hallways comparing their weekend conquests at Lujo. Lujo was not really a Nikki Kill kind of establishment. Actually, it was not *at all* a Nikki Kill kind of establishment. But I wanted to talk to Dru. I wanted to find out more about what had gone down with his dad. Maybe he would help me figure out who was in the photo.

See you then.

17

HAD EXPECTED Lujo to be swank, but this place was swank to the extreme. I could practically smell the money when I walked in, and had the lights not been turned down so low, I might have been blinded by all the ice draping the customers. So many of them. Young ladies hanging all over old geezers. Older ladies surgically made young again. Middle-aged men in suits, their hair slicked back with product, their money clips flashing as they motioned for waiters.

It wasn't the kind of place where you might spot Lindsay Lohan or a Kardashian, but it wasn't stodgy, either. Not like the golf clubhouses that dotted the suburbs or the old-world Italian restaurants with their candelabras and red velvet. Lujo was modern, plush, with black, angular booths and white suede seat cushions. Trendy tableware and flashy drinks. The thump of EDM beneath the conversation as waiters hurried, their eyes turned upward in a way that suggested they saw and knew nothing.

I stood in the doorway, tugging on the hem of the denim miniskirt I'd put on. It was the nicest item of clothing I owned, and it was so far beneath Lujo, it wasn't even funny. I scanned the crowd for Dru, but didn't see him.

"May I help you?" a snooty hostess wearing all black asked. She wrapped her stilettoed black fingernails over the edges of a menu, smiling at me as if to humor me.

I stepped toward the podium, wobbling a little on my heels. "I'm here to meet someone."

Her eyebrows arched, but she didn't consult any sort of list.

"Dru Hollis?" I said, my voice turning up into an annoying question mark as I said his name. As if I were unsure that Dru was who I was actually meeting. I cleared my throat. "He's expecting me."

She studied me for a moment longer—very skeptically— and then nodded. "Right this way."

I followed her as we wound through the tables, the music getting louder as we made our way toward the back corner of the room. She stepped to one side and waved her hand toward the table.

"The Hollis booth," she said.

Jesus, they had their own booth? Suddenly the black sequined tank top I had paired with my skirt felt as shabby as a garbage bag. I tilted my chin upward and scooted past her, my bare legs sliding over the suede of the bench. "Thank you," I mumbled.

"Can I get you something while you wait for Mr. Hollis?" she asked, the note of bitchiness still saturating her words. "Something to drink?"

"Just, um . . . water," I said, hating the way her pert little smile seemed to be mocking me. I wanted to get up, yank her perfect blond ponytail right off her head, and feed it to her. *You're no better than me,* I wanted to scream, and I wanted to do something to prove it. But in a place like Lujo, there really was no proof. Here, everyone looked better than me. "Thank you," I said again, trying to convey everything I was thinking by making my eyes as dead as possible.

The hostess scurried away, and a few moments later a waitress arrived and plunked a sweating glass of ice water on the table in front of me. She walked away without a word. I sipped the water and checked the time. If Dru didn't arrive in ten minutes, I was out of there. We could meet somewhere more my speed, like a food truck.

To while away the time, I pulled the photos out of my purse and flipped through them again, pausing for a long time to study the blurred man walking through the open door. I squinted, trying to make out the details of his wrist.

Maybe there was a bracelet there. Maybe it was the same man. Maybe someone was cheating, and Peyton had caught them. Maybe that was who had beaten her. It was a working theory, and, really, the only thing I had at the moment, with Gibson Talley cleared. I felt like I was starting back at square one, especially if I ignored my doubts about Dru. Which Detective Martinez was making easy to do, given how much he was still watching my every move.

But no matter how hard I looked, I couldn't see any jewelry on the man's arm. All I could really make out for sure was the shoe lifted in midstep as the man disappeared into the doorway. I thought maybe I'd seen it before, but I couldn't place it for the life of me. I had no color to anchor it to. If only it had writing on it.

I flipped over to the photo of the hand holding pills. A drug deal. I was sure of it now. No bracelet, of course. Nothing to help me, although I'd memorized every detail of the hand, even down to the nail jewelry.

I was staring so intently at the photos, I never even sensed anyone approaching me, until a blond blur planted herself in the booth seat across from me.

I looked up, startled, jamming the photos back into my purse.

"Someone's doing something naughty," the blonde said. "What's got you so oblivious, Nikki Kill?"

I'd never been this close to her, but I would have

recognized Luna Fairchild anywhere. She was a sophomore, elfin and ethereal, always dressed as if she were heading for a music awards show. Often, Luna showed up to school in outfits Peyton had worn only days before, and I'd heard her on more than one occasion imitate Peyton's laugh to a T. Until Peyton cut and dyed her hair, Luna was a convincing Peyton stand-in. It was creepy.

"Excuse me?" I said.

She pointed toward my purse. "You looked pretty intense there," she said. "I thought maybe you were doing something you weren't supposed to." She flashed a perfect-toothed smile. "Just kidding, of course."

The waitress who had all but ignored me earlier was instantly at our table, practically out of breath from rushing so fast to get there.

"Vodka cranberry," Luna said, without even making eye contact with the waitress. She waved her hand, sending the waitress away.

"Yes, of course, Miss Fairchild," the waitress said as she left. If the Hollis family was full of privilege, Luna was the most privileged of all.

"If you want a real drink, it will be fine," she said, as if reading my mind. "They know me here. They won't question you."

"I'm waiting for Dru."

"Yes, I know," she said. "I saw the texts. My brother is

really bad about leaving his phone lying around where anyone can see it. Cute, the two of you. I had no idea he was settling down and, like, actually dating someone. So good to see him getting serious with someone his own age for a change."

"We're not dating."

Luna leaned forward on her elbows, resting her chin on her hands, pinning me with a look of fake innocence that made my blood boil. "Interesting. Tell me, then, Nikki Kill, how come you're here?"

"Dru invited me," I said. "But you already know that if you saw the texts."

"You do know the definition of *date*, don't you?" she asked. I didn't respond.

She continued to stare at me, and then took a deep breath, leaned back, and fiddled with a cloth napkin. The waitress came back with her drink.

"You're a doll, Liv," Luna said, and I swore the waitress practically melted under the compliment. She floated away, and Luna picked up her drink, sipped it. "Yes, I know my brother invited you to Lujo. It's really nice here, isn't it? So much better than some of the other clubs, where you can't even dance without getting elbowed by somebody's body-guard. And not too many photographers here. We're old news." She looked me over. "Or no news."

"It's a bit much," I said, not wanting to fall into whatever trap she was setting.

Her lips turned down as she assessed the room. "Maybe, but I don't mind a bit much. Not at all." She laughed loudly, then sipped her drink again. "Anyway, I wasn't asking why you were here at Lujo. As you said, I saw the texts. You are clearly here at my brother's request. My real question is— and we are all kind of wondering this—why is he requesting, Nikki? How do you know my brother? And how do you know Peyton?"

"*All* wondering?" I asked. "Who is all?"

She shrugged. "My parents, too. They're a little concerned for his safety right now. For obvious reasons. So what's your deal?"

I blinked. "I don't understand your question."

She took a bigger drink and set the glass down, the fake smile dropping from her face. "It's a pretty easy question."

I shrugged. "I know Peyton from school. Everyone does. I met Dru at the hospital."

She nodded. "Ah. But you seem so much more involved than that. You know? You can't blame me for being curious. I mean, after all, someone did try to kill my sister." She leaned forward, slid her elbows across the table. "Do you think she's going to die? God, can you imagine? Peyton Hollis, dead. How my mother would mourn the loss of her best asset."

Again, I wasn't sure how to respond. Luna seemed to be laying land mines all around me, waiting almost giddily for me to step on one. I couldn't figure out where this was coming from, or where it was going. And I sure as hell wasn't going to tell her the truth about what I saw in Peyton's monitors when I was in the room. This obnoxious little turd didn't need to know the first thing about my crimson.

"I hope not," I said. "She doesn't look good, though."

"Oh, well, she stopped looking good a while ago, with the haircut and tattoo." Luna sipped again. Her drink was already half gone. "I'm joking, of course."

"Of course," I repeated, but not even the tiniest smile ghosted across my face. Who jokes about someone who is fighting for her life?

"Anyway. So Peyton. I really hated the way my mother doted on her. Everything was about how she was so beautiful and so talented and blah, blah, blah. There've been times I would've given anything just to be Peyton. And then she did all that weird stuff right before this happened," Luna said. "The tattoo, the hair, the band. Got a new phone and stopped answering her old one. She was in real trouble. We're all very sad, of course, but I can't say we're too surprised, given the path she was taking. I think we all knew she was just asking for something awful to happen."

My mouth went dry. Everything about Luna was abrasive. Why would she be telling me this? And did she really just blame Peyton for her own beating? "She was asking to be beaten?"

"Well, I mean, I wouldn't wish what happened to her

on anybody, but it had gotten impossible to be close to her anymore. Did you know that she was an escort?" Shock must have registered on my face, because she nodded vigorously. "Yeah. A hooker, some people might call it. And she was selling drugs, too. Pills. Molly. People who do that are sort of asking for bad things to happen to them, don't you think?"

I didn't know how to answer. Was Luna telling the truth? Peyton, an escort? I immediately thought about the photo in my purse—the one with the hand holding out pills. Molly, Luna had said. Peyton had been selling drugs. Good God, there were so many more possibilities of who might have attacked her now. How would I ever figure out who it might have been? Maybe it was time to admit I was in over my head. Maybe it was time to cry uncle, go ahead and let Detective Martinez take over, no matter how wrapped up in this mess I had gotten.

Luna settled back into her booth, looking smug. "So I guess you don't know her all that well, then," she said.

I shook my head. "I never said I did."

Luna sipped her drink again. "It's all very unfortunate. I feel sorry for Peyton. She really got herself into a mess. And I feel even sorrier for Dru. I think someone's setting him up."

"Who? Why?" I asked.

She shrugged. "I don't know. Maybe one of Peyton's suppliers." She rolled her eyes. "Maybe her pimp. Dru and Peyton were two little peas in a perfect pod. Maybe that pissed off one of her johns and he came after her in revenge. Who knows? Poor Dru. I worry he'll be next." Her eyes darted across the dining room. "Oh, and speak of the devil."

I followed her gaze. Dru was walking toward us, looking amazing in a pair of chinos and a crisp pink button-down, a Zegna tie bringing out his eyes. But, unlike me, he also looked like he fit in. He gazed at us curiously. Luna stood, greeting him.

"There's the man of the hour. Dru, Dru, Dru, you have never been very good at being on time. Nikki was sitting here all by her lonesome. Thank goodness I just happened to accidentally see your texts, so I could keep the poor girl company."

"What are you doing here, Luna?" he asked.

"I just told you. I'm entertaining Nikki. And I'm having a drink. Is there something wrong with that?"

He plucked the nearly empty glass out of her hand. "Actually, yes. You're sixteen."

The waitress breezed through with a fresh drink for Luna. Luna took it, all smiles. "Since when did you get so legal, Dru Hollis? It's really very unbecoming. You don't want Nikki here to think you're an old poop."

Dru didn't respond, but I could see his jaw work with displeasure.

"Well," Luna said brightly. "I guess I'll leave you two

lovebirds to it. It was good to meet you, Nikki. Maybe I'll see you again sometime."

I nodded to her; she waggled her fingers at me.

"And I'll see you later, big brother," she said to Dru, pinching his cheek.

And that was when I saw it. A flash of turquoise at the tip of her pinkie finger.

I'd seen it before. I'd practically memorized it right before Luna had arrived.

Someone's doing something naughty. What's got you so oblivious, Nikki Kill?

I'd been trying to shut out my synesthesia since I was eight years old. Trying to be able to concentrate on things without seeing colors. I'd been so focused on the pills, my brain didn't even register it. But it was there. Seeing it in person, I was sure I'd first seen it in the photo.

An outstretched hand full of pills. The fingers splayed. A delicate charm pierced through the pinkie fingernail. A tiny chain.

The letter R dangling at the end of it.

The R flashed at me, *turquoise, turquoise, turquoise.*

Luna had tried to convince me that Peyton was selling drugs. But if that were true—if Peyton had been the one doing the selling—why did she have a photo of Luna's hand, full of pills?

"I'm sorry about her," Dru said, sitting where Luna had just been. "She's a pain in the ass." He assessed the look on my face. "Do I even want to know what she had to say before I got here?"

I took a drink of my water, trying to get control over my thoughts, tamp them down. My mind was spinning. I needed to look at the photo again, be 100 percent certain that I was right before I said anything to Dru about what I'd seen. But there was no nonchalant way to go about that, not with him sitting right there, gazing at me like I was behind zoo bars.

"She wanted to know how I knew you and Peyton," I said. "I didn't tell her about . . ." I trailed off, unsure how to put it. Using my forefinger, I gestured between us, leaving a violet trail in the air, which was quickly flooded over by a wave of pine-colored embarrassment.

He smirked. "You mean what happened at Peyton's apartment?"

I nodded. "Yeah, she doesn't know. She thinks we're dating."

He reached across the table and took my hand. A jolt of the same chemistry I'd felt at the apartment ran through me, the white suede rippling purple, the pine gone. "It doesn't matter what Luna thinks. I don't regret it." I ducked my head and he tipped his lower to catch my eyes, looking devilish.

Purple. Turquoise. Orangish pink. Crimson. It was never-ending when I was around these people. My feelings, my intuition, my curiosity, everything. It all swirled together into an impossible tornado, and I no longer knew what exactly I was doing here. First it was Gibson and then not Gibson. It was Dru. It was the shadow man with the bracelet. It was one of Peyton's johns, it was Luna. Every moment it changed. I was confused, and I hated the way my gut twisted every time I looked at Dru Hollis, every time I caught his scent on the air. Every time I touched him. And I hated the way Chris Martinez's warnings crept into my head every time I was with Dru. And I especially hated how somewhere deep down it was those warnings—that possibility of danger—that made me want Dru even more.

I knew the things that I knew. I was certain about them. But they were right and then wrong. I was learning that I couldn't trust myself; how could I trust anyone else?

"She had a good question, Dru. Why am I here?" I waved over my shoulder. "Obviously this is not my usual hangout. I'm so out of place here, and you have your own special table."

"We can go somewhere else," he said.

"No, it's not that. It's the bigger question. Why me? That seems to be the one thing I can't answer when it comes to your family."

He wrapped his fingers solidly around my hand and used

the fingers of his other hand to trace lightly up the length of my arm and down again. I shivered. "Because you're different. You care about Peyton, and you weren't even friends with her. You don't fit in here, and that's exactly why I like you. I don't fit in here, either."

With horribly poor timing, the waitress reappeared. "Mr. Hollis? Bourbon neat?"

"Not now, Liv," he said, without looking at her, his voice cold and robotic, somehow reminding me of Hospital Bill Hollis, and she vanished like mist. The tingle in my arms moved up my neck as he kept the longing gaze.

As much as I was learning that I detested everything the Hollises—and everyone like them—stood for, I would be lying if I said the control that he exhibited didn't turn me on just a little. Funny, the thing that made me stay arm's distance from Peyton, the thing that scared me about Bill Hollis, the thing that put me off Luna . . . made me want Dru.

Even though I desperately did not want to, I pulled my hand free of his. It shook as I picked up my water and took another drink. "Luna said some things about Peyton."

Dru's expression clouded as he leaned back, just as Luna had leaned back minutes before. "Such as?"

"She said Peyton was an escort and that she sold drugs."

"She said that?"

"Is it true?"

Dru raised an arm to get Liv's attention and made a motion with his finger. She nodded and hurried to the bar. I guessed he'd changed his mind about that drink. He folded his hands, tapping his thumbs together contemplatively. When Liv arrived with his drink, he pushed it a few inches away from him and shifted in his seat again.

"Listen, Nikki. My family is anything but perfect. Everybody thinks it would be so great to have Bill Hollis for a dad, but there's a lot of pressure. The bastard can't just let us be who we are. We have to make him look good. We have to show the world how important we are. It's unrelenting, and he doesn't care about us as anything more than accessories that support his image. Sometimes, when the pressure gets to be too much, you . . . do things you aren't proud of. My sister understood that. She got the same pressure, and even more from our so-called mother."

"So it's true?" I asked. "Peyton was a prostitute?" I tried to imagine the girl who lorded over the hallways of our school selling her body at night. I couldn't do it. Peyton was too perfect for that. But, like Dru had just said, pressure made people do strange things.

He made a face, waved me off. "Who knows? Luna is a liar, and you never know what kind of bullshit is going to come out of her mouth next. If Peyton was an escort, and selling drugs, like Luna says, she did a hell of a job covering it up. I was the only one close to her, and if I didn't know, I don't know how in the hell Luna would."

"I thought you said your dad was the one closest to her."

He gave me a blank look.

"At the hospital. You said your dad was going to be shattered. You said he was super close to Peyton."

He let out a snort. "My dad. No, my dad isn't close to anyone. That's just not the way the Great Bill Hollis gets ahead in this world."

My hands instinctively pulled away from the tabletop and the white tablecloth that stretched over it, and reached across the booth bench and curled protectively over my purse. I couldn't pinpoint what it was I was picking up on. The way his eyes flicked to the side while he was talking. The fine mist of sweat that edged along his sideburns. The slight tremor in his hands while he rested them on the table.

For the first time since this all started, I saw gray tinging the corners of my vision, smoldering in like the filter of a burning cigarette. I wanted so badly to believe that Dru was innocent. But I was beginning to suspect he was also lying.

18

HALF AN HOUR later, Dru led me to the parking lot behind Lujo, his hand between my shoulder blades.

"You got your Spyder," I said, pressing my back against the driver's side. The evening light made Dru's tan skin stand out even more against his pink shirt. He'd loosened his tie, and it hung seductively around his neck, the first two buttons of his shirt undone.

"Yeah," he said, moving in close. "My dad was flipping out about it being in an apartment building parking lot. He's already had Peyton's apartment emptied."

"Already?"

He nodded. "Cleaned out. After the cops got done with

it. Her living at a place like that was an embarrassment to him, I'm sure."

"Yeah, but how'd he find someone to clean it out so fast?"

Dru laughed, but there was something sharp behind the laughter. "He's Bill Hollis. He can find anyone to do anything at any time. For the right price. You would be amazed at what, and who, can be bought in this world."

"You are not your father's biggest fan," I mused. I reached forward and fiddled with his tie. I couldn't help myself.

"Not at all." He leaned in closer to me, putting his weight on his hand, which he'd rested on the car just above my head. I could feel his thighs near mine and smell the bourbon on his breath. "Don't get me wrong. I like a person who's tough." He palmed my side with his free hand. "But with a little softness, too." He moved his hand up my side so tenderly my insides melted.

"You're in luck," I said, but I didn't get to finish before his mouth was on mine, his entire body pressed up against me.

"Come home with me," he whispered against my mouth.

I wanted to. I really, really wanted to. But I knew that going home with him would mean falling into bed with him, and I couldn't help hearing Chris Martinez's warnings in my head again. And seeing that gray.

Plus, I really needed to look at those photos again. Needed to see the one of the hand full of pills again, just to be sure. And not just those. I needed to look at the ones on

Peyton's photo-sharing site again. Things were needling the back of my brain. Things that I'd seen but couldn't quite pinpoint. Answers were in those photos. I knew it. I just had to find them. I gave Dru a soft shove.

"Not right now," I said. "Maybe I'll come by later?"

He groaned, pulled away from me. "My apartment. Tonight? We'll be alone."

"Deal," I said. "I'll text you."

THE HOUSE WAS quiet when I got home. Dad was out, and as the night wore on I began to wish more and more that he was home. I hadn't heard a word from Gibson Talley since our altercation in the parking lot, but I was still sort of waiting for him to come exact his revenge for what had gone down out there. Gibson Talley didn't seem like the type to let things go easily. He definitely didn't seem like the type who would let a girl get the best of him and then just brush it off as if nothing had happened. He had face to save.

I realized I hadn't eaten, so I grabbed a bowl of cereal and headed upstairs, the whole time trying to make sense of the things I'd learned at Lujo. Trying to clear my mind of my encounter by the car with Dru and my promise to meet up with him later. Not an easy task. I could still feel his feathery finger brushes against my side.

But I had to focus. I shoved a spoonful of cereal into my mouth and chewed.

There were secrets, that much I believed. But whose secrets were the deadly ones? That was the question. Who was telling the truth and who was lying? Who was covering up for what?

And was it possible that a Hollis was behind Peyton's attack?

The thought had begun to whisper to me.

Luna had guessed it could have been a john who'd beaten up Peyton. She'd said she thought Dru was being framed. Dru had made it sound like Bill Hollis was power hungry enough to possibly be the culprit. Detective Martinez had seemed to be pinning it, at least in part, on Arrigo Basile, Dru's alleged puppet thug. And, of course, I couldn't forget the mystery man with the bracelet. And the claim Luna had made about Peyton selling the Molly while it was her hand full of pills in the photo.

All the arrows seemed to be pointing in opposite directions, but one thing had continued to come up again and again: escorts.

Arrigo Basile was known for his involvement with prostitutes. Luna had said Peyton was an escort. Bill Hollis's license plate read DREAMS, which just happened to be part of the name found on a flyer in Peyton's apartment. Hollywood Dreams Ranch. The word Dreams glittery lavender. I looked at the flyer for the thousandth time.

The glitter reminded me of something.

I had seen something else recently that had stuck out to me because of its glitter and glitz. Yes . . . glitz. The thought made it click. The color I'd associated with it was something about the word *glitz*.

Glitz. Glitzy cherrybomb. That was the phrase that had come to mind.

I logged on to Peyton's Aesthetishare site and scrolled to the photo of her and Luna. They were standing in front of a sign that promised SEXSEXSEXSEXSEX and were both seriously flirting up the camera. Luna had her lips and hips pushed out. Peyton was wearing a T-shirt with a dollar sign on it.

I scooted away from my desk, staring at the screen as it all became so clear to me.

The dollar sign. The SEXSEXSEXSEXSEX. The way they vamped for the picture.

Maybe Luna hadn't been full of shit. Maybe Peyton really was an escort.

Why? Why would someone who had it all need to accept money from strange men for God-knew-what? It made no sense.

But again, it made all the sense in the world. Peyton, wearing the dollar-sign T-shirt in front of the window advertising all that sex. It was so obvious it was almost too obvious.

I scrolled to the post details. Peyton had titled the photo *Double Rainbow*. Was this a play on her new tattoo?

Was she trying to say something more?

Live in Color. Double Rainbow, only not regular rainbow colors. Glitzy cherrybomb *Rainbow*. Call-girl-colored *Rainbow*.

I sifted through papers on my desk until I unearthed the Hollywood Dreams flyer. I picked up my phone and dialed the number, chewing on my lip while it rang. This was an outside chance, but . . .

"Dreams," a voice purred on the other end.

"Um, hi, I'm looking for Rainbow?" I asked, my voice sounding way too high-pitched and nervous. I tried to lower it, sound more confident. "Is she working tonight?"

"I'm sorry, Rainbow's not available for a while," the voice said. "Can I help you with something?"

I hung up, silver squiggles I associated with excitement wriggling in the air.

It had been an outside chance, but now it all made sense. The clues added up perfectly.

Rainbow was Peyton's call-girl pseudonym.

I lit a cigarette, pushed up the window with one hand, and then rolled back to my desk. Pieces of the puzzle were clicking into place.

The photo above *Double Rainbow*—the first photo of Peyton to catch my eye—filled my computer screen. Black and white, Peyton looking like a starlet as she stood, sultry, so angular she looked broken-boned, in the water, a life preserver dangling over her arm. The first time I'd looked at the photo, I'd noticed the yellow-and-pink *SO* written on the preserver. But now I knew the rest. *S*. The preserver had *SOS* written on it.

What was it her Facebook status had said? The one right before she moved away? *Must get to the bottom of things.*

I gazed at the photo again, noticing something else for the first time. Her other hand was clutching the life preserver, mostly covering tiny writing—what was maybe the name of the company that made the preserver. All that was showing was *nik.*

My cigarette trembled between my fingers as I squinted at it, the copper that I usually associated with my name there, but just slightly off. It wasn't *nikki* . . . it was just *nik.* Brownish, but not quite copper. Something that would stand out to me.

Something that someone else with synesthesia would have known would stand out to me.

She wanted me to know she was making changes. But she wanted more than that. *Must get to the bottom of things.*

Nik. Must get to the bottom of things. SOS. Separately, each had their own colors. But together they were one. All in orange.

It was a colored banner that might as well have read, *Help me, Nikki.*

■ ■ ■

I WAS STILL puzzling over the photos—looking for more of Peyton's clues, something I might have missed in the SOS photo—when my phone buzzed. I'd been lost in the photos for hours now. But I felt like I was on the edge of figuring it out. So close.

"Hey." It was Dru. "I thought you were going to text."

"Yeah, sorry. I was busy."

"Any progress?"

"Huh?"

"You're still working on Peyton's case, right? Have you made any progress?"

I rubbed my eyes. "She knew she was in trouble," I said. "She was reaching out to me. But I still don't know why exactly."

"You two must have some connection," he said, but his voice sounded distracted—almost as if he was talking to himself, rather than to me.

If only you knew, I thought. I tabbed back to Peyton's photo site and found the family photo on the pier. I liked this photo. Dru looked amazing. Damp and sculpted, sun-kissed.

You could tell by looking at the photo that this was one powerful family, and you could tell by looking at Dru that he was comfortable with his power. He stood at the opposite end from his father—not a surprise, given what I'd seen—but also at the opposite end from Peyton. Luna and Vanessa were pressed in close to him, the small blond woman's arm wrapped around his waist. He wasn't reciprocating the hug. He stood confidently apart, even while being together.

There was something else about the photo that I couldn't quite pinpoint, but his unbuttoned shirt distracted me. I couldn't help it. And hearing his voice on the other end of the phone only made it worse.

"Hello?" he asked, jarring me away from the photo. I closed my laptop to shut out the distraction.

"I'm still here," I said.

"So it's gotten pretty late. You coming tonight? I really, really want you to. We can pick up where we left off earlier."

Still in my skirt, I slid my bare legs over the windowsill and sat in the night air. I lit up a cigarette. A part of me wished that this was a normal night. That Dru Hollis was calling me to come over just as Jones had always done, and that I was about to go over for a good time, without all the drama and nerves of this weird shit I'd gotten into.

But I feared that longing for my relationship with Dru to be normal bordered on having feelings for him. I didn't want to go there. He was a hot guy. A guy who wanted me as much as I wanted him. That was it. Who wanted normal when the drama and nerves amped up the sex all the more?

"Give me half an hour," I said.

I smoked the cigarette down to the filter, and then lit another just to keep him waiting.

■ ■ ■

DRU'S APARTMENT WAS almost as big as my house, taking up the entire top floor of a ten-story loft-style building on Sycamore Square.

It was also pitch dark inside.

"Hello?" I said as I pushed open the door. The elevator door slid shut behind me, stranding me there. "Dru?"

There was no response, so I stayed in the doorway, blinking to try to adjust to the darkness. I heard a noise—a thump—off to my left. I jumped, flexing my arms protectively in front of me as I faced that direction.

"Dru?" I asked again. No response.

There was another thump, and I flinched again. Could the same person who hurt Peyton have hurt Dru, too? Could the person have known we were meeting here and had been waiting for him?

I thought about how Luna had read his texts earlier in the evening and had intercepted me at Lujo. Maybe she was playing the same game twice. *Dru, Dru, Dru. You have never been good at being on time.* Maybe she knew he was going to be late. Maybe she knew I'd figured out about the drugs. Maybe she was here to hurt me.

There was no way I was going to let a skinny, entitled bitch like Luna Fairchild scare me off. I walked toward the sound. "I hear you," I said, holding my fists out in front of me. Now there was a noise at my back and I swiveled. "Come on out. Why are you hiding?"

A louder thump this time, closer. I turned again.

Someone hit me hard, wrapping me up and knocking me backward onto what felt like a couch. I let out a gust of air, but immediately pulled my legs into my stomach to put distance between me and my assailant.

"Hey, hey, hey," the figure who'd just tackled me said. It was Dru's voice, so close I could feel his breath tickle my cheek. "Why so feisty?" He grabbed my wrists and pinned them to the cushions on either side of my head. He leaned into me, full force. "You look amazing in shadow, by the way. Your hips curve just right." He ran one hand down my hip, hooking his thumb into my waistband.

"Goddamn it, Dru," I said, ripping one hand out of his grip and punching him in the chest. "You scared the hell out of me."

He laughed, pulling away from my punch and rubbing his chest, allowing just enough slack for me to free my other hand and hit him with it, too.

"It's not funny," I said through gritted teeth. "You're lucky I didn't kick your head in."

He groaned, leaned into me again. "I love it when you talk tough," he said. "So hot."

"It's not talk," I said, hitting him again and again.

My fists slowed as he began to nuzzle my neck.

"Don't be mad," he said into my hair. "I just wanted to have a little fun with you. You're so serious all the time. A mystery." He pulled my earlobe with his teeth. "I love mysteries."

I let my hands drop at my sides, let him glide closer and closer, the heat of his mouth against my skin leaving pulsing violet drops across my shoulders. Soon I was pushing my hands through his hair, kissing him back.

He straightened his arms, pulling up above me. I still couldn't see his face, but I could make out the angle of his silhouette.

"What?" I asked, impatient.

I saw his silhouette move, as if he were shaking his head. "You are something else, that's what," he said. "Any man would want you."

And as he leaned in to kiss me again, I knew what move I needed to make next. *Any man would want you.* Just as any man would have wanted Peyton. *Nik.*

Must get to the bottom of things.

SOS.

I felt Dru tug at my shirt, but in my head I was already at Hollywood Dreams.

I was already following Rainbow's trail.

I was already going to find the john who'd hurt Peyton.

TURNED OUT, THE hardest part about getting a job at Hollywood Dreams was finding it. But once I located the nondescript glass front door and pulled it open, I knew I was in the right place, because I'd seen it before. This was the same door in the blurred photo I'd found in the suitcase at the bottom of Peyton's closet. Whoever the man was who had been in that photo, he'd been entering here. I got goose bumps following in his steps. What if that man had been Peyton's attacker?

The door opened onto a staircase—just as unremarkable as the door—and I climbed it slowly. I felt so uncomfortable in my hastily bought outfit—a stretch royal-blue dress a size too small, so tight and short it felt like I was wearing nothing at all. I wobbled on six-inch sequined heels. I was all legs and boobs and pissed-off awkwardness. Whatever connection Peyton and I might have had, this was not it. I would have made the worst call girl ever.

I tried to imagine what Dru would think if he saw me dressed like this. Or even better, Jones. Jones would probably have a heart attack and die.

I tried not to imagine how on earth I would defend myself in something so uncomfortable. My only solace was that one of my heels would jab out an eyeball nicely. Gunner would have been proud of that line of thinking. That knowledge made me more comfortable.

At the top of the stairs was yet another ordinary door—this one wooden with mailbox number stickers adhered to the front. I tried the knob. It was locked. I knocked, wiped my sweaty palms along the (not long enough) length of my dress. I considered turning around and leaving, thinking of another way to get the information that I needed. I had to bite my lip hard and remind myself that nothing was ever going to get anywhere near an actual transaction just to get myself to stay there. I would bolt if anything weird happened. I would punch and then I would run. And this blue dress was as naked as I was going to get, period.

After some time, there were footsteps, and then the door opened. A statuesque girl with doll eyes and perfect skin stood on the other side. She wore a simple black tunic and impossibly clingy jeans, the cuffs rolled to reveal a towering pair of cork wedges. Her long red hair swished over one eye seductively. When she moved, I could see a scar that had cut a line through her eyebrow.

"Can I help you?" she asked in a voice I recognized as the voice that had answered the phone when I'd called earlier that day.

"I think I talked to you," I said. "I'm Nikki."

She stepped aside, opening the door wider. "Yep, come on in. I'm Brigitte." I followed her down a short hallway into a perfectly plain reception area—a pockmarked wooden desk, a basic computer, a printer, a coffeemaker on top of a scratched file cabinet. This was anything but Hollywood. Or dreamy. "Actually, I'm Sarah," she said over her shoulder. She motioned toward a chair and I sat. "But the boss likes us to have special names. Something sexy or mysterious or playful, you know. Brigitte, Celestia, Cinnamon. The clients are in it for the fantasy—they don't want to be with a plain Jane girl, even if that's who we really are off the clock." She flashed a smile that was anything but plain Jane. I pondered anyone accusing Peyton or Luna of being plain Janes. I couldn't get there. "So, Nikki Kill, is that what you said your name was?" She opened a file with one sheet of notebook paper in it. I nodded, she made a note. "Almost good enough on its own, right? Maybe Killgirl or something super tough-sounding. You look the type."

"I'm a type?" I asked, pulling the front of my dress up over my cleavage for the millionth time.

Brigitte assessed me, biting on her lower lip. One of her front teeth was slightly crooked, a flaw that somehow managed to make her even more gorgeous. "Definitely. Black fringe, thigh-high boots, bustier, the whole nine. I could see some of our clients going for the bad-girl vibe. You could really play it up. You know, when you're alone. But I could see a lot of them wanting that innocent bad-girl thing. You know, the juxtaposition, like with a slutty librarian. That kind of thing."

"Okay," I said, although I had no idea what she was talking about. I could do the bad-girl vibe with no problem. But I had no intention of playing anything out while alone with a client. I still had yet to figure out how that was going to go.

Brigitte continued looking me over. She must have liked what she saw, because she finally gave a definitive nod. "Yeah, you'll be popular. We just lost an escort whose image was sort of a punk rocker type. The guys loved her. Constantly calling for her. More requests than she could possibly take."

I sat forward. "She quit?"

Brigitte wrote a few notes in my file. "Yeah," she said absentmindedly. "Was too bad. She was one of our best. The boss had been grooming her for a while."

"The boss?"

"Don't worry, she's not as intimidating as she sounds. Come here, I'll show you her office. But she's out today. She's been out of town. And having some . . . family problems."

She plucked a set of keys off a hook on the side of the file cabinet and I followed her down the hallway, past a modest kitchen and supply area, to a door at the other end. Brigitte opened it. It was like opening a portal to a whole other world. Thick pink carpet flowed across the floor, a shining ship of a desk taking up the back, flanked by bookcases filled with crystal figurines. A zebra-print chaise lounge took up one corner, next to a Tiffany floor lamp, which bathed the room in a comforting amber light. There was a night-and-day difference between this office and the one Brigitte occupied out front. Whoever this madam was, she definitely wanted to let the support staff know that she was in charge.

"Very nice," I said.

"Yeah," Brigitte said. "She doesn't like the front office to be flashy, just in case the cops decide to be curious or something, but she likes her expensive things. And you'll make money, too. Lots of it, so don't worry about that." She closed the door and locked it. "Anyway, she keeps it locked unless she's here. She's had some problems with . . . things . . . getting stolen lately." She winked at me. "Pharmaceutical enhancements," she whispered. "Some of our clients figure if they're already tempting the law, they might as well get a good buzz off it." We walked back to the front office and sat down. "It's just me in here, anyway, and not very often. Only when someone like you is coming in. You probably won't really see any of the other girls. Not usually, anyway, unless someone books a double or something, which hardly ever happens. Most clients don't like anyone to know that they're having to pay for it. They want all their friends to think they can get girls like us all on their own." She laughed. I laughed along with her, but the sound wanted to get stuck in my throat. The reality of the situation—that I was now officially an escort—had started to set in. "So," Brigitte said brightly, closing the file. "Any questions?"

I shifted in my seat. I had so many questions. My mind was swirling with them. But I reminded myself that I was there for Peyton. "The punk rock girl. What was her name?" Brigitte paused. "It might help me choose one," I said.

"Oh," she said. "She called herself Rainbow."

I already knew this, but it still felt like a victory to hear her say it. I didn't know if I wanted to jump up out of my seat in triumph or if I wanted to cry.

"Do you have any, like, bodyguards?" I asked.

Brigitte smiled a knowing smile. "We have one—Rigo— but we don't ever need him. Hollywood Dreams isn't a place to pick up a cheap hooker, Nikki. The kind of guys who can afford us are usually a little more elevated than that."

"Usually," I repeated. Score one for Detective Martinez. I was guessing Rigo was short for Arrigo Basile, but that was one question I wasn't going to ask. Guess Dru wasn't the only one who was chummy with Arrigo. Peyton must have known him, too.

"There have been a couple of instances," she said. She busied herself with gathering papers on her desk. "But let's be honest. Women could be attacked anywhere."

"That's a pretty defeatist way of looking at it."

Brigitte smiled at me again, but this time the smile had gone thin. "Realist," she said. "Don't worry. We will only set you up with regulars for a while, anyway. You won't have any problems. In fact . . ." She thumbed through the papers she'd just gathered, pulled one out. "I have one for you tonight if you'd like to start right away. He was supposed to meet with Rainbow, but . . ." She handed me the slip of paper. "His name is Stefan. Of course, most of our clients use fake names, too. He's been one of our regulars for years. Owns a dot-com, has a wife and three kids in the valley, but loves his Hollywood whores." She laughed out loud. "He's short, bald, kind of fat. You can imagine. Anyway, looks like this time he just wants some dinner and some company. Wouldn't surprise me if dinner is room service. But don't worry. Stefan is a real teddy bear. All our girls love him. You'll have a good time." She winked.

All our girls love him. "Perfect," I said aloud. "I'm excited."

"Great. Meet him tonight at eight in the hotel lobby. The address is right there on the paper. And what you're wearing will be fine for tonight, but we will want to start thinking about getting you some other clothes. Unless you already own a lot of leather and stuff?"

I shook my head no.

"Well, after Stefan pays for tonight, you will definitely want to go shopping."

Brigitte was all smiling teeth and encouragement now.

Little did she know, I had no intention of giving Stefan the opportunity to pay for anything, especially not anything I had to offer.

20

THE HOTEL LOBBY was super classy. Marble and mahogany and crystal and brass so shiny it hurt your eyes. A doorman in full uniform opened the door for me. He seemed to have a knowing look in his eye, and I wanted to both die of embarrassment and punch his eyeballs right out of his head. But I couldn't blame him. I knew what I looked like. I didn't look like the kind of girl who could afford this hotel, that was for damn sure. I looked like the kind of girl who was getting paid to be here.

How could Peyton have done this? She had everything. How could she give herself up for money, and, more importantly, *why* would she? She could have had any boy in the school—hell, any man in the city. Her family was loaded. It made no sense that she would choose the life of an escort.

I tried to walk as confidently as I could across the marble floor, weaving, wobbling, and praying that my heel didn't slip and send me sprawling. I picked out Stefan before I even began looking for him.

Brigitte had given the perfect description. The man was at least four inches shorter than I was, and that was before my heels. I towered over him, getting a bird's-eye view of his freckled scalp. He wore thick glasses with marbled plastic frames and a ratty polo shirt with frayed sleeves. His brown shoes curled up at the toes, giving him an elfin appearance. He was the kind of guy that no girl would look at twice. The way he beamed at me, I could tell he had spent plenty of lonely nights by himself. I would almost have felt sorry for him had Brigitte not told me that he had a wife and three kids at home. How lonely were they right now?

He closed the space across the lobby between us surprisingly fast.

"Prism?" he asked.

I nodded. Despite Brigitte's desire that I use a tough name with the word *Kill* in it, I had decided to go with the one thing that definitely tied Peyton and me together— color. It helped me stay focused on what I had to do.

He reached over and let his hand fall the length of my arm. Ordinarily, any man who dared touch me like that at our first meeting would be taking home his spleen in a plastic bag, but I couldn't do that to Stefan. He was paying for the right to touch me however he wanted. The thought made my stomach turn, and I had to curl my toes inside my shoes to keep my feet grounded. *It's just an arm,* I reminded myself. *He gets no farther than an arm.*

"Aren't you a fine addition?" he said. "Great skin."

"Thank you," I said. *Creep. Jerk. Disgusting, nasty, creepy jerk.*

He stared me down until I was beyond icked out, and then finally—thankfully—swept his arm out to one side. "I thought we would have dinner here tonight, if that's okay with you."

"Sure," I said, stepping around him, glad to be out from under his unsettling gaze and clammy hands.

We were seated immediately, even though the hotel restaurant was packed, with people spilling over into the bar area. Stefan clearly had some clout. I was starting to learn that money could buy a lot of things.

"You take many of the girls here?" I asked as the waiter scooted me in and placed my napkin on my lap.

Stefan's face clouded over. "I've never been asked that question before," he said.

"I was just curious. I'm new, so I don't know what the other girls have done."

His cloud turned into a deep frown. "Since you're new, Prism, I will cut you some slack. But I must tell you it is very poor form to inquire about other women while on a date." His tone was clipped, displeased. He looked like a mild-mannered, meek little guy, but I could see a dangerous side underneath. *Or maybe you just want to see that, Nikki. Maybe you want the first guy you meet to be the one who hurt Peyton.*

"Sorry," I said. "I didn't know."

He softened, barely. "That's all right. Like I said, I'm willing to give you a break. Would you like an appetizer? How do you feel about shrimp cocktail? In truth, I don't like it. But there's something sexy about it, don't you think?"

I felt his foot brush the side of my leg when he said that. The dumbass hadn't even bothered to take his shoe off. I forced myself not to flinch under his touch. Instead, I wrapped my hand around the handle of the table knife, slid it off the table, and held it at my hip. It made me feel better to have it there, even if I would never use it.

"Shrimp cocktail is fine," I said, trying to sound sweet.

He motioned for the waiter and ordered the shrimp, plus steaks for both of us. I wondered how I would ever gag down all this food, but reminded myself that I had to if I was going to get alone with him. I needed to be alone with him. Even if he wasn't the guy who'd hurt Peyton, he might know who was.

The waiter left, and it was just the two of us. I had no idea how to make small talk with a guy who grossed me out and made me angry all at the same time, especially not with my mind in a totally different place.

What was Dru doing right now? Was he sitting by Peyton's bedside? Was he talking to his lawyer? Was he battling his father? Was he regretting being with me the night before? What would he have thought about me now, a call girl getting ready to eat something sexy for a married guy who was paying to be with me?

"So, Prism," Stefan said, cutting into my thoughts. "If you don't mind my saying, your name doesn't suit you very well."

"No?"

He picked up the bread basket, plunked a roll on my plate, and took another for himself. He bit directly into it, spilling crumbs down the front of his shirt.

"No. Not nearly as well as the others. Why do you call yourself Prism, anyway? Seems like you could come up with something a little more creative. Prisms are colorful and shiny. They evoke a certain image in the mind of the person choosing."

"I see. I didn't think about that. I've never had to . . . choose."

His eyebrows shot up, coming to a point beneath his nonexistent hairline. But then they relaxed into a devilish smile. "Snarky. You're a hateful little vixen, aren't you?"

I tore a piece off my bread, tried to act casual as I poked

it in my mouth. "I'm sorry," I said, trying with all my might to sound repentant. "I don't mean to be. I guess I'm not very good at this yet."

"Well, nobody said you had to be good at small talk." He laughed, snorted, laughed some more. "I'm not paying to listen to you chitchat." He took another large bite of his roll and leaned forward, laying his chest across the table.

My hand tightened around the knife handle. With little effort, I could drive it right into his leg under the table before he even realized it was missing.

He chuckled, chewing, looking way too much like a child. I imagined his short legs swinging back and forth under his chair. "Maybe I should rename you. Stormcloud. But I'm guessing you are a lot more than a little thunder, aren't you, you sexy thing, you?"

I fought the urge to roll my eyes. Who talks to people like that? "You have no idea," I said.

He swallowed, his face flushing a deep red, suddenly looking serious and swimmy. I'd seen that look before, on Jones. "You keep talking like that, and I'm going to skip dinner altogether," he said.

Please do, I thought. But instead, I smiled demurely, nibbling on more bread. "But the best things come to those who wait," I said. "A good storm has to build up, and the clouds haven't even begun to roll in yet."

"I think I like you after all," Stefan said, just as our

shrimp arrived. He pushed the plate toward me. "You first."

I tucked the knife under my thigh, leaving the handle poking out for easy retrieval if it should come down to that. I picked up a shrimp and brought it to my lips. I didn't care for them in any case, but especially after he'd called them sexy, my stomach clenched in on itself, trying to refuse entry.

Had Peyton done this? Had she felt her face burn as this disgusting little Stefan leered at her like she was only there for his pleasure? Had she gotten hateful and caused him to be gruff? Too gruff?

Dinner passed in a long, tormenting series of innuendos and waggling eyebrows. I pasted a smile on my face, acted like this was the best time I'd ever had, and prayed that the meal would get over with quickly so we could be alone, where I could get the information I needed and be on my way.

Finally, we were done. Stefan pushed away from the table, tossing his napkin onto his crème brûlée ramekin. "Bill my room," he said curtly to the waiter, gazing at me instead of talking to him. It was different from the way Dru had dismissed the waiter at Lujo. When Dru had done it, it had been a powerful, sexy move. When Stefan did it, it was a rude display of inner powerlessness.

"Are you ready, my little dark rain cloud?" he asked.

"Of course." I slid the knife into my purse and pushed my chair back. *More than you know.*

"You are about to see some extreme atmospheric pressure,"

he said, coming up behind me. Sweat popped out on my forehead instantly, my body ready to hand this evil little jerk his ass in a doggie bag.

Instead, I played along, trying to flirt, which I didn't do well under any circumstance. "Forecast says to take shelter. The system that's moving in could be very dangerous."

He laughed, a low, guilty laugh. "I like that," he whispered. He pulled my chair out and stepped back so I could stand.

Don't hit him, Nikki. Not here. Not now.

He didn't even bother to hold the door open for me when we got to his room. He was too busy kicking off his shoes the moment the door opened. "Bathroom's in there if you have any special props or anything. I didn't request any, but you never know when someone's going to give you a freebie," he said. He unbuckled his belt and untucked his shirt. I was still standing by the door, disbelieving what I was seeing.

Was this how it always was?

A part of me wondered if maybe I should just turn around and go right back out the door, before things got too serious for me to handle.

He gave me a sarcastic look. "Hello? Let's get on with this. I'm not paying for you to stand around looking stupid."

"Sorry," I said. I let the door snap closed behind me, a bumpy, silvery squiggle sound—a jolt of fear and a jolt of excitement all at once. It was do-or-die time. It wouldn't get too serious, because I wouldn't let it. This was my chance.

Just don't kill him, Nikki, I could hear Gunner saying in my ear. *You can come close, though, if you want.* "Nervous, I guess."

"Well, get over it," Stefan said, stretching back—still fully clothed, thank God—on the bed. "I don't have time for first-timer jitters." He closed his eyes, stretching his arms back behind his head. "You bring any Molly with you?"

"Sorry," I said, stalking toward him, stepping out of my shoes as I approached him. I opened my purse and dropped it on the floor next to the bed.

"Should've requested it." He let out a disappointed sigh. "What are you, seventeen?"

"Eighteen," I corrected.

He shook his head slowly. "Girls these days. I hope my daughter has better morals than you."

I tipped my head to one side, flirty, and gave him a patronizing smile. "I doubt that," I said. "Not with a horrendous scumball like you for a dad."

His head whipped up. "Hey, now," he said, actually having the gall to sound offended. "Who the hell do you think you are, talking to me like that? Your boss is going to hear from me about this. I'm one of her best customers. I don't pay to listen—"

I lunged for my purse and grabbed the knife, but I wasn't quick enough. Stefan caught the movement and sprang into action.

"Hey, what do you . . . ," he began, but he didn't finish because he had reached across the bed and grabbed a fistful of my hair.

I let a squeal escape, knife clunking to the floor as both of my hands clawed at his. He pulled me across the bed with much more force than I ever would have guessed a guy his size could muster. I rolled across his body and landed on my back next to him, still struggling to free my hair from his grip. The reality that I was under his control began to seep in, and I flashed back to the feel of Gibson Talley's hand over my mouth, arm around my neck, in the parking lot. Panic set in and wiped all my knowledge away in a haze of gray-black fear. I batted at his hands, legs pressed into the mattress, back arched, unsure how to move.

"Stupid bitch," he wheezed, and before I could get my wits about me at all, he balled his fist and punched me below my right eye.

A flash of neon-green light, throbbing pain. A sting that suggested a cut of bone against thin skin. Nothing I hadn't felt before. Sparring could sometimes get pretty tough.

Something about the feeling brought me back to my senses. I saw Gunner in my mind, warning me to be careful, but also reminding me that I knew what to do. *Just do it.*

With a grunt of rage, I backfisted Stefan right across the bridge of his nose, his glasses crunching into my knuckles, but I didn't care. He howled, and, fast, I backfisted him a second time. This time the crunch was his nose itself, and my hand came back to me bloody.

I rolled, digging my forearm into his to force him to let go of my hair. He did, both hands flying to his gushing face, his words unintelligible as he shouted into his palms.

I didn't want to touch him. Just the sight of him nauseated me. But the knife was on the floor and he was between me and it. I rolled across his body, hit the floor, picked up the knife, and in one fluid movement brought it to the base of his throat.

Just to show him that I didn't appreciate having my hair pulled, I jammed my right knee down into his groin, putting all my weight on it and keeping it there. He coughed, long and throaty, and tried to grab at the knife, so I pinned his forearm to the bed with mine.

"Stop," I said. "If you're smart, you will just stop."

"God," he wailed. The blood poured from his nostrils down the sides of his face.

"Oh, don't be such a baby. It's a broken nose," I said. "But if you touch me with your free hand, this knife is going in."

"What the—what the hell?" he yelled. I could see him consider swatting at me, so I pressed the knife harder into the skin of his neck. He sucked air, his hand going slack at his side. Sweat had joined the blood on his top lip, though it appeared his nose had stopped bleeding some. "Are you going to rob me now, is that it? I thought Hollywood Dreams was careful about white-trash criminals like you. Fine. My wallet is—"

"I don't want your wallet," I said. "I want information."

He blinked, swallowed. "What kind of information?"

"Rainbow. I want information about Rainbow. Who hurt her?" I growled, gripping the knife so tight my hand hurt. "Was it you?"

"I don't understand," he blubbered, his stubbly neck jiggling. "Is this part of your shtick? I don't like it."

"This is not shtick," I said, breathing heavily, half out of exertion and half out of adrenaline over finally getting to pin this freak down. "There is going to be no shtick. I'm not an escort, and this is the closest you will ever get to me." Colors burst around me, taking on the fireworks quality of adrenaline but with a kaleidoscope of hues—gold, neon green, ragemonster red. Had I not been so in the moment, I might have been distracted, even dazzled, by them. "Someone hurt Rainbow, and I think you know who it was."

"Which one? There were two," he said.

"What do you mean there were two?"

"An older one and a younger one," he said. "They looked like twins. Sisters, at least."

Half sister, my brain nagged. Hadn't I had the same thought not that long ago, that Luna could have been Peyton's twin?

"The older one. The one who's almost dead now," I said.

He shook his head. A bead of sweat dripped down toward his ear. "I don't know what you're talking about. And that's just a table knife."

"You knew her. You're a regular here, so you knew her. You were with her. Did you beat her up? Did you decide to play rough and go too far?" I dug the knife deeper into his neck, puckering the skin around the rounded tip. "And don't you dare doubt my ability to pop your jugular with this table knife."

"I never slept with her," he said. "I never got the chance to."

"I don't believe you." I pushed harder, and his face pinched with pain and rage. Three lambent flashes of green—*pop, pop, pop*. I blinked them away.

"The little bitch wouldn't put out, okay? I tried, but she got all sloppy drunk and started in on some sob story about how she was supposed to be an actress and she refused to whore herself to get there. You're hurting me!" I dug my knee into his groin.

"I'm trying to hurt you, you idiot. Keep talking."

He made a face. "Jesus, you smoke, don't you? I can smell it in your hair. I told them no smokers."

I punched his ribs. He made a hissing noise. "I said keep talking."

"Okay. Okay. I tried to at least get dinner out of the deal, but the bitch got into some daddy bullshit and then walked out on me. I asked for a refund, and they told me they'd send me someone else next time, on the house. I thought it was a joke, because the next time this other blond chick shows up, and she's clearly trying to look exactly like the first one. She even sounds just like her. And she called herself Rainbow, like I wouldn't notice the difference. But she had Molly at a discount, so I went with it. That's all I know."

"She sold you Molly?"

He swallowed miserably. "Could you let up on the knife? Usually I can get it from Brigitte, but Brigitte said they were out, and this new Rainbow chick showed up with it and was selling it at a good price. Every time I saw her after that, she sold it to me cheap. Said she had a big plan."

Suddenly it all made sense. *Double Rainbow*, the photo had been titled. The other photo that depicted a drug deal with Luna's hand. Peyton had known Luna was pretending to be her. She was trying to lead me to her.

But Stefan had said she had some sort of *big plan*. What was Luna's big plan?

"Can you let up on the knife now, please?" he asked angrily.

I squinted at him. "And that's all you know about her?"

He nodded as best he could without poking himself. "I swear."

"Did she ever tell you her real name?"

He thought, his eyes roving wildly, and I could see panic budding in him again. I wasn't sure how much longer I had until he began to fight me again. "Something that starts with a P. Paige? Peggy?"

"Peyton?" I interrupted.

"Yeah. That's it." He picked up his hand and waved it in the air weakly. "And she had a little charm on her pinkie finger."

Luna. Yet she'd told him her name was Peyton. She looked and sounded just like her, used the same call name, and sold him stolen Molly. Was she trying to set up Peyton?

Stefan started to buck underneath me, and I had to push my weight into him harder than ever. "Stop moving."

He let his head flop back onto the bed. "I've told you everything, okay? I bought a couple of whores and some Molly, but I didn't beat anyone up."

I shook my head in confusion. "Wait. You said the first Rainbow talked about daddy bullshit. What did you mean?"

"Jesus, you are relentless," he hissed, a bead of spittle flying off his lips and landing on my chest. I resisted the urge to wipe it away. But the revulsion of it being there made me loosen my grip a little, giving him a chance to take a deep breath. "It apparently really bothered the poor little whore that Daddy is a client."

Of course. The photo of the man coming through the front door of Hollywood Dreams. The well-shined shoe.

I'd seen it before. On Bill Hollis the day he picked up Dru from the police station. No wonder his license plate said *DREAMS*. He was a regular. How did a man hire girls from the same place where his daughter worked as an escort? Or did he not know? I pulled the knife away from Stefan's throat but kept my knee in his groin to keep him in place.

"I don't know why, though," he said, huffing and clawing at the space where the knife had just been. "With her mom being the madam. Where the hell did she think the two of them met?"

"Whoa, back up a minute," I said. "What do you mean her mom being the madam here?"

He rolled his eyes. "Get your knee off my balls."

"No."

"Vanessa is Rainbow's mom, you stupid bitch, now get off me!"

There was a knock at the door, and both of us looked toward it. I shook my head at him. "You make a noise and I'll kill," I whispered. I readjusted my grip on the knife to show I meant business, even though I was trembling, my insides feeling like liquid at the very thought of doing anything more than I'd already done.

"I've told you everything I know," he whispered back, foam collecting on his teeth.

There was another knock, and we both froze.

"I'll say you tried to rape me and it was self-defense," I warned.

"I hired you. It's not rape if I hired you."

"Also illegal, dumbass," I said. "Just be quiet and they'll go aw—"

A third knock interrupted me. And then a familiar voice from the other side of the door. "Nikki? It's Detective Martinez. You in there?"

Stefan's eyes got big and alarmed. "You brought the fucking cops here?"

I shook my head, shushing him. "He must have followed me here."

Holy Christ, what had I walked into?

"He followed you? Jesus, are you a cop? You have to tell me if I ask you directly, right?"

There was another knock.

"Technically, I never paid you," Stefan said. "Nothing ever happened."

I backed off him. "Okay," I said, smoothing the front of my dress, which had gotten wrenched up into a wad during the scuffle. "No, I'm not a . . . Just shut up, would you?"

"Nikki? Answer the door."

Stefan scrambled to his feet much faster than I ever would have guessed he could move. His broken glasses hung askew on his face, but he was too busy tucking in his polo and fumbling with his belt to notice. "You're going to turn me in to the police. I should've known not to trust you. I saw it on you the moment you walked in. Prism, my ass. I have a family. A family, damn it."

"Chill out," I said. I picked up my purse and headed for the door, smoothing my hair and wiping the mist of blood off my chest on the way. "I'm going to take care of this. Trust me, if he was here with other cops, they would have busted in by now."

I bent to pick up my shoes on the way to the door. I couldn't even fathom putting them back on, especially not as sweaty as I was feeling at the moment.

"You'll ruin my children's lives," Stefan was saying, as if he hadn't heard me speak a word.

"Shut up," I snapped, and he did.

I opened the door and stepped through it before Chris Martinez's angled neck could see Stefan inside.

"What's going on in there?" He scanned my face with worried eyes. "Are you okay? You're bleeding. Did someone hit you?"

"Is this a good use of taxpayer money?" I pushed past him and headed toward the elevators.

"I asked you a question," he said as he followed me down the quiet hotel hallway. "What happened in there? Are you okay?"

I turned and faced him. "Why?"

He cocked his head to one side. "Is that a real question?"

I turned my palms up, my shoes hanging off the fingertips of one hand. "Yeah, actually, it is. Why do you care so much? I've told you everything I know. I haven't done anything wrong. You said I was free to go, but you keep showing up in my life. From what I can tell, being followed by you isn't exactly freedom. I didn't realize the police were so into harassment."

"I'm not following you as a cop. I'm following you as someone who is interested in seeing you not get killed." He gestured toward Stefan's door. "What was going on in there?"

"Absolutely nothing," I said.

He shook his head. "Not true." He got a serious look on his face, his cheeks even reddening a little bit. He scratched the back of his neck, nervous. I could practically smell the dark lemon radiating off him. "You haven't—you're not—"

I grinned. "Having sex? It's okay, you can say it. And no, everything but the shoes stayed on."

"I could arrest you. Prostitution is illegal in this state," he said.

"Not a penny changed hands," I said. "And no sex. So what about this was prostitution? I was just having a conversation, that's all."

He stepped closer to me, dropped his voice. "Then this was about Peyton Hollis, wasn't it?" I didn't answer. "Come on, Nikki, help me out here."

"Miss Kill," I reminded him. He planted his hands on his hips and lifted his head, tilting his chin to the ceiling in exasperation.

"Right."

I pushed the elevator button with my free hand. "Yes," I said. "It was."

"And?"

"And what?"

"And what do you know?" He stepped toward me, whispering. How many times had Dad asked the police that very question over the years? *What do you know, what do you know, what do you know?* And never, not once, did they know anything.

"I don't know who did it," I said sourly.

He shifted, put his hands on his hips, and once again I noticed his badge. So very truth, justice, and the American way. He was a good cop. He deserved better than I was giving him.

So why was he following me? I thought the answer might have been the bite to his bottom lip outside the *dojang*. It might have been the way his voice quavered when he said he wouldn't stand back and watch something happen to me.

"What did you do?" I asked.

He gave me a quizzical look.

"You're a very by-the-book kind of guy, Detective Martinez. But you're breaking all kinds of rules here. I think you're hiding something. You keep letting me get by with stuff you shouldn't." I stepped closer to him. "This is personal, isn't it? Tell me, Detective, is there a little bit of trouble in your golden past?"

His eyes narrowed, got serious. "We're not talking about me," he said.

I laughed, just as the elevator arrived and the doors opened. I took two more steps toward him, so close I could smell his aftershave. "Well, I'll tell you what. You spill your secrets, and I'll spill mine." I tugged his collar to straighten it. He followed my fingers with his eyes, the intensity never fading. I leaned close to whisper in his ear. "In the meantime, step off."

I turned and got into the elevator, leaving him in the hallway. Just as the doors began to slide shut, I pressed the button to keep them open. "Oh, and Detective?" His eyes flicked up to meet mine, but he didn't say a word. "The guy in that room? Total john. Figure out who he's buying from, and you'll know some of what I know. You might even find your connection to Arrigo Basile." The doors began to slide shut again. I waited until they were almost closed, smiled big, and waved. "You're welcome."

I WAS WAY too ramped up by my run-in with Stefan to go home. I had so many questions and so few answers. Peyton was an escort, but she didn't want to be. Luna had been pretending to be her, had been selling Molly, and, judging from the photo I'd found in the suitcase, Peyton knew it. Brigitte had said Vanessa had been having "things, pharmaceutical enhancements" go missing from her office, and Stefan had been certain that Peyton's mother was the madam of the business, which would mean Vanessa Hollis had a big secret nobody knew about. Peyton's situation was starting to look a whole lot more complicated than just a few song lyrics and a haircut and tattoo.

Chris Martinez was busy at the hotel, which left me safe to go wherever I wanted without being tailed. I headed toward where I thought some of the answers I needed might be: Hollywood Dreams.

The front door had been left unlocked, so I walked right up the stairs, leaving the high heels in my car. To my surprise, the door to Hollywood Dreams was unlocked, too, but the front office was dark, the only light coming from Vanessa's office. I crept inside and slowly made my way down the short hall. If I could hide under Brigitte's desk, maybe I could wait out whoever was in here. But just as I tiptoed into the office, a file drawer slid closed with a bang. I saw movement by Brigitte's desk. I gasped.

"Hello?" a voice said. I squinted into the darkness. It was Vanessa Hollis. "Who's there?"

"Sorry," I said, letting out a breathy laugh, feeling the tingle of adrenaline rush through my veins. "You startled me."

She came around the desk, her blond hair a fluffy halo around her head. She wore painted-on leggings and a puffy-sleeved sweater that showed her midriff.

"Who are you?" she asked. "I recognize you, don't I?"

"I don't think so," I lied, hoping she wouldn't put it together that I'd been at the hospital. "I'm Prism. I just started here."

"Prism? We have to do something about that. Sounds like a common hooker. Did Brigitte give you that name? I'll have a chat with her."

"No, I came up with it on my own," I said. "Sorry. Maybe Stormcloud is better?" There was a part of me, though, that was incredulous that the owner of an escort service who also sold "pharmaceutical enhancements" to her clients was worried about one of her escorts having a "common hooker" name.

"Well, Brigitte is gone for the day, so why are you here, Prism?" Vanessa said. "I don't have all the time in the world." She checked her watch. "I've got somewhere to be."

"Of course," I said, fantasizing for just a moment about roundhousing her to the back of the head. "I just forgot where I was supposed to meet Stefan tonight."

Her eyes widened as she looked me up and down. "You have a date?"

I nodded, shifting, uncomfortable. "With Stefan."

"You're a bit of a mess for a date, wouldn't you say,

Prism?" Again she scanned me. "Your dress is ripped, your makeup is smeared, you're bleeding. And where are your shoes?"

My hand automatically went to the cut under my eye. I'd tried to wipe myself up as best as I could while sitting in a dark car, but apparently I hadn't done a great job of it. "The date's later," I said. "I'm going home to clean up first. I . . . fell."

She gave me one last long stare. Her expression said she didn't believe a word of what I was saying, but she checked her watch again and seemed to shake off her doubt. Apparently her plans were more important than trying to get the truth out of a new hire. "Brigitte should have written the address down for you," she said.

"I lost it. Sorry."

She blew out a gust of air and marched to Brigitte's desk, acting very put-out. "We can't hold your hand, you know," she said. "You've got to learn to figure this stuff out for yourself. And present yourself like someone with class. Stefan is one of our best clients. If you didn't show up, I would be very angry."

"Understood," I said.

She searched through several papers, scribbled the hotel address on a Post-it note, and handed it to me. "You're late," she said. "Lucky for you, Stefan is easygoing." She hooked her finger in the neckline of my dress and tugged it downward.

"A little word of advice, Prism. You can't expect to get ahead in this world if you hide your assets. Show them off. Use them to your advantage. I don't care if a man is sixteen or a hundred and sixteen, he will do things for a peek at a little skin. He will do just about anything if he thinks he can own it. I didn't get my beach house in Monaco by wearing turtlenecks, if you get my drift."

"Okay. Thanks," I said, resisting the urge to pull the neckline of my dress back up. Up close, Vanessa was a lot more calculated than she'd seemed in the hospital. "And sorry again."

She waved me off, leafing through some papers and then heading to her office.

I waited until she sat at her desk, then slipped over, grabbed the keys off the hook on the file cabinet, and hurried out.

It was another hour before she left the office, toddling on impossibly high heels toward a parking garage nearby. I watched from my car, slouched low in the seat, so she didn't see me.

I waited until the same SUV I'd seen at their house pulled out of the parking garage, and then got out of my car and ran across the street toward the nondescript office door, carrying the keys in my hand.

I didn't know what I was looking for, but I knew it was in Vanessa's office. I let myself in, using my phone flashlight instead of turning on the overhead light, just in case.

Unlike Brigitte's desk, Vanessa's was carefully organized, her keepsakes dusted and placed just so. The only paperwork on her desk were scraps filled with addresses and phone numbers, no names, nothing identifying. Just jumbles of oranges and pinks and blues and greens that made it hard for me to concentrate. I opened a desk drawer and found a cache of pens. Another desk drawer was completely empty. And a third was locked. Undoubtedly where she kept her Molly.

No photos of her family. Nothing that indicated she had a daughter in the hospital, or even a daughter at all. It was like a showroom office—the look of habitation without actual habitation.

There was a closet on the other side of the room, and in a last-ditch effort to find something, I went to it. It yawned open, a black chasm, and when I shone my light into it, I found a wardrobe of skimpy clothes, the kind that I was wearing right now. Some fetish costumes. A ton of shoes. And . . .

I paused, my light freezing on something black and smooth, tucked behind a pair of patent-leather boots. A locked box.

I reached inside and grabbed it, kneeling, and shone the light on it. Of course, it was locked, but this was an easy lock to break. I used a shoe to pry the lock open.

Inside were papers. Lease agreement for the address of

the service, paid in cash. Bank account papers, written in a different language.

And, at the bottom, two birth certificates. I picked up the top one and studied it in the light of my phone.

Peyton Harlow Hollis. I ran my fingers over the raised seal and studied the details of her birth, immediately going back to the day Dad had brought home Mom's death certificate.

Can I have a copy? I'd asked him.

Why?

I'd run my fingers over the raised seal, just as I was doing now. *Because it's the only way I'll know it's real,* I'd said.

He'd never given me one. And it turned out I didn't need it anyway. The reality of Mom's death was proven to me over and over again, every time I needed her and she wasn't there.

I dropped Peyton's certificate back in the box and kept going. Beneath her certificate was Dru's. It looked the same. But something about them was off. Something about the font didn't match all the way through.

I dug through the box some more and found out why. There, beneath credit card statements from 2006, were two more birth certificates for Dru and Peyton. Only these had been doctored.

The names of the parents had been whited out.

21

ON MONDAY MORNING, I waited for Luna outside the side doors of the school, which were just across from where most of the sophomores parked, but also just happened to be a secluded place where the smokers could light up a quick one before diving into their stressful school day. I stood with my back pressed against the wall, the threads on my jacket catching against the rough brick. I didn't like brick—it reminded me of shame, and sometimes anger. I cupped a lit cigarette in my palm by my side, every so often stealing a drag.

There was a deep gouge in the toe of one of my Chucks from rolling around on the gravel with Gibson Talley, and there was a cut under my right eye from where Stefan's fist had met it. My entire cheek was tender and swollen, and the back of my head ached where the little runt had grabbed my hair. Even the palm of my right hand felt sore from gripping the knife so tightly. And I was terrified that someone at Hollywood Dreams would notice that all four of Peyton's and Dru's birth certificates had been removed.

It had been a rough few days.

Sophomores poured from their cars and streamed into the school, most of them chattering in that annoying sophomore way, without even noticing me standing there. I didn't care. I was there for one person and one person only.

Just when it seemed like Luna wouldn't show, her mystic-brown Mercedes screeched into the lot and squealed into a parking space. A sixteenth birthday gift from Daddy, no doubt. Or maybe a hush gift. *I'll buy you a Mercedes, darling, and you don't tell the world about our little family business, okay?*

Luna got out of the car, giggling and talking over two of her friends, who had also piled out of the car. They moved slowly, as if they were heading to a social gathering rather than school. I watched as other girls, standing by their ordinary cars or getting off the school bus, stood and watched her. Luna was the next Peyton Hollis. The next reigning royalty of her high school class. All hail Queen Hollis the Second.

Only, unlike Peyton, whose coolness was her popularity,

Luna was aggressively unlikable to those she didn't care for. There was something almost reptilian about the way she moved through her world. Something sideways about the way her eyes worked, as if she was always looking over her shoulder, over your shoulder. As if she was always on the make. Predatory. Something about her made me think of the rough grayish green of crocodiles, the cold scaly gunmetal of snakes.

They reached the alcove, a little hurricane of decibel-shattering snark, one of them pulling open the door without so much as a nod toward me. Luna's two friends slipped through, and Luna started to follow. I pushed away from the wall.

"Hey, Rainbow," I said. She didn't hear me, so I repeated myself, louder. "Hey, Rainbow."

Luna turned, the smile on her face changing to a look of bemused surprise. She seemed to take me in slowly, as if she knew she'd seen me somewhere before but couldn't quite place who I was. Then it dawned on her. "Excuse me?" she asked, all well-bred innocence and politeness. "What did you say?"

"That's who you are, right? Rainbow?" I didn't return her smile. "Well, the second Rainbow, anyway."

She seemed torn by the gravitational pull of her friends, who had now turned and were waiting for her a few steps down the hallway.

"I'll see you in class," she told the girls, waving them on. She let the door close. She dropped all pretense of giggly sophomore as she faced me full-on. "Who told you?"

"Who said anyone had to?" I said.

She clenched her teeth. "I don't know what you're talking about."

"That's not what Stefan says," I said. She narrowed her eyes, and I could almost see her turning over my words in her head, trying to suss out if I really knew what I was talking about or if I was bluffing. "What do you want?" she asked. "Money, is that it? Predictable. I don't have any on me now, but I can get some." She had the gall to look weary of the process. "How much do you want?"

"I'm not after your money. Not everyone works like that, Luna. And you know exactly what I want. I want to know who hurt Peyton."

She touched her fingertips to her chest, her eyes opening wide and innocent. "And you think I know?"

I rolled my eyes. "You're a terrible actress. Stefan told me a lot of things. I can sink you and your entire family with a single phone call. First, I'll tell Mommy that you're the one who's been stealing drugs from her office and selling them right under her nose. She'll love that. And then I'll talk to my friend Detective Chris Martinez at the police department. I'll let him know all about the family business, and dear old Daddy's favorite pastime, which appears to be paying barely of-age girls for sex. Wow, won't that change the way the world looks at him when the media gets ahold of it? I know all about you, Luna. You've been doubling as Peyton, selling drugs as her, meeting up with clients as her. I just don't know why. What were you setting her up for? And I don't know what it has to do with her lying in a hospital bed clinging to life right now. But I promise you I will figure it out."

"You don't have any proof of anything," she said. "You're just a jealous, delusional girl, out to extort a rich family, who, by the way, is grieving their daughter's assault. We will make sure everyone knows that. What do you think the media will do to you, after you stalked and terrorized Peyton's sister?"

I nodded thoughtfully, flipped my cigarette to the ground, and stepped on it. I let the last drag flow through my nostrils. Luna was a lot of things, but *grieving* didn't really strike me as one of them. Neither did *terrorized*. If Luna wasn't off-putting enough on her own, her lack of concern for Peyton made her downright ugly. "If you want to risk it . . ." I started to walk toward the parking lot.

She grabbed my sleeve. "Fine. I'll tell you. But you're not going to like it." She had a maniacal look about her—feverish, desperate. "Yes, I've been taking the Molly and selling it to my clients. But it's not like my mother is missing it, and she's the one who got them hooked in the first place. I was trying to help Peyton. She wanted out. I thought I could get her fired if our mother found out she was stealing." She bared her teeth. "But it never got to that point, because of what happened to her. As for who beat up Peyton . . . Dru did it."

I must have looked shocked, because she picked up steam, nodding. She held her fingers to her ear as if she were holding a phone. "Hello, tips hotline?" she said in a squeaky voice thickly laced with an East Coast accent, sounding nothing at all like Luna Fairchild. "That girl who got beat up in the school parking lot? I overheard a guy telling someone that she was his sister, and that he beat her up. Yeah, he said he wanted to kill her, but it didn't work and he was worried he was gonna get caught. Yeah, I don't know why, but you should check him out." She pretended to hang up the phone, a smug look on her face.

"You set Dru up?" I asked. "Why?"

"No, I turned him in. There's a difference," she said. "He did it. He found out about the escort service, and he was so pissed he wanted her out. He thought she was the one selling Vanessa's precious Molly, which is actually his good buddy Rigo's precious Molly. He found out she was sleeping with turds like fat Stefan. So he went after her. Dru is vindictive and dangerous, Nikki, and you need to stay away. I would have warned you right up front, but you got all up in our business and messed up everything."

"I don't believe you," I said. But the truth was, at this point, I had no clue who to believe.

"Why would I lie?" She flipped her hair over one shoulder, haughty, daring. "He's my brother."

"*Half* brother," I reminded her.

"Aw, it's cute how well you know the family tree," she said, giving a sweet smile, her eyes narrowed in a glare. Again, I was reminded of something reptilian.

"What is that even supposed to mean?"

She shrugged. "Nothing. But you may want to be careful about how far up in our family tree you climb. You may not like what branches will hit you right in the face."

"Is that a threat?" I felt my fists clench and stuffed them into my jacket pockets to keep myself from ripping out all her hair right there in the sophomore parking lot.

She stepped right up to me, so close I could smell wintergreen gum on her breath. "Sister, that's a promise," she said. "You're going to want to leave me alone." She turned and pulled open the door, then sashayed into the school without so much as a look back.

I had come into this meeting certain that I would have the upper hand. Certain that I would be able to tell her what I knew, and that she would buckle. Instead, she'd fed me a mouthful of bullshit about Dru and turned the tables around to threaten me. Not at all what I'd expected.

Luna Fairchild wasn't the delicate little innocent she made herself out to be.

Luna Fairchild was scary.

I decided that I wasn't going to walk through the same hallway that she just had. One, it was full of obnoxious sophomores, but two, I didn't want Luna to have the impression that I was going to follow her anywhere. I hoped that despite her threats and bravado, she was maybe the tiniest bit intimidated by me. That she was thinking Nikki Kill was scary.

I walked through the grass toward the front of the building, where the buses dropped off and the doorway bottlenecked with kids who didn't want to go inside. I wished I could stay back at the side doors and sneak another cigarette, but there wasn't time. I needed to get to class.

The first four hours of school were pretty much torture. My eyes swam with colors every time I entered a room, most of them bringing back to mind something to do with Peyton's attack. Turquoise: Luna's pinkie charm. Glitzy cherrybomb: Rainbow. Soft orange: SOS. Crimson, crimson, crimson. I was completely lost from having skipped so much, and I couldn't concentrate on anything.

Mrs. Lee called me to her desk during study hall, where I was busy rubbing my temples miserably, my eyes squeezed shut against the world.

I approached her desk in a slump.

"Everything okay?" she whispered. A kid in the front row looked up, and then quickly down again, but I could tell from the cast of his eyes that he was just trying to look like he wasn't listening. I recognized him as someone I'd seen in Peyton's orbit.

"Yeah. Fine," I lied.

She tilted her head to the side, scrutinizing me. "You sure? You look like you're in pain over there. Do you need to see the nurse?"

"No, I'm good."

She pointed to her computer screen, which was now dark, in sleep mode. "I was noticing that you're having some attendance issues."

Nice. She didn't notice when I wasn't here, but the minute the freak was back, she suddenly wanted to get all up in my life. "Sorry."

"You know, Nikki," she said, lowering her voice, "study hall is a gift to someone on academic probation. I want you to succeed. But there's only so much I can do. I can't help you graduate if you don't show up."

"I know," I said, mostly tuning her out.

She leaned over so her temple was in the palm of her hand, her elbow propped up on her desk—the universal teacher I-care pose. I wanted to throw up. "I've heard that your friend Peyton was in a pretty bad accident," she said.

I gaped at her. "My friend?" I asked. "Where did you hear that?"

She looked confused by the question. "I may be a teacher,

but I do know some things. Have you been spending a lot of time at the hospital?"

"I have homework to finish," I said, turning away.

"I think it's really loyal of you to be by your friend's side," she said at my back.

I noticed that several faces were pointed toward me now. And the ones that weren't were trying to look like they weren't listening, just like the boy in the front row was doing. I whirled to face her, and then positioned myself so I was talking to the whole class. "Look, I never met Peyton Hollis before the attack, and any of you who hung out with her already knew that. So I don't know why all of a sudden everyone is talking about me, but I can assure you there is nothing to talk about. Okay?"

"Not what Vee says," a girl in the back murmured.

"Excuse me?" I asked, craning my neck to look at her. I didn't know her, but recognized her as one of Viral Fanfare's many groupies.

She at least had the decency to look embarrassed about being overheard. "Just that I heard you jumped the Viral Fanfare guitarist and beat the crap out of him with a tire iron."

I laughed incredulously. "A tire iron? Is that what he's telling people?"

"All right, everyone, we should be working," Mrs. Lee said.

The class shuffled uncomfortably and bent their faces to their books. I made my way back to my desk, feeling much better now that I knew I clearly no longer had Gibson Talley to worry about. He was definitely afraid of me and embarrassed about what I could do to him. I would have almost felt bad for the guy if he hadn't jumped me first. A tire iron. Ha.

I slid into my desk, feeling pretty proud of myself, and got comfortable. I shut my eyes and reopened them, thinking maybe I could get into reading a little, with that much, at least, off my mind. But as soon as I opened my eyes again, the cheerleader across the aisle leaned over toward me. Her face was split in a giddy smile.

"So, is it true?" she asked.

"Is what true?"

"Are you really dating Dru Hollis? You know, he dated my older sister for a couple of weeks. He is so hot. I never thought he would go for someone younger than him. According to my sister, he likes real women." She leaned back and crossed her legs, her posture so filled with self-importance it sickened me. Everyone wanting a piece of Hollis to rub off on them. And Luna so happy to provide it.

Fortunately, the bell rang, and I didn't have to answer her. I gathered my things and blew out of class before anyone else, cruising through the mostly empty halls before the classroom doors had even been opened.

I had fifth-period lunch shift.

Just enough time to get to the hospital and back.

Jones intercepted me halfway across the parking lot.

"Going out for lunch?" he called as he cut through the line of cars to get to me.

"Yep."

"Want some company? I could go for some pizza."

I kept walking, digging my keys out of my jacket pocket at the same time. "I don't want pizza."

"I'll eat a burger," he said. "Listen, I'm sorry about all those things I said the other day. I was being territorial. Let me make it up to you. Where are you going?"

I sighed. "Jones. Don't make me tell you where I'm going."

His face fell, and then hardened. "Right," he said. "Have fun, then." He walked briskly away from the car, and for a fraction of a second, I felt bad.

Even though it was fall and the temperature outside was pretty mild, it was toasty inside my car when I slid in. But I welcomed the warmth, not realizing until it began to seep into my skin how chilled my fingers and toes were. Like the freezing-out from the others had somehow wormed its way into me. *Well, screw them,* I thought. They could judge all they wanted. They could accuse me of whatever they wanted. They could talk. I had work to do.

I fired up my engine and drove straight to the hospital.

■ ■ ■

DRU WAS SITTING by Peyton's bedside. I didn't realize until I was in the room that I'd expected to see him there.

He looked up when I came in. His face was weary but brightened with a smile as soon as he saw me.

"Hey," he whispered, getting up. He hadn't shaved, his stubble reminding me a little of Chris Martinez. I felt choked with violet and yellow and gray shards flying at me in a confusing blast. Who was Dru, really, and who was I when I was with him?

"Hey."

He came around the bed and, with no hesitation, scooped his arm around my waist and pulled me into him. His arm was strong and warm against my back, and while it still felt weird to be doing this at Peyton's bedside, it felt comfortable now somehow, blasting the shards away. Like I belonged there, in the crook of his arm. He leaned in and kissed me, both of us swaying a bit, my back arched over his forearm.

"Hey," he said again when he was done, his lips still close enough to tickle mine when they moved. He relaxed his arm so that I lowered myself off my toes. "I wasn't expecting you yet." He looked at his watch. "Isn't school still on?"

"Technically," I said. "But it's lunch shift, and I wanted to see Peyton."

His arm slipped around me again, and he pulled my hips to meet his. "I think you meant you wanted to see me."

"You, too," I said. "But I did come to see her. How's she doing?"

He released me and went back to his chair, shaking his head. "No change. I thought maybe she fluttered her eyelids earlier, but I guess I was wrong. Maybe I was wanting it too much."

I glanced at the machines behind her bed, hoping that maybe he had seen movement and she had taken a turn for the better. But the crimson still bled from the readouts. *My mom's arm, flung sideways in a pool of her own blood, the numbers on her watch pulsing slower and slower . . .* I squeezed my eyes shut and concentrated on Peyton's face when I opened them again.

"So where have you been?" Dru asked. "I tried to call you last night."

I had decided that I wouldn't tell Dru about where I'd been. I had gone back and forth with it in my mind. I didn't know how much of what Luna said was true. Maybe he knew about the business, about Peyton, and was keeping it a secret from me out of embarrassment. Or maybe she was lying and he knew nothing. I had suspicions, but no proof that his mom's business was directly related to Peyton's attack. What right did I have to yank his family skeletons out of their closets?

But then there was the Luna problem. I wondered if Dru knew that she was an escort. A master at imitating people. A drug dealer. I wondered if anyone in the family knew. And I especially wondered if he knew that she had turned him in.

But, again, no proof. Not yet. Just a hunch, some cryptic information from a john, and a threat that Luna would undoubtedly deny until the day she died if I were to out her. Oh, and my synesthesia. I was not about to open that can of worms. Not with Dru.

"Nowhere," I said. "I was tired. I went to bed."

Dru cocked his head to one side disbelievingly. "Nikki. You have a black eye and a cut on your cheek. You didn't get that in bed."

I touched my cheek tenderly. It still hurt like hell, and just touching it reminded me of that disgusting slug Stefan. I wanted to jack his nose again, watch the blood spurt, just for fun.

"Oh," I said. "The *dojang.* Sparring got a little out of hand, I guess. No big deal. I've been hit harder."

He stared at me for a moment longer, and I could see the wheels turning inside his head. Mint-green clouds above us. He was trying to decide if he should believe me. I set my jaw and stared at him until I'd pushed the clouds away. Eventually he turned his eyes back to Peyton.

There was a rustle of movement in the doorway. "Oh, gosh, what a surprise," a familiar voice said. I turned just in time to see Luna coming into the room, carrying a giant stuffed bear. "The two lovebirds getting their mating dance on at my sister's deathbed. How very white-trash romance of you."

Dru's eyes hardened. "Don't be gross, Luna."

She sat the bear in the other visitor's chair and brushed her hands off, her Cartier bracelets clinking together with the movement. "I'm not the one using Peyton's hospital room for a motel room. Talk about gross. Ghoul."

"What do you want?" Dru asked in a tired voice.

Luna slipped me a sideways glance. She wanted to send a message that she was watching, I knew. She wanted to ferret out what I had told him. But of course Dru knew none of this. She pinned a brilliant, very whitened, smile to her face.

"I just want to see how my sister is doing," she said. She walked over to Peyton and stroked her hair, pushing wisps of it behind Peyton's ears. She even leaned in and kissed Peyton on the cheek. It might have been tender and sweet had it not been Luna. "She looks god-awful," she said, and while she said it in a concerned voice, I could hear the cattiness beneath. The playacting. Damn, Luna was one hell of an actress.

"I should go," I said, pointing toward the door. "I should get back to school."

"Already?" Dru asked, but at the same time, Luna, who was still looking down at her sister, said, "Yes, you should."

"What the hell, Luna?" Dru said, but I had turned to leave, and I let it go. Let them have their family squabble. If

I got too in the middle of it, I would spill what I knew.

It was a good time for me to leave anyway. Lunch shift was long over, and already I was late to sixth period. Not that I cared much about Shakespeare or whatever the hell we were learning in that stupid class, and at least I was going back, which was better than I usually managed.

I hurried through the hospital, my stomach rumbling from missing lunch, and headed toward the parking lot. I unlocked my car, got inside, started to put my key in the ignition, and stopped cold. There was a Post-it note stuck to the ignition.

I pulled it off.

Don't ever doubt where and how I can get to you, it said, the bumpy gray-and-black words undulating on the pink scrap of paper.

Luna had been in my car. My locked car. How had she done that?

Clearly, Luna was out to prove to me that her threat was not idle. She could get to me. And she would, if that was what she needed to do to protect herself. Luna did not want to be found out. And she was willing to go to pretty great lengths to keep it that way.

I balled up the paper and tossed it backward out the window so that it came to a landing out in the center of the parking lot aisle.

Luna had her messages to send; I had mine.

22

LUNA SHOWED UP pretty much everywhere for the rest of the week, which meant she was willing to go way out of her way to make her point.

One day, I came out of a bathroom stall, and there she was, drawing lipstick on her fragile little mouth—*ragemonster red*—watching me in the mirror as I washed my hands.

"Boo," she said, twisting her half-lipsticked mouth into a grin.

"Fuck off, Luna," I said, ripping off a paper towel and pushing back out into the hallway. I tried to look as if I couldn't care less that she was following me, but on the inside I was a little disturbed. I could kick ass, but there was a difference between Stefan the Slug and Luna Fairchild the ghost.

The next day, she appeared outside my seventh-period classroom, leaning against a locker, not even bothering to hide the hatred in her eyes.

"How does it feel to know someone wants you gone?" she asked as I walked by. I ignored her and had to restrain myself from peering back over my shoulder to make sure she hadn't followed me.

I had gone to my locker and gotten my stuff, and by the time I got to my car, she was already there, sitting on the trunk.

"Get off," I said, again trying to be nonchalant, but feeling a little like I was failing.

"I would love to see you do something about it," she said. She lay back against my rear window, resting her head in her hands.

In my mind, I took two steps toward the car and axe-kicked her right in the gut, so hard it dented the trunk lid beneath her. But in reality, I simply got into my car and started the engine.

She still didn't move.

God, the girl had balls.

I sat for a second in the driver's seat, unsure what to do. Unsure what war I was willing to wage here. Every day, Luna proved herself to be scarier than the day before. But every day she tempted me to be scary, too.

I finally decided to put the car into reverse and ease out

of the space. Luna felt the roll of the wheels and hopped off the trunk, storming around to my side of the car, muscles bulging on the sides of her neck.

"You have no idea who you're messing with!" she screamed, and even though my window was rolled up, I heard her loud and clear.

ON FRIDAY MORNING, there was a pot of coffee already brewed when I came down for breakfast. Dad must have gotten up early. Thank goodness. The stuff with Luna had me more than a little freaked out. The thought of Dad being up and able to protect me while I slept comforted me.

I hadn't talked to Dru since the hospital on Monday afternoon. He'd been in meetings with his lawyers but hoped to be able to get together over the weekend. We had plans to meet up at his apartment like we had before. I tried to wave off the dread of a long school day ahead of me, knowing that the payoff would be to see him again. I could almost smell his skin if I thought about it really hard. I could almost taste the salt of his sweat. I wanted to taste it again, even if part of me was unsure what I was doing with him, and who he really was underneath.

I'd made up for missing Dru by going to see Peyton every night. Of course, there was no change, except most of the flowers had begun to wilt and had been removed. Someone had given Peyton a bath, had cleaned her up a little. I almost thought I saw some makeup on her face again and wondered if Luna had done it. Maybe the girl had one tiny devoted bone in her body.

Still, when I left the hospital, I felt followed. Could almost hear footsteps behind me in the parking lot, starting when I started, stopping when I stopped. Stealth wasn't exactly Luna's style, though, and there was the little matter of Peyton's attacker still being out there. I knew Luna was somehow behind it, but there was no way the girl had done it herself. Peyton was small, but Luna was smaller.

Dad came into the kitchen, smelling like his morning shower, just as I sat down with a muffin and coffee.

"Good morning, Sunshine," he said, opening the fridge. He began assembling a green smoothie, his usual. "You're ready to go early."

I took a bite of the muffin. "Want to get this week over with," I said around the bite. I took a sip of coffee.

"Hear, hear," Dad said, capping the blender and starting it up.

I took another bite, washed it down with the coffee, then dumped some extra sweetener into the cup. Dad must have gotten overexcited with the grounds again—it was bitter. "Listen, I have a shoot in San Diego this weekend. I'm leaving this morning. Will obviously be staying down there. I won't be back until Tuesday. I trust you will still go to school while I'm gone?"

"Would you stay home if I said I wouldn't?"

He poured the smoothie into a cup and sighed. "Come on, Nikki. You know I can't."

"I know," I said, disheartened. Dad wouldn't stay around to parent me even if I desperately needed it. I looked him over—jeans and flip-flops, a V-neck tee that showed off a little tuft of chest hair, tan face with a boyish look to it. He was handsome. Still looked young. Why wouldn't he just settle down already? "Don't worry. I'll go. I want to graduate and get the hell out of there."

"Good, that's the spirit," he said. He came over and planted a kiss on my head. "You sure you're okay?"

I sipped my coffee and took another bite of muffin. I was starting to think neither one of them tasted all that great after all. "Yeah, why?"

Something felt funny about my mouth. My lips. They were numb. My thoughts were slow. And the sunlight streaming in through the kitchen window suddenly seemed very bright, and like it was dripping in through the windows rather than shining through it.

"Just not like you to be up early enough to make yourself coffee before school," he said as he disappeared behind me. "I'll see you Tuesday." I heard the front door shut, struggling all the while to make sense of his words. I knew what I'd just heard was bad but couldn't quite pinpoint why.

"Dad," I said, or maybe I only thought I said it, because I wasn't entirely sure that my mouth was working. The room had begun to spin. "Dad," I tried to say again, but he was gone.

I tried again to stand up, my hands slipping on the table and knocking the coffee to the floor. The plate that the muffin had been on shattered on the tile, but the sound came to me muted and from far away. Panic set in as I tried to move my legs around the chair, catching the chair leg and sending it clattering backward as well.

"Oh, God, help," I said, but my breathing had gotten too shallow to put any effort behind the words.

My heart pounded and my ears rang, but suddenly I felt so weak, so very weak. I vomited down the front of my shirt, felt my legs give out beneath me, and then everything went black.

THE NEXT SENSATION I was aware of was something hitting my face. Repeatedly. Hard. But I couldn't feel any pain. Just the movement, the pressure of being struck.

"Jesus, wake up already. Why the hell won't you wake up? I didn't put that much in it."

I tried to open my eyes, but they felt cemented shut. My head ached, too, as if it was being pried open like a cantaloupe. I groaned.

"It's about time," the voice said, and I felt the sensation of being struck again.

I put all my concentration behind it and finally opened my eyes. Luna Fairchild was bent over me, her blurry face taking up all my vision. Immediately, the panic was back, but my limbs still weren't working. I needed to be ready to fight, but how could I?

"Wakey, wakey," she said, her sweet voice sounding almost shrill as my ears cleared from whatever drugs I'd been given.

"What—" I started, with no clue of how I was planning to finish that question. I closed my eyes again, swallowed. Thirsty. I was so very thirsty.

"Shut up," she said. "You don't get to talk here."

"Where—" The word tumbled out of my mouth. This time the slap hurt, but only in a distant sort of way. I whimpered and brought my hand to my face. It rested against my cheek heavily. Thank God, my arm was working now.

"I said shut up," she said. "Of course you don't know where you are. That's the point. You are not a Hollis, no matter what you might think."

"Who—" I winced before the slap came. In a weird way, the pain was bringing me back to lucidity.

"If you were truly my sister's friend, you would know where you are. You would have been here before. Clearly, my brother doesn't think enough of you to bring you home to meet the family. Which I think is kind of piggish, but whatever floats your skanky little boat."

Home? I was in Hollis Mansion? I turned my head and blinked hard. An ornate bookshelf filled my vision, leather-bound books and gold paperweights and little porcelain doodads lining it, but they were undulating, switching places. A dormant fireplace hunched next to it, the brass tools reflecting the lamplight she'd turned on, looking very serpentine. A rainbow floated above me, twisting, surging, bursting, my colors exploding in confusion.

She slapped me again. I felt the itch to slap her back but knew my limbs would never cooperate for such a movement. "Are you listening?" I turned my eyes to her, managed a nod. "Good. So here's the deal. I've been warning you all week to stay out of my family's business. Have you listened? No. There you are, hanging out at Peyton's bedside, just like two happy little twins. Did you know that people used to think Peyton and I were twins? We looked so much alike. Don't you think that's weird? We're not even related, right? But we were sisters. Sisters."

"*Half* sisters," I corrected, my voice croaky and dry.

Again with the slap, and this time my hands jerked up. I was thinking clearer. I was hearing clearer. I was getting angry. Who the hell was Luna to sneak into my kitchen, drug me, and kidnap me? I'd played along with her game up until now. But I was done letting Luna win.

"I said shut up!" she yelled. "I spent my whole damn life with my useless father in his disgusting little rental house, knowing I belonged somewhere better. Somewhere that lived up to my lifestyle demands. My mother was here, beautiful and rich and perfect and happy, and raising two kids. They had what I deserved, and I did everything I could to get it."

"And now you have it," I said, shocked to hear a full sentence come out of my mouth. I also felt like I could maybe lift my throbbing head now. I could feel my elbows and heels pressing into the floor. Things were coming back into focus.

Her eyes, which I'd once thought of as reptilian, narrowed into reddening slits. "And Peyton was taking it all," she said. "She had to stick her nose into business it didn't belong in. She knew too much, and I was going to lose everything I'd worked for to some ridiculous half sister."

I knew it. Luna wasn't trying to help Peyton get out of the escort business. She was trying to take over her life. "So you attacked her. Why? Because you're selfish?"

Luna's face split into an evil smile, and she laughed out loud. "Aren't you listening at all? Or are you really so stupid you think that this is all about me?" She slapped me again. It burned, and the anger seethed inside my chest. I had to wait for just the right time to pounce. "Peyton Hollis, the perfect, knew too much. And now, guess who else knows too much, Nikki Kill?" She leaned in close. "This is your last warning.

Get out of my business. Leave my brother alone, leave me alone. Or next time I will kill you."

There was the dull thud of a door shutting somewhere in the house, distracting Luna. She looked away, cursing under her breath.

"Luna?" a voice called. A female's voice.

Luna looked torn. She reached down and pressed her palm against my throat, momentarily cutting off my air. I held my breath, readying myself. If she was planning to kill me, she was first going to have to fight me.

"Don't you dare move. I will find you and kill you right now," she said. She pressed down into my throat with one final jolt and got up, leaving the room.

I barely waited for the door to close before I got up. My limbs still felt rubbery, and as if they were moving of their own accord, and my muscles felt stiff and achy. My head pounded and I swooned with dizziness. I held on to a nearby desk—a giant glass-topped boat of a thing that matched Vanessa's desk at Hollywood Dreams—to keep myself steady. I could hear voices—Luna's and the other female's—echoing from elsewhere in the house. Now was my chance to get out of there.

Slowly, my legs building strength beneath me, I made my way to the door. I pushed my ear against it. Nothing. I opened the door a crack and peered out. Nobody.

I crept into the shadows of the endless hallway. At one

end, I could see part of a den, a shiny black baby grand piano the centerpiece, looking spiderish, its fangs clicking at me. I blinked away the hallucination. At the other end, I could see that the hallway emptied out into what was maybe a vestibule. The house was so enormous, I had to blindly choose a way to go. I made my way toward the vestibule, lurching and grunting and sweating.

As I got closer, the voices grew louder. Across the vestibule was an archway to an ornate living room, complete with a brass-decorated wet bar and what looked like an authentic bear rug—which almost appeared to be breathing—sunken two steps below the vestibule. The room was dominated by a cavernous fireplace, the mantel adorned with dozens of brass statues. Beyond that was what looked like a kitchen, the voices emanating from within.

I gave the front door a longing look, noting the enormous chandelier that hung directly over my head, and between the kitchen and living room, on the far end, a spiral staircase that led to an upstairs loft walkway. Instead of turning toward the front door, I went right, drawn by the voices, thanking God for the plush bone-white carpet in the living room, so soft that even in my half-drugged state I walked soundlessly, like walking ankle-deep through snow.

". . . much does she know exactly?" a woman's voice asked.

"Enough. She knows about Hollywood Dreams. She got

hired there, Mother. You really need to fire Brigitte."

A sigh. I snuck closer to the kitchen doorway. "Prism. I knew I'd seen her before. Okay, but that's it? We can handle that."

"I don't know. She's relentless. Always at Peyton's bedside. Sleeping with Dru. She needs to be stopped, Mother."

I took a chance and craned my neck around the corner. Luna stood with Vanessa Hollis in a shadowy corner of the state-of-the-art kitchen, the morning sunlight doused by blackout shades, the stainless steel appliances dully gleaming, the marble countertop looking like wool to my foggy eyes, my still-confused colors smearing across everything I looked at. Luna's back was to me. Her mother, wearing a skintight pink satin minidress and leopard-print heels, leaned backward against the wooden cabinet behind her.

"Luna, we have to be careful about these things. We can't just—"

"Shush, did you hear something?" Luna interrupted.

Quickly, I ducked my head back around the corner as the two of them listened for me.

"You didn't leave her there, did you?" Vanessa asked. "For God's sake, Luna, of course she's going to run."

"She can't run; she's too out of it," Luna said, her voice moving closer to me.

I dropped low and crab-walked behind an easy chair, which dwarfed a corner. I watched between the arm of the chair and a ficus tree branch as the two bolted through the living room toward the hallway. It was now or never.

But there was no way I would make it to the front door without them spotting me from the hallway.

As I clawed my way out from behind the ficus, I was struck with a realization. I was in Peyton's house. She'd lived here until just a few weeks ago. Dru had said she'd barely taken anything when she moved out. She might have left behind a clue. If Luna had her way, I would never step foot into this house again. Now was my chance.

The spiral staircase waved and dipped beneath my feet, making me sick to my stomach as I tried to quickly navigate it. I stopped, gagged, covered my mouth, and kept going, churning my leaden feet as fast as I could until I was on the landing up top. I dropped to my knees and peered through the wooden railing, listening as Luna and Vanessa yelled at each other about where I might be and whose fault it was I was now missing.

I closed my eyes and took two deep breaths to clear my head and my stomach, and then opened them and looked down the hallway ahead of me. It was dotted with doors on either side. I got up and headed toward them, holding my breath and praying for an empty room each time I opened a door. Bathroom, another office, boutique, some room with a giant pink couch, generic bedroom, generic bedroom. And then a bedroom that looked like a tornado had hit it.

I knew right away I'd hit pay dirt when I saw the Forgotten Rebels poster stapled to the far wall. It had been half ripped down and seemed to dance in front of my eyes, but it was still unmistakably punk. Unmistakably Peyton. There were also boxes strewn across her bed and floor and stacked in the closet. These must have been the things Bill Hollis had cleaned out of the apartment.

I stepped into her room and closed the door behind me. I wanted so badly to take my time, to pick through her things methodically, discover her one piece of memorabilia at a time. But I could still hear doors being slammed downstairs, and I felt like I was moving through quicksand. I pushed myself to move faster.

I pulled open boxes and checked the bottoms of each and every dresser drawer. I felt behind the half-affixed poster. I rummaged through books on her bookshelf. Nothing. Nothing, nothing, nothing. Dru had said Peyton had barely taken anything when she moved out, but that wasn't quite the truth. She'd taken everything important. She only left behind the pieces of her life she didn't want anymore.

I was just about to give up and make my way back downstairs, when I saw a rainbow-colored box tossed haphazardly into the bottom of one of the moving boxes in her closet. Somehow I'd missed it when I'd searched the apartment.

Rainbow. *Live in Color.*

I opened it, and there inside were mementos—the kind

of things kids keep from elementary school. Field day ribbons, burnt birthday candles, photos of classmates. Nothing that made any sense to me. I sat on the closet floor and dug through, using every ounce of concentration I had to understand what these things meant. I had been hoping the rainbow was significant, the box a clue, but I guessed I was wrong. It was just a conglomeration of childish crap.

And then my hands landed on something solid on the very bottom, beneath an old, folded Girl Scout vest. I pulled it out.

It was a cell phone.

My heart leaped into my throat. This wasn't a childhood memento—I was sure of it. This was what Peyton had wanted me to find. This was the cell phone everyone had been talking about—the old one she ditched right before moving out. This was why she'd left the rainbow box in her apartment. I pushed the power button, but nothing happened. Dead. I would just have to take it home and—

"There you are," I heard. "I should have known you'd be too stupid to listen to my warning."

My head whipped up to find Luna standing outside the closet door, her legs spread wide, her arms outstretched to come after me. From my vantage point, and to my drugged head, she looked like a giant standing there. A big, bulging, terrifying giant.

I didn't wait for her to make a move. I already felt slow

and stupid. I only hoped my training would kick in automatically. *Take her down and get out,* Gunner's voice said in my head. *Use what you have on hand.*

I only briefly glanced down at Peyton's cell phone—Luna's eyes following mine—and then I wrapped it tight in my fist, reared my arm back, and drove it into the side of her knee with everything I had. She let out a surprised squawk, her leg buckling, and I used the moment to then drive the edge of the phone down onto the arch of her other foot.

She squealed, so loud I felt my eardrums vibrate, and I knew then I had to move. I jumped up, the top of my head catching her chin, and used my arms to push her back like a football player hitting a dummy. She went flying, and I raced out of the room, running for the stairs.

I could hear Vanessa calling out Luna's name from somewhere downstairs, getting closer with every step. I missed one of the stairs and hit my knees, sliding down several steps, but got up again and ran, my shins and ankles crying out with dull pain.

"Luna?" Vanessa's voice was coming from the entryway as I hit the living room floor.

"She's upstairs!" I heard Luna shriek, and I turned just in time to see Vanessa storm into the living room. There was no way I was going to get to the front door, and the last thing I wanted was to have to fight Vanessa. My muscles were already screaming. My hand that had hit Luna's leg and foot throbbed. And my knees ached from falling down the stairs. The rainbow that had swirled my confusion before was now mostly the green of a bruise.

Instead, I turned through the kitchen. Surely, there had to be a door somewhere.

I found it, behind a long blackout shade. A set of French doors that led out to the patio. A pool, and pool house, straight ahead. The door squeaked as I pulled it open. I wasted no time slipping through the tiniest opening I could manage and ran like hell out of there.

I didn't stop until I was two blocks over, which was precisely when I had to bend forward and vomit again.

MY HEAD WAS much clearer by the time I got to Dru's, though my stomach still cramped in on itself over and over again. I burst through the door the moment he opened it.

"She's crazy," I said, panting.

"Whoa, what?" he yelped, shutting the door and trying to catch up with me. I was already pacing his living room, back and forth, back and forth. In the light, his apartment was all bachelor opulence—browns and grays, tribal artwork, a kayak standing on end in one corner.

"Luna. She's insane," I said.

He came to me, a worried crease in his forehead. "What happened this time?"

I stopped pacing. I was hot. So hot the sweat felt like

it was pouring off me. And my mouth was drier than ever. "She drugged me."

He stepped back, looking incredulous. "Drugged you? Are you sure?"

"I'm positive," I said. "I passed out, and when I came to, I was in the mansion. She said it was a warning. She's going to kill me if I don't stay out of your family's business. What is this business, Dru? What is going on that I haven't figured out yet?"

He shrugged, shaking his head, palms up, as if he were as in the dark as I was, but I could sense that familiar wall going up between us, just as I had before. He was shutting down, closing out the parts of himself he didn't want me to see.

"Come on, Dru," I said, throwing my hands up. "You'll sleep with me, but you won't tell me why your crazy sister wants me dead?"

"I don't know why," he said. "Did she say anything else?" He licked his lips, and if it had been anyone else, I would see chipped slate that meant nerves. But Dru wasn't anyone else. Dru was a mystery. Instead I saw slate marbled with turquoise. *Cheater blue,* my mind singsonged. *Cheater blue, cheater blue.*

My stomach cramped in on itself again and I doubled over. He wrapped his arms around me from behind. "You okay?"

I gasped, gulped. "I need to use the bathroom," I said.

"Okay, I'll get you some water."

I headed toward the bathroom, passing Dru's office on the way. Because his apartment was so open, everything was in view. Had it been in a shut room, I might not have even seen a color jump out at me as I walked by. On his desk, tucked half under a paper, maroon and black shiny letters— the color pattern I associated with electronics. I looked back over my shoulder. Dru was still in the kitchen area, an open cabinet door shielding his face. I crept toward the desk, my stomach forgotten.

The desk was littered with papers, books, electronics, and cords. It all looked like the usual household paperwork— travel website printouts, a couple of résumés, some bills. But when I moved an application for a modeling school that had a Post-it stuck to it (*You have an interview Monday. GO TO IT.—V*) the maroon and black blazed out at me.

I picked it up and turned it in my fingers. SanDisk. Just what I thought.

A camera memory card.

Suddenly the ailments from the poisoning were such a distant memory I didn't even feel them anymore. Dru had a camera memory card here. Peyton had a camera memory card missing from her car. Was it the same one?

I was just about to pocket it, take it home, when Dru came up behind me, silent as a cat.

"I thought you were going to the bathroom."

I jumped, gasped, nearly dropped the card. "Oh. Yeah. It passed."

His eyes landed on the card. He handed me a glass of water and took the card from my hand. "What's going on?" he asked, his voice slick and cold. Again, I had a sense of Bill Hollis lurking under there somewhere. *Cheater blue, Nikki. Slate with cheater blue—you can't ignore it.*

"I just didn't realize you like photography," I said, trying to keep the water in the glass steady.

He turned the card over. "I don't. This is just from a trip to Vail. Did some hiking there last summer. It was really beautiful, so I took some pictures."

His face gave away nothing. My legs started to shake, since I wasn't allowing my hands to do so. "I'd love to see them," I said, offering a small smile.

"Sure," he said, offering one back.

"Now?"

He frowned. "Maybe not. You're pretty pale. You look sick."

I looked sick, or he was hiding whatever was on that disk from me? I put the water on his desk. "You're right. I should go. I don't feel very good."

"You sure? Sounds like you've been through a lot today. You can stay. You can tell me more about what Luna said. Sounds traumatizing." He brushed his palm down the back of my head, threading his fingers through my hair on the way down. Sparks flew up the back of my neck as his fingertips touched it.

I disengaged myself and headed toward the front door. As tempting as it was to spend some time with him, my head was way too foggy to even consider it. I had to do some thinking about who Dru Hollis really might be. *Slate and cheater blue! Slate and cheater blue!* "Maybe next time," I said, stepping out into the hallway and pushing the elevator button.

"Okay, if you're sure," he said. The elevator opened and I stepped inside. "And, hey, let me deal with Luna. I'll take care of it." He slipped the camera card into his front pocket as the elevator door slid closed.

23

I HAD TO see Peyton again. I wasn't sure why I felt so
compelled—only that sitting next to her bed was now
familiar to me. I understood why I was doing this, following
these clues to nowhere, a little bit better when I was staring at
her rainbow tattoo. Not to say that I understood fully just yet.

Funny how attached I'd grown to someone who'd literally never spoken to me, except through photographs. But
somehow I felt connected to Peyton, and it wasn't just the
Dru connection.

It was Saturday, so I didn't have to deal with Luna at
school, which was a good thing. But not being in school
meant I had no idea where Luna was at any given moment,
which was a bad thing. It was hard to protect yourself against

someone when you didn't know where in the city they were. I felt like I was on high alert every second.

I had the whole day, so I decided to stop at the *dojang* first thing. Gunner was standing at the front desk.

So was Chris Martinez.

Gunner took one look at my bruised face—the cut on the cheek from Stefan's hit a week ago scabbed over and fading, and a fresh blackish splotch above one eyebrow from falling in my kitchen, along with a faint yellowing along my jawline where Luna had repeatedly hit me—and dropped the pencil he was holding.

"What the heck happened to you?" he asked, hurrying around the desk. He was in his *dobok* but was wearing flip-flops. A junior instructor was assisting the kids on the floor.

"I'm fine," I said, but even I didn't believe me. Detective Martinez didn't react, but I could see him studying my face from where he was standing, too.

"What's he doing here?" I asked, though at this point I wasn't really all that surprised to see him pretty much any-where in my life. That seemed to be his specialty—always being right in my way.

"Open gym today," Gunner said. "He wants to work out. Why? Is there a problem?" He looked from my bruises to Detective Martinez, and back again.

It was only then that I noticed Detective Martinez was wearing a pair of navy sweatpants and a white tee so tight it showed off the shadow of a tattoo across the left side of his chest. I shook my head, resigned. "Of course not. It's open gym. I didn't know you were into martial arts, Detective," I said.

"I'm into protecting myself," he answered. "But yes, I do okay in the *dojo*, too."

"Good," I said, grinning. "I won't have to worry about you getting in my way too much, then. But just in case, the junior instructors are over there." I pointed to where the kids were practicing their moves.

I thought I heard a low chuckle come from Detective Martinez. He looked down at his shoes, and then back up at me, nodding. "I'll keep that in mind. But just out of curiosity, where is the sparring mat?"

"Got to have a willing partner," I said. "Sometimes hard to come by someone who can keep up on open gym day. But maybe one of the nine-year-olds will go easy on you."

He stepped forward, folded his arms across his chest, and looked down at me. "Or maybe I'll go easy on you."

We locked eyes for so long, wordlessly challenging each other, I almost forgot Gunner was standing right there until he cleared his throat. "Nik? You sure you're up for sparring today?" he asked. "You look like you've taken some shots already."

I answered him but refused to take my eyes away from

Detective Martinez's. "Would love to spar the detective."

Ten minutes later, we stood in the middle of the mat in our sparring gear—padded headgear, gloves, shoes, shin guards.

"Okay, you two, try to keep it civil," Gunner said. We bowed to him, and then to each other, and then dropped to our fighting stances, hands up at the ready, as Gunner backed off the mat.

"Just so you know," Detective Martinez said, "these marks on your face are not fine, Nikki. I thought we talked about you being safe."

I shrugged, tried to make a lame attempt at lightness. "I can't always promise safe. I can only promise trained." I threw a high kick—a roundhouse, but he saw it coming and backed off.

"Who did it? Who hit you?"

"Which one?" I threw another high roundhouse, faster this time. He got his arm up just in time to block it. I sank back into my fighting stance, hopping on my toes, determined not to let him distract me.

"Jesus, you are stubborn," he muttered under his breath. I threw another roundhouse. He ducked, blocked it with his arm, and shot out with a quick left jab, tagging me in the mouth. I felt the sting on my lip. "Does your dad know what's going on?"

"Cute," I said. "And no. He's in San Diego."

"So you're alone. Don't you have anyone you can stay with?"

"I'm fine," I repeated, only more strongly this time. More believably, or at least I thought so. "I've got the house all locked up. Nobody can get in. Plus, I'm here, right? A little fight is nothing." I chose to ignore the tiny detail about Luna getting in before, drugging me, and hauling my passed-out ass to her house so she could warn me off. Remembering my confrontation with Luna, combined with my stinging lip, irritated me. I swung my back leg high in an inside crescent. He ducked, just as he'd done before, but I was ready for it. I let my toe touch the mat, then, as if on a spring, arced my leg back around the other way. Outside crescent to the jaw. His hand went to his face, surprised, and then we both dropped back to our fighting stances.

"Not bad," he said. "But you're all up top. What happens if someone gets you on the ground?"

I jabbed at him with my left hand. He blocked it, so I jabbed again. And again. "I seem to do okay," I said. One more jab, and then I spun around on my left heel—wicked fast—and hook kicked him right in the ribs.

Air escaped through his teeth with the impact, and for a second I thought I had him. But he was faster than I'd bargained for, and when I advanced on him with another inside crescent, he grabbed my leg and yanked it up against his hip, pulling me in. "What if 'okay' isn't good enough?" he asked, his face inches from mine. He grabbed my lower back, stepped behind me, and leaned forward so that we both tumbled to the mat. He was on hands and knees on top of me, my leg hooked over his arm so that my calf was draped over his shoulder. He had a smug look on his face. "This is what I'm talking about, Nikki. You're tough, but you're not invincible." He got a serious look on his face. "I wasn't always a cop in Brentwood, you know. I grew up on the east side of South Central. I know what tough is. And I know there's no such thing as invincible."

For a moment, we just breathed, staring into each other's eyes, the connection between us reminding me of spilled wine. Reminding me of when my mother curled me up tight, rocked me, and sang into my hair, still wet from the bath.

If crimson scared me, spilled wine terrified me.

I wriggled under his grasp, at first unsure what to do. He was right about me—I was trained to fight standing up, using my legs, my feet, and distance. This close, I was going to have to rely on gut instinct, or I was going to lose.

Damn it, I hated to lose.

I wrapped both of my arms around his neck, pulling his face in close. I could feel his sweat on my skin, but had no time to let it distract me. I wrapped my left leg around his back, pushed hard with my right leg—the one he was holding— and rolled with all my might. It worked—Detective Martinez flipped and suddenly I was the one on top—but I refused to show my surprise that I'd been successful. I held his wrists down on the floor, both of us panting. A drop of sweat fell from my nose onto his chest. We stayed that way for just a beat, and then I got up and held out my hand to help him up.

When he was standing, I bowed to him and left the floor.

My arms and legs still felt stiff and unusable this morning. My head still felt unclear. But at the moment I felt like I could conquer anything.

"I'm as close as you're going to come to invincible, though," I said over my shoulder. I tossed a wink at the detective as I sauntered away.

He shook his head. "You are definitely the hardest-headed woman I've ever met."

"I'll take that as a compliment."

TWO HOURS LATER, my muscles were warm and taut from work, and I had a faster roundhouse than ever. Powerful. Aimed just right, I could knock someone out cold with that kick.

I'd come home to clean up, the exercise and the shower chasing away the last of the drugs and making my head crystal clear. I even wrote the word CRYSTAL in the fog on the bathroom mirror just to see what happened. Almost immediately, it blinked at me like a diamond hit with sunlight. I was back to normal.

I pulled on a pair of my most comfortable jeans, a worn black T-shirt, and my Chucks—the ones with the scrape on the toe from my fight with Gibson Talley—clothes I could move in. I felt stronger than ever. Let Luna come at me. She would be a challenge I would gladly accept.

I spent the afternoon Googling everything I could find about Bill and Vanessa Hollis. Vanessa, perhaps not surprisingly, turned up almost nothing. A couple of photos from a celebrity party, Vanessa on the dance floor, a drink in hand. A piece on interior decorating, where Hollis Mansion was featured. A photo accompanying the article showed the office Luna had dragged me into, and I was shocked at how many details I'd missed while I was in there. Pieces of furniture I hadn't seen, art on the walls. In some ways, it looked like an entirely different room from the one I'd been in the day before.

But there was still something about it that bugged me. A familiar itch that tugged at the back of my memory.

On the other hand, there were more articles about Bill Hollis than I could even count. No way could I read them all, so I skimmed a few. For the most part, it seemed like the features about Bill could all be summarized like this: Bill Hollis, the most amazing movie exec to ever grace Hollywood, might actually be the second coming of Christ. He was to be loved—no, revered—and every move he ever made was either (1) groundbreaking, (2) genius, or (3) so astoundingly philanthropic it was a wonder that the Hollises weren't living in a dirt hut so that others might live in the lap of luxury. And, speaking of the lap of luxury, Bill Hollis actually was the physical lap of luxury. Every suit he wore became the must-wear suit of the century, every cigar he smoked was notable to anyone who knew their ass from a cigar, and every bottle of wine he touched must be hundreds of years old. Maybe thousands. I rolled my eyes as I scrolled through the articles. Photos of him with his arms around Angelina and Scarlett, photos of him shaking hands with Bono and drinking scotch with Seth Rogen. A photo of him leaning against a Lamborghini, the license plate on that one screaming out at me in neon blue, *HLYWD*.

I sat back. So he had two cars, their vanity plates reading *HLYWD* and *DREAMS*. He was flaunting his dedication to an escort service to the whole world, and everyone was too busy kissing his boots to notice.

There was not one mention of him having a connection to an escort service. I even plugged in the search terms "Bill Hollis" and "scandal." Nothing. He appeared untouchable.

Except for the most recent news entries, of course. The ones about him bailing his son out of jail. But all those articles spun Dru to be the unappreciative son of a devoted father. One headline even dared proclaim, "When Rotten Apples Fall Far from the Tree."

Ugh. More like rotten tree.

The thought of how very untouchable this family was chilled me. Was there a prayer that I could come near someone like Bill Hollis, or would he crush me like a bug? There was something that Peyton knew—Luna had made that clear, and it wasn't all about her—and look what happened to Peyton. I shuddered at the thought that Bill Hollis might have had something to do with his own daughter's attack.

I shut my laptop, rubbing my face with my palms. I'd plugged in Peyton's phone before falling down the rabbit hole of researching her parents. I was eager to find what clues it might hold.

I turned it on, unsure what to expect.

Peyton's wallpaper was the SOS photo, which told me she'd meant for me to find her phone. She'd left it as a clue. But a quick look inside told me that it was not much of a clue to have. The phone was wiped totally clean.

There were no contacts in her list. No photos. No videos. Not a single app. Her call history had been deleted, as had her voice mails. Had she deleted everything, or had someone else done it when they cleaned out her apartment? It seemed unlikely that they'd found the phone at all, given that it was buried under all those childhood mementos.

I closed my eyes and tried to remember the night of

her attack, the phone call that I'd gotten, letting the color orange that I'd seen on the numbers lead me back there.

I remembered thinking it might be Jones calling. Being impatient when I answered. But then I remembered the impatience being whisked away when I heard shallow breathing on the other end. "Hey," a voice said, childlike, frightened. Peyton. "Listen, I . . ."

But then there'd been something else. A voice in the background. I hadn't been able to make out what it was saying.

"Nikki," Peyton had said. Definitely calling me. Not just reaching out blindly in fear, but reaching out to *me* in particular.

The voice in the background spoke again, and this time I could make it out clearly. "Put the phone down," it had said.

It was a man's voice. The significance didn't sink in until that moment. It was a man's voice threatening Peyton, not Luna's.

I looked again at the SOS in the background, but I was confused. How was this supposed to lead me to anything? There was nothing left on this phone.

I switched over to her texts. To my surprise, there was one, sent to a phone number I didn't recognize.

I know everything. I need to see you.

There was no response. A few minutes later, she'd sent another to the same number.

Call me for time and place.

Still no response. Ten minutes later, she'd sent a third.

I wouldn't chance it if I were you. Call me or I will take you all down.

Wait a minute. *You all?* I tapped the phone number at the top, and three other phone numbers dropped down. It was a group text. The numbers all shimmered in their individual colors, settling into disjointed patterns. All except one.

The one I recognized.

Dru Hollis's phone number.

24

I JOLTED OUT of my chair, dropping Peyton's phone on my desk, staring at it as it bounced and fell to the floor, all the while Dru's number sending a beacon of lies at me. Turquoise, gray. *Cheater, liar.*

She was threatening, in those texts, to take them all down. Including Dru. Had asked them to call to set up a place and time to meet.

Put the phone down.

A man's voice. Was it Dru's? I covered my ears, paced the length of my room and back, hearing the voice over and over in my head, trying to place it, to match it to his. I didn't know. It could have been Bill Hollis's voice. For that matter, it could have been anyone else's. Gibson's. Arrigo Basile's. Or one of Luna's friends.

I left the phone on my floor.

I'D SAT THERE so long, researching the Hollises, combing Peyton's phone, it was evening before I left the house. By the time I reached the hospital, it was full-on dark. I hurried through the parking lot, looking over my shoulder the whole time for Luna, or Vanessa, or both. I was hungry, but afraid to eat anything in my house, afraid to stop anywhere, to walk through a parking lot. Nothing seemed safe to me anymore. Nobody.

I had plans to see Dru that night, to meet him at his apartment. It was supposed to be an intimate meeting. A good time.

But how could I have a good time with him now?

Yet, I wanted to see him, to hear his explanation of why he'd never told me about the text, even after I told him about Luna. I needed to see how much he knew about the family business, about Hollywood Dreams, the Molly, *Double Rainbow*. But I needed to see him for other things, too. I needed to be reassured by his touch, by the colors that would swamp the room when we touched, that he wasn't involved in this. That he hadn't gotten the text. That he'd talked her out of whatever she was planning. That . . . something. Anything.

Otherwise it would mean I'd placed my trust—what little of it I had—in the wrong person. Again. It would mean Detective Martinez had been right, and that I'd been stupidly playing with fire all along. It would mean I'd chosen violet lust over myself, over Peyton.

Surely this made me one of those dumb, mooning girls. Surely this made me the very kind of girl I hated. The kind whose headlines would make me shake my head and goggle at their stupidity.

I headed straight for Peyton's room, not even pausing to listen for the footsteps that seemed to follow me everywhere. The closer I got, the more the urge to see her pressed in on me, and I found myself jogging down the hallway by the time I got to her floor. Nurses stopped and stared at me. I rounded the corner into Peyton's room and skidded to a stop.

Vee was sitting next to her bedside, tears streaking down her face in long lines of jet-black mascara. Behind her stood the guy I recognized as the drummer from Viral Fanfare but didn't actually know. On the far end of the room, sitting on the heat register, his arms folded, sat Gibson Talley.

"Oh," I said, my hand covering my heart without my even realizing it.

Gibson Talley stood up, uncrossed his arms. He glared at me.

"I didn't expect . . . ," I said. My throat had gone dry. "Why are you here?"

"I would ask the same of you," Vee said. Her top lip was swollen and red from tears. "But we know that you're all up in Peyton's business. Never hung out with her once, never came to a single show, yet here you are again. Can't even let the poor girl die in peace."

"Die?" I said, taking three hurried steps into the room.

"Don't get your hopes up. She's not dead yet. You still have time to pin this on any number of people in Brentwood," the drummer said. He chewed on the inside of his lip piercing, making the skin surrounding it wiggle up and down in a deepening dimple.

"Listen, I know it wasn't you," I said, turning to Gibson.

"No shit," he said, his face hard. There were stitches on the side of his head, though the cut that they'd sewn together looked mostly healed. I felt a small pang of guilt.

"I'm really sorry, but you came after me."

"I came to talk to you," Gibson said.

"You put me in a choke hold. I had no other choice." I turned to Vee. "And someone said you'd been asking about a will. Surely you can see how you guys looked guilty."

"I just wanted to know what to do with the songs," she said. "Especially the ones that Gib cowrote. Just in case something terrible happened. The band has a right to them." She looked down at Peyton, and her eyes filled with tears again. "It was bad timing. If I'd known there was a real possibility that she could die, I would never have asked. We can write new songs. All that stuff was stupid. I wish we hadn't ever fought. I think we all wish it." She leaned miserably into the drummer. He wrapped an arm around her shoulder as she sniffled.

It was the softest and most genuine I'd ever seen Vee. I hadn't known she could do that.

I sat in the chair on the other side of Peyton's bed and leaned forward to get right in Vee's line of vision. "She was in trouble," I said, a whisper. "She maybe still is. And now I am, too. I can't figure out why she was reaching out to me before her attack, but I know now for sure that she was."

"How do you know?" Vee asked. "Maybe she wasn't and you're just butting in."

"She left me some clues. And if she left them for me, it must have been because she wanted me to know something. I can't figure out what the missing link is, and it's driving me crazy. If I don't get it soon, the police will take over and that will be it. I'll never know what Peyton wanted me to know. Please. I'm sorry that I hurt you." I looked over at Gibson. "But I'm desperate. What do you know?"

Vee sniffled some more, and I could see her fighting with herself over how much to let me in. Chameleonlike, her shirt slowly shifted to the green of lime sherbet. She clearly didn't trust me—clearly didn't like me—but she wanted to do the right thing by Peyton. Deep down, despite the argu-ments and the threats, she loved her friend.

She shrugged helplessly and looked at her two band-mates, who seemed to acknowledge something without moving a muscle. The three of them were that close. "All I know is that she started acting really strange. Started talking about not being able to trust people."

Immediately, I heard Jones in my head, standing outside my classroom door, telling me about a party he'd been to at Peyton's house. *She kept saying all this weird shit . . . some shit about not being able to trust anyone . . .*

He'd seen Dru and Luna carry her away, joking about Peyton being groomed to be a soap opera star. He'd later seen them fighting with another blond woman. Dru. Luna. And Vanessa, I was sure of it now.

I will take you all down.

What had they done to blow her trust in them?

Vee continued, "She moved into Fountain View, and even though it meant we couldn't practice at the mansion anymore, we were all like, okay, this is going to be good, because now she'll be living close to Gib." She reached over and touched Peyton's tattoo, running her finger along it like she was tracing the lines. "She and Gib even got new tattoos together. We thought this was a step in the right direction, because her family . . . Something was going on. She was bothered by it."

"What was it?" I asked. "Did she ever say anything about the name Rainbow?"

Vee shook her head. "Not really. She loved rainbows—that was why she got the tattoo. She loved colors in general."

She loved colors. Shocked me. I didn't realize until Vee said those words how much I'd come to hate colors over the years. I'd always equated them with bad things—sadness, death, worries, stress, bad grades, feeling like an outcast. It never occurred to me to embrace them, to see them as a gift. Look at what I was able to do—I was able to communicate with a comatose girl because of my colors. That was pretty amazing. Why was Peyton able to love her colors and I wasn't able to love mine?

Vee sniffed again, long and hard.

"Tell her about the rest," the drummer said softly. He seemed to be the quiet one of the group, but I didn't dare mistake that for weakness. He was still hard as rocks.

"I already told her," Gibson chimed in, his voice stone.

Vee glanced at him, then back at me.

"She walked out on you," I said. "And took all her songs with her."

Vee nodded. "And refused to cut a deal with her dad's friend. She had gotten so weird. Cutting her hair, moving out. She got a new phone so none of us could get ahold of her. She never called anyone on it." *Not true*, I thought. *She called me.* "She was all of a sudden so paranoid," Vee continued. "It was like she knew this was going to happen to her."

"She did," I said.

Vee looked startled. "She knew?"

"I think she did. That's why I'm here. She knew, and she tried to call me right before it happened."

"It doesn't make any sense," Vee said. "Who would want to hurt Peyton?"

My mind swam. How many times had Dru said those very words? Only now I had no idea if he really meant them, or if they were a cover.

It's not like Peyton's attacker is going to be hanging out at the hospital, Dru had once said, sarcastically. Though every moment it was looking likelier and likelier that her attacker had been doing just that. The question was, which one of them was it?

I felt Gibson's eyes bore into the top of my head. I reached over and grabbed Peyton's hand in mine. "Turns out, a lot of people wanted to hurt her," I said. "Too many to keep track of."

Viral Fanfare stuck around for a few more minutes. Mostly we sat in silence, only occasionally interrupted by loud sobs from Vee. The girl was taking this very hard.

"We were like sisters," Vee said, as she stood to go, propped up by the drummer. "She always said I was her third sister."

"Third sibling," I corrected.

She shook her head. "No, third sister. Peyton had two sisters. The blond chick who looks just like her, and another one. I never met her or anything, so I assume she's older."

I froze, my hand gripping Peyton's. Probably if she'd been awake, she would have winced under the pressure.

There was another sister? One that Peyton, Dru, and Luna hadn't mentioned? A secret sister? Was it possible?

They headed for the door, a bundle of leather-clad sadness. I swiveled in my chair.

"Did she say the other sister's name?" I asked.

Vee turned, looking confused. She shook her head. "She only really talked about her a few times." Her chin crumpled and her lip quivered. "She said something about how they used to watch movies together all the time. They had a favorite. What was it called?"

The drummer shrugged, but Gibson Talley spoke up. "Some Harrison Ford movie."

Vee pointed. "Yeah, that's it. She said they'd watched it a million times and that they liked to sit in her sister's window and smoke. Said her sister always chucked the butts into the bushes, and if anyone ever looked inside those bushes, they would be shocked."

They turned the corner, and I was left alone with Peyton, wondering how everything fit together. A sister nobody had said anything about? A Harrison Ford movie? I felt like these were important details, but I couldn't quite put them together.

I got out my phone and pulled up IMDB. I plugged in "Harrison Ford" and began scrolling through his acting credits. He'd been in so many movies, and I'd seen most of them. Everyone had. But none of them sounded important. None of them rang any bells or set off any alarms. Maybe Bill Hollis had produced one of them and I would have to go through, one by one, to discover which movie it was.

"If this is another one of your clues," I said to Peyton, "I'm missing it."

Almost as soon as the words were out of my mouth, I saw it.

My mouth hung open, and I felt like I was spiraling down a long tunnel. I could only sit there next to Peyton's bed, my whole body numb, my mind racing, my ears ringing. The urge to sneeze pressed in on me, distant, familiar. The urge I always got when I saw the dusty word *beneath*.

What Lies Beneath.

Harrison Ford had starred in a movie called *What Lies Beneath*.

I'd stared at that photo for more time than I wanted to think about. I'd looked so hard for clues, for anything to make sense of it. I'd assumed it was a mistake, a throwaway. But I should have known. In the clues that Peyton had laid down for me, there were no throwaways.

They liked to sit in her sister's window and smoke. . . .

Dusty, sneezy *beneath*.

I could see the image clearly in my head now, and it all made sense. The stucco wall, the pinprick of orange light, the bushes.

That photo was a photo of me. Me, sitting in my window—my favorite place—and chain-smoking when I should have been studying for chem or history or God-knew-what.

I felt like I was floating across the room toward Peyton, the crimson pushing, pushing, pushing in on me, tinged with whorls of confusion and spikes of anger and curling snakes of shock.

It made sense. Of course it did. Synesthesia tended to be genetic, my doctor had told us. Had I had any siblings, the chance was good they would see colors, too. But I didn't have any siblings.

Or at least I didn't think I did. Until now.

Peyton saw colors. Peyton talked about a third sibling. Peyton took a photo of me in my window and then told Vee that her sister sat there, referencing a movie she'd titled that very photo. Peyton tried to call me moments before her attack.

I know everything, her text had said. I could see the colors behind those words, the colors behind all her words. *What Lies Beneath. I know everything.* And in her Facebook post, *Must get to the bottom of things. Nik.* And when her friends had pressed her, she'd answered in a single word. A brilliantly colorful one: *Family.*

Nik. Must get to the bottom of things. Family. What Lies Beneath.

I was the third. The one who smoked on her window ledge.

Peyton Hollis thought she was my sister.

25

I SANK INTO the chair by her bed and picked up her hand again. I didn't realize tears were streaming down my face. I didn't feel sadness. Not yet. I felt so many emotions, but sadness wasn't one of them. They all tornadoed into something that was too big to label.

I was bewildered more than anything.

It didn't seem possible. Peyton was wrong. She had to be. Just because we both saw colors didn't have to mean we were sisters. There were lots of synesthetes out there, all blissfully and beautifully unrelated. It couldn't be. The odds against Peyton and me being sisters were just too astronomical. My parents were in love. I didn't remember much about the time before Mom's death, but I knew that much. They loved each other. They held hands and cuddled and smiled at each other and called each other *babe*.

But if this were true—if Peyton and I were actually sisters—one of my parents had to have cheated on the other.

Which one? My dad, who was still so devoted ten years after his wife's death? No way. My mom? God, could my mom have had a baby with someone else? I refused to believe that could be true.

Maybe I was wrong. Maybe I'd misread the clues. Maybe Peyton was trying to tell me something else—that we were connected in a different way. Or maybe she was telling me that her sister—Luna—had two sides to her, almost like a third sister. That the dangerous side of Luna was who she'd been afraid of.

But then I couldn't help remembering what I'd found in the Hollywood Dreams office. The birth certificates, one set of which had the parents' names whited out.

I rubbed my hands over my temples, groaning. How would I ever know for sure what any of this meant?

"Peyton," I whispered. "Peyton, please wake up." My nose ran, and I let it run over my upper lip. "Peyton, I need you. I'm so confused."

I hated crying. I prided myself on rarely shedding tears. Crying was for weak girls. Crying was for girls with dead mothers.

Suddenly the lack of change in Peyton, the crimson that

was her constant companion, was more than just an annoy-ance, more than just a reminder of a bad time.

It was a reminder of the most devastating loss of my life.

The last time I spoke to my mother, that last day before I went to my friend Wendy's house, she was putting pigtails in my hair, humming a song while she worked. I loved the sound of my mother's hum. I loved her voice. I wanted to sing like her someday. I imagined us singing together, two grown women with stunning harmonies.

You are so lucky to have this beautiful hair, she'd said. I remembered that part clearly.

It looks just like yours, I'd said, and I'd really believed it had. People told us all the time that we looked alike. *You could be an older sister,* they would say to my mother, and she would touch her neck shyly and laugh, a breathy laugh.

Mine's got all this ugly gray, she'd said, although I never could find any. My mom still looked like her high school photos, except the smile in her high school photos was wider than I'd ever seen her smile at home. Her high school smile was an easy smile. *But you do have my nose and my thick eyebrows.*

I remembered examining my face in the mirror, leaning so close I could see the pores in my skin. *Do you think if I had a sister she would look like me?* I'd asked, and I hadn't noticed it at the time, but remembering the moment now, I could see it plain as day. Her face had darkened. She'd faltered. She'd pulled my pigtail tight and patted me on both shoulders. *You ready to get to Wendy's?* she'd asked. Was I remembering that darkening, or was I only imagining remembering it now that I was searching for lies?

I knew that my dad didn't see colors. He would have told me. He wouldn't have been so confused by my ability. He wouldn't have been so worried about it. But did Mom see them? I remembered asking Dad about it once, on our way home from the doctor's office.

"I don't know, sweetie," he'd said, hands gripping the steering wheel.

"But wouldn't Mommy tell you if she did?" I asked, unable to understand how someone could keep their colors secret.

"I'd like to think so," he said.

"But how did I get it, if neither of you have it?"

He'd glanced at me, reached down and patted my knee softly, and smiled. "You're just special, I guess," he'd said, and we'd let it drop.

Since then, I'd learned that it was more than possible to keep your synesthesia a secret, and, with neither parent admitting to being the source of my "specialness," I would never really know where I got it.

If it was true . . . if Peyton was my sister . . . did that mean Mom was Peyton's mom, too? How was it even possible? Or could Dad be Peyton's dad? I tried to imagine him having anything to do with another woman, but all I could ever conjure were images of him holding Mom in a hug. Still, at least if Dad was the cheater, he could have a child resulting from a one-nighter and not know it. If Mom was the cheater, that would mean she *knew* I had a sister out there. She knew about Peyton. And had never said anything.

If only I could have seen beneath the Wite-Out on those birth certificates.

And I didn't even want to begin to think what that meant my true relationship with Dru was.

No matter who had done what, there was one truth—if I was Peyton's sister, my life was a lie. A complete and total lie. My parents were liars. Cheaters. Abandoners.

"Peyton," I said again. I placed my hand on top of hers, sandwiching her palm. I rubbed it. It was so soft and warm. She was in there somewhere. "I need you to wake up. I need to know what you know. I don't understand and I need your help. I've done everything I can." I felt a tear slip down my cheek. "Please, Peyton," I begged. "Please wake up."

As if on cue, just like in a movie, Peyton's eyelids fluttered. My heart stopped. I held my breath and sat up straighter as the blue of her eyes began to show. Silver squiggles danced in the air. Her eyes rolled and then shifted to my face. When they landed on me, her lips twitched into a serene smile.

"Oh my God," I whispered, letting my breath out. "Oh my God!" I shouted. "Peyton? You're awake! Oh my God!"

Just as quickly as they had opened, her eyes slid shut. I fumbled down the side of the bed, searching for the nurse call button, found it, and pressed, wiping the wetness from my cheeks even as startled new tears flowed. I pressed the button over and over, my thumb jamming it so hard I thought I might break it.

"Can I help you?" a nurse asked, her voice bored.

"She's awake," I said excitedly. "You need to come in here because she's awake."

The nurse didn't respond, but I soon heard footsteps coming down the hallway toward the room. A large nurse came in, belly first, and made her way toward the bed.

"She woke up," I said breathlessly, jumping back so she could get at Peyton. She did, picking up Peyton's wrist and checking her pulse, then looking her over, attending to the monitors. "Her eyes opened," I said. "She smiled at me."

"It's not unusual for there to be involuntary muscle action," the nurse said. "She's been twitching for days."

"But her eyes opened. It wasn't a twitch. They were open. She smiled at me."

The nurse shook her head. "I'm sorry. Not of her own volition," she said. "You're not the first one to be fooled, so don't feel bad. Her brother was very excited for a few moments earlier this week."

I remembered Dru saying her eyes had fluttered while he was there, too. It had been nothing. It was still nothing.

"But she smiled." I could hear the whine in my voice, the disappointment, as the squiggles died out and fell to the ground like broken balloons.

The nurse placed her hand on my arm. "Honey, it's very important that you keep up this hope. Your positive energy might help a miracle happen."

"It's not positive energy and hope," I said, whisking my arm away angrily. "She woke up. I was talking to her and she smiled at me. I saw it. I know what I saw."

"Let me know if you see it again, and I'll come check her out, okay?" the nurse said as she waltzed out the door, as if nothing astonishing had just happened.

"I know what I saw," I said to her back. *Yes, Nikki, you know exactly what you saw,* my brain supplied. *The same thing you're seeing now. A sea of blood so deep and thick you can't help but think of your mom. You can't quit going back to that last day. You're seeing it, Nikki. You can't not see it.*

I pressed my fists into my eyes, shaking with rage, hating my synesthesia with everything I had. Hating Peyton for first making me fear her, then making me love her, and now making me face telling her good-bye.

I wouldn't do it. Not yet.

I stumbled out of the room, crying, seething, leaving Peyton behind. Fuck it. Fuck *her.* You didn't just become sisters with someone and never tell them. You didn't leave a bunch of bullshit clues lying around in colors so that she would follow them like an ignorant dog. You didn't set people up to be beaten and drugged, terrified. You didn't do this to people, and the fact that Peyton thought you could was exactly what made her a Hollis rather than a Kill.

If all this was true, either my dad had an affair with Peyton's mom, or my mom had an affair with the wretched Bill Hollis. Either way, I didn't want to know. I didn't want to know any of this anymore. I wanted out.

I pressed the elevator button with the same force and repetition that I'd pressed the nurse call button. "Get me out of here. Just get me out of here," I whimpered to myself as I pushed and pushed.

The doors opened and I jumped on. As soon as they closed, I made a fist and punched the elevator wall. The car didn't even shake from the impact, so I punched it again, harder. I felt the jolt through my fingers, my hand. I punched harder still to feel it in my arm. "Screw you, Peyton," I said to the empty elevator. "Screw you and your involuntary twitches. Screw you and your movies. Screw you and your stupid pictures." I pulled out my phone and called up her photo-sharing site. There it was, so obvious, as plain as day. I felt the urge to sneeze and scrolled away from the *What Lies Beneath* photo to the one of her family standing on a pier. I could see it. Something in her eyes. Something that set her apart from the rest of them. Something that reminded me of me.

The doors slid open, and a familiar face greeted me from the other side of them. I let my head drop back against the wall in frustration. Of course.

"What are you doing here?" I asked Detective Martinez. I gestured to his suit jacket. "You're dressed like a cop this time, so I guess you're not here to spar."

"I came to see how Peyton was doing." He squinted at the streaks that the dried tears had left on my cheeks. "Are you okay? Did something happen up there?" he asked.

"She didn't die," I said. "If that's what you're asking."

"It wasn't." A flash of yellow from his badge area. Whatever. Who cared anymore? "I meant did something happen to you?"

"Is it not okay for me to mourn the loss of a classmate?" I snarled.

"Yes, of course it is. But I thought you weren't friends."

"Oh, if only you knew," I said. The doors started to close, so I stuck my arm out to make them jump back, and then piled out of the elevator, which meant I had to slide way too close to Detective Martinez once again. This guy had serious personal space issues.

He reached out and took hold of my wrist. "I would love to know," he said. "I've been begging to know. You could tell me."

"What's the point, anyway?" I asked. "You've got all the

answers. Why even bother to follow another lead?" I started to walk away.

"You mean like Vanessa Hollis's little Molly enterprise?" he asked at my back. I stopped and came back to him. "Like Bill Hollis's ties to some very popular escorts? I'm not as in the dark as you think, Nikki. I haven't been able to pinpoint anything, but I'm getting close, aren't I? I can tell by the look on your face that I'm a lot closer than you thought I'd get."

I licked my lips. The yellow was reminding me of lemonade and making me thirsty. It was emanating from his badge and dissipating into the air like gas. What should I tell him? Everything? Just open up and spill my guts, which would lead to discussions about my synesthesia, my link to Peyton, my mom? And what about Dru? In all of what Detective Martinez said, he was the only one whose name hadn't come up. And the one who Detective Martinez was so eager to pin this on. "You can't even begin to imagine the mess this is," I said. "You're so not close, you're not even in the same stratosphere. I'll tell you again. I know nothing. Stay out of my life."

This time when I walked away, I vowed to keep moving no matter what he said at my back. But it turned out he said nothing, so I was free to go.

I walked across the parking lot, unsure what I was going to do next. There was something Vee had said that had perked my ears. Something about if Peyton's sister ever looked in the bushes she would be shocked at what she'd find there. Had Peyton hidden something in the bushes beneath my bedroom window on the night she was attacked? Was it really that straightforward?

But I didn't care. I didn't want to do this anymore. I wanted to walk away. If I looked in the bushes . . . if I found something there, I would only be enmeshed in this thing even further.

I kept walking, and when I turned the corner into the shadows of the parking lot, I noticed the light of my phone in my hand. Idly, I looked at the screen, at the Hollis family photo, taken on a pier. What had always stood out to me in this photo was Dru. He was so gorgeous, so at ease, so set apart from the rest of the family.

This time I noticed something else. Vanessa Hollis. Something about the way she leaned slightly backward over the railing sparked a memory. I'd seen a blonde in that pose in another photo.

A blonde, leaning back over a desk in a shadowy office, deep in a kiss with a man. A young man.

I stopped in my tracks, using my thumbs to enlarge the photo. How had I never seen this before? How had I over-looked it all this time?

The easy way Vanessa scooped her arm around Dru's back in the pier photo. The way Dru was pulled away from her just slightly, his right arm held up in what looked like a defensive posture. *Dru. Baby. Have you eaten?*

I enlarged the pier photo even more, and moved the photo around so that I was getting a close-up of that arm.

Dru wore a sapphire ring on his finger.

And a Figaro chain bracelet around his tanned wrist.

26

DROVE HOME in a dream. When I pulled into my driveway, I honestly didn't even remember how I'd gotten
there. Had I taken the highway? I couldn't recall.

The entire way home, all I could think about was Dru.
That bracelet. My brain tried to come up with reasonable
excuses for what I'd seen. Maybe it was a different bracelet. There were probably thousands of them sold every year.
Maybe millions. Could one bracelet be the evidence to
damn him?

But then again, I'd never seen him wear a bracelet. If he
still had his, wouldn't I have seen it at some point by now?
Maybe not. People's fashion tastes changed all the time.

Of course, there was the most perplexing evidence of all. Even if Dru's bracelet had not been the broken bracelet I found in Peyton's car, it had definitely been the same bracelet that I'd seen on the arm of the man in the photo. Kissing Vanessa Hollis. Peyton's supposed mother. Which would, in a normal family, make her *his* mother, by extension. But this family was anything but normal. And the thought was so revolting, I could only assume that somehow Dru was in this mess, too, and that Vanessa wasn't his mother at all. The birth certificates. The whited-out names.

There were a lot of messed-up things about my family. My mother, murdered. My dad, broken, too much of a friend to be much of a father. Synesthesia. Academic probation. Not to mention the fact that I couldn't trust anyone long enough to let them anywhere near my heart.

But my mom was my mom. My dad was my dad. And the chances that either of them would ever be in a photo like that—in a position like that in first place—were absolutely zero.

I parked my car and went into the house, making a beeline for my bedroom, where the photos I'd taken from Peyton's suitcase still sat. I knew it was dangerous for me to just barge in here, lights out and house empty, but I wasn't thinking about safety at the moment. Gunner would have a shit fit if he knew, but I was too distracted to worry about whether crazy Luna had gotten in while I was gone. Plus, I had a feeling Luna was not one to retry a failed attempt. She was craftier than that. She would be lying in wait for me somewhere else. Somewhere I didn't expect.

I paused before shutting my bedroom door, but I didn't hear anything other than the regular sighing and breathing of a house at night. I closed myself in and went for my desk, rifling through the photos before I'd even sat down fully.

There it was, third one, the now unmistakable image of Dru and Vanessa leaning against what I now recognized as the desk that I had been lying near in the Hollis Mansion the day before. His hair was longer, brushing the top of his collar, and darker in the photo. They were almost sprawling backward over the desk, or at least that's where it looked like this kiss was heading. Dru's hand searching Vanessa's waist, low; Vanessa's hand tangled in the hair at the base of Dru's neck.

God, how could I not have seen it? I was sleeping with the guy. I'd gotten as up close and personal as you could possibly get, yet I'd been wondering about the wearer of that bracelet all this time. I felt like such an idiot.

Surely I was wrong. Surely it was a mistake. But the longer I stared at the photo, the more convinced I became of what I was seeing. This was Dru, without a doubt.

As if on cue, my phone buzzed. A text from Dru.

We still on for tonight? My place in 30?

I studied the words, even the *30—purple, black*—to try to pick up on something. Anything. An innocence or a message or something that would tell me that what I'd seen in the photo was easily explained. But nothing came to me. I couldn't feel emotions behind a text. It was just impossible. If I could just somehow see that everything was fine, I could go over there, I bargained with myself. Or my colors were a fucked-up system of making decisions. Something akin to using tea leaves. Which was way more likely. Purple and black, two colors with no meaning whatsoever. It was what it always was, and what it always would be.

"Ah, God," I said, letting the hand holding my phone flop onto my thigh. "What have I been thinking?" *You haven't been thinking*, I told myself. *You've been coming perilously close to love, Nikki. Admit it. You've almost committed the L sin. See where that gets you? In the middle of a sketchy family drama.*

I pushed the phone back into my pocket without answering his text. I didn't know if I could do it. If I could face Dru after knowing what I knew. There were so many lies, so much stuff covered up. He had to at least have known about some of them. He had to know that his affair with Vanessa would be something I'd be interested in hearing about. How could he keep these things from me? And, more importantly, why?

Out of habit, I pulled open my window. I still had half a pack of cigarettes left. I dug them out of the top desk drawer and lit one up, inhaling deeply as I made my way to the windowsill. I needed to think. I needed to be in my space.

The air was crisp again, just the way I liked it, and I could almost detect the sound of traffic on the highway in the distance. The wings and whines of a few bugs and frogs wrapped around me, and if it had been any other night, I might have felt like I was in the middle of perfection. In fact, other than the chem quiz that had been dogging me the night Peyton was attacked, I had felt like my life was just fine. I took another drag off the cigarette and blew out the smoke, frustrated that my life had taken this turn when all I'd been doing was minding my own business.

Wasn't that the way it always went? You were eating Tootsie Rolls, having the greatest day, and *bam*, your mom dies. You were smoking a cigarette and thinking about how much you love the nighttime in the fall, and *kaboom*, you're in the middle of a disaster, people out there wanting to actually kill you.

They say tragedy strikes when you least expect it. And they were totally right. Because when you expect it, you're watching. You're vigilant. It was when you started to take the good parts of your life for granted that you let your guard down. It was when you started to trust someone that you left yourself open for that unexpected life changer.

I should have stuck with Jones. No matter how magenta he got on me, I would never have fallen in love with him.

I could resist him. I couldn't be blinded by him. Jones deserved better than me, but I deserved happiness, and happiness could have come through him. The occasional booty call. The good-looking trophy on my arm. The knowledge that the poor puppy would have done anything for me, and all I would have to do was every now and then play catch with him, and everything would be good.

I'd let my guard down. I wasn't being vigilant. I didn't watch what could be coming for me, and *pow*, tragedy.

I was so sick of my life being about tragedy.

I took one last inhale and flicked the butt to the rocks below. It shot up a tiny bloom of sparks, snuffed by the thick bushes that had been in the *What Lies Beneath* photo. I chuckled, and then threw my head back and laughed out loud at how obvious it had all been. Peyton had taken a photo of me sitting in my favorite spot at my own house. Had posted it online. Had led me to it. And still I hadn't seen it.

Said her sister always chucked the butts into the bushes, and if anyone ever looked inside those bushes, they would be shocked.

At this point, I didn't think I would be.

I thought about my dad in San Diego. Normally, I would be hoping he was meeting someone who could make him happy. Someone who could make him laugh the way Mom used to. I thought about the last time he and I went to the beach together, how self-conscious he was, how he seemed to constantly be looking over his shoulder for something that would never come. But now, I just wanted him to come home so I could ask him about Peyton. Dad had to know what was going on. He had to have answers, and this time I wouldn't let him shut me down with a knee pat and a comment about how special I was.

I smoked another cigarette, this time working very hard to clear my mind of all things Hollis. I even recited a few chem formulas out loud, watching their colors drift up in my mind as I said them.

I felt totally relaxed by the time I went back downstairs, my keys in hand.

But instead of going to my car, I walked around the side of the house.

It was funny how different my house looked from the outside. Generic, angular. Nothing bespeaking the comfort you find inside a home.

My bedroom window appeared to be higher from down here than it did when I was sitting in it. I supposed I'd just gotten used to the height, had enjoyed the feeling of being on top of Brentwood. But from down here it looked like a speck of a square, somewhere that no one in their right mind should ever sit. I wondered if I looked startling to passersby. I wondered if the neighbors held their breath and waited for me to fall.

It didn't take me long to identify the bush directly below my window. It was surrounded by old butts, including the two I'd just thrown. The others had been weathered by sun and rain, and I wondered if the gardener had given up on cleaning up after me. I wouldn't have blamed him if he had.

"What lies beneath, Peyton?" I asked out loud, the sound of my own voice giving me a chill. "Besides the bushes, I mean."

I bent and began pulling the branches apart with my hands, searching the bush for something obvious. I didn't find anything. Perhaps the gardener had already been here, and while he didn't want to clean up my ashtray, he'd thought nothing of taking something hidden inside a bush. Did it matter if whatever she left here had been intercepted by a hired hand? No, probably not. In the end, she would still die, the crimson would win, and I would still be in the dark.

Perhaps I'd misread the clue entirely. It was just a lie that Peyton told her bandmates, maybe to make her sound even more important than she already was.

But then my hand landed on something. Hard, plastic, small. Resting against a larger branch in the center of the bush. I pulled it out and held it up for the streetlamp to illuminate.

It was a digital voice recorder. A tiny, skinny one, like the kind people use when they want to record something without anyone knowing about it. I turned it over, flipped the power switch, and it came to life. This. This was what Peyton wanted me to find.

I started to feel really exposed in the massive side yard between our house and the neighbors'. They looked to be home, but no lights were burning on this side of the house. Would they hear a scream? Probably not.

I took the recorder to my car and locked myself in, after checking both the front and back seats.

Once inside the car, I could really get a look at the recorder. It appeared to be new—unscratched, black, cheap. So this was it. This was what all those clues Peyton had left behind led to. This small bit of electronic machinery designed to explain everything. This smoking gun that would lead me, or police, or whoever to the person was who'd attacked Peyton.

But for the first time, it really dawned on me that for Peyton, this wasn't about finding her attacker. She knew something was coming for her. She suspected that she might not be able to speak for herself. But that hadn't been why she'd been reaching out to me.

She'd done that because I was her sister. And because she thought knowing that was something important to my life.

I wasn't a detective out to solve her crime. I was her witness. I was the one with the story now.

I pressed play. At first there was just a muffled sound like the recorder being jogged around inside clothes. But then there was a voice. A voice I recognized instantly.

"What is this about?" Dru's voice. Unmistakable. My stomach tightened. "Mom and Dad are freaking out, Peyton. You disappear, then you send a text like that. What is going on with you?"

A door closing.

"Good to see you, too, big brother," Peyton's voice said, much closer.

"Well, you can't really expect me to be happy about this. We need to meet? Call for a date and time? What is that?"

"I said to call me, not bust in on me at my new place. How did you know I was here?"

"I followed you from school. It's not that hard."

"Do not tell anyone where I live, Dru. I mean it. Nobody. I left because I didn't want to be found. And I'm not staying here. I have bigger plans."

There was a hesitation. "I won't. I promise."

Well, you would be happy to know that he didn't, Peyton, I thought bitterly, remembering how shocked he seemed to be about finding Peyton's apartment. He'd had me completely conned. I'd never have guessed he'd been there before. Just days before, in fact.

I felt like such a fool. He'd lied to me, and I'd totally bought it.

And I felt even more foolish because a part of me thought

that Dru's lying to me about Peyton's apartment somehow proved he was trustworthy. He was a guy who kept his word. He'd promised her, and he'd kept his promise.

There were footsteps, the clink of ice cubes hitting the sides of a glass, the sound of a couch cushion sighing.

"So what is this all about, then? What is it that you think you know?"

"First of all, I don't *think* I know anything. I know. And I've got evidence."

"Of what?"

"Of all of it."

"That tells me nothing."

"Dru. I saw you. You and Vanessa. I saw it. I know it happened."

For a long moment of silence, I thought I could almost hear Peyton's heart beating. Had she carried this recorder in a shirt pocket? In her bra? My own heart sped up to beat in time with hers. I sat forward, hunched over the speaker, as interested in hearing Dru's response to this as Peyton was.

Finally, he spoke. "It wasn't supposed to happen. I was drunk. I was . . . I don't know, pissed off at Dad. He won't leave me alone. He's always pressuring me to 'be a Hollis.' He won't accept that I am who I am and will never be him. And she was all over me, telling me all this shit about Dad's affairs and his power trips and how he'd ruined the lives of her escorts just because he could. She wanted revenge on him, and . . . I guess part of me did, too. She was begging me, and it doesn't make sense now, but it did at the time. It was like both of us were against him, together. Like I said, it was stupid and it shouldn't have happened."

"But it did. It happened, just like Luna happened. And Hollywood Dreams happened. God, have you even thought about the affairs? Have you ever wondered how many there were? Have you wondered if we have siblings, Dru? Someone out there who shares our DNA? We already know we don't have the same mother. How many other mommies are out there? How many babies? Have you ever thought about any of this? Because you should. I mean, what if my real mother had another baby with another man? That's a half sibling I could have out there, Dru. Jesus. It's all so . . . sick."

She was hinting. She already knew about me at that point, and she was trying to tell Dru. Trying to get him to divulge what he knew. She trusted him. Even though she'd seen what she'd seen between him and Vanessa, she still trusted him. It was a relief to know that I wasn't the only one.

"And even if that—"

But Dru interrupted her. "You're making a big deal out of nothing."

Peyton laughed, long and loud, resentment ringing through the recorder. "It's nothing? He stole us, Dru. He *stole* us. Vanessa isn't our mother—clearly you believe that, or you wouldn't have had your tongue shoved halfway down her throat. Where are they? Where are our mothers? What did he do to them?"

"I don't know what you're talking about," he said, but his voice was very low.

"Luna and I were supposed to be actresses, not escorts. Luna knew Vanessa's plans and I didn't. I thought we were going to be stars, and the whole time we were being groomed to take over Vanessa's disgusting business. I spent my whole life believing in this lie. I thought I would be on the big screen someday. Not on my back." She said this last with such venom, I actually eased away from the recorder just slightly.

"It's not too late," he said. "You can still—"

Peyton interrupted him. "That, my friend, is where you're wrong." Her voice had turned cold, clinical. "You used to be with me. You hated Daddy Dearest just as much as I hated Vanessa. When I told you what I'd found out about the affairs, you said you were going to take him down. But now that it's all getting real, big brother, you just can't force yourself to make the break, can you? You're just not strong enough. I thought you would have my back, but I guess I was wrong. It is definitely too late for me and this family. I am done."

Dru's voice came back, half mocking, half uncertain. "What do you think you're going to do?"

"Bug out."

"You already have."

I could hear a long swallow through the microphone, followed by the tinkle of ice on glass again. "Not good enough," Peyton said, her voice wet. "I don't just want out of that house. I want *out* out."

A slight pause. "What does that mean?"

"It means money, big brother. I want money, or I will sink every last one of you. Bill Hollis, the perfect, impeccable filmmaker, will lose his career in a flurry of whores and affairs, not to mention abuse. Vanessa will find out all about Luna's extracurricular activities with drugs and johns. They will both look fabulous in orange, don't you think? And, by the way, I will tell Dad about your little affair with his wife. Just see how much of his precious inheritance you receive after that. Not to mention, no job in the industry for you, which you'll need when he cuts you off. You'll be just another uneducated pretty face waiting tables in a chain restaurant. Pity."

"You can't do that," Dru growled. I had never heard anger in his voice before, not even when Detective Martinez was hauling him out in handcuffs. It was an unsettling sound. Reminded me of just how much about him I didn't know.

"Oh, but I can," Peyton said, her voice calm and steady. And equally unsettling. In a way, I was overhearing the most awful conversation of my life. I was overhearing hatred. "And don't doubt me. You had your chance, and you were too cowardly to follow through. I, on the other hand, have already left home. I literally have nothing to lose."

Not true, I thought. *You had Dru.* There was affection there, I could hear it behind the shock and the anger and the doubt.

You had me.

Although I supposed she wouldn't be worried about losing something she'd never actually known she had until now.

"How much?" Dru said tightly.

"Five million," Peyton answered without hesitation. I heard the ice on glass again. "Enough, for now, to get me away."

Dru made a balking noise.

"Laugh all you want. Daddy has it. He can shit out five million without breaking a sweat. If I keep thinking about how easy it will be for him, I might have to ask for more."

"He'll never go for it."

"Make sure he does, Dru. There will still be a few million left for you, then."

Another pause. The sound of footsteps moving away. "When do you want it?"

I sensed movement from Peyton as well—a shuffling of clothing just like before. "Here, I wrote it down for you on this." A brief pause, and then an evil giggle. "What? You don't like the flyer I chose? It's just an advertisement for the family business, Dru. You and Vanessa are so close, I would think you'd be in support of it."

No answer.

Peyton spoke again, the merriment gone from her tone. "You are the only one I want there, understood? If I see anyone else, I'm out of there and we renegotiate a much higher amount."

"Why me?"

"Because, believe it or not, big brother, I actually trust you. I think that down deep you're still on my side. Here, take the flyer."

"I've already read it. I know where to go. You keep it."

"Suit yourself," she said. There was the sound of a door shutting again—no, slamming—and then the recording shut off.

For a long while, I held the recorder in my lap, wondering if I should play it again, or if I should listen longer just in case there was more, or if I should simply put it back in the bushes and pretend I'd never seen or heard a thing.

I understood now what had happened. Peyton was blackmailing her family. But someone had gotten one up on her. She had thought it might go down that way and had enlisted me to be her witness.

She had intended for me to see this through to the end. So I would.

I tossed the recorder into the passenger seat.

I straightened one leg, leaning over to one side, and dug my phone out of my pocket.

I pulled up Dru's text and answered it.

Meet me at the mansion instead. Pool house. 30.

I tossed my phone in the seat right next to the recorder and put the car into gear, pointing it toward Hollis Mansion.

27

THE MANSION WAS dark, the only lights the landscaping lanterns shooting up the white stucco in ominous beams, the windows a line of black holes punched in the walls. No sign of life within. A little disconcerting. Where were all the Hollises? More accurately, where was Luna? Vanessa didn't impress me as the kind who liked to get her hands dirty, and to hear Peyton talk on the recorder about Bill's reputation, there was no way he was going to risk bad press on little old me. He had people for that.

And from what I'd witnessed last time I was here, Luna was his people.

I looped around the block and parked the next street over, figuring my best asset would be the element of surprise.

If Luna didn't see me coming, she couldn't be waiting for me. Gunner would have been proud of my planning.

I sat for a few minutes in my car, listening to the tick of the engine cooling and thinking it wasn't too late to just turn around and go. . . .

Go where, exactly? Back home? Luna knew I was there. She most likely knew I was alone at home, too. To Detective Chris Martinez? He would probably arrest me for aiding and abetting Dru. To my doting parent who would forever and always keep me safe? Yeah, as if. I ached for my mom. If what Peyton had hinted at in the recording was true, Mom was her real mother, too, and if she were here, she would be able to clear things up. Maybe she could even have protected Peyton. Maybe she could have protected me. Putrid yellowish brown, the color of vomit and rotting garbage, began to overwhelm me. It was a color I knew well but hadn't seen for years—the color of bitterness over Mom leaving me. I had to get moving before I got sick.

Besides, I needed to talk to Dru. I needed to tell him what I knew, to ask him for clarification. To confront him about the kiss. Why was his bloodied, broken bracelet in Peyton's car? If he was so up to his eyeballs in this mess, why did he keep sleeping with me? Why did he act so clueless when I was around? What was he afraid of?

I waited for a car to pass by and disappear down a long circle drive at the other end of the street, and then I got out of my car and headed toward the mansion. In order to get there, I had to go through two yards, which meant scaling a fence, where I was greeted by a white puffball of a dog who barked at first, but then came running to me excitedly, the bells tied into the ribbons on his ears jingling in the night.

I scratched him behind the ears, whispering softly to keep him quiet and ducking behind a massive hot tub until I was certain his owners weren't going to come out to investigate. When they never came, I raced across the yard and climbed the fence again, this time emptying myself out into the beam of a motion-detector floodlight. Another dog—much bigger, two yards over—began barking then, and I moved as fast as I could out of the floodlight's reach, my path lit by gold-and-slate fireworks, which had appeared with my nerves and adrenaline.

The next yard, fortunately, didn't have a fence, a dog, or any illumination, but I found myself almost walking right up on top of a couple making out in front of a dying fire pit in the backyard. They were too hot into it to notice me, so I veered over one yard and ran to the front corner, which faced the Hollis mansion.

The fence wouldn't be nearly as easy to scale—wrought iron, tall—but I found a tree that hung over it on one side. It had low branches, made for climbing. I scurried up the tree, hugged the trunk as I edged around to the other side, then dropped into the yard, imagining the Hollis family safety consultant shaking his head at the overlooked breach.

The house was still dark. It gave off a creepy vibe, for some reason not looking empty, but the opposite of it. As if there were Hollises on the inside, peering out at me, waiting for me to trip so they could pounce.

"Don't be stupid, Nikki," I told myself. "She didn't beat you before, and she's not going to now." I tried not to think of all the possibilities of what she could do. Although I'd run through the backyard the day Luna had drugged me, I'd never actually approached the house from this side before. But I was pretty sure I knew where to go, so I stuck to the shadows and made my way around a delicately manicured side garden, several fountains, and an aggressively obnoxious gazebo, the home of a ridiculous armless statue. Jesus, it was like these people had everything, just to prove that they could. I wondered if the neighbors thought all this money was made in the movies, or if they knew that a good portion of it was earned, literally, on the backs of young women. Did they know that the armless statue might have been bought with drug money?

The pool was lit up and shimmering in the breeze, making soft ripples against the steps. In any other world, the sound would be comforting to me. I loved swimming. I preferred the beach, but the scent of chlorine and sound of a gurgling pool pump held a special place of excitement in my heart, too.

Mom had loved swimming. She was practically a mermaid. She despised swimming in public, though, because all the men were constantly ogling her. *Some men have no respect,* she used to say. Or at least those were things I remembered, sketchy, disjointed, and out of context. It was the worst part about losing my mom at such a young age. I couldn't trust my memories.

I waited by the gazebo, just watching, searching for something out of place or dangerous-looking. Listening for footsteps or breathing or a voice. But other than the gurgle of the pool pump, the night was still. The pool house was dark, but the door was cracked open. I thought I saw the curtain on the door flutter, but the movement was so slight it might have been a trick of my mind.

I walked around the pool, past the lawn chairs, and approached the pool house door. My heart began pounding with anticipation.

I pushed, and the door popped open with a small squeak. I stepped inside and listened. Nothing. The door swung softly shut behind me. Immediately, I tensed.

"Dru?"

Still nothing.

I took another step inside. I could feel a presence, the faint smell of soap or shampoo or something on skin, the air disturbance of another body. My eyes wouldn't adjust, though. "I'm here," I said. "I need to talk to you."

I heard a noise—a thump—and saw a shadow move, positioning itself in front of me, near the far end of the room. I had a sense of more than just darkness now—the sensation of bumpy gray and black pressed in on me, too. I breathed deep, trying to calm my fear.

"For real, I just need to talk to you about some things, okay? No games this time. Please?"

Something was wrong. I could feel it. I could see it begin to roll in from the corner shadows, like freshly poured asphalt progressing toward me. I rubbed my hands together. Dry, papery. I swallowed, my eyes darting for possible places to take cover. There was a bulky shadow to my right. An easy chair, maybe? I took a step toward it.

"Dru?" I slid my hand into my pocket and wrapped it around my cell phone. If nothing else, I could use it as a weapon. Slowly, I pulled it out of my pocket as I edged another step closer to the chair.

This time the noise I heard was different. Coming from the shadow at the end of the room. Metal clicking on metal. I flicked on my cell phone flashlight.

The room was flooded with light, so bright and unexpected, my free hand flung involuntarily in front of my eyes. I squinted against the ache.

But even in the short amount of time it took me to shield myself from the light, I could see the blond hair, the wafer-thin body, the crocodile eyes.

And a gun, pointed right at me.

"Look at you, Nikki Kill, right on time," Luna Fairchild said, her hands gripped around the gun, her smile steady and cold. "And my brother is late. Just like always."

*R*UN, NIKKI.
Run.

Gunner's voice echoed through my mind, dark bursts of brown. *Be safe. Turn around and get the hell out of there.*

He would have been right to suggest I run. He also would have been so disappointed, because I didn't do it. I wasn't *rooted to my spot.* I wasn't *paralyzed by fear.* I wasn't *taken back to my childhood, frightened that I would meet my mom's fate, blanked out by crimson at an impossibly young age.*

I was just fed up.

I wanted this to be done.

I was pissed. *Ragemonster-red* pissed.

"You don't want to kill me," I said, working to keep my

voice steady. I was no longer messing with Luna, but that didn't mean she didn't terrify me. I could feel her calculated fury pulsating across the room.

She laughed, tossing her hair back without so much as twitching the gun out of place the tiniest centimeter. "Oh, you're so wrong about that. Not only do I want to, I actually need to."

"Why? Because Peyton figured out that I'm her sister?"

Her smile fell the tiniest bit.

I used my momentum to my advantage. "Yeah, I know, Luna. I know all about why Peyton was suddenly acting so strange. She wanted out of this family, she was planning to run with the money she was extorting from you, and she was reaching out to the one blood relative she thought could help her. Me."

"Lies," Luna said, the gun as steady as a rock. "She was reaching out to you so she could blackmail you, too. Peyton likes money, and you were just another source. When she was done bleeding us dry, she was going to go after you. *Sister.*"

"Why would a Hollis come to me for money? And what could she possibly have on me, anyway?"

"Because she could," Luna said, as if I were the dumbest person she'd ever encountered. "Peyton was a scammer. A user. She always knew what everyone's weak spot was the instant she met them. She knew all about your sweet little family, that's what she had on you." She turned her head to the side, her blond waves cascading beautifully down one shoulder. With the gun in her hand, she truly did look like a movie star, like she was simply playing the part of a psychotic killer. "She knew that somebody did the naughty with someone they shouldn't have and, oops, out popped a baby. How embarrassed your devoted little daddy would be for the world to find out. Are you sure he's even your real daddy, Nikki? Or was he the naughty one? How are you so sure your mom was the skank?"

I ground my teeth together, forcing myself not to let her push my buttons. Not to rush her. There was too much distance between us, and I had no idea how good of a shot she might be. As fast as I was, a bullet could close the distance much faster.

Luna's smile spread wider. "Aw, did I hurt your feelings? So sorry. It must hurt to hear that your new sister was only in it for herself."

Only in it for herself. I saw a brief flash of Peyton in the hospital, her hair fanned out against the pillow. I saw the way she opened her eyes, tentatively, in response to my voice. I saw the smile she gave me.

It's not unusual for there to be involuntary muscle action, the nurse had said. But she was wrong. I knew it then and I knew it now. Peyton was responding to me, to my voice.

She'd smiled. She'd told me in that instant of "involuntary" movement that she'd meant to be sisters, not that she'd meant to squeeze me for cash. She was trying to protect me.

"You're wrong," I said. "You don't have any idea what Peyton would have done."

"Honey," Luna said, removing one hand from the gun to swipe her hair back over her shoulder, "nobody knew Peyton Hollis better than I did. I have *been* Peyton Hollis, practically more often than she has. My mom always liked Peyton better. She thought Peyton had so much more potential than I did. So I proved her wrong. I was better at being Peyton Hollis than she ever could have been. What Peyton could never accept, I took advantage of. She didn't want to be an escort? Fine. I'll be one for her. I like money, and I love fucking over my mother by selling her drugs to her own clients right under her nose. Peyton thought she was the better actress? Please. I never shared her dreams of getting an Oscar, but I think we both know that I could." Her eyes grew wide and sad, her full bottom lip quivering. "I don't know, Officer," she said in a bereft voice. "I don't know why Nikki Kill would commit suicide in my pool house. She's been dating my brother. She must have needed attention."

The red deepened, mixed with the gray and black, and shot up in gold-tinged fireworks. This was all about sibling rivalry? Peyton was dying because her sister was jealous?

She took a step toward me, and then another. Her hands gripped the gun more tightly. I could see the whites of her knuckles.

"Nobody would believe you. Chris Martinez would not believe you."

"Oh, wouldn't he, though?" Her face grew hard again. "I had it all taken care of. All of it. But here you come along, a new sister, who thinks she suddenly knows everything there is to know about darling Peyton. Fucking Dru. Trying to be a Hollis. I don't care whose mommy and daddy are whose. You are not one of us, no matter how much you pretend."

"You're not a Hollis, either," I pointed out. I found that my free hand was rising, palm out, surrender-style, as she continued to walk toward me. I didn't intend to surrender. I needed a plan. My mind raced for one, but all I could come up with was *keep her talking.*

"I went through hell to be reunited with my mom. And Peyton tried to screw it up. And now, when it looks like things are going to be resolved, here you come to screw it up. I am not going to lose my place here because of you. Do you understand?" Her controlled voice had gone shrieky. "You will be just another stain on the carpet. Carpet that we will have replaced before your sad daddy puts you in the ground. That's right. *We.* My parents are fully aware that you need to disappear, just like Peyton, and they have just the resources to make that happen."

"Dru will turn you in," I said. She was so close now I could see her arms trembling. The gun was heavy and she was slight. She couldn't hold it out in front of her like that forever. If I could just get it away from her . . .

"Lover Boy Dru has too much to lose," Luna said. "You think I set him up? *He* set *us* up. We all met. All of us, right here in this very pool house. We agreed."

I shook my head, confused. "Agreed on what?"

She swung the gun down in short jabs as if pounding on an invisible table. I jumped every time, convinced she would accidentally pull the trigger. She was just feet away from me now. "You know exactly what. To get rid of Peyton. She wouldn't let anyone come with the money but one of us. Guess who?"

"Dru," I said. I knew it because I'd heard it on the recording. She'd asked Dru because she trusted him.

Luna was nodding, looking thrilled that I finally got it. "And we all agreed, Dru would take his good friend Rigo."

"Arrigo Basile?" I asked through numb lips.

She nodded again. "Ding, ding, ding! Rigo was going to kill her. The five mil was for him all along. Hit money. Dru knew it, we all knew it. We all agreed."

"But she didn't die."

Luna's triumphant look turned sour. "No, she didn't. Dru said Rigo got soft, took the money, and ran away. But if you ask me what happened, Dru turned on Rigo, beat the crap out of him, and gave Rigo the money to run. My parents think so, too, but what can we really do about it? If we made Dru disappear, it would start to look really fishy to the cops, now, wouldn't it?"

I thought back to the bruises I'd seen on Dru at the hospital, and the ones I found later at the apartment. He'd said he'd gotten them playing basketball. He'd said something about Hollises leaving it all on the court. "Uh-oh," Luna said, bending slightly to look in my face. "Looks like I touched a nerve. Are you starting to lose faith in your innocent little boyfriend? You should. He wanted her murdered just as much as the rest of us."

"I don't believe you," I said, but the words were weak. What had I missed? *I didn't hurt her,* Dru had exclaimed when Chris Martinez showed up to arrest him. *I didn't touch her.* But that was really a technicality, wasn't it? Dru didn't touch her—he simply hired Arrigo to do it—so he was innocent? "I don't . . ." But I couldn't finish the sentence. My hands shook. My knees wanted to buckle.

Luna actually had the guts to look gleeful. "Aw, I'm sorry to be the bearer of bad news. Not only is your boyfriend one of us, he actually screwed up the one job he had." She giggled. "He's not even a successful murderer."

"He lied to me about everything," I said, my voice flat, numb. For the first time, it was really sinking in how stupid I had been when it came to Dru. I'd gone from curious about why Peyton had called me to jumping in the sack with her brother, thinking blissful violet thoughts, without knowing much of anything about him. And the one thing that I did know about him for sure was that he was closed off. Angry. Mysterious. Yet even after I'd found the camera card in his apartment, even after I'd found the bruises on his ribs, I'd continued to trust him.

Why?

I didn't trust anyone. That was what I'd told myself back when I was eight years old and tucking myself into bed at night because my mother was gone. Don't trust anyone. Don't fall in love. Love and trust get you hurt. They get you killed.

Suddenly, I was washed over by a deep indigo wave, standing under the foaming crest, in front of me an endless nighttime on the sea. I'd never contemplated betrayal before—not on any real level—but I knew instantly that this was what I was seeing. Deep indigo, deep betrayal.

God, I was the biggest idiot in the world. I felt like a failure. I'd failed Peyton. She'd given me all these hints and clues, and I'd been literally sleeping with the person who'd tried to kill her.

Chris Martinez had been right.

Luna had been right.

I was the only one who was wrong.

"He lied," I repeated.

"Oh, please," Luna's voice cut in. "Spare me the drama. You knew what you were getting into the first time you stepped foot into Peyton's room at the hospital." Had I? I specifically recalled seeing the crimson and getting the hell out of there with my heart in my damn throat. I remembered feeling faint, sitting in a rolling chair, Chris Martinez getting me some water. And . . . yes, I also remembered thinking this was a mess I didn't want to get into. Peyton Hollis was not my problem, I had thought. I didn't need this shit.

Luna was right. A part of me knew this from the very beginning. A part of me ignored the trouble that was surely coming my way.

I fell into bed with Dru Hollis despite my own misgivings.

"Anyway, I think we're done here. Say good-bye, Nikki," Luna said, leveling the gun right at my chest. I aimed the light at her again. Even though she was only a few feet away, seeing where the gun was pointing made me relax a little. A confident shooter would have aimed at my head. She was a bad shot and she knew it.

I squeezed my free fist together, pushing away the indigo, fixed my eyes on her hand, and settled back on one foot, ready to roll at the slightest movement of her finger.

There was a noise outside the door at my back. A shuffling noise. Footsteps. Both Luna and I glanced at the door. And then everything seemed to go in slow motion.

The doorknob turned. Luna and I locked eyes. Her lips curled into a smile that looked more like a snarl, and I swear to God I could see her palm flex as her finger began to put pressure on the trigger.

"What—" was all Dru got out before I turned and bolted right through him, knocking him backward onto the pool deck and tumbling on top of him just as the boom of Luna's gun deafened me. I felt wind, and then splinters, caress my right cheek, and a blanket of warmth sluice down the side of my face. I didn't even pause to check the damage.

"What the hell are you doing?" I heard Dru yell, his voice bubbly and foggy and faraway, as if he were talking from the bottom of the pool.

"Don't let her . . . ," Luna screamed back.

I scrambled to my feet, droplets of blood making the deck slippery under my shoes, and hurried around the lawn chairs. There was nothing but open space between me and the fence. I would be target practice, and Luna had proven that she wasn't afraid to shoot. And that maybe she wasn't as bad a shot as I'd originally taken her for.

Panicked, I whipped my head left and right for an escape. To go back the way I'd come in, I would have to traverse my way around the pool again, which meant I would have to run past Luna. I gulped in air, trying to slow my breathing, trying to calm myself. I couldn't fight if I was too frightened to move.

I thought about Gunner, who'd said the best offense was a good defense. *Be safe, Nikki,* I could hear him say. Gunner wouldn't stay out here like a sitting duck any more than he would go back inside that pool house. He would find a safe place to be, where he could see and hear his threat, and then he would deal with it.

I raced for the kitchen door that I'd scrambled out of, half drugged, just yesterday. The house was dark, empty— I'd noticed it when I arrived—and at least I knew what was on the other side of that door. I'd beaten Luna once inside that house; I could do it again.

The door was locked. Damn it. I whipped my head around, searching for an open window or a secluded path out of here or . . . anything. But there was nothing, and I could hear, through the dull ringing in my ears, Luna's and Dru's voices coming from the pool house.

Without thinking, I grabbed a paving stone from the landscaping. With two hands, I hoisted it above my head, and then brought it down with all my might on the door- knob. It made what sounded like a monstrous noise, and when I glanced back over my shoulder, Dru and Luna were coming. I hefted it over my head and brought it down again. This time the monstrous noise was accompanied by the sound of metal clanging on the porch. The doorknob. The door sprang open and I ran inside.

If the blackout shades had made the kitchen shadowy

when I'd been in here last, it was downright cave-like now, the clock on the microwave glowing in gold, giving off little bursts of color. I saw shapes hulking tidily on the counters—coffeemaker, blender, toaster, knife block—and started toward them, working my way around a small oak kitchen table, hoping I could get to a weapon before Luna got to me. But I had only just rounded the table when I heard footsteps.

"What the hell? Luna!" Bill Hollis's voice.

I wanted to freeze. All the bones and muscles in my body wanted to turn to jelly. I wanted to put my palms up, surrender. But something inside of me told me there would be no surrendering here. Bill Hollis was not a man who liked to lose. I had to act.

I could just see the silhouette of him rounding the corner into the kitchen, and I slipped through the other doorway to the living room. I found myself at the foot of the spiral staircase I'd been up before. I couldn't see the steps very well, which was almost a relief, given how they'd danced under me last time.

Bill Hollis lumbered to the back door, assessing the damage to the doorknob. "Luna!" he called again.

"Nikki Kill! She's in the house!" I heard her call back, and my spine turned cold. Bill Hollis got very quiet. I could hear the light shuffle of his feet, but even that was so soft it was hard to tell where it was coming from. I tried not to breathe.

"Stay outside, Luna," I heard him say, quietly, calmly. "I'll take care of her in here."

I could see his form come from the den doorway across the room and stop. He seemed to be looking right at me, but it was impossible to tell for sure. He didn't move; I didn't move.

"I see you," he finally said, in a regular talking voice, but it sounded like a sonic boom in the silence. "You aren't getting out of here, you understand? You're an intruder. I have every right to protect my family from an intruder."

I swallowed, feeling his words all the way to my toes. My breath sounded incredibly loud to my own ears. I could sense, more than see, asphalt-like fear rolling under my feet.

"All you had to do was stay out of our business," he said. "I might have even made it worth your while. Gotten you and your pathetic father a real house. One on the beach."

I licked my lips. Tried to keep my footing on the roiling gray and black.

"But you just couldn't stay away, could you? Sleeping with my son, hanging out at Peyton's bedside all the time. Messing with Luna. With our house. I could have had you arrested ten times over. But now I'm glad I didn't, because I get to deal with you myself. Tell me, Nikki, was it worth it?"

Immediately, I thought of Peyton turning her head and smiling at me in her hospital bed. Her face faded into Mom's face, turning her head and gazing at me from the pool of blood. The crimson surrounded both of them, and the memory nearly bowled me over. But I got to look into the eyes of my mother and my sister as they faced the reality of leaving this world. I got to see that they loved me. "Yes," I said. "It was worth it. Peyton is my sister."

"She is Luna's sister," Bill snapped. I jumped. "She is Dru's sister. She is my child. A Hollis. Being a Hollis is a privilege. Peyton didn't appreciate the privilege, but she's learned her lesson. I've worked my ass off my whole life to have what I have. I can't let some snotty teenager take it all away from me, turn me into a laughingstock no better than some working-class family. You can bet Peyton won't be looking into your tramp mother again."

His last words hit me like red—*ragemonster*—arrows to the chest. I felt my breathing get faster, my fists clench harder. "Don't talk about my mother," I said.

"Truth hurts, doesn't it?" he said, and I could see his teeth flashing white from across the room. And then his voice went into a low growl. "Don't worry. You won't be in pain for very long." His shadow shifted as he began to advance toward me.

I had to do something, but he was between me and the front door. Luna was outside the back door. Dru was God-knew-where. I wished more than anything that I'd called Detective Martinez before coming over here. The image of him finding my body, thinking that he'd repeatedly warned me and if only I'd listened, having to tell my father that the only other person in this world who he loved had been murdered, too, was what finally loosened my feet.

I turned and bolted up the stairs, unsure what I would do once I was up there, but certain it was safer than where I was at the moment.

Or so I thought.

Waiting at the top of the stairs, her face peeled back in a snarl, was Vanessa Hollis.

"We tried to warn you," she said, planting her hands on my shoulders. Letting out a roar, she shoved forward, with far more might than I would have ever expected out of someone so tiny, and I went reeling. My arms windmilled as I tried to regain my footing, but she'd pushed too far.

I fell backward, my legs snapping over my head and turning me into a backward somersault, and then another, and another. I was distantly aware of pain as my ribs cracked against the edge of a step, my head and shoulders and hips and legs bouncing off hard wood and wrought iron, neon green flashing behind my eyelids.

And then my head came down on the floor at the bottom, and everything went black.

29

AT FIRST I wasn't sure where I was. I was only distantly aware that I was moving. Or being moved, that was more like it. I could feel a burning wetness on my cheek, and my limbs throbbed. Colors wiggled and hopped inside my head, a shifting kaleidoscope of confusion. My side split with fire every time I breathed in. I pressed my arm into my ribs and nearly shrieked as they thunked and crunched together in an unnatural way. My other arm found its way to my head, which was foggy and disoriented.

"Get your things," I heard. A command, but I wasn't sure what things I was supposed to get. "I'll take care of this and then we'll go."

I opened my eyes, and that was when everything started

coming together again. I was being pulled by my feet, the back of my head sliding on tile. A stainless steel refrigerator hummed by my ear. When I turned my head to look at it, the surface was a shifting checkerboard of neon green and orange, the squares trading places over and over again. I closed my eyes and opened them again. The person dragging me had silver hair and was wearing a ring that glinted in the shadows.

"Okay," a female voice said. "I'll be ready. Make it fast."

All at once I understood what was going on. Bill Hollis wasn't commanding me to get ready. I was what he was going to take care of first.

He was going to kill me.

Come on, Nikki, move. Gunner's voice in my head. *Defend. Get to where you can fight.*

That meant I had to get up.

Summoning all the strength I had, I pulled my right foot free of his grasp and kicked at his knees, one, two, three times. On the third, I connected, eliciting a growl. He let go of my other foot and stumbled backward. My opportunity.

Clumsily, I pulled myself to standing, still pressing my arm into my ribs. My head ached and my eyes swam, and I could only take shallow breaths. I couldn't focus on anything other than what I was doing, except I was aware that Bill Hollis was coming toward me again. I backed up until the small of my back hit the kitchen counter, and then I turned and scrambled for a weapon, blearily peering through my out-of-control colors. My hands landed on the knife block I'd seen when I'd first come in. I grabbed the first one I could get to and held it up in front of me.

"Get away from me," I said, my voice coming out breathy and scratchy.

I saw a flash of teeth. The man was actually smiling. "You're an intruder," he said. "A stalker. You had a weapon. I was scared for my life."

He lunged toward me and I swung the knife at him. He dropped back, just barely missing the blade, and then came at me again, his hands outstretched to grab me.

I swung the knife again, this time making contact, slicing deep through one of his palms. He roared—a bellow that cleared my head a bit—and I instantly heard the patter of blood hitting the tile floor. I swiped again, this time catching his other forearm. He stumbled away from me, staring at his palm in shock. *Do what you know to do, Nikki*, I thought. I threw a front kick, closing my eyes from the pain that wrenched up through my knee with the movement. I connected somewhere solid—his upper chest, maybe. He let out a strangled cry and then went down, his head hitting the marble counter on the way. He was out.

I stood in the middle of the kitchen, panting shallowly,

watching him, my hand still gripping the knife so tight it was cramping, my hair stuck to the side of my face with drying blood.

I had to get out of here.

I would have to go the long way around, unless I wanted to step over him, which I didn't. I wasn't sure if I'd have the strength to fend him off if he were to grab my leg a second time.

But I had only taken two steps when I heard a scream to my side. I barely had time to react before Vanessa Hollis came barreling in from the living room, holding a brass statue in both hands. She said nothing intelligible—only that primal scream—as she came at me with it, swinging it down from over her head just as I had brought the paving stone down on the doorknob earlier.

I lifted my arm to block the blow, the crash making my entire arm instantly numb, my entire field of vision flash green. My fingers let go of the knife. It clattered to the ground, skittering away to where I could no longer see it. I cried out in pain, holding my throbbing arm.

Ignore the colors, Nikki. Put them out of your mind.

I glanced up, and Vanessa was still coming at me with the statue. All I could think was *cover your ribs, cover your ribs, cover your ribs.* Holding one arm tight over my broken ribs, and the other up in defense mode, I bent my knees and waited for her, pulling up one knee at just the right moment to connect with her stomach.

Vanessa Hollis flew back, landing on her butt, coughing and gagging from the wind being knocked out of her. *Go, Nikki,* my brain told me. *Get out.*

But I had only turned halfway when Vanessa let out a yell. "You nosy bitch!" She threw the statue, and it hit me in the temple. I reeled, my vision going swimmy again, my head bursting with fireworks of pain. I felt warmth trickle down my ear, and when I touched where the statue had connected, my hand came away dark with blood.

Unbelievably, Vanessa was pulling herself up and coming at me again. I only had just enough time to sink back into my fighting stance, letting my training take over. As soon as she was close enough, I shin-kicked her to the knee and then pulled my arm back to use a technique Gunner had only shown me once and I'd never had a chance to try in practice—an ear slap. I cupped my hand and let it fly, catching her squarely over her right ear.

Her hand flew to her ear as she fell back nearly on top of Bill, who was just starting to rouse. I had no time. I had to get out.

I zipped through the back door, feeling the dread of knowing that I was right back at square one. But now that I knew what was inside the house, I knew my chances of surviving outside were at least a little bit better.

I slipped behind a bush next to the back door and looked

for Luna or Dru. I could see neither, though I could still hear both. I dropped to a crouch and ran to the side of the pool house, pressing myself into the shadows. I ran the length of the pool house until I found a corner with a trash can parked in it, then climbed behind it. I was covered, hidden, huddled in the dark, pressing my palms into my eyes, hoping for the confusing hues to stop battering me, hoping my ears and my head would clear so I could listen for Luna.

Every inch of my body screamed with pain. I was bleeding and broken, and every breath brought white lights to my eyes. I wondered if this was how Peyton felt the night of the attack. I wondered if she'd fought back as I had, if her colors had gone crazy like mine were doing, or if she'd just accepted her fate the way Mom had accepted hers. Or if she'd had a chance to even realize what was happening. If either of them had.

Peyton had called me before her attack. Maybe she'd been begging for help.

Maybe I needed to ask for help, too.

I pulled out my phone. I'd never programmed Chris Martinez into it, but I'd looked at his business card so many times, I'd memorized the color pattern anyway. I hoped I was remembering it correctly through my injured haze.

The phone rang for what seemed like forever.

"It's Nikki Kill," I whispered, after he finally answered.

"Nikki? Are you okay? What's going on?"

"I need you," I said. "Hollis house. Now."

"Get out of there. I'm nearb—"

But suddenly I could hear Luna's and Dru's voices, so I ended the call and slid the phone back into my pocket. He would be too smart to call me back. He would know from the way I sounded that I was hiding.

He was the one cop I could trust.

Their words sounded like mumbles to me. I caught only partial sentences.

". . . told her everything . . ."

". . . don't know what went down that night . . ."

"Did you like jail? Because if you don't . . ."

". . . has to be another . . ."

"Shut up, do you want her to . . ."

The voices went farther away, as if Dru and Luna had gone into the pool house, and I thought I could hear the sounds of things being moved inside. Maybe fighting, a crash here, a thud there. I straightened, shimmied toward a window, and peeked inside. Suddenly everything seemed too silent. I could hear everything and nothing. My ears were still betraying me. My cheek ached, and I could feel blood dripping from my chin. I couldn't think about it. I couldn't let myself see the color of that blood, that crimson, not even in my mind, or I would lose it. I needed to keep my calm. I needed to be aware of other things.

I thought I heard shifting leaves behind me. I tensed,

crouching into a ready stance, but the sound stopped, replaced by the beating of my heart.

A few minutes passed. Just when I began to think maybe I should come out of hiding, I heard them again, whispering. Fighting about how best to find me.

"I'm telling you, she's over by the gazebo," Dru said. "I saw her go."

"Bullshit," Luna hissed. "She's hiding out here somewhere. I can smell the smoke on her."

Shit. I'd never thought about that.

"Let's at least just look." If I didn't know better, I would think Dru was trying to lead Luna away from where I really was, so I could get away. But Dru was not the man I'd thought he was, so for all I knew he was trying to find me right along with her.

"Chill. We will, but we're going back here first."

"She might get away."

"I'm the one with the gun, so we do what I say."

"I'm going to look for her in there."

"Fine. Go. I don't need you."

The voices were getting closer now, and then the footsteps softened, swooshed through grass. They were coming right for me. Again, I thought I heard a swishing noise behind me, and realized it must have been a trick of acoustics. Their footsteps ricocheting off their privacy fence.

"Come out, come out, wherever you are," Luna sang,

and then giggled, sending chills rippling up and down my spine.

I crouched deeper, pressed my elbows into my sides, and strained my eyes, trying to make out the shifting shadows in the yard. My cheek itched. The kaleidoscope had slowed down, honing itself into a few colors—black hate, orange danger, so much red—that I could mostly ignore.

Just when I thought I heard a footstep behind me again, Luna's face popped up over the trash can.

"Boo!" she crowed, bringing the gun up to point over the trash can at me. "Found you!"

30

I DIDN'T THINK. There wasn't time to think. Luna had already proven that she was willing to shoot, and behind the trash can I was a fish in a barrel.

I took a breath, which hitched with my aching ribs. Springing up with a yell, I hammer-fisted Luna's forearm, feeling a dull crack under her skin. She yelped as the gun flew through the air, bouncing in the grass. She sucked in air and grabbed for her arm, but I didn't give her the chance. Anchoring my back against the wall, I front-kicked the trash can with everything I had, shoving it into Luna, who fell under the force. Empty beer and wine bottles rolled out on top of her.

I sprang out of my corner, leaping over the trash can and

landing in a fighting stance, turning left and right, watching for the others, hoping Chris Martinez was near enough to be arriving soon. Dru was still nowhere to be found. Every noise on the night air made me swing toward it, my breath ripping out of me so hard, spit collected on the front of my shirt.

Luna was crying, babbling, rolling around under the spilled trash as she spat out threats. I didn't have much time to get away, but I was afraid to move. There were so many places for Dru or Vanessa or even Bill to pop out at me. Catch me off guard. Finally, Luna untangled herself and got to her knees, holding her arm to her chest. She slipped, but then found her footing and lurched toward the gun.

"You will regret that, you bitch!" she snarled.

I reached the gun first, scooping it out of the grass and holding it in front of me, but my hands were shaking with so much adrenaline—*gold bottle rockets, kapow, kapow, kapow*—I couldn't point it at her. I had been trained to use my body to fight. I had no idea what to do with a gun, other than keep it away from her.

I started to back up toward the fence line. "You don't want to do this, Luna," I said. "You're already hurt. Just let me go before this gets any worse." The wind shifted and a pool raft rattled across the deck, causing me to flick my eyes worriedly that way. Where the hell was Chris Martinez?

Luna laughed, looking completely unhinged with a twig hanging in her hair and sweeping like a pendulum across her forehead. "Bitch, you're the one bleeding."

"Your arm is broken, Luna," I called. I swallowed, tried to tighten my grip on the gun. "I felt it. Let me go so you can get it fixed. We can be done with this."

She continued walking toward me, completely unfazed by the gun in my hand. "Oh, we will never be done. Not until you're permanently gone. Don't you understand?"

"Dru!" I shouted. I licked my lips, but I didn't dare take my eyes off Luna. "You better come out or I'm going to have to shoot your sister!" One of the dogs I'd dodged earlier began to bark again, setting off a chain of barks throughout the neighborhood.

"Yeah, Dru," Luna said in that singsongy voice again. "You should come out so you can say your last good-byes to your sweet little Nikki." She cupped one ear. "What? You don't care what happens to her? Oh, yeah, that's right, because you're in it as deep as the rest of us!"

"Come out, Dru!" I yelled.

"Come out, Dru!" Luna mimicked right after me. She let her hurt arm drop to her side and rolled her eyes. "Okay, this shit's just getting boring now." She rushed at me.

I stumbled backward two steps, trying to convince my fingers to pull the trigger. But the gun was so heavy and I was so filled with confused energy, I couldn't relay the message from brain to hand. Bumpy black and gray swirled in my mind, silver, flashing oranges and yellows and ragemonster red, and mists of green. Fear, mistrust, danger, pain, fury—a palette of awful. I couldn't concentrate. I'd never done this. I'd never thought I'd have to. And Luna was moving so fast.

She was two steps away, and then one, and I still hadn't done anything with the gun. I took another step back, my arm cocking backward to do what I did best. I hit Luna across the temple with the butt of the gun, but she was too close for the connection to do any real damage. She let out a squawk, dug her claws into the side of my neck with one hand, and grabbed at the gun with the other. She was moving with too much force, and I was off balance from not being ready. We both went down, Luna on top of me, the back of my hand smacking the ground and the gun flipping away about three feet. My ribs screamed, taking my breath away.

I tried to sit up, to go after the gun before Luna could get it again, but she was tearing at my neck, my arm. She reared back and, with a yell, slammed her forehead into my right eyebrow. I saw a flash of light and felt the neon pain of a new wound opening. My eyes immediately flooded with tears, making it impossible to see. I covered my face with my free hand, but when I felt her rear back again, I grabbed a fistful of hair, just the way Stefan had grabbed mine that night in the hotel. With all my strength, I brought my elbow across her jaw. I heard her teeth click together, hard, and a grunt escaped her. I straightened my arm to roll her off me.

Luna screamed and scrambled, flailing, both hands scratching at the hand I had buried in her hair.

"Let me go, you bitch! I will kill you!"

She peeled deep trails through the back of my hand that felt like fire. I had no choice but to let go, but to make up for it, I turned and axe-kicked her to the ribs, just as I had fantasized doing to her on the back of my car that day at school. She bent her legs to deflect most of the impact, though, and rolled away, reaching for the gun.

"No!" I yelled, grunting, trying to get up, to figure out some miracle way of getting to the gun first. But I was too late. She was already there.

I heard footsteps pound across the patio, around the pool, coming toward me. I still couldn't see because of my watering eyes and the throbbing in my cheek and forehead, but I could make out what looked like Dru, coming toward us fast, his arms outstretched.

This was it. I couldn't fight them both off. I was too tired, too confused, in too much pain. Whether Peyton and I were real sisters, we were sisters in this. We were sisters in giving ourselves for the secrets and the truth. I supposed, blood or not, that was what made a connection matter, anyway.

Luna staggered to her feet, panting, bleeding, her shirt ripped, her hair wild. She had the gun held in her good hand, low, pointing to the ground. She started to level it at me, still on the ground, too weak and disoriented to stand. I dragged myself on my elbows and feet, trying to get away. If I didn't get up, I was going to die right here.

"Luna!" Dru yelled, and the footsteps got closer. But instead of coming at me, he got between us and faced Luna, shielding me. I was almost numb with shock. "Run, Nikki! Get out of here!"

I backed into a tree and somehow used it to pull myself to my feet.

"Go, Nikki! Now!"

Luna turned, brought the gun to shoulder level, and fired.

I gasped as I saw Dru drop to the ground, instantly quiet.

He'd been trying to stop her. He'd been trying to save me.

It felt like Luna and I stared at Dru's limp body for hours, but it was probably only the span of two heartbeats before I felt my feet propelling me forward, my body rigid with red rage. *Fire engines. Cherries. Lava.* Fast, faster, dead run. Luna only had time to turn her head before I reached her.

You know what to do, Nikki. You've done this a million times before in the dojang. *You've trained for this. Just do what you do.*

I stopped, put all my weight on my back foot, turned my whole body, and then brought my leg up, extending my foot. Roundhouse kick. The best I'd ever landed. My foot hit

Luna's head with a hollow thud, and she dropped like a sack of sand. All my colors blinked out at once.

I took a few breaths and then grabbed the gun out of her hand. The barrel was hot. I turned and threw it with a grunt. It skidded across the patio, then plunked into the deep end of the pool and sank to the bottom.

IT WAS ONLY then that I heard the sirens. The lights bounced around the backyard in fits and starts, and for a moment I was unsure if I was the only one seeing the colors. Police cars out front. I staggered in a circle so that I was facing the mansion.

"Back here!" I yelled.

In moments, three cops stormed the yard. I held my hands up in surrender, but the fourth cop to come around to the backyard ran straight to me. It was Detective Chris Martinez.

"You okay? You okay?" he asked, checking me over. "Jesus, you're bleeding everywhere."

I nodded. "But Dru . . ."

Martinez hurried over to Dru's body and knelt beside him, tearing open his shirt and pressing both hands low on his chest. Another officer radioed in for an ambulance. It seemed impossible to me that he could still be alive. There was so much blood. And he was so still.

My foot ached. Hitting the heavy bag was not the same

as hitting the back of a human head. But I limped my way over to Dru as well and knelt beside him. He was in bad shape, but he was still conscious. He saw me and tried to sit up, but failed.

"I tried to stop him, Nikki," he said. "I tried to . . . save her . . . she . . . was right about . . . us. I changed my mind." A tear slipped from the corner of one eye. His face was so pale it looked waxy. He swallowed, wincing. "I . . . moved her . . . I called the . . ."

"Okay," I said. I pushed his sweaty hair away from his forehead. The letters on his T-shirt slowly soaked through with red, but I was afraid to look closely enough to tell if it was the red of his blood, or the crimson I'd gotten to know so well. Luna had come to and was instantly making a hell of a fuss. "Help is coming. Just hang on." He didn't need to finish. I knew what he was going to say. He'd tried to save Peyton. He was just a little too late.

"I'm so sorry, Nikki," he said. I noticed blood begin to ring his bottom lip. I still couldn't bring myself to look at the gunshot, to look at Chris Martinez's hands as he pressed into the wound to stop the bleeding.

"I knew it!" I heard Luna yell from where the officer had sat her up on the lawn. "I knew you betrayed us! Bastard!"

"That's enough," I heard the officer say. I wanted to go over there and yank every hair out of Luna's head, to tell her to shut the hell up, that this was no longer about them.

I wanted to show her the crimson, all the crimson that had now shaded the pool water, unmistakably the synesthesia making its statement about Dru.

But I was too spent, too tired, too focused on keeping my eyes on Dru's to do anything.

It hadn't been just a technicality. Dru had been innocent. He'd changed his mind when they met up with her that night. The bruises I'd found on his hands and face and side weren't from Peyton fighting him off; they were from him fighting Arrigo Basile. Either way, he hadn't been the one to attack her. He'd tried to stop her attacker. He'd moved her car and taken her to the elementary school and called for an ambulance. He'd tried to do the right thing, and he ended up making himself look really guilty. Luna had seen that and did what Luna did best—take advantage. She'd set him up for the fall, but he didn't deserve it. Ultimately, he'd sacrificed himself for Peyton. He'd decided that she was more important than all that he had to lose.

All at once I felt vindicated and defeated. Because I knew, before the paramedics stormed in, pushed me away, and started shouting, "coding," that Dru wasn't going to make it.

"It's okay," I said, stroking his hair again. "She opened her eyes for me. She's going to be fine." It was the truth, and it was also a lie. But it was a lie I thought he needed to hear at the time. It was the lie that allowed him to let go.

■ ■ ■

THE PARAMEDICS WERE a blur of activity, and I was outside of it, my limbs suddenly so weak and tired I couldn't even stand up, my foot throbbing with my pulse, my ribs aching, my head pounding. I was dimly aware of neon green lighting up my foot with every pulse, of putrid brown filling my heart, but finally I was able to ignore my synesthesia. I scooted on my butt to the pool deck and propped my back against a lawn chair. I hugged my knees to my chest, nestled my face on top of them, and cried.

I felt a shoe scuff on the patio next to me. I didn't look up.

"Hey."

I continued crying, letting my tears wet the knees of my jeans, letting my nose run freely.

There was a shifting, a sound of keys and things jingling with the movement. "Hey," the voice said again, much closer to my ear this time.

I finally turned my head, taking in Chris Martinez's face through slitted and blurry eyes. He was crouched in front of me.

"We need to get you checked out," he said softly.

"I'm fine," I said, trying to turn my face back to the safety of my knees.

"You've got a nasty gash on your cheek. You've been shot, Nikki. And you've got a cut on your head and I can see that you're in pain. You have to get that taken care of."

"Why do you even care?" I said angrily, my words muffled by my jeans. "Aren't you here to tell me you were right about Dru?"

He was silent for so long, I chanced another look at him. "I wasn't," he said. "Not entirely. I didn't start to piece it all together until that night at the hotel." He turned his face upward. The moon shone on his forehead. "I wouldn't have figured it out without you, Nikki."

I made a snorting noise. If he was trying to praise me, it was too little, too late. I didn't want praise. I wanted to go back in time to before this happened to Peyton. I wanted to warn her not to try to do this on her own. I wanted to save her from herself.

But that could never have happened. Peyton wouldn't have listened to a girl like me. Not until we were sisters.

31

THEY OFFICIALLY RULED Dru as "dead on scene." Which meant that I'd held the last of his life, literally, in my hands. I sat in the emergency room bay staring at my palms, trying to piece together what I could have done differently. How I could have saved him.

It turned out Luna's first bullet had definitely grazed my cheek. Another inch and I could've been the dead one. It wasn't lost on me as I sat there numbly, letting the nurse bandage up my cheek, that had I just stood still at the pool house, Dru would have lived. I felt partly responsible for his death.

The nurse took me to X-ray, wrapped me up, gave me instructions, had me sign papers, whatever. I was mostly just remembering the way Dru's hands felt as they slid down my waist that first day in Peyton's apartment. How his skin smelled like expensive soap. How his hair was soft and feathery and lay perfectly across his forehead, always. How he'd said he liked me because I was brave, and that I didn't really understand then that he'd tried to be brave for Peyton too late and felt responsible for what happened to her.

I remembered how boyish he'd looked as his father led him from the police station to the DREAMS car. How cowed. Defeated. I felt sorry for that boy. I didn't blame that boy for what had happened with Peyton.

Had Dru not been a Hollis, he might have been a dream guy.

Which, of course, meant he would have had nothing to do with me.

I slept for a solid day after I got home. Now that Luna was locked up, I no longer had to worry about anyone getting into my house. I no longer had to be on high alert. When I woke up, I went downstairs and ate, then went right back upstairs and fell asleep again.

Dad came home at some point while I was sleeping, and I had a vague memory of him sitting on the side of my bed, brushing my hair back. Maybe I'd dreamed it, or maybe it was real, but I could have sworn he was crying. Later, he came up with some soup and made me take what seemed like a hundred pills. He didn't ask questions. But for once I didn't think it was because he didn't care. For some reason, I had a feeling he wasn't asking because he already knew.

I got up on that second day and started the shower, not remembering a word of instruction about what I was supposed to do about my wounds. I peeled away the bandage that the ER nurse had plastered over my cheek, sucking air in through gritted teeth from the pain. The wound was stiff, ugly, burnt-looking. My cheek puckered around it. I touched it gingerly, the pain shooting through my entire head. It was going to leave a hell of a scar. Wait until Gunner saw it. He would flip.

The shower stung, and the water ran red around my feet. I still had dirt caked under my fingernails and found a smear of blood across my chest. I scrubbed at my skin until it tingled. I got out looking flushed and clean. I rebandaged my cheek, not doing nearly as good a job as the nurse had, pulled my wet hair up into a loose ponytail, and headed downstairs with my chem book. It had been a hell of a few weeks, and now I was in real trouble with graduation. If I didn't get my shit together soon, even Mrs. Lee would give up on me. I would study a little with lunch, and then I would head to the hospital, see if I could get Peyton to open her eyes again. I wanted to tell her that everything was over and it was safe for her to come out now.

No sooner did I get downstairs, though, than the doorbell rang. I was surprised by the jolt of fear that ran through me at the sound, but then I shook it off. It was going to take time to get over the feeling of being hunted.

I set my book on the bottom stair and opened the door. Detective Chris Martinez stood on the other side, scratching the back of his neck. He was in his casual clothes today. I leaned one hip against the door, giving him attitude, but I found that I didn't quite feel the attitude as much as I used to. Chris Martinez was a pain in my ass, there were no two ways about it, but he'd also saved my ass, and I supposed I owed him at least the tiniest bit of friendliness.

But not too much.

That night, on the patio, I'd filled him in on everything I knew about the Hollises and their conspiracy to get rid of Peyton, so I couldn't figure out why he would be at my house.

"Miss me already?" I asked.

He chuckled. "Can I come in?"

"Good. I didn't miss you, either," I said. But I shuffled away from the door, pulling it all the way open and gesturing for him to come inside.

He stepped into the foyer, looking uncertain and awkward. I could see him glance around, taking in photos and knickknacks and the stuff that made my life mine. Having him openly ogle our stuff made me uncomfortable. I shut the door and stood there, my arms crossed over my chest.

"So, you just here to make sure I'm not doing anything

illegal? Or do you need me to solve another case for you?"

"Actually," he said, "can I get a glass of water?"

I rolled my eyes. "You want me to make you lunch, too, Your Highness?" But I brushed past him and down the hallway toward the kitchen. He followed me and seated himself at the breakfast bar, even though I didn't ask him to. I poured him a glass of water and placed it on the counter in front of him. "Comfy now?"

But he didn't look comfy. He looked pretty miserable, actually. He stared at the counter, pink circles breaking out on his cheeks. "I'm afraid I have some bad news," he said.

I felt the energy drain from my head all the way down to my toes. "What now?" I asked.

His eyes finally lifted to meet mine. I could see his misery in them. "Peyton died this morning," he said.

I pulled out a bar stool and sank onto it, feeling dizzy. "But she opened her eyes," I said in disbelief. "She smiled at me."

He nodded. "The nurse said she'd been doing some of that, but it was all—"

"Involuntary," I finished. "I know. She told me that, too. But I was there. I saw it. It didn't look involuntary. It looked like . . ." I felt my eyes well up and blinked them hard, refusing to cry in front of him again. "I was going to visit her today."

"I'm sorry," he said. "I wish I had an answer for you. She'd just suffered too much damage to her brain. Here. The water was for you," he said, sliding the glass toward me.

I touched the sides of the glass but didn't drink it. I didn't want water. I wanted Peyton to wake up. I wanted more than photos. I wanted there to be a reason to have gone through this whole thing. I wanted a payoff, damn it.

"So does this mean the Hollises will all be charged with murder now instead of just assault?" I asked, their name coming out bitterly.

He stroked his top lip and down his chin with his thumb and forefinger. "I don't know," he said. "They left the house before we got there that night, which is pretty miraculous, given the amount of blood on the kitchen floor. Yet it seems Bill and Vanessa Hollis got on an airplane yesterday morning."

"To?"

"Dubai. No extradition laws. And it would appear that they took a healthy amount of money with them."

"So they just get away with it? With everything?"

He turned his palms up. "For now, yes. But believe me, Bill Hollis is not the kind of guy who can walk away from Hollywood forever. He will come back. We will get them eventually."

"What about Luna?"

"Well, she also had a ticket to Dubai, scheduled to join them the next day."

"Sounds pretty planned out. Where was Dru's ticket?" I finally picked up the glass and sipped the water, just to give myself something to do.

"He didn't have one."

"Interesting," I said, trying to sound nonchalant. But the truth was, knowing that Dru wasn't planning on running brought his innocence home to me. Again, my heart squeezed at the thought of him dying to save me. The feeling made me seethe. I hated being sentimental. Sentimentality was for ignorant people. I knew better.

"So what about Luna, then?" I repeated.

He shrugged. "It's going to depend on what the prosecutor thinks he can do. Right now, he can only get her on the accident in the backyard of Hollis Mansion."

I slammed the water glass back onto the counter. "Accident? It was no fucking accident!"

"She didn't mean to kill Dru."

I almost laughed. "No, you're right. She only meant to kill me."

"But she didn't," he said simply. "She's claiming self-defense. We're still rounding up facts. Right now we can definitely nail her for assault and battery, and I'm fairly certain we can get her for attempted murder. But she is a minor."

"And what about what she did to Peyton?" I asked.

"We don't have any real evidence," he said. "We can't

find Rigo or a murder weapon or anything that wouldn't be considered circumstantial. Without evidence, it's all just your word against hers, because the only other two people involved . . ."

"Are dead," I finished for him. He nodded. I stood up suddenly, knocking my bar stool over. "It's not fair! They killed her. They can't just . . . walk away."

"I know," Detective Martinez said, standing up and coming around the counter. He put his hands on my shoulders. "But I'm determined to see this through, Nikki. I won't stop until I have evidence on all the Hollises and I find Arrigo Basile. You have my word on that. It would help the process tremendously if you have some real evidence you can show me. Something that will let me know how you solved this."

"The escort service? The one I handed to you at the hotel?" I asked, knowing what he was going to say before he even spoke a word.

He shrugged. "Entire office cleared out by the time we got an address. Nothing but pink carpet, a few bits of paper, and an empty filing cabinet. I do have this for you, though. It's a copy. I had to keep the original. And I could probably get into huge trouble if anyone found out I gave you a copy. It was in Peyton's bedroom. Taped to the bottom of a box colored like a rainbow." He handed me an envelope.

Of course. The bottom of the box. I'd forgotten to look there. Or been interrupted by Luna was more like it.

I opened the envelope and pulled out a photocopied letter.

Nikki,

    I'm putting a ton of faith in your synesthesia right now, but if I'm right about what you can do, you're reading this letter.

    So basically this is one of those if-you're-reading-this-I'm-probably-dead letters. I've known you were my sister for a while now. I even watched you a little at your house, at school, stole your records from the guidance office, that kind of thing, trying to decide how, and when, to tell you. But I started discovering other things, too. Things about my family. I was afraid of putting you in danger. I finally decided I would write this letter and leave you clues, and would only bring you into this if things had gone really wrong and my life was on the line. So you'd think I'd be really scared writing this letter, but I'm kind of not. I've been scared for a long time. Scared of where my life was going, thanks to the people who raised me. Scared of who, or what, I will become. Writing this letter is actually a relief.

    Everything about the Hollis family is a lie. We are not who the world thinks we are. We have secrets, Nikki, and they're bad. And when I say "we" I actually mean we. Including you, Nikki. Maybe you've figured this part out already, but if you haven't, I'll tell you now. Your mother, Carrie, was my mother, too. I know this because I've followed a very long trail of deceit. But I've included in this letter a lock of my hair, just in case you want to have it tested for DNA to be sure. I don't need to see a DNA test. I already know.

It all started when a woman named Brandi Courteur came to one of Viral Fanfare's shows in Long Beach. I can't tell you anything more about Brandi because it will be very dangerous to her if this letter should fall into the wrong hands. I know that sounds very mysterious, but if you're reading this, you obviously can do mysterious. Let me just say that what Brandi told me after that show changed my whole life. My entire life was a lie. Fake. A show. Everything started to make so much more sense. And I learned things about my father, about Vanessa, that could ruin them.

Find Brandi, Nikki. When you do, you will understand everything.

Also, take care of Dru. I've told him about his own mother, but he's still in denial. He's still trying to please dear old Daddy. He doesn't know what he's doing, but he's good on the inside. I know this because we've lived the same lie.

Peyton

I folded the letter and placed it back in the envelope, not even realizing that I was crying until I was wiping the tears.

"You ever heard of this Brandi person?" Chris Martinez asked.

"No. Nothing."

"Do you have anything else that will help this case? Anything at all?"

I shook my head sadly. The only real evidence I'd ever had was a recording of Peyton blackmailing her brother, and Martinez had taken it out of my car the night Dru got shot. "It was mostly hunch," I said.

Martinez stood there for another long moment, eyeing me skeptically. Finally, he let go. "I just wanted to let you know about Peyton," he said. He walked toward the door, but halfway through the entryway he stopped, his shoulders slumped, his hands on his hips. He stared at the floor for a moment, and then turned back to me. "Listen," he said. He cleared his throat, definitely uncomfortable. "You asked what was in my past."

His eyes flicked up to mine, and I nodded.

"I didn't grow up in a house like this." He gestured around him. "It was just my mom and three kids." He cleared his throat again, looked back at the floor. "When I was fifteen, my older brother, Javi, got mixed up in a gang. Really bad people. I knew he was in it, and I knew he'd gotten into some bad shit, but I didn't tell my mom or anything."

"You don't have to—"

He held up his hand to stop me. "He killed some punk named Leon. He told me. Shot him in the chest over some stupid grudge. But I still didn't say anything to anyone. I kept my mouth shut because I thought that was what you did. I thought I was going to follow in his footsteps, you know? I was going to join his gang, too, and I had to prove myself. So I said nothing."

I tried to imagine Chris Martinez, with his blazing yellow badge, in a gang, selling drugs, stealing cars, killing people. I couldn't do it.

"Two weeks later, Leon's boys went after Javi and shot up his car." He ducked his head, scuffed one shoe on the tile, and then looked up again. His jaw was square and tense. "Only it wasn't Javi in the car. It was our sister. Ada."

"Oh my God," I whispered. "I'm so sorry. You didn't know. . . ."

He closed his eyes. "But I did know. And now Javi is in prison and Ada is dead and it's just my mom in that house. And she lives with that pain every day. And so do I. You asked why I was so busy following you? Because I swore to myself I would never stand by and let someone get hurt again. Not if I could stop it. Especially if it's someone I care about."

We stood there awkwardly for a beat. I didn't know what to say. Putrid brown puddled around our feet, and I squeezed my eyes shut to make it go away.

Finally, he turned. "Anyway, I owed you that. I should go."

"Wait," I said, and he stopped. I went to the kitchen desk, found a scrap of paper and a pen, and jotted down an address. I handed him the paper. "In the trees behind the Dumpsters, you'll find her car. It'll have my fingerprints in it, just so you know."

He held the scrap of paper up for a few seconds, then folded it and tucked it into his pocket. The address was no longer coming at me in blacktop black and gray. The fear was gone.

"Thank you," he said.

My fingerprints weren't the only part of me Chris Martinez would find in that car. He would also find my stolen school records, filled with the counselor's details about my synesthesia.

It would take Martinez a while to understand what he was looking at, but he was a pretty good detective. He would eventually get it.

If we were going to finish this out, he was going to have to get it.

But I felt confident that he would. That we would. That eventually Vanessa and Luna and Bill would have to own up to what they did. To the prostitution and the drugs and the murder. I owed that much to Peyton. And to Dru. They died for their family secrets. For *our* family secrets. It was up to me to expose them.

I followed Chris Martinez to the front door and watched him get into his car. The license plate glowed bright yellow at me. Just as it had from day one. I had a feeling Chris Martinez was nothing if not reliable. But there was something else there, as well. When I remembered sparring with him, or sitting with him on the Hollises' pool deck, I thought of violet things—flowers, grapes, purple crayons. I pressed my eyes shut, tight, and reopened them. The color was gone. But it had been there. I had seen it.

I stood by the door, leaning my temple against the door frame, as he pulled out of the driveway. My cheek throbbed. I thought about the night that Dru died. How I'd sat against the lawn chair, sobbing. Everything I'd known about my life had been a lie. I wasn't sure who my parents were, who I was. The confusion was overwhelming. And while, with Luna being handcuffed and hauled away, it looked like this was all over, in reality, it had only just begun. There were still so many questions I needed to ask. Starting with my dad. He would try to evade—that was his style—but Chris Martinez wasn't the only one determined not to give up until there were answers. I wouldn't give up until I knew who I was, who Mom was. I *couldn't* give up.

I shut the front door and then, instead of going back to the kitchen to study, snatched my chem book off the stair where I'd left it, and took it back upstairs. I grabbed my tae kwon do duffel off my bedroom floor and stepped into some shoes.

I threw on my jacket, which smelled faintly of cigarette smoke, and remembered seeing Peyton for the first time in the hospital bed. Even in all that crimson, with her chopped hair, with her battered head and arms, she still looked beautiful.

I could see her. Her soft skin, her small nose, her long eyelashes. Her tattoo, a black-and-gray rainbow with words underneath.

Live in Color.

I walked out the front door, shouldering my duffel and digging out my car keys at the same time.

I intend to, Peyton. I intend to.

ACKNOWLEDGMENTS

Always first, I would like to thank my friend and agent, Cori Deyoe, for encouraging me to take leaps and try new things, and for having my back no matter what happens.

This book literally never would have happened without the vision, belief, and help of the amazing Claudia Gabel, Melissa Miller, and Katherine Tegen. Thank you to all of my wonderful HarperCollins family, especially Joel Tippie, Kathryn Silsand, Valerie Shea, Roseanne Romanello, Lauren Flower, and Alana Whitman.

Thank you to Scott Brown and Alex Tison, for helping me choreograph Nikki's badass fight scenes ("Do it again, only slower"), and to Paige Wood for helping take notes while I was on the ground patting out ("Did you get that?").

As always, thank you to my family and friends for forever supporting me. Scott, Paige, Weston, Rand, and Preston, I love you all.

And thank you, dear readers, for following me into my colorful make-believe worlds. You are my rainbow, and you are beautiful!